Before the Apocalypse

Book Two

Haven

Quest

Kepler Nigh

McDougal Publishing
www.mcdougalpublishing.com

ISBN: 978-1-58158-175-1

Published by:
McDougal Publishing
P.O. Box 3595
Hagerstown, MD 21742-3595
www.mcdougalpublishing.com

Printed in the United States of America
For Worldwide Distribution

Acknowledgments

It is appropriate to note that everyone whose names appeared on this page in the first book of the trilogy could once again be included in this second book. I am extremely grateful to all those who have participated in this project through the years. I will not repeat that list here, but I do emphasize my gratitude to each one.

I must especially express my gratitude to the Bulley family, especially Connie, for all of her input and kind encouragement as this project moves forward. I also mention Alan, whose friendship is priceless.

Again, I mention Jerry and Debby Smith, who have been a vital part of helping me make this series a reality. Thank you, and may the Lord bless you as you touch nations with the Gospel.

Clark Vaughn, we're pals! Thanks for keeping up the good fight and blessing the children of Ecuador through your ministry, "For His Children-Ecuador."

A special thank you is in order for Harold McDougal, whose effort has been essential in the task of bring this edition to print and to a verity of electronic mediums. I owe him more than I can ever repay. His efforts in ministry through many years have given much fruit in the Kingdom. Thank you.

Pat Myers provided proofreading, for which I am very grateful (as are all of my readers).

Diane McDougal, thank you for helping make this edition possible!

To the Iron Men, as iron sharpens iron: I really appreciate your courage to stand for Christ and thank you for your prayers! I especially wish to mention Dan Poyner, Allan Bare, Mani Bhaskarla, Bob Fahey, Pat Moler, Steve Parlato and Connie LoPresto.

Again I must remember my family and the support they have provided. Blanca is a fine wife and woman of God. I am proud of each of my three children and their spouses. Keren is our middle child, and in this "middle" novel of the trilogy, it is fitting that she be given a special mention as the design artist for the cover, and for all her help in reviewing the content. It has definitely been a father/daughter project. David and Kimberly have also been part of the project in more ways than they can know.

Dedication

To Dr. Steve Haynes, a man of science and a man of God,
and to Sarah, who knows how to play real monopoly.
They are truly live action heroes.

Chapter 1

Escape

On the whole, human beings want to be good, but not too good, and not quite all the time.

— George Orwell

February 16, 1992 — Quito, Ecuador, South America

Having grown accustomed to the heat of Manta, Ashley shivered in Quito's cold night air. The skimpy sweater that María had given her wasn't enough for the fifty-degree temperature. Initially, it had felt refreshing, comparable to air-conditioning, but the feeling didn't last long. When she stepped out of Dan's vehicle, she momentarily felt woozy, for at nearly two miles high it's not as easy to breathe as it had been at sea level, in Manta, where she had been that same morning.

Ashley found herself content that James had left her alone with the *outers*. With his absence it would be easier for her to escape and find Nova Mundi's office.

Jon, James's missionary friend, led her to the door of his house and Judy, his wife, greeted them. It was a pleasant place, wide marble-topped stairs leading to a solid dark wood door with many flowers in permanent planters on each side of the entrance. They were fuchsia orchids. She wished her vision enhancements were working so that she could see them better, but the light from the porch light was enough to preview the beauty that daylight would accentuate. She was tempted to stop and smell them, even in the cold, but Jon had already opened the door and called his wife, who was ready to be introduced. After the initial exchange, he told Judy, "Ashley is a friend of James." Then he left her with Judy and went back to talk to Larry, who was still waiting in the Jeep on the street.

Judy led Ashley into the house. She had expected it to be warmer inside, and it was, but not enough to be comfortable.

"You're shivering?" Judy asked.

Ashley laughed as she said, "Yes, I am! It's cold here."

"May I get you a jacket?"

"Please," Ashley responded, unable to say much more, for trembling.

Judy signaled her to follow. Moving up to the second floor, Judy soon had her standing in front of a closet, and it didn't take long for her to find a jacket that fit. Judy was tall, but not as tall as Ashley. Happily, there wouldn't be a fashion contest.

"You came up from Santo Domingo?" Judy asked.

"Yes," she answered simply.

"You knew James?"

"We're friends."

"Did you come from Novus Ordo, too?"

"He told you about Novus Ordo?"

Seeing Judy pause in answering, Ashley realized that she had asked her question too intently, and she was probably making the outer dwell on the subject more than necessary.

Judy, having delayed, answered, "He mentioned it to us."

Ashley worried to herself — James told these people too much. And I just confirmed there's a Novus Ordo. I should have asked her, "What is Novus Ordo?" Then I wouldn't be confirming any secrets.

"So you found James?" Judy asked.

"Yeah," Ashley said in a drawn-out fashion that could have sounded Southern, and was out of character for her, but reflected her recently engaged caution. Speaking to outers could lead to trouble.

"Had you been looking for him?"

"Oh, no. It wasn't planned at all. I didn't even believe it when I saw him."

By now, the ladies were downstairs and Jon was still outside talking with Larry.

"Could I get you something warm to drink?" Judy offered.

"Thank you. I would like that."

Judy started the propane fire under the kettle. "Excuse me for asking, but you look a lot like James. Are you family?

"Oh, no. At least not brother and sister, if that's what you mean." Ashley reflected. She hadn't ever thought of how similar Alpha Force members probably look in the eyes of outers.

"Did you work with James?"

Judy's interrogation bothered Ashley, but before she could answer, Jon walked in and said, directing himself to Judy, "I see you've got Miss Brown something warm. I was afraid she was going to turn purple." Jon chuckled. The ladies mutely joined him.

"Oh, yes. First thing. I saw the poor girl was freezing to death. It seems that she and James are friends?" Judy inquired.

"Not only friends," Jon answered, "but they worked together. She was the first officer on James's spaceship. They've been to Mars together."

Hearing this nearly made Ashley burst out with a threat; she had trouble containing herself. They know! — she thought. *Inflict* James! What's wrong with him? Can't he keep a secret? He's going to get himself killed.

"You've been to Mars, too?" Judy asked innocently.

What should I say? — Ashley asked herself. Apparently the outer woman noticed her hesitation in giving an answer because she changed the subject and made another comment, "That's such a beautiful dress," she said, in an adoring tone.

"Thank you," Ashley responded, welcoming the change.

"It looks like it was made for you."

"It was. A friend made it for me in Manta." Hearing her own words, she began to think — I'm divergent. I'm calling outers friends. Then she reversed herself — So what! They are friends! Then a terrible thought struck her like a bolt of lightening — The Plan says I'll have to kill my friends. She lowered her head as she pondered the weight of her conclusion.

"Is something wrong, Ashley?" Jon asked, seeing the change in her expression.

Is something wrong? — she asked herself, sarcastically. Realizing that *cleaning* would mean eliminating her outer "friends" — even María, and Pepe, who was the very man who had saved her life, she let out a false laugh and said, "Oh, I'm fine. It's just the cold."

Jon shifted the conversation and began telling Judy about the trip to Santo Domingo and the decisions for Christ that were made in the street meeting. This made Ashley feel greater alienation. Apparently they noticed, for it wasn't long until they showed her to the guest room behind the house.

Judy gave her some things for the night, and Ashley was able to take a hot shower. It felt good — the first one since leaving DEEP 1 (Dimensional Electro Ether Propulsion Unit). In Manta, María had only had cold water, which Ashley had enjoyed in the hot climate, but hot water in Quito's cold air felt good. After the shower, she found her way under the covers, where she lay, hating herself. She thought — I can't win. I'm not strong, like James. I can't just decide to be an outer. I've got to return to Novus Ordo. Maybe they'll inflict me and I'll have to tell them about James and my friends. Then they'll come and *clean*.

Such was the torment within her, as she thought about the implications of returning to TerraNova, that tears came to her eyes. Why will I go back? — she asked herself. There's no point in it, and they'll inflict me, I'm sure.

However, she couldn't answer her own question. She simply knew that she was going to go back to TerraNova and that as much as she may have wished to resist her conditioning, she couldn't. She felt driven, like a salmon fighting its way upstream, returning to its spawning ground, even if death awaited her. She eventually reached the conclusion that James was doing the right thing by not going back to TerraNova. He would escape infliction, and she really wanted to do the same thing, but training and conditioning bound her powerfully, and she knew she couldn't break loose. At one point, during the long night — while she twisted, scratched, turned and rolled over back-and-forth and from side-to-side — she came to the conclusion that James was right. She decided she was wrong. But it didn't matter. She would surely go back. She didn't sleep, not one wink, and the hours passed slowly.

* * *

The next day

Dawn's first hazy light slipped through the window into the guest room. Ashley got her things together, stepped out the door into the cool morning air, and moved towards the perimeter wall. It was quickly turning into a brilliant day. The room was in the back, away from the house, and so she decided to jump, and escape onto the back street before anyone saw her. It would probably be a couple of hours before they discovered she had left. By then she hoped to have made contact with the Nova Mundi Foundation office in Quito and be on her way home. James wouldn't dare come after her, and besides: What could he do to stop her?

About that time, one of the morning's first flights was approaching on its glide path. She realized, as it thundered by, that she was near the airport, and she thought — Excellent. There'll be telephones there. She watched carefully as the 737 landed just a few blocks away. She began to walk in the direction the plane had gone, and inside of ten minutes she found herself by the end of the runway, which sat behind a large fence. It would be easy to follow the fence to the terminal, but she wasn't sure on which side she would find it. Guessing from what she could see, she began to follow the sidewalk on the western side, which ran beside a heavily traveled road where numerous cars had already whizzed past her.

She realized that she had chosen the correct route when she walked into the airport terminal five minutes later. Public phones were plenty, but there were no phone books. She tried to ask at the information booth, but they weren't working yet. She took a seat, guessing it wouldn't be much longer until they started to open.

* * *

JAMES AWOKE, got up, and started dressing. He was eager to speak to Ashley. He decided he would beg her to stay, and not go back to TerraNova. He would tell her to think about her decision for a few days. He would tell her not to make a rash decision. She needed to realize that if she returned, TerraNova's people would probably kill her by infliction.

He felt terribly concerned. He knew he had to go to the Whittens before it was too late. He knew that she was entirely capable of leaving there without even saying good-bye. Though he had been free for several months, he still felt the urge of his conditioning propelling him to return to TerraNova, and the battle of his will against his conditioning wasn't easily fought. It reminded him that staying free of the grip of TerraNova's Alpha Force was very difficult.

* * *

ASHLEY TRIED not to think. A blank mind was much better for the task before her. Just be a good soldier — she told herself. Don't ask questions. Obey orders. Inflict the cursed orders!

More and more people filled the airport. Eventually a lady took her position at the information counter. Ashley walked over.

"Good morning; may I help you?" the woman asked with a heavy accent.

"May I see your phone book?" Ashley requested.

Once it was in her grasp, she flipped through to the "F" section. It was there, "Fundación Nova Mundi," with number and address.

She had to buy a *"ficha"* – a little token – to be able to use the phone. It didn't cost much and she still had enough from the collection they had taken for her in Manta. She dialed the number and two rings later there was an answer. A recorded voice spoke, "You have reached Fundación Nova Mundi. Our office hours are from 9:00 AM until 6:00 PM, Monday through Friday. Please leave your message and your number after the tone, and we will return your call as soon as possible." The message had been in Spanish. After a moment there was a tone, and she spoke, mechanically, "I am Ashley Brown. Alpha Force. First Officer. Serial number, A0549. I'm calling from the airport. Please come get me."

She hung up, feeling as if she was a walking corpse. It won't be long now — she thought, as she took a seat. A blank look still filled her empty face. That was the best expression for the occasion and it best expressed how she felt.

Maybe an hour had gone by, probably more, but nothing happened. She looked up at the big flight board; it was 9:30 AM. She thought — They aren't in much of a hurry: like when they never came when I was drowning in the Pacific. Maybe they won't show. Then what will I do? Why do I even bother? But the *"why"* had nothing to do with the choice, which had been made for her by *inflictions* past.

* * *

"SHE'S NOT HERE"; these were words he wished he had never heard. Jon's solemn word and his somber expression let James know that he wasn't happy about the news himself. Judy had the same look. They all realized that Ashley's disappearance wasn't good for any of them.

They had been sitting around the kitchen table for some time without talking when Jon began speaking with conviction, "We can't let this affect us!" And then, after a pause, he looked around as Judy and James raised their eyes to meet his. He then continued, and said, "Daniel kept praying even when he knew they'd toss him to the lions. God saved him and He can save us too. If He wants us to be martyrs, then so be it. But we can't live in fear. We've just got to snap out of it, and he finished telling them, "It's Sunday morning. Let's go to church as planned."

"Good idea," Judy answered.

But James, who still felt like someone was about to inflict him, began speaking, slowly and seriously, "I'm so sorry I've brought this on you. I think we should leave Quito."

"Well James, if you feel you have to leave town, you probably should, but Judy and I will stay here. We're sure that God will keep us out of harm's way, and if not, we're ready for whatever He wants."

James wished he could make Jon understand just how dangerous it would be for him to stay, but he had already explained the power of TerraNova, and how they worked, so it would be useless to repeat himself. With this in mind, James said, "If you feel you must stay, just remember, I advised against it. I'm going to go back to the man I told you about, who helped me on the mountain. They won't look for me there. I haven't told you much about him. So if they come here, just say I left town. I pray they take your word for it and don't try to force you to say anything. But you all need to know something. It's possible they'll use something really dramatic to scare you into talking."

"Like an alien abduction?" Jon questioned with a chuckle.

"Yes, Jon. Take it seriously," James said, waiting for the proper change in Jon's expression before continuing, "How can I stay in touch? Maybe Ashley will reintegrate without saying anything. Maybe they won't question her much. If they haven't come around in a few weeks, they probably won't. And even if they come around, and I'm not here, they might leave you alone."

"I don't know, Jim," Jon said gravely, looking a bit shaken, "maybe we should come with you."

"That would be good," James answered.

Jon looked to Judy. She looked hopeful and said, "When we decided we were going to be missionaries we decided we wouldn't give up, no matter what. We decided that even if it meant death, we were going to share the Gospel. God hasn't told us to go anywhere else, so I think we should stay here. If James feels he needs to leave Quito for a time, then he probably should. I don't think we need to be any more afraid of this enemy than we have been of any other. With Jesus, we need not fear! Our real enemy isn't flesh and blood. If it's God's will for us to die in the hands of these TerraNova people, then it won't save us even if we flee; they'll find us no matter what. But if God wants us alive, they won't be able to touch us, no matter how powerful they think they are."

James, touched by her simple faith, considered aloud, "Maybe I should stay here, then?"

"I think you have to do what you feel you have to do," Jon said; "Judy's talking about us, and the call God has given us. I think she's right. We'll just sit the storm out. Maybe it'll blow over quickly."

"Let's hope so," James replied. "I think I'd better get moving then. But is there some way we can communicate?"

"You haven't told me much. I just have a general idea where you're going, and I know you crashed on Antisana, but I don't know who the man is that helped you. There's a church though, in Talontag, near where you got the bus into town. The pastor's name is Bautista. I don't think he has a phone, but I could probably get a message to him. So, you could check with him once in a while," Jon explained.

"I guess that's about as good as we can do," James said, reluctantly. "I'll be gone. I can find my way to the bus station. I have money from Jack. It should be enough for some time. I won't need to spend much out in the country. I sure thank you, and appreciate you."

"We'll be praying for you, James," Judy affirmed.

"That would be good," James said, thinking — God saved me once; He can do it again, but I prayed for Him to keep Ashley from going back. Why did He let her go? Is He really so all-powerful? Maybe He just saved me to mock me? He kept me alive long enough for Ashley to tell the others, so they can come and get me, and inflict me to death!

James's questions were serious, and he soon found himself on the edge of incredulity. What was the point! Things had been going fairly smoothly until Ashley came along. It seemed like every time he started getting closer to her, everything disintegrated. When he was a kid, his attraction to her was terminated by infliction; now it would probably end with premature death.

* * *

ASHLEY, STILL BLANK-FACED, sat staring. Eventually she looked over at the clock on the wall. It was 10:00 AM. Where are they? — she asked herself, feeling disgusted. She felt as if she couldn't sit still any longer and decided to walk some.

Getting up, more than a few men's eyes followed her figure. She wasn't used to it, and felt uncomfortable, as if she would rather hide, and thought — Everyone in the world sees me, everyone except TerraNova — *inflict* them! They've taught us to fear them. Ha! They're supposed to be everywhere. They sure seem lost!

She walked out of the terminal doors and started to walk around the parking lot. After she had walked aimlessly for couple of blocks, a chubby (probably because of parasites) little native boy ran up to her and tugged on her dress. She stopped and looked into his dark eyes. His face looked so sad and he said, *"Déme un regalo."* There was a whine in his voice. He wanted a gift. He was just a beggar. Dirt was ground into everything he wore, including his skin. He had a runny nose, and a large drop of mucus hung under it.

Ashley jerked away and kept walking. We'll clean the scum from the Earth — like beggars, and Jews, and Christians too.

She decided she should start hating them, to make it personal, and she continued her list: And Pepe, and María, and those foolish missionaries, and James, inflict them all; we'll clean up the scum. We'll bring a New Age, and Therion will reign for a thousand years. It'll be glorious — she knew it would, but she wanted to cry.

I'm tired of hating! — she exclaimed to herself. They've all loved me. Everyone wants to help me, everyone but TerraNova. But I've got to hate them, and then destroy them too!

She remembered watching the writhing victims in Iraq, and imagined James's face on one of the scattered corpses — it was a bitter memory, a bitter plan, and a bitter future.

I'm sick — she told herself and added — They've betrayed me! TerraNova has betrayed me. Now, can I betray them? She laughed in her tired mind, wishing she could, knowing she couldn't.

Then the little beggar came up to her again and yelled after her, *"Ayuda a los pobres"* — "Help the poor." She stopped and looked around at the pathetic creature. It surely isn't human? — she asked herself. But the sun twinkled in a special way, and the *thing's* eyes sparkled. She looked a moment longer. *It* started moving towards her, slowly. An image of her own pathetic self came to her mind — when she had fought so hard to stay awake in the Pacific, and had cried out to God to save her — and He had. She stood there, safe and sound. God did His part, but she hadn't done anything.

She looked at the helpless child. He couldn't escape his world any more than she could break away from hers. Reaching into her pocketbook she pulled out a few coins which she extended to the child. He reached out and took them, and said, "*Gracias,*" and turned away.

He told me, "Thank you." I just took my gift and ran. I owe all of them: Pepe, María, the foolish missionaries, and, curse him — James too! I ran, as quickly as I could, back to my own sick life, and my owners won't even come to get me.

Using every swear word she knew, invoking ill favor upon, and countless inflictions for her tormentors, she continued her aimless walk. Within herself she could find no power to keep herself from returning. It didn't make any sense. She didn't even want to go back, and they'd probably inflict her to death, but she would go back — as sure as day turns to night.

* * *

JAMES WALKED BACK to his small rented apartment. Jon promised he would check on things in James's absence. Once inside, he put on blue jeans and a sweater and stuffed everything he had, that he thought would do him any good, in his backpack — especially his poncho, along with the RSB (Reentry Survival Bubble) blanket that he still had, and the PLOT (Portable LOcator Tablet). He tried to make sure that he left nothing that would identify him, but he knew his effort would probably be useless, since the others would be able to identify his DNA quickly, and he didn't have a good vacuum sweeper to use for cleanup.

Briskly, he moved out onto the sidewalk and walked three blocks. He caught a bus going south.

* * *

That same day — Novus Iridium

JANICE ALLENBURG lay in pain, which was about the only thing she could do, and had done, for weeks.

She remembered some guy in a black suit, and walking towards a helicopter, and then a brilliant flash. Before the explosion, she remembered being in NHMI (New Horizons Multinational Industries) Siberia. Maybe the guy's name was "Chenskosky?" Or something like that — Russian? But she hadn't seen anyone she knew since then. When she asked to make a call, they ignored her. She even demanded that they allow her to call NHMI, and threatened their jobs if they didn't, but they disregarded her. She could barely walk to the bathroom under her own power, but they told her that thanks to their operations, she could walk, albeit with great difficulty. And what little she was able to move, it felt like something, or someone else, was doing it for her. It was different — jerky — like a robot. She even thought she must be moving a bit like Frankenstein. They told her that without all the operations she would've been a quadriplegic, which was a good description of how she felt — immobilized. They said that with physical therapy she would walk smoothly, and have less pain. She wished.

She dreaded the thought of more physical therapy. It was torture, and she thought — They promise me that I'll be as good as new, but my body's nothing more than scar tissue. All this pain! I wish I was dead! They force me to move, and it makes me hurt. I hate it! — she exclaimed to herself, and occasionally to the walls, thinking there was a better chance they were listening than the nurses.

No one tells me anything! They say I'll be fine, and to keep my desire to live, but why? I don't see any reason. Why should I? She hated herself, and she thought — I haven't got the guts to end it all, either. About the only thing that encouraged her, thinking of how terrible the accident, or whatever it was, must have been, was that when she looked in the mirror she saw that her face was still clean and unscarred. She had been told she was beautiful, and in that sense, if indeed she had ever been "beautiful," then she still was — for whatever good it would do her.

But there were times when she would bitingly tell herself — So what if I'm "beautiful"? I'm trapped in this prison. Where is this infernal place? What country is it? It seems like it should have something to do with NHMI, but no one will talk to me. They speak English — at least the ones who speak. But most of them act deaf and dumb, especially when they're around me. I've seen them talking, though. And the strange uniforms? And sounds? Like a science-fiction movie. No windows! No sunlight! Yet it's so bright all the time, but it feels dark! The air smells fresh, but it's stale. It doesn't make any sense, but that's the way it seems.

I'm confused. They've operated on me so many times, and the doctors keep telling me, "You'll be fine." But when I ask, "What's wrong with me?" they give me the silent treatment. I ask, "Where am I? Is this NHMI?" And they just continue their work, speechless. "What are you doing to me?" I ask. And they tell me, "You'll be fine." Curse them! I'm not fine. I want to talk to someone I know. As soon as I can walk a block, I'll find out where this penitentiary is!

Chapter 2

Suicide, Murder, or Life

I FEEL AS IF I were a piece in a game of chess, when my opponent says of it: That piece cannot be moved.

— Søren Kierkegaard

February 17 — That same day — Quito

ON SUNDAYS buses weren't very full, and though it was cramped (because of the lack of space between seats), James found a seat on one. He had some serious questions running through his mind. He kept asking himself, if the Almighty outer God had gone to so much trouble to save him, and apparently to save Ashley also, then why would He let her ruin everything?

Suicide seemed like a viable option, for a moment, but it didn't take him long to get over it. He wanted to live.

James toyed with the idea of turning himself in to TerraNova and thought — Maybe, if I go back and pretend that things are like they used to be, then I could scheme something and escape with Ashley later, after I convince her that being outer isn't bad. But he knew it wouldn't work. Things had changed for him. He didn't act the same. He didn't think the same, and he didn't even look the same. His time with the outers had changed everything about him. If I do go back — he considered — they'll probably make me murder some outer. But outers are my friends. I couldn't do it — he concluded. However, the thought of going back did have some merits — If I did it right, I might be able to save some lives. I could take charge, like a captain should. He almost liked the idea, but he knew he couldn't. Perhaps the hardest thing was that he was feeling himself to be a Christian more all the time. He found himself asking what Jesus would do when confronted with different situations. He had read much of the New Testament, and he remembered the prayer he had prayed back in the plaza. According to the missionaries, that made him a Christian, and even though he didn't quite see how, or understand it, they seemed to be right. They said he was born again, and even though it was obviously a metaphor, he really didn't understand why. About the only thing left was to simply confess his new faith openly, as they had told him he should. But he wasn't ready for that — not yet.

Lumbering along, the bus didn't seem to be in any hurry. James figured — I'm probably safer here than in most places. A SAO (Special Affairs Operative — pronounced Say-Oh, or "sow" by outers) would be too arrogant to get on one of these behemoths.

* * *

ASHLEY WALKED AIMLESSLY. Suicide seemed like the best thing. It would solve her problems, save lives, and end her torment. She swore and asked herself — If God is so good, why didn't He let me die at sea? Why did He let me see James? It would've been easier if I hadn't seen him. Then I could've turned myself in without a hassle.

Circling back around, she walked into the terminal again. It seemed as though all the men in the place saw her, with their eyes following her every step. She wondered — Don't they feel embarrassed, to look at me like that? Then she thought — Well, Nova Mundi isn't here. They wouldn't have any trouble seeing me, and the place isn't very big. She walked in farther, self-conscious of every move. She could tell that some of the men tried not to stare, by looking the other way or sticking their noses deeper into their newspapers. They're the more civilized of the bunch — she told herself. But it seemed that even they couldn't avoid an occasional glance. If given the benefit of the doubt, they were probably looking at other things, but she knew otherwise. She was the object of attention.

She looked up on the big board, where all the flights were listed, and she saw the clock. It was 11:00 AM. However, this time her eyes caught something else. It was Sunday.

SUNDAY! — And she cursed to herself. No wonder they haven't come: They don't work on Sundays! We never had Sundays free. I wonder what they do, *go to church?* — she asked herself sarcastically. *Inflict* almighty TerraNova; I hate them. They never sent the trucks, and now they can't even keep an office open. I know Ecuador isn't important. They don't have drugs, like Colombia. It's just a small country, but if TerraNova is as almighty and powerful as it pretends, why can't they keep at least one lousy office running — just one — in the whole country?

Sunday... she considered once more, turning to walk out of the terminal, with at least a dozen pairs of male eyes following her turn, precisely in synchronization, as if they were watching a tennis ball in match play.

Once on the sidewalk, she started pacing, but without any idea where she was going. She moved with determination though, as if she had found a cause to champion.

They'll hear my message on the answering machine tomorrow morning, and then they'll be here, swarming the place like bees, but I'll be gone! — she told herself, not knowing what "gone" meant in her context, just knowing that it expressed the way she felt.

* * *

JON AND JUDY had followed their convictions and it was about 12:50 PM as they returned from church. Still about ten blocks from home and near the airport, Judy suddenly spoke out, "There she is," and pointed in Ashley's direction.

She was walking with her head inclined, as though she was thinking, and her arms were crossed — she didn't lose a single step.

"Should we ask her if she wants a ride, or something?" Judy wondered aloud.

"I guess we'd better, but you never know: Those Nova Mundi people might be around."

"Oh, Jon, don't be paranoid."

"Maybe I haven't been paranoid enough," he answered, pulling the Jeep close to Ashley, knowing it was the right thing, even if it was against his better judgment.

Judy quickly rolled down her window and yelled, "Want a ride?"

Ashley looked up, obviously not expecting them.

A horn went off right behind them. It seemed that it could have moved them by its blast. Whoever it is, some "person" — Jon thought with sarcastic note, not wanting to vocalize what he would have preferred calling them. Jon wondered how much longer he would be able to take it — the "honk" was many decibels louder than it should've been.

Ashley hadn't moved; she stood like a statue. But Judy opened her door and stepped into the back seat so that their guest could get in quickly if she was so inclined.

The deafening horn kept roaring. Judy motioned to Ashley to get in. Jon waved to the "gentleman," indicating he could go around, but he stuck to them like a wad of gum on good shoes.

Ashley stood frozen, which gave Jon the feeling that she must have reported them. Why else would she resist their invitation? Or did the roar of the horn paralyze her?

Judy called her again, now from an open back window, "Come on, Ashley. Let's go!"

Jon's nerves wouldn't take much more; he continued to signal for the "jerk" (even if he had just left church, it was hard for him to think politely about this "person") to pull around.

Ashley began to step towards the open door and Jon felt relieved as she responded to Judy's encouragement. Reaching the Jeep, she hopped into the empty passenger seat.

"I'm sorry," Ashley began, as Jon quickly pulled forward. The loud blare stopped. "I was surprised to see you."

"Well, we're surprised to see you; we're sorry you left us so early. We felt like we hadn't been good hosts," Judy said.

"I've just had so many things on my mind. I wanted to get out and have some fresh air," she answered.

Jon knew there was more, and he tried to get her to talk by advising, "James was concerned that you went to see your Nova Mundi friends."

Judy looked at Jon, and he saw her mouthing the word, "Careful," in the rearview mirror.

Ashley answered, gagging a bit, "Oh — " and after she paused, "Where is James?"

"He was concerned, and left town," Judy said.

"Left town. Where?" Ashley asked.

"That's hard to say. He was going back to visit a friend, but he didn't tell us much," Jon explained.

By now Jon was parking in front of their home.

"I've got lunch ready," Judy informed. "I'll just warm it up. You'll join us, won't you, Ashley?"

"Yeah," she answered in a reluctant tone.

Soon they were inside. Judy showed her a seat. Jon went to help Judy. They wanted to keep things moving lest their guest escape before they'd had a chance to find out what was going on.

"Please come on in," Jon invited her, as he pointed the way to the kitchen.

Ashley accepted, and soon they were seated around the small table. Jon began to pray, "Heavenly Father, thank You so much for Your provision for our bodies' needs. And thank You for Ashley. Help her, Lord, as she deals with decisions about her future. In the name of Jesus. Amen."

JON'S PRAYER didn't make things any simpler for Ashley. She had nearly resolved that TerraNova's line was the only one she would ever know and that Christians were a momentary accident in her life. She owed them nothing. But when Jon prayed for her, and thanked his God for her, she couldn't help but remember all of the prayers they said for her in Manta.

I can't stand it — she thought. I'm about ready to have these people decapitated and cleaned, and they're praying for me, feeding me, and treating me so well. They aren't dumb. They know what I've been up to. That's why James fled — blast him! — and here they are: just so nice. I hate it!

When Jon finished, Ashley felt the silence; it was only a moment, but she felt awkward, as though Jon wanted her to say something, and she thought — He probably wants to know why I left this morning without saying good-bye.

The silence was broken when Judy passed her a bowl, which was filled with soup. There were tuna salad sandwiches also. When Ashley had taken several bites from her sandwich, she couldn't resist complimenting, "This is good, Judy."

"Glad you like it, Ashley," she replied.

"Will you be with us for a while?" Jon asked. "We'd love to have you another night."

Ashley had to think a moment, and answered, "I don't think so. I'll probably keep going after lunch."

"But, do you have anywhere to go?" Judy asked.

By now they were mostly finished; it hadn't been a heavy meal, and conversation had been spaced, considering the tension that all three felt. Ashley didn't like facing Judy's question. She had been arguing with herself all day. She knew it made sense to forsake TerraNova. Therion hadn't ever done anything for her. At this point she had no desire to go back. She had lost her desire when she was treading water in the Pacific. But desire had nothing to do with her situation. I just don't have any choice — she told herself. Tomorrow, when they listen to the recorded message I left, they'll have this place crawling with SAOs. They'll fly them here in DEEPs. A few flying saucer reports won't hurt their cause. They'll set up so they can check everyone entering and leaving Quito.

Judy's question had led to a long delay. Ashley was silent. She didn't have an answer and she didn't want to reply.

Jon said, "Ashley, please. You're welcome here. You can stay as long as you need."

It finally got to her. She was being forced to a decision. In her frustration she decided — I'll tell them, and spoke, "Can't you see it?" Her voice was harsh. The change in Jon and Judy's expression cued her that her words were affecting them. "You want to save me from them, but you can't! And about this time tomorrow they'll be carrying you out of here in body bags. It'll look like some accident — gas or something. Face it. You can't help me! I can't even help myself."

Having spoken these words, Ashley realized the severity of her decision to return. She had realized it before, but now, with the mention of body bags, the scene became much more graphic in her mind. The bodies would be those of her friends. The killing would continue with Pepe, María, and then James too. And they might kill her also! She knew how they worked. When would it end? When they had exterminated all of the outers? Of course, she knew the official answers: that all outers who are exposed to the knowledge of TerraNova's secret world, and all Alpha Force who are AWOL, and all Jews, and all of those who would not deny Asmina, were to be cleansed and forever eliminated from Therion's kingdom. But there wasn't any really good reason for it. At least it didn't seem like it to her at this juncture, now that the victims wouldn't be nameless faces. She had become too attached, and it no longer seemed to her that the good of Therion's kingdom would really be served by eliminating so many people.

Ashley saw Jon's face take on a soft, perhaps fluid brilliance. Her words had been intended to scare him, but he appeared more courageous than ever. He began to answer her in a controlled voice, "Ashley, we love you. We'll help you. Jesus loves you—"

"Oh!" she said as she cut him off. She exclaimed, "Fool! You think I won't hurt you?" She was shocked by her own words. She knew it wasn't really her that was speaking, but her conditioning. And she knew that she had already reached another conclusion, but it was as if she couldn't stop herself.

"I'm sorry, Ashley," Jon said. "If you feel like you need to hurt me, then let's get it over with." With these words, Jon held his arms towards her, as if giving himself to her. "Just let me tell you: Jesus loves you and I forgive you. Even if you kill me, Jesus can still save you — if you'll let Him."

Ashley looked into his eyes. She saw, as though it was a reflection, a quality that she knew she needed. She knew that whatever it was, it would satisfy her and give her the strength to do as James had done. It was what she needed, but the voice of conditioning screamed at her once again, and said, "The Plan says to kill the Christian slime. Do it! Grab him. Break his neck. You've got bioenhancements! Just twist his neck off. He won't be the first. You've done this before. You're trained for it. Do it! Then you can finish the woman, and you'll have the house to yourself. You can call Nova Mundi tomorrow and they'll come to clean up, and send the proof of your loyalty to the morgue. If you kill them, you won't be inflicted. If you kill them, you can prove your loyalty, and maybe they won't question you. Maybe by killing them you can save Pepe and María."

The voice had made an interesting offer. It seemed like a good idea: Kill the missionaries, and life would be better. But what about James? The voice hadn't mentioned him, because she knew that he would have to be sacrificed. As much as she wanted to save him, her conditioning told her she couldn't. She reached a moment of silence in her mind. It wasn't peaceful though. "Well, what are you going to do?" the voice asked.

Ashley blazed silently back at the voice, "No! I won't!" Inner turmoil weakened her. She even felt herself losing ground to insanity — as if she was entering the realm of the mad and the jester of derangement was laughing at her hysterically. She desperately wanted to escape his grip.

She barely heard as Jon offered, "Look Ashley, don't listen to the evil voice that's speaking to you. It's wrong. Jesus really wants to save you."

"Can He really?" Ashley asked. Can He keep me from going back to TerraNova? God knows I don't want to. But I've been trained, and conditioned, and inflicted, and I've got to go back. Can't you see? I'm under their control. Nothing can change that!"

"Ashley, Jesus can. He can change everything. Just let Him. Give Him a chance. Pray with us and invite Him into your heart."

Judy added, "Yes, Ashley! Give your heart to Jesus. He'll give you peace in your heart."

That's what I want – Ashley told herself. Peace! She looked for a moment at a large knife that was in the sink. For a moment, she felt just as predisposed to use it on the Whittens as she did on herself. She felt so miserable. Jon's gaze caught her again. Yes – she told herself – he's got that peace he's talking about. Oh, James – she thought. She wanted to love him. She had always wanted to love him. Even if loving him meant becoming an outer, she had wanted it. Conditioning had told her no! And the jester's voice pounded, "Don't listen to the stupid missionary. Just finish him off, and TerraNova will promote you to captain."

She saw Jon, still looking deeply into her eyes. He encouraged her again, "Let's pray. Will you do that? Pray with me?"

But she sat in silence, not even blinking, fixing her view on Jon. Again the jester of madness spoke to her, "You're weak. Terminate the Christian worms. That will give you peace. Don't pay attention to them. They can't give you any peace!"

She thought – But James has peace! I could see it in him. I want James! I want what he has! I've got to get hold of myself. I can't let conditioning control me anymore.

Jon asked her again, "Ashley, would you pray with us?"

She felt like her tongue had returned to her mouth, but it still felt like a foreign object, heavy and dry; however, it seemed she might be able to make it speak. It took a monumental effort, but she forced herself, trying to speak. She coughed dryly, still trying to start. And then, as if it was the first word she had ever spoken, or perhaps more appropriately, her last word, uttered in a gasp from a deathbed, she said, "Yes."

She saw big smiles come on Jon and Judy's faces, and Jon said, "Then repeat after me, with all sincerity, and say, 'Jesus.' "

That was a hard word to say. Ashley delayed.

Judy said, "Go ahead, Ashley. You want to be free. You don't have to be in bondage to them anymore."

Ashley knew she wanted to be free and said, stumbling in tone, "I've … got … to be free."

"Okay. Ashley. Let's try again," Jon guided. "Say, 'Jesus' …"

But she continued in silence.

Jon prayed aloud, "Father, help Ashley …"

In her mind the jester's face turned into Master Teacher's, and she was pointing an infliction control right at her. *Infliction* — she thought. And basely, Ashley reacted to her conditioning, answering, "No! I can't do it."

JON ALMOST HEARD the devil laugh in his ear, and say, "You can't have her. She's mine!" But he became more determined, and commanded in prayer, "Evil power of hell, I bind you in the name of Jesus. Release your grip on Ashley. Be free! Ashley, in the name of Jesus," he prayed intensely. Judy joined him as she gently touched her shoulders and comforted her.

"I want to be free!" she voiced with emotion.

"Okay, Ashley. Now's the time; just pray with me," Jon indicated. One moment it seemed they had her, and the next it seemed she was headed back to the enemy's camp. Jon knew they had to help her cross the line, and gently commanded, "Now say, 'In the name of Jesus,' "

A tear trickled from her eye; then another. Judy passed her a handful of tissues, and Ashley wiped her face. She began to sob, and to repeat Jon's words. She said, "In the name … of Jesus."

"Say, 'I'm free!'" Jon led her.

"I'm free."

Jon and Judy continued ministering to her. Eventually she began to show peace in her countenance.

"Would you like to ask Jesus to come into your heart?" Judy questioned in love.

Ashley was still whimpering, but there was conviction in her voice when she said, "Yes. I want Jesus."

Jon wondered if he was hearing a heavenly chorus. Could it have been that the veil pulled away, and an angelic choir sang in celebration? He felt glory, as if it was dripping on him. He had prayed with many to receive Jesus, and he knew one person wasn't more important to the Lord than another, but this was different. Maybe it was the battle they had won? – he couldn't tell.

"Ashley, Jesus died for you because He loves you, and He's your friend. Now, please pray with me."

Jon led her, and she repeated each phrase, "Wonderful Lord Jesus... I come to You, a sinner ... I repent of my wrong way ... Have mercy on me, Lord ... Help me ... I believe in You... I believe You died on the cross for my sins ... And You rose from the dead on the third day... I confess with my mouth that You're my Lord and my Savior... Thank You, Jesus, for making me a new person... Come into my heart... Thank You for Your precious blood that You shed for me... Thank You!... Help me, Jesus, to be faithful until You return..."

ASHLEY KNEW that she wasn't the same woman. She hadn't understood certain parts of the prayer, but she had peace – she knew, because the jester had left the stage of her mind. She felt like the atmosphere – the air itself – had changed. It had a new freshness.

"How do you feel?" Judy asked.

She began shaking her head, but with a radiant smile, and she began to explain, "I realized that no matter what, TerraNova would try to kill me. I also realized that they would kill James and everyone else. So I decided I was going to do like James, and get out. But it was hard. It seemed like I couldn't, even if I wanted to. But I couldn't do what they wanted. I couldn't hurt you, because, if I did, I'd have to kill everyone else: Pepe, María, and James too. So I decided I had to be free. I had to at least try to be free."

"James is going to be surprised," Jon commented.

"Can you reach him?" Ashley asked, a spark in her voice.

"It's not that easy," Jon answered. "I wasn't lying. We really don't know where he is. But we told him a place where he could get messages from us. We'll just have to send him a message and ask him to call."

Ashley looked a little downcast again.

"You really would like to talk to him?" Judy asked.

"Yeah ... but there's something else," she said reluctantly.

"What's that?" Judy asked.

"I left a message on Nova Mundi's answering machine. I told them who I was, and to come get me at the airport."

"And what happened?" Judy asked.

"They never came. I didn't realize that today was Sunday. And they don't work on Sundays," she said with a laugh.

"So the tape's there," Jon resigned, understanding Ashley's mood.

"Yeah. It's there, just waiting for them to come in tomorrow."

"But you say you told them to get you at the airport?"

"I did."

"Well, then. Relax. You don't have anything to worry about. Just don't get near the airport tomorrow," Jon recommended naively.

"No," Ashley began, "that's not the problem."

"What is, then?" Jon asked.

"They'll know I'm alive, and that I was here in Quito. They'll start asking around for people who have seen me." Ashley didn't say it, but she thought — And every guy in that whole airport had his eyes on me.

"And that jerk who made such a thing about us stopping to get you, with his horn blaring — why, he probably drew enough attention for half of Quito to know you got into a gray Jeep. They may've even gotten our license number," Judy summarized.

"Well," Jon began, "there's not much we can do. Except, maybe, you could travel out in the direction that James went, but we don't even know where to tell you to go."

"No, that won't work. I've got to do something that will fix the mess I've made," Ashley said.

"What?" Jon asked, and then said, "you can't just call them up and tell them you aren't really here."

"But I can go there and get the tape," Ashley said with a sly smile.

"Won't that be dangerous?" Judy asked.

"Not as dangerous as waiting around here."

"So you're saying you want to steal the tape?" Jon asked.

"Jon," Judy declared, "be polite."

"Oh, excuse me. So you want to go and remove your tape from their premises?"

"Right," Ashley answered resolutely.

"So, how will you do it? Just walk in the front door and ask for the tape? Do you even know where it is?"

"That's easy. Their address is in the phone book. The hard part will be breaking their security. Nova Mundi has super-tech. So it won't be just any regular alarm system."

"And do you think you can do it? If they catch you, we'll all be in trouble. Don't you think it would be better just to stay here and not make waves? Besides, I'm sure you're exhausted after what you've been through," Jon said.

"I am," Ashley confessed. "And I haven't even had a decent night's sleep. But if I don't do something about this, I don't know if I'll ever get any rest again."

"Ashley, just turn it over to Jesus, like you gave Him your life," Judy counseled.

Ashley began to think — I'm different. I don't want to go back. My conditioning has been broken. So Jesus *has* changed me. But I've got to do something. They just don't understand. TerraNova will kill us all. I can't just sit here and do nothing.

Then Ashley progressed in her thought and realized that as much as she had feared TerraNova before, she didn't fear them now. Then she asked herself — Why do I want to go after the tape? But she couldn't explain. She just knew she had to try to get it.

Chapter 3

Burglary

Still bent to make some port he knows not where,
Still standing for some false impossible shore.

— Matthew Arnold

February 17 — That same day — Worldwide

"Weller, don't you think you're devoting too many resources to finding a dead man? Smith's no more than an oil spot. If he'd lived, he would have turned on his transceiver," Stonefell complained, trying to get Weller off his fixation, and move him on to some productive work. I can't let the kid have his way on this one — Stonefell considered. I've got to dominate him before he makes himself Chairman. Smith can't be alive. Why waste our time?

"If it so pleases the 'Chairman,' " Weller answered, with a sarcastic bite, "I appeal to the Committee to continue the search. We know from

Chief Jones that Smith was a bit unstable just before the explosion. Our calculations show he would have been in the same storm that killed Brown, but in his case, since he ejected last, he would have fallen nearer the Ecuadorian coast, and therefore, his chances of living were greater. It's likely that his RSB washed ashore. We should try to find it, if for no other reason than to keep some outer reporter from getting to it."

"I do believe, Stonefell, that Herr Weller has reason to continue the search. It shouldn't be too hard to find an object as big as an RSB. It gives a distinct reflection on an ionic-meson scan," Watkins observed, and continued in a cool tone, not wanting to inflame Stonefell, but Weller, indeed, had a point, "and he's right, you know. If the press finds an RSB, we will be cleaning up for a long time. You know how hard it is to shut down a free press. It's much easier to keep them from finding it. Perhaps, finding the RSB is more important than finding Smith."

Cyzack added, "Please, Irving, with all due respect, I agree with Weller in this case. We should be able to find it. And it seems that we have ample reason to do so. I know it's just one RSB, but what if the other equipment is in it? Sure, we could explain away a big shiny bag, but what if there's a body? A neat Aryan in a uniform. And if they do an autopsy, they'll find his enhancements. Then there is all the other tech, and black boxes — micromechanics and nanomechanics — the PLOT, even his watch. We don't want all that technology falling into the wrong hands. It's not likely an outer would know what they'd found, but we can't take any chances."

Gernik agreed, and added, "Remember the slobs who went to the press with their discovery of cold fusion? We're still working on that one — trying to convince people it was a fraud."

"Gentlemen — enough. If it's the consensus of the distinguished Cosmokrators that Weller should continue his search for Smith's RSB, then I join the majority." Stonefell looked loathingly into Weller's holographic eyes and told him, "You have your mandate; so find the inflicted RSB, and Smith too — if he's alive." And after he dictated his orders, he thought — Curse Weller. I'll have to get him later. He's already acting like he's the boss.

* * *

Quito, Ecuador

IT WAS DECIDED. Jon wasn't quite sure it was a good decision, but it was apparent that Ashley wouldn't be happy with less. Besides, if she was successful, they wouldn't have to worry about a swarm of those people called "sows" (Jon's purposeful mispronunciation of SAOs) and all of their terrible technological gadgets that James and Ashley had talked about.

At first Jon had been hesitant, but he was a firm believer in doing whatever he did to the best of his abilities. So whether he liked it or not, he fully committed himself; and it did seem exciting: a little James Bondish — he imagined.

THEY DIDN'T have much time to come up with a very thorough plan, and Ashley had no idea what she would run into once she was inside the building, but she was a well-trained guerrilla fighter, industrial spy, agent at large, or whatever TerraNova needed — Alpha Force was the best. She knew the tricks and felt confident that she could do the job — a simple one at that, if compared with many previous assignments.

But this would be different. She didn't have all the toys: like a PHENIX (Portable High ENergy Ion eXterminator) that could be used as a harmless stun gun, or for more sinister purposes. She didn't have anyone to watch her tail. There were many other difficulties: Some were as simple as not having the right shoes and camouflage. But she weighed the risks and decided — It won't be hard.

Judy frequently evangelized with mimes, and had plenty of black and white makeup, which Ashley used to make a spotted dark-gray camouflage for her face. Judy also had a black hair net, and a dark scarf, which would cover her brilliant blond hair. It was also fortunate that Judy was fairly tall and her clothing mostly fit Ashley. The black pants were a bit short, but the blouse fit well. Jon sacrificed a few pairs of heavy black socks, and she cut open the toes of one pair. He had a couple of old inner tubes, which she cut into strips in several different shapes.

It was late afternoon and they had to keep moving. Ashley wanted all the time she could get, if she needed it, before office hours Monday morning. It might be a long night.

"I'll pull the Jeep into the carport so Ashley doesn't have to parade in front of the neighborhood," Jon indicated.

"Okay," Judy approved.

He backed the Jeep inside, near the door, to reduce the distance she would need before getting in the vehicle's back end. He then put the seat down, making a larger area where she would be able to lie down and hide under a blanket.

Ashley got in and under the blanket. Jon pulled out — Nova Mundi's address in hand. Now in traffic, they headed south towards the main business section of town. Being a Sunday afternoon meant that there wasn't too much traffic.

Nova Mundi's address was in one of the better-known office buildings. The plan was for Jon to "check it out." All he would do was find out if the address was correct, and find out what floor the *others* were on, along with any additional details — if he could.

IT WAS A twelve-story building. Several of the surrounding structures were taller. They didn't have any trouble parking, and Ashley remained covered. It was about 6:15 PM and Quito's short twilight was beginning. Judy sat in the passenger seat and Jon got out. He walked around the corner to the main door. A guard, with a mean-looking short-barreled shotgun, stood in a station by the door. Jon knew the man could be the worst shot around, but if he just pointed that thing in the general direction and fired, whatever was there would be killed.

Jon tried to play the part of an innocent nobody who had some business with Nova Mundi. He started to open the door, but it was locked. The guard was immediately standing on the other side of the smoked-glass entrance.

"Nova Mundi?" Jon inquired, speaking loudly so he would be heard through the door.

The guard answered him in Spanish, saying they would be open tomorrow but that no one was there now. Jon got closer to the door and shaded his eyes, trying to see the building's directory and get the floor number. The guard didn't seem to like his movement, and turned to face him with a nasty expression.

Jon asked him, "I'm just curious which floor they're on — for when I return."

The guard turned around and pointed to big letters that read, *"Nova Mundi, sexto piso"* – "sixth floor."

Then the guard gave him a jewel of information. He said, "Take the elevator, and it'll be the door to your right. They should be here tomorrow morning at nine."

This was exactly the information Jon needed. He thanked the guard, thinking — Maybe I could be a spy and — walked back to the Jeep, content with himself and his successful mission. Once inside, he informed the ladies. Ashley was still under the blanket.

"Maybe you ought to move on," Judy suggested. Won't you look suspicious, just parking here? No one else is around."

"You're probably right," Jon answered, and pulled away.

"But Ashley," Jon began to ask, with a concerned voice, "how are you going to get past the guard and all? He looked mean."

"Guards are supposed to look mean," Ashley answered, "but I'll never see him. If he's the only one, it'll be a cinch."

"You know," Judy spoke in a sorry-to-have-to-tell-you-this voice, "but isn't this breaking and entering?"

"Why?" Ashley asked. "I'll just pay them a visit. I'll try not to break anything, and if I do, you know, accidents happen. Besides, I *am* part of Nova Mundi, so it's sort of like my own office. And I'll not take the tape. That would be too suspicious. I'll just erase it. So don't worry, Judy. Okay?"

With reserve, Judy smiled at Ashley, who had gotten her head out from under the cover. She really looked the part of a cat burglar.

"Jon, maybe you could drive me around to the back of the building or one side. I'll stay down, but I'd like to get a view of it to pick out the best place for you to leave me."

"Okay, but what are we going to do about picking you up?"

"Just go home. I'll take care of myself. If I need it I've got a change of clothes in my bag. When I'm done, I'll call you and I'll tell you where to find me."

"Simple enough. Are you sure you can do it?" he asked, thinking — This sounds like fun. I wish I was going.

"I have to," Ashley answered, "and yes, I can."

They came around to the side of the building. There was an alley, but Jon felt it would look too fishy if he drove into it. Ashley agreed, and instructed, "Drive back around the block and come by this corner again. I'll jump out."

"How will you get out of the Jeep, doll?" Judy inquired.

"Oh, I'd better open the door," Jon remembered aloud, realizing he had locked it from the outside.

Traffic was very light and Jon pulled over, got out, and moved around to unlock the back door so that she would be able to open it. He then drove on around to return to the point she had chosen. When he pulled to the curb, she jumped out and streaked away, disappearing like a panther in the night. Judy commented as she watched her go, "My, that girl's quick."

Jon had been too busy driving to notice, but when he looked, she wasn't anywhere to be seen.

ASHLEY COULD MOVE rapidly, with stealth — her nerve-pulse accelerators allowed her to calculate movements with far more precision than an ordinary person. She could make swift movements, but without stepping on things that would make noise. Only two pairs of socks covered her feet, making her step even quieter.

Moving around from the side to the back she saw there wasn't any easy way inside — without breaking down a door — and that would draw attention. So she decided to go ahead with what had been her main plan. The building was dark gray, which would help. She sat down quietly, opened her little bag, and dug out the strips of inner tube she had cut. Removing the outside pair of socks, her toes were exposed. She wrapped the rest of her feet with the inner tube, as well as wrapping parts of her hands. It was makeshift, but it was a short climb — only twelve floors to the roof — and if she was lucky, there might be an open window or some place to get inside, on, or near, the sixth floor.

She didn't want to enter just any apartment, though, and would take care to get into a stairwell, giving her access to the whole building.

The building's downtown location was advantageous for her Sunday-evening job. There was little traffic, no one was walking about, few windows in any of the surrounding buildings were lit, and her target looked as though it would be easy to scale. Numerous windows with small sills would allow her to, for all practical purposes, jump from one floor to the next.

With bioelectomechanics functioning optimally (except for her vision enhancements, which would have been useful), she bent her knees, extended her arms upwards, fixed her eyes on the first ledge, about twelve feet up, and jumped. It was easy. Her fingertips latched onto the protrusion and her implants actuated, lifting her entire weight smoothly. She made it to the ledge and stood fully balanced, thanks to enhanced inner ear processors. Not one nervous twitch, not one false move — vertigo wasn't an acceptable trait for an Alpha Force troop. None of them even talked about being afraid of heights. All she needed was a good toehold and she could balance her entire weight.

Other parts of the wall enabled her to climb like a spider, but instead of eight legs she had twenty points of contact (ten toes and ten fingers). She didn't have proper equipment, but powerful implants, pulling on genetically reinforced tendons, gave her all the sheer power she needed. However, she had to take care not to rip open her own flesh. It would have been easy for her to abuse her unprotected fingers or toes. Even though she had to move slower than good equipment would have allowed, she still averaged a floor about every ten seconds.

Having climbed four floors, she found an open window to a stairwell, just as she had hoped. Pulling herself up, with fingers on the ledge above, she penetrated the dark passageway, feet first, attempting to be quiet. It was doubtful an ordinary cat burglar would have been able to match her abilities. She had the power to be gentle and sure at the same time.

Once inside, she sat in the dark stairwell in a corner and, pulling the dark gym bag off her shoulder, she unwrapped her feet and hands, stashing the rubber strips and slipping the outer pair of socks back on her feet. She sprang up the stairs, and ascended two more floors. There were little windows on the doors, allowing her to look through into the hall before entering. Her way was clear. It was just a stairwell and the door would be open, she hoped, and it was. She stood in front of the elevator door, but the door to its right wasn't Nova Mundi's, as Jon had said. Now what! — she thought. What should I do?

Then she remembered, in Latin America and parts of Europe they count floors in buildings differently, so she still needed to ascend. Agilely, she moved back through the door into the stairwell and climbed another story. There wasn't any sign that anyone else was in the building, but she knew otherwise. There was at least one guard, and likely more. Reaching the next floor, she moved into the hall, and there it was: a simple-looking door, but well sealed and locked. On it was an elegant, though not ostentatious, plaque, and inscribed upon it were the words *Fundación Nova Mundi.*

Ashley looked around and decided that the floor was empty. Sheer force would have been sufficient to breach the door, but a deed of that nature would have left evidence of her visit, and trigger the alarm.

There wasn't a demodulator box on the outside of the door, so this wasn't the ingress to the maximum-security area. This arrangement was consistent with other countries where Nova Mundi retained a small presence: a low-security outer office to receive the general public, but inside, a hidden area that was off limits to most anyone, except approved personnel.

If she could get past the door, she knew she would only have about ten seconds to disarm the alarm system. But the door was a formidable foe. It had a dead bolt and an ordinary lock too. Picking them required a simple tool she didn't have — a PARASITE (Programmable Aeronautic Robot And Semi-Intelligent Tactical Explorer). She checked to see if there was any ventilation duct work big enough for her, but that would have been too good to be true. She decided she would have to take a risk and go back outside. Would someone have left a window open or unlocked? — she doubted it, but it was worth a look.

Moving back to the stairwell, she opened the window and lifted herself through. Soon she had moved around the corner of the building and had Nova Mundi's windows in view. She carefully checked, trying to be quick, since the last thing she needed was to be seen. There was a section of louvered windows. She approached them, moving along the windowsill — balanced on her toes. There were eight pieces of glass altogether. If she removed each one, she would have enough room to get inside. From the bottom to the top, she checked each pane to see if any were loose — no luck.

With the curtains drawn, she couldn't see what was on the inside, but she could guess: They would probably have a motion detector, at the very least.

It looked hopeless. She began to debate her apparent options: bash in the door and trigger the alarm; break a window, same result; or simply give up and let them hear her message. None of the options were agreeable to her.

I'll try the windows again — she decided, and began to go back over each one, shifting each pane up and down, left and right: anything that would allow her to remove one. She applied more force — to the point that she became concerned that it would break the glass. If it does break, what will I do? — she asked herself, trying to make a scheme. I'll break them all, and then jump in and the alarm will go crazy. I'll make it look like a cheap robbery and get out — not a bad idea. I'll probably be gone before the guard, or anyone else, gets here.

As she thought about it, frustrated with all the time she was taking, she nearly decided to go ahead and break the small pieces of louvered glass, knowing it would be too good to be true — that she would find one that was loose. Properly fastened windows would be one of the first things the security people would have insured. However, she attempted to remove them; since it was a low-security area — and just an outer office — maybe they had missed one. Eight windows meant there were sixteen edges that had to be tight. If only one was loose, it might be enough. She tried the last pane, for the second time, but it didn't budge. It looked as if she should either abandon her effort or break in. She had been on the sill most of a minute, and knew that every second increased the chances of being seen. It was time for a decision and she wished James was there — he would know what to do. Partially in frustration, and partially because she wasn't satisfied with the other possibilities, she tried again, forcing harder, depending on her rapid sensory perception to push each piece to the limit, though not totally sure she wouldn't break one. She decided to try again, and instead of pushing against the exposed edge from the middle of the pane, she powerfully pushed on each end directly, concentrating the pressure at the point where it was most likely to give her the maximum benefit. She gave up on the first pane and tried another — nothing. Any harder and, she felt certain, it would break. With hearing enhancements, she tried to tell by the sound when it was almost cracking, but not quite. At that point she would stop applying pressure, and move her thumbs to try the next piece.

Testing each one took valuable time. A cool breeze swept against her, which was welcome. When she finally reached the last one, she decided she was out of luck, and the chances of it snapping out were less than being struck with lightning on a clear day, but she would try, having gone this far, since there was this uncanny thing — something a guy named Murphy had noted in one of the corollaries to his law, which seemed stupid, but often proved itself true. In the law he had stipulated that if something could go wrong — it would. The corollary indicated that no matter what order you decided to use for a trial-and-error test, it would always be the last possibility tried that worked. Murphy was an outer, who had been a scientist at White Sands, but his law was universally known — and respected — even by scientists in the New Order.

So she tried that last pane, pushing with all the might her strong thumbs could apply without cracking the glass outright. Nothing. Curse Murphy — she started to think, but caught herself, and laughed silently — Yeah, if anything can go wrong, it will: Even the blasted corollary to his law didn't work right! The last one tested didn't budge.

Looking at the pieces one last time, she nearly broke one, but then thought — What if I heat the aluminum support? It will expand. The force of expansion might be enough to crack any sealant they've used. That could give me enough room to jimmy it out. She hadn't brought anything to heat with, but then she thought — Friction.

She pulled the gym bag around, and reached in the bottom, removing the base support, which was little more than cardboard covered by nylon. Ripping the nylon off, she removed the cardboard, tore off a piece, and began to rub the exposed portion of the aluminum frame that held the edge of the middle pane. Her powered movements — several times quicker than ordinary hands — worked well, but it was noisy.

At least it didn't seem as though anyone was close enough to listen. She looked around, and didn't see anyone on the street or in the alley, but she knew her activity could draw attention.

The metal was getting warm, but she wondered if she would be able to get it warmer than it would be on a sunny day? That noise! — she exclaimed to herself, feeling embarrassed: as if all the eyes in the airport were staring her way again. It was getting warmer; it even started to feel uncomfortable to her touch. She had been working on it about ten seconds, and kept on for a moment more before deciding to try to see if she had made any progress. She forced again with her thumbs. The left side snapped! Yes!

She looked around. Things still looked clear. It had only taken about fifteen seconds in all, so she decided to try the right side.

Again, rubbing with quickened motion, she worked to get it hot. Then she tried forcing again, but nothing snapped. Yeah, Murphy — she silently told his ghost, and looked about, before rubbing once more — as hard as she dared. It was getting hot. She rubbed harder. It was painful.

Her fingertips, despite enhancements, were tired and boiling too – she knew it was about time for a good first-degree burn, and relented.

Rapidly, before losing the heat, she started to force the bottom edge of the glass. Right and left, up and down: Come on! – she told it, to herself, and prayed – Help me, Lord. But it didn't snap.

On the street below, some cars had zoomed by, but as far as she could tell, she was still unseen. She thought a moment more – Is it worth it? And resigned – So what! I might as well get out while I can, and she started to pull the bag around to her back and stood on the sill, looking at the silly windows – hating herself for giving up. She started to turn away.

But I've got to get that tape! – she thought. I'll break the glass! Turning back and squatting on the ledge, she started pushing up on the edge of the pane, and decided it would either snap loose or break! With ever-increasing pressure, and the tips of her thumbs bent back in pain, she forced. Any moment she was certain she would hear the sound of shattering glass, but it snapped loose! Yes!

Both sides were free and the pane moved – though hardly at all – but it moved. She started working with it, jimmying it up and down. She could hear the glass scraping – nearly cracking – but she tried to control the amount of pressure she exerted with her tired fingertips. Thankfully, her enhanced sense of touch gave her the necessary control.

When the segment slipped out of the louver frame, moving upwards, she reached through to the inside, being careful not to touch the curtain – she didn't want to activate the motion detector, yet. With the one pane free, the others were only a matter of seconds each; as she pried – powerfully pried – her exhausted fingertips kept working, snapping back the tabs that held each piece, and breaking the sealant.

She gently laid each of the eight panes of glass, one on top of the other, on the sill. For her next step, she wished she had vision enhancements, for it would be dark inside, darker than it was outside. Her best guess was that she would have about ten seconds to reach the demodulator. She also knew it would record her implanted electronic identification, but if she was successful, no one would ever know she had been there, and therefore, no one would check the record. If she failed to reach the demodulator, then she would go with Plan B: Let the alarm sound and the security cameras film and call Novus Ordo, and everyone else, the local police and the inflicted local sow too — she thought, kind of liking Jon's mispronunciation of SAO.

She had been on the sill too long. She couldn't waste any more time. She burst through the curtains as quickly as she could without tearing them from the rail. Sure enough, she saw the little red light on the sensor, located on the ceiling, blinking as she moved. The demodulator would be near the main door. She could barely see her way there. Each step seemed to endure, as if made for keeping in a museum, and with the darkness she wasn't sure she would make it without tripping on something.

Where's the demodulator? — she asked herself, finally moving into the entranceway. It should have some indicator — some light — something! But she didn't see anything. She hadn't been counting seconds, but she knew the alarm system would trigger any instant. Where is it! — she demanded. Feeling and groping, her hand touched a coat stand. It moved and she saw the digital display. It showed "01." That was all the time she had left, and with accelerated reflex she snapped her wrist against the box. "PROCESSING" came on the display, not an instant too soon. A moment later, "CONFIRMED" — and displayed her serial number, and then "SAFE" appeared.

Ashley breathed easier. The display flashed the time back on — 19:33. She thought — So far, so good, and she began to look for the telephone.

Chapter 4

Failure

WE ARE ALL FAILURES — at least, all the best of us are.

— J. M. Barrie

February 17 — That same day — Quito, Ecuador

"SEÑOR WALKER," greeted the guard at the building's entrance.

"Buenos noches," he answered in return, and told the guard he needed to leave some boxes in the Nova Mundi office — for work tomorrow. He asked the guard to help him, to avoid making two trips.

The guard slung his shotgun over his shoulder, behind his back, and helped Walker, who always gave him a good tip. Together, they got the boxes loaded into the elevator, four in all. They were heavy and awkward. Walker made some joke about the current government and the guard laughed wholeheartedly.

ASHLEY'S HEARING ENHANCEMENT assisted her in distinguishing the sound of laughter coming from the elevator shaft. She doubted it had anything to do with Nova Mundi. She had seen the phone, but it didn't use a cassette tape. It was a new solid-state model that used memory instead. She would have to do more than just grab a cassette. Removing the battery for a while would do the trick — she imagined. Taking the whole phone would be the easiest. However, her purpose was to remain undiscovered.

The fax machine sat near the window and there was enough light coming through a crack in the curtains that she noticed a message. She started reading, before tackling the phone. It said, "From: Nova Mundi, New York. To: Nova Mundi, Quito. Mr. Walker, prepare to receive large contingent of representatives. Make reservations for 12. RSB has been located. Investigation is Alpha priority. Obtain cooperation from local military and requisition all-terrain vehicles. Helicopter support also solicited."

About then, she heard the elevator motor start, and decided she needed to hide, just in case they were coming her way, and asked herself — Where? Behind the curtains or back on the windowsill? And if someone comes, will they notice the window's been opened? She looked quickly to see if the curtains were drawn and the windows hidden. And the alarm? — she remembered. Is it disarmed? Dashing back to the door, she put her wrist back on the box: ARMED — printed on the little screen. She reentered the office where she then lay on the floor between a couch and the wall. If someone came in — and they probably wouldn't — she figured they would occupy themselves on the other side of the office.

Sharply, the elevator stopped. From the sound, they were in the hall. Just my luck — she thought. Hopefully, they'll do what they've got planned and get out fast — she aspired.

She could hear them outside of the door. She wondered if there wasn't something else she could do — but decided to wait. She heard the door open and the alarm chime, indicating that it had been deactivated. She heard them piling the boxes through the door. It didn't take them long.

She glanced around and saw the back of the man, who must have been a SAO, as he handed the guard about a dollar's worth of the local currency. Stepping back, the security man took his gun in hand and pulled it around to a position of greater readiness. The SAO came back into the office and turned on the lights. His feet came into her field of view, at times, but not his face. Her angle was too low. She didn't fear him seeing her; as long as he didn't come over and specifically look behind the couch.

Ashley cursed in her mind when he pressed the play button on the answering machine (as if he made a habit of it, and he probably did). He was a SAO — but an Alpha Force first officer was more than a match for him. Maybe I'll have to take charge — she considered, knowing she could've whipped any five, hand-to-hand, but he likely had a PHENIX. Even so — she figured — he would be dead before he could get to it.

The machine rambled on, two messages, and Ashley still didn't hear hers. The SAO didn't seem to be paying much attention to the recorded "orders" and went to the WC. The third message came — ramblings — a pick-this-up, take-that-there message.

It wouldn't be long. Saturday's messages had almost finished. Sunday's would be coming. She began to think — I'll break his neck. Do Christians do that? — she questioned. It seems like they must — she decided, remembering her history classes. She thought — They've fought many a war in the name of Christ. She didn't feel good about her conclusion, but there wasn't any time for philosophy.

Walker finished his visit to the bathroom about the same time Saturday's last message finished.

This is it — she thought. There was a hiss. It's coming — she knew it was. The hiss seemed to get louder ... and then ... all too quickly, she heard, "Walker," and the machine's tiny speaker went on with another get-this-and-that.

By now he was out of the WC and he walked around the back of the desk. He stood momentarily, his back to her, and his arms crossed.

Was it instinct? Could it have been fear? It probably wasn't either. It was training and reflexes. She had to do something, and it had to be now — before her voice came through the speaker. Jumping, with a powered leap, she sprang like a mighty black feline and landed upright on both feet — behind the SAO. He wasn't slow to react, but she had all the advantages. She grabbed his head and twisted it violently, but he was already turning the same direction, which saved him. Both were moving at the limits of heightened reflex. He came around and delivered a powerful blow directly to Ashley's stomach, which he found to be as hard as a board — leaving his hand in throbbing pain. She was hurt also, but she didn't have time to notice.

She twisted and leaped, coming up under him with a powerful kick — right in his Adam's apple. He staggered backwards and fell, while reaching into his coat pocket.

Ashley saw him, and knew he was after his PHENIX. She vaulted towards him and, with her shoeless foot, kicked his hand away.

He rolled over, attempting to get to his weapon.

Diving, she grabbed onto his arm and twisted it back. She ripped open his pocket and the PHENIX fell out as he rolled over violently, throwing her off to one side. He attempted to reach back into his suit pocket, not yet realizing it was empty. She sprang back, over top of him, and landed on his PHENIX. She grabbed it up. In a maneuver she had practiced more times than she knew, she popped it open, armed it, and aimed at the desperate agent, who came — as a thrown lance — right at her. She pulsed the firing button. A short burst, less than a millisecond, brought the big man down.

He fell, crashing hard onto the floor — stunned. Ashley pressed the coded points on the PHENIX, setting it for full vaporization. She pointed it at the SAO and started to aim. Her arm locked in place. Her expression was cool. She was well trained and her action was spontaneous. She would finish what she had started —

But she paused … though still ready to fire … she hesitated … she would do it … but she couldn't — it wasn't right. Her arm dropped and she disarmed the PHENIX.

She heard her message finish playing.

The SAO would be out for a few hours. But when he regained his senses, he would know that a woman, camouflaged in black, had attacked him. He would also know the woman had nearly twisted his head off. He would know she had bioenhancements. He would conclude she was from Alpha Force, because he would have been the victor in a fight against anyone less. Ashley figured that vaporizing him would solve some problems — it was the expedient thing to do — but she couldn't. She had never had such a problem before, but she couldn't execute the helpless man — her newly operational conscience told her so.

Her debate with herself didn't last long. She heard the elevator again. Who will it be now — she thought with discouragement. I've failed. My message from the airport was probably recorded on the security camera's sound track. But I'll have to think about that later. And then she lamented — If I'd been successful in breaking the SAO's neck, like I wanted, I would have been able to shut the recording off before it was too late. If I'd thought I would fail, I would have gone after him sooner. Then she thought — It's crazy, but I'm really glad I didn't snap his neck, or vaporize him. I don't think that Christians would do that. Or would they?

She didn't have time to think about it anymore. Whoever was coming, if they were coming her way, probably knew that the SAO was in the office and they would expect to find him. She rushed to take position and readied herself behind the entrance door — which the SAO had left closed, but unlocked.

While she stood, in a moment of pause before the elevator stopped, it occurred to her that something was wrong with the picture — I haven't seen the surveillance cameras — she told herself.

The elevator stopped. I hate it! — she exclaimed to herself; for, sure enough, it stopped right on her floor. She heard heavy, unconcerned footsteps coming towards the door. She was ready, PHENIX in hand — armed and ready to stun. The door beside her reverberated with a couple of hefty bangs and a voice spoke up, *"La pizza, Señor Walker."*

Pizza — Ashley thought. So he was planning to work late.

After a moment the guard banged on the door again. Would he come on in? — or walk away? — she wondered. I'll have to stop him either way.

"Señor Walker, la pizza llegó."

Again there wasn't any answer.

The guard mumbled to himself, *"¿Por qué no contesta?* — Why doesn't he answer?" and decided to see if the door would open.

Ashley saw the knob turn and she stiffened. The door opened inward, hiding her.

The guard called again through the door's open crack. Still, there was no answer.

Opening wider, he started through; the box of pizza preceded him. Then the tip of his shotgun, and finally his somewhat overweight body followed. Pizza … smells good — Ashley thought. He chugged a couple of steps through the door into the short hall and started to turn to close the door.

She pressed the PHENIX button. There was a sound, almost too brief to be heard, like a welder's torch. He fell forward on the pizza, squashing it. She would just leave him there to enjoy it when he recovered.

Then she moved back into the office, looking carefully, trying to discover where they had hidden the security cameras. Then it came to her, and she hated herself even more. She just remembered that Nova Mundi had been changing their regular cameras to SPARQs (Singular Photon Abstraction by Reflected Quanta) — in most of their offices.

With this realization, her stomach began to sicken and she remembered another incident when a SPARQ had ruined her dreams — back in the closet.

She looked at the ceiling censor. Sure enough, a small diamond-shaped protrusion glistened with a rainbow of colors. It stared ominously throughout the room, seeing behind corners, out into the hall, into the bathroom, under the desks, and probably behind the curtains too. Its vision, within a range of ten yards, or so, was limited only by the processing time allotted to it by the supercomputer, and it couldn't be blinded easily. The only consolation was that they wouldn't be watching a live image, since the crude data would have to be processed. They only bothered with the task of processing if there was a good reason, which she had certainly given them.

Of course; Why didn't I remember? – she asked herself, feeling stupid. To get its data I'd have to break into the high-security area.

The entrance was visible on the other side of the desk, and another demodulator box was beside it. However, she knew, that unlike the outer door, if she used her demodulator there, it would require reconfirmation from Novus Ordo, and they would know she was there – in real time. Besides, if she even made it to the computer, it would require her to log on, and again, they would know she was present.

So, the SAO was going to work late – she reasoned – because they found James's RSB. They're going to have a big mobilization. That's why there were so many messages on the phone. He was going to work late, getting help from the Ecuadorian military and government on a Sunday night. He would just cash in a few favors. Nova Mundi always had plenty of "good will": new loans, better payment plans for the national debt – whatever it took.

She tried to think of some way to tie the SAO down, which would give her more time. It would take her a few more minutes, but it could be worth the effort. She ripped the upholstery off of the plush black leather couch, and tore it in long strips. It would take some significant binding to keep him from breaking free.

For the guard it was just a few simple wraps around his wrists and ankles, but for the SAO, she bound his arms from his wrists to above his elbows, leaving them behind his back, and his legs, she tied from his ankles to above his knees. It was a significant chore and took about ten minutes, but she figured it might give her a few more hours.

By the time she finished tying him up, she was even feeling a little guilty for having beaten up on the poor devil. But she asked herself – Why should I feel guilty? I'm hurting too. She could feel her blows starting to throb with pain; at least infliction had given her good pain training, and she could forget her hurt, for now.

She realized that she was giving whoever played back the SPARQ's data a good show, but her actions would delay the premiere viewing for a few hours. By now, it was obvious to her that if she had killed the SAO, it wouldn't have aided her cause — the SPARQ had her, anyhow.

It was a temptation for her to think that her effort had been a waste. She wanted to curse herself — and did — thinking of herself as having the intelligence of a worm. She started *iffing* — If I'd been a little quicker... If I'd thought of heating the frame sooner... If God would've helped me... If... If... If... Training told her not to *if* over spilt milk, but to clean it up. In this case it didn't look like the mess she'd made would clean so well — it could leave a permanent stain. The most she could hope for was to extend, by a few hours, the time it would take for her employer to issue a pink slip with her name on it. They wouldn't even need to order a coffin: vaporization would be adequate — after prolonged infliction.

Despite her bungling, she had found out they were after James, and her effort would give her some time to reach him — she prayed. Despite His seeming absence on this mission, God had proven to her that He could do miracles. She didn't know why He hadn't done one that evening, but she figured that He probably had His reasons, and after all, she was still alive and well, and had a chance to save James — so maybe He had helped. Maybe that was the miracle.

She reasoned — In two or three hours the SAO will awaken. By the time he has his wits, figures how to free himself, and calls for help, it'll be morning — she hoped, and finished the task of tying him.

She picked up the handset on the stupid telephone that was "responsible" for her ordeal — although she knew it was really her own mistake — and started to dial Jon's number, but then suddenly stopped — realizing that the SPARQ was registering her every movement. They would be able to see the number she dialed, and even without a SPARQ, they would have been able to trace the number she dialed through the local phone company, so she hungup, and moved towards the door. There wasn't anything left for her to do in the office.

In her hand she carried a trophy from her visit — a PHENIX. For stunning, it could probably be fired twenty or more times; for vaporization, maybe only two or three.

She nearly armed the alarm before leaving, but decided it wasn't a good idea. If the SAO, or the guard, started moving, it would trigger the alarm and bring Nova Mundi much sooner. She locked the door behind her, and ran down the stairwell with the step and grace of a ballerina, the speed of a feline, and the mastery of an eagle. There might be other guards, so she would be careful.

Reaching the first floor, she opened a window and escaped from the building. Once in the alley she hid herself in a stairwell, between walls, and quickly pulled off Judy's black blouse. She wiped off her blended camouflage makeup with a washcloth. Then she slid on her dress, which she had already taken out of the bag, and unbuckling, she dropped Judy's black pants and stepped out of them as her dress fell about her. In less than a minute, she finished her transformation and was, again, an elegant blond, but she didn't want to be seen, not just yet. She yanked off Jon's socks and slipped on her medium-heeled shoes. She shook her hair out and puffed it with her hands, giving it some body.

Feeling presentable, she looked to see if the way was clear. It was 8:20 PM. She moved into the alley, and suddenly a door burst open and a shotgun pointed her way. Facing the thing wasn't pleasant. Behind it was, indeed, another guard.

Does he know what's happened in Nova Mundi? — she asked herself. But she doubted the guard would fire without saying something, and by then she would have stunned him — the PHENIX was now in her fingertips, and armed. She held it to her side, out of the guard's view (but it wouldn't have looked like anything more than a cigarette lighter, in his eyes). Besides — she figured — he probably wouldn't be looking for trouble. If he had found the bodies, or knew something, he would have called the police and would have been waiting for them in the office. She concluded that he was a second guard making a routine check.

"*Que...,*" he started, but then held his tongue, apparently expecting to see something else.

Ashley answered, taking advantage of his surprise.

"*Estoy perdida* — I'm lost," she said, with as much accent as she could, without being misunderstood, and making her voice a bit seductive, but not too much (she didn't want to carry it too far). Certain aspects of "*seductive*" were a mystery to her, but not its effect on outers. It had been part of her training. She also knew that it would work on Alpha Force troops, save for the threat of infliction. A part of her had always wanted to do it, she knew, to James, but that had been off limits, until now — perhaps — if she found him before Nova Mundi did. For the moment, she would practice on the shotgun jock, and added, "*Hotel?*" with just the right touch of *seductive* and a questioning inflection.

The guard pointed in the direction she had been headed — out of the alley. Whatever he had been expecting, she wasn't it. She began walking slowly and deliberately. As long as he didn't do something stupid, like accidentally pulling the trigger while her back was turned, she would be gone before he knew he should have done any differently.

Ashley turned the corner, desperately needing a plan. By now, she had come to the conclusion that Quito wasn't going to be a friendly place for her to visit any longer, and she and James were going to be objects of a massive manhunt. She had to reach him, and they both had to get out of there. But how?

She saw no choice but to persuade Jon to help — quickly. So instead of walking away from where she imagined there might be people, she turned and went the way she had pictured as being closest to a phone, and about three blocks away she found a restaurant.

She entered and asked to make a call. They dialed the number for her. Jon answered, "Hello."

"I'm ready, but I'm here ... just a second," and she asked where, and then continued, "on *Amazonas,*" and she told him the name of the restaurant. "May I please ask you to come get me?" she said, with the note of a teenager needing a ride home.

"I'll be there in about twenty minutes."

"Thanks Jon, but I think we need to take a trip, right away, so could you come prepared?"

"What do you mean?" he asked, puzzled.

"I can't explain too well on the phone, but if it's possible, just come — ready to travel, out in the country, to where James is."

"Tonight?" Jon asked, protest evident in his reply.

"I think so," Ashley answered, trying to be firm but not demanding.

"Ashley!" Jon exclaimed in a voice that was trying to say, "No way!" But then, as if he had taken a moment to think about it, he said, "Okay, I'll do my best. But we only know the direction he went. How will we find him?"

"I'm not sure," she answered. "But we've got to try."

"Okay," Jon said. "But we might be a little longer getting you if we're going to make a trip?"

"I understand. I'll be waiting, but please hurry."

We've got to get out of town while we can — she told herself as she gave the phone's receiver back to the man behind the cash register. She turned and walked over to one of the tables and sat down and ordered a cup of coffee. It had been a long day, but rest wouldn't come soon.

"THAT GIRL," Judy expressed, with surprise, shaking her head from side to side. "What's she expecting?"

"I don't know," Jon answered, "but it seems like we'd better try to help her through it."

"Fine, but this is getting to be just a little too much," she said, at once realizing the poor girl probably didn't have any other option, and feeling sorry that she didn't feel more motivated to help, but she was tired. And it was Sunday. We have a right to rest! — she exclaimed to herself. But it wasn't the first time they had been inconvenienced by an opportunity to do a good deed, and it wouldn't be the last, she was sure.

"It is!" Jon agreed, confirming that he too felt inconvenienced, but then he charged, "Let's get moving." He began loading the back of the Jeep with sleeping bags, a toolbox, a propane lantern, flashlights, a first-aid kit, and numerous other things he kept ready for trips to the mountain villages. Judy said "Amen" when he commented, "I sure hope we don't need to use any of these things." He even tossed in a jug of water and some dried food.

ASHLEY FELT CONSPICUOUS, waiting in the restaurant. She had been to the WC, and finished two cups of coffee. She was running out of reasons to be there. So she was glad when Jon and Judy appeared at the door. Fortunately, it hadn't taken them as long as she thought it might.

She stood and joined them at the door, after paying her bill. They left, walked around the corner, and got in the Jeep — exchanging only a few words. Jon started the engine and began driving.

"Ashley, how did it go?" Judy asked.

"I failed," she said, lowering her head.

"What happened?" Jon asked.

"I don't want to talk about it now, but I found out that they've found James's RSB on the mountain, and they are going to begin a search to find him."

"Did they see you?" Judy questioned.

"Yeah. Or I mean they will," she answered reluctantly.

"So they're after you now?" Jon asked.

"Not yet, but they will be — I'm sure of that."

"They know you're in Quito, then?" Jon asked with a troubled voice.

"They will," Ashley answered with diminished pride, starting to feel upset with all the interrogation.

"Now what? This could be dangerous?" Jon stated with interrogative inflection.

"That's why I want to get out of town and find James."

"Well, it's not going to be easy. There aren't any roads where he was headed, or so he said. And it's a long walk. The way he told it, some of it was really rough."

"We'll have to see what we can do, but right now; I've got to get out of this town. And tomorrow they'll have people all over that mountain where James is. We've got to find him tonight, and be on our way out of there before morning."

"Ashley," Jon said, "I think we'd better pray, because you're going to need a miracle."

She paused, and thought about it. She remembered how the "M" word had been so trite to her, but he was right — they needed a miracle — and with that in mind, she said, "God saved me when I was lifeless. They saw me floating like a dead man and fished me out of the Pacific. I should've been left for the sharks. But before I went unconscious, I prayed, 'God, if You're real, save me,' and He did. I tried to deny it had been a miracle, or that God had anything to do with it, but I couldn't. I know God does miracles. I just wish He'd have done one back in that office," she said as she savored her letdown.

By now, they had made significant progress towards the edge of town.

"Okay," Jon said, as he pulled over, "let's pray."

"Good idea," Judy echoed.

They bowed their heads, and he prayed, "Father, in Jesus' name, we ask that You would be with us on this trip and keep us from harm on the night road. We ask that somehow You would help us to find James before the *others* do and that we could warn him so he and Ashley can escape. Amen."

After lingering a moment, Jon — who hadn't turned off the motor — pulled back onto the highway.

Ashley said, "We'll make it — I know."

"Jon, you said it's a small country and all the Christians know each other?' Ashley reminded him.

"Well, that's sort of true, but if you think it means I know everyone, then I didn't mean it that way."

"Oh, no. I understood. But you said you'd told James a place where he could go to get messages from us. Maybe someone there will know the man James went to visit?"

"I doubt it. James didn't even give me a last name. All I know is the name, Juan José. That's a common name, and it would be like trying to find a Smith, or a Brown, somewhere east of the Mississippi."

"But it's all we've got, isn't it?" Judy asked, worrying about some way to help Ashley accomplish her goal.

"It sure isn't much," he answered. And then he continued, "Besides, by the time we get there, it'll be ten, or so, and people will be in bed. In the country, they go to sleep early. We probably won't be able to ask Pastor Bautista anything until tomorrow."

"God will help us," Judy affirmed, as her eyes caught Ashley's.

Chapter 5

Juan José's

THE LIFE OF MAN is a long march through the night, surrounded by invisible foes, tortured by weariness and pain, ... and where none may tarry long.

— Bertrand Russell

February 17 — That same day — Juan José's house

IT'S REALLY DARK and almost too quiet — James thought. He lay on a couple of mats that covered the wooden floor, with his poncho for a pillow, and a woolen blanket for covering. He had all but forgotten how peaceful life was in the silence of the country.

Juan José had acted as if a long lost brother had returned when he saw James coming over the ridge, and he had greeted him warmly. James, now that he wasn't in a rush to return to Nova Mundi, had time to share with his "old friend" during dinner. To James, Juan José was an old friend. He had known him since the day he had begun life as an outer. Juan José had shown himself willing to receive him, so he felt grateful to God that his trip out of town hadn't been in vain. He was surprised to find that Juan José was a Christian. James looked forward to being there — helping out on the farm — but it was cold.

Yes — James thought — it's cold. How did I ever survive on that mountain? It's even worse up there. And there aren't any conveniences — not even an outhouse. The only available "plumbing" at Juan José's was the cornfield, and squatting in the cold wasn't civilized, cultivated, or enlightened, or anything else that TerraNova promised humankind. He wished he had thought to bring a roll of soft paper from his apartment — the corn leaves scratched. He wished he hadn't had to leave Quito so suddenly, and that he would have been able to plan his trip. Even a bar of soap would have been good to have. And his stomach was rumbling after the meal with Juan José — Would diarrhea come next?

It wasn't going to be much fun. In fact, it was going to be tough and dirty. Which led him to think — Ashley, Ashley... Why? Why did you go back to them? Couldn't you see? They'll inflict you until you tell them everything, and then they'll discard you like an empty throwaway bottle, after sucking you dry. Ashley, Ashley... Her name kept running through his head.

That tear! Ashley... And a tear came to his eye. He couldn't forget. He felt tempted to question God. No — not tempted — he did it ouright: Why God? Why did You let me see her again if You were going to take her away so quickly? But he felt uneasy questioning God, and had a hunch that everything that happens isn't necessarily the way God would've liked it. Life as an outer would have been a lot easier with Ashley — he mulled.

Why not just go back? — he asked himself. TerraNova can give you the good life. Captain was the highest rank, and everyone in Alpha Force was under my command. They promoted me after I wrote that stupid book, but I was so young. If only I could burn it! They'll probably use my tactics to hunt us down.

The hardness of the floor started to feel as if it was flattening his bones. My! — he exclaimed to himself. It's so hard ... and cold!

After he turned to his other side, he began to remember Juan José's testimony, which he had shared with James earlier that evening. It made him wonder if he was making a good decision, to become a Christian, since it looked like it could be dangerous. Not only did TerraNova hate Christians, but apparently many outers did too. James wondered what it would take for a man to say, "Father, forgive them," as Juan José had, when the stones were striking him, or as Jesus did, when hanging from a cross. He had assimilated enough outer thinking to actually admire the strength of character that would be required to make such a statement under such circumstances, but he doubted that he would ever be able to do it himself, even if he really did decide to believe in the outers' Jesus.

* * *

Talontag

ENTERING TALONTAG in the pitch black of a cloudy night wasn't something Jon would have planned for himself, but he knew it could be done. When he was younger, and less cautious, they would go to meetings and come home in the dark. There had been a bridge, about fifteen years earlier, which amounted to little more than a few logs. Everyone would get out and walk across, presumably to make the vehicle lighter, but the logs would've held a semi. The real reason was to reduce the body count if the driver had a nervous twitch and stirred his way off the edge into the canyon — which wouldn't have been difficult — about 80 feet down. It was sort of like driving onto a grease rack at a service station, only longer, about twenty-five feet. But if you missed on a rack, you could try again. And the service station always had someone telling you how to turn your wheels, but here, it had been a matter of fixing your wheels straight, looking to the other ledge — saying a prayer — and hoping for the best.

However, thank God, and indeed Jon thanked Him, there was now a real bridge, which they easily crossed without delay. His estimate had been about right, and his watch showed 10:00 PM as they pulled around in front of the church. It hadn't been many years before that the road didn't reach that far.

"It looks like there're still people here," Judy observed.

"Maybe God's heard our prayer," Jon commented. "Now, we only have to find Juan José, which shouldn't be difficult. Our problem will be in finding *the* Juan José."

The ladies stayed in the Jeep and Jon got out to investigate. It turned out they were just finishing a late Sunday evening meeting with a special evangelist, and Pastor Bautista was away on a trip. Initially this was disheartening, but when Jon asked them about Juan José and a tall *gringo*, he was surprised — it seemed to be common knowledge that a tall gringo had been through town that afternoon and had headed for Juan José's place — back over the ridge towards Antisana. It was evident if Nova Mundi was after James, he didn't stand much of a chance. Because it was a small community, everyone knew everything.

Jon walked down the incline in front of the church and opened the Jeep's door.

"What did they say?" Judy asked impatiently.

"It's too easy," Jon answered.

"What?" Ashley asked.

"Everyone knows where he is."

"Good," Judy said, with delight.

"But it's too easy. If Nova Mundi's looking, they won't have any trouble finding him."

"If we keep moving, we can beat them," Ashley said.

"But how? There's no road. They told me there isn't even a good Jeep trail."

"We knew that. That's what you said. But that's no problem for me," Ashley affirmed. "Just point me in the right direction and I'll be gone. I might even be back by midnight."

"You can't do that," Jon said with a snicker.

"I can," Ashley affirmed. "Listen, I know what I'm doing."

Jon felt tempted to remind her that she had said the same thing about the office in Quito, but he decided to keep quiet and avoid needless antagonism.

"Okay," Jon said. "The people said to follow that path to the end." And he pointed in the direction they had indicated. "They said it's just one path and Juan José lives near the end, about three huts from the last one, on the left."

"That's easy," Ashley said. "You can wait here, and I'll be back with James before you know it." Then she paused, and with humility, announced, "I've got a problem. I'm going to need some shoes."

Judy looked down at hers and offered, "I'll let you use mine if they fit, but I don't think they'll do any better than what you've got on." She stooped and pulled off one to show Ashley. It had a lower heel, but it looked small and wouldn't be good for the path.

"I need something I can jog in," Ashley said.

Judy offered, "Jon has something, but they'll be too big," and immediately Jon felt that his personal space had been invaded.

"Maybe not," Ashley said.

"They'll be too big," he affirmed, with levity of tone, hoping the whole thing was a joke. "I wear men's size eleven. Your foot will be floating in such a big shoe."

He pulled off a shoe and handed it to Ashley, confidant that she would decide not to take it. But then she said, "It looks perfect," and in a moment her foot was inside. "Fits like it was made for me," she said with a laugh.

Jon wanted to resist giving her his other shoe, but he couldn't find any good reason for it, and turned the other shoe over to her with the same fervor with wihich he sent checks to the IRS.

"You have a big foot for a woman," Jon said, with a shade of derision.

"Jon!" Judy said with chagrin.

"I suppose I do," Ashley answered, realizing that Jon felt ridiculed, but that was just the way it would be. She had to hurry, and she advised, "Now, I need to change."

"You can do it while I hold a blanket," Judy offered.

It didn't take too long, and Ashley was ready. Judy opened her door to let her out.

"Are you sure you can handle this alone?" Jon asked, trying one last time to salvage some dignity.

Jon saw Ashley start to grin as she began to answer, and he thought — She must be "liberated." But then he figured — It's probably just the way they trained her in that army she belonged to.

"Jon, I appreciate that you want to take the lead, but I've been trained for this and I have experience. There's only one pair of shoes. I can move fast and I'll find him quickly."

"But in this dark? There aren't even any stars tonight. And the fog on those ridges will be thick," Jon noted, as if it was his hidden ace.

ASHLEY WAS REMINDED that she no longer had vision enhancement contacts and that night vision wouldn't be any easier for her than it was for Jon. This made her consider just how quickly she had lost the advantages of TerraNova. But she knew, despite the difficulties, she had to reach James, for if she didn't, the enemy would. Then she realized — I'm calling them enemies. And her thought progressed — Even if they "made" me, they're my enemies. She finally realized — They've always been my enemies! I just didn't see it until now.

Jon asked again, "So, what about it? Should I go with you?"

"I'd feel better if you just stayed here," Ashley replied, while not wanting to sound harsh, yet knowing that she would have to convince him to stay. He would slow her down too much, but she didn't want to tell him that, at least not in those words. She said, "Jon, you're right. It won't be easy in the dark and fog. But I've got to do it." Ashley told him, looking directly in his dimly lit eyes, and then she added, "You really wouldn't want to leave Judy here alone? What if TerraNova's people come?"

"Okay," Jon began, "I guess I should stay here." Then he indicated, "There's a propane-cartridge-lantern in back, and a flashlight. There're a couple of extra canisters of propane and a few extra batteries. That should be enough to make it through the night."

Ashley, having been accustomed to the benefits of night vision, frowned on the idea of carrying a lantern and everything else, but Jon's forethought, she conceded, could make the difference between success and failure. "Good, Jon. I'm glad you thought to bring everything. It'll sure make it easier."

Jon pointed her to a pack. In it were the lantern, the canisters, a flashlight, a small first-aid kit, a sleeping bag, a jacket, and some dried food and drinks. He explained it all to her and when she had the propane flowing out of the miniature tank; she ignited it using the built-in lighter.

"My, that's bright!" she exclaimed.

"Does pretty well," Jon said. "Just turn it down as far as you can so you don't use up the propane too quickly."

They exchanged farewells as if she was going on a long journey. She walked off, with a point of light gently swinging, her figure both silhouetted and lit by the lamp.

"She sure moves quickly," Judy observed.

"They must have something different. Remember how James played basketball?" Jon asked.

"Really," Judy agreed.

They shared a moment of silence, and then Jon reached over and touched Judy's hand. It would be romantic — Judy considered — but it's too cold and too dark. We'll have to sit here all night.

"My feet are cold," Jon declared.

Judy couldn't keep from snickering as she reached back over the seat to get one of the sleeping bags and passed it over to him.

Ashley moved briskly along the path. Implants did little for her. It was impossible for her to move any faster on this terrain without more light. The lantern was bright, and lit the area where she was walking, but its light didn't reach far enough ahead to help her anticipate her maneuvers.

But the lantern did give her enough light, with her inherent strength and her nerve-pulse accelerators, to keep her moving along at superior speed, faster than an outer would have been able to travel. Another factor that influenced her to go slower was a fear that vibrations could damage the sensitive mantle of the lantern.

As it was, she was moving along at over twice the average outer speed for the path. She calculated that it might take her about two hours to make it to the area where James was supposed to be. For now, she would concentrate on keeping one foot moving in front of the other, as quickly as she could.

But she was hungry, not having eaten since the light lunch at Judy's, and so she stopped for a moment. She found a candy bar, some juice in a box, dried bananas, and peanuts. Thanks, Jon! Lunch seemed as though it had happened in some other lifetime — centuries ago. After "dinner," she covered a significant amount of territory and was about 45 minutes along the path — near half way — she calculated. So far it had been mostly uphill. From the way she imagined the landscape (she couldn't see a thing — at least not a global view), most of the trip would be a climb. After all, she was heading towards a place that wasn't far from where James said he "landed," which had been on a snowcapped mountain, and certainly the path would be uphill.

A few minutes later she began to breathe moist air, which had thickened into a fog. Since she entered the dense white cloud, her lamp wasn't effective, but if she turned it off, it would be worse. She had to slow down and take one step at a time, struggling just to see the path under her own feet. Indeed, it was nearly impossible to tell the difference between it and the rest of the landscape.

Ashley's triumphal can-do attitude was hastily vaporizing into the night's haze. It would be easy to get lost or even turned around. She wished she had a PLOT, or even an old-fashioned compass. She decided — At this rate, it'll be morning before I get there, if I don't get lost. I don't even have a watch, but it's about midnight, I guess.

* * *

The next day — Grand Central Hotel, Guayaquil, Ecuador

LÓPEZ HAD HAD A LONG DAY and things weren't getting any easier. They had spent over two months searching for a shiny bag, or a tall *gringo* – in forlorn fishing villages, while suffering tropical heat – and hadn't found even one clue. He logged in to communicate his lack of findings to Weller. It was near midnight, but Weller kept hours to 2:00 AM, Ecuador time. He wished he had something to report, and was dreading the conversation.

When Weller's picture came on his screen from Novus Ordo, he had an impassioned look, like something big was happening, and asked, demanding, "How fast can you get to Quito, López?"

"I'm not sure. There should be flights tomorrow, but they'll be booked up."

"I could send a DEEP for you, but it would be better for you to make a call and bump a few reservations. Get your people to Quito. Things are happening. Chief Jones found a way to allow scans from space and we were able to locate Captain Smith's RSB. It's on Antisana, east of Quito. We DEEPed in to check it out, and the cursed thing is empty. There was no body. There are some signs that he just walked away, although none of our people believe it. Among other things, it seems that Smith buried his RSB to keep it from being seen. He might have been trying to hide it from outers. It looked like he smashed his transceiver, but maybe the crash damaged it. It's hard to say."

"There must be some mistake," López began. "He couldn't have lived through a crash into a land mass."

"That's what the experts say, but I was there and saw it for myself. Maybe the snow on the glacier saved him. I don't know. But if he's alive, we'd best find him and find out. Someone said, 'He probably hit his head after a fall like that, and maybe that's why he broke the transceiver and walked off.' He was probably so badly injured he didn't walk far, if he walked at all. He might have crawled. He surely would have died on that inflicted mountain."

"Okay, then. I'll get our people moving and we'll begin working out of Quito. With Walker?"

"Right, López. He should be expecting you."

* * *

That same day — Between Talontag and Antisana

I'VE GOT TO SIT DOWN — Ashley told herself. There's no way to keep moving. How can the fog be this thick? She saw what appeared to be a ledge a few feet away, protruding just a bit, in the canyon wall she was walking through. There wasn't any way to know for sure; the murk was so heavy. Approaching, she decided it would be a good place to sit a spell. There was little point in walking — moving only inches at a time.

Sitting there, she started to feel cold and fished for the jacket. She found it and bundled herself as best as she could, pulling the collar up around her neck.

She decided to turn off the propane lantern, but first she put the flashlight in the jacket's pocket. When the light dimmed, it was as if she was in a cave. Incisive blackness — humid non-illumination — pressed heavily around her, and she couldn't see anything. Perhaps my eyes will adjust — she thought — and then I'll see something. But she really didn't think so.

She started wondering — Why God? But there wasn't any answer. However, she did feel that somehow He had everything under control and was aware that she was sitting there in the dark haze — and that He heard her now, like He had heard her in the Pacific.

Her eyes did adjust after several minutes and there was a hint of light from above, but from no direction in particular, and not enough to see anything, except a faint outline of what must have been the canyon's ledge. Maybe it's moonlight? — she asked herself. If so, I'll only need to climb a little bit more to get out of this cloud. The path is uphill, so I'd better start moving again. I might be able to climb out of the haze.

With renewed hope she began the taxing climb. Not that it was steep or difficult, but it was like trying to swim in mud — or maybe quicksand — it was nearly impossible. She kept telling herself — Just a little higher.

Had another hour gone by? She had no idea, but it seemed that way. Had she made any progress? Perhaps. She had the faintest notion that she was able to see a bit more than before. About then there was a breeze; she felt it on her face and looked upwards. A sliver of the moon could be seen looming aloft and gradually fading into the darkness as the smoky haze leisurely moved under the distant satellite's winking eye — an illusion created as the quarter slice of white light was rhythmically veiled and unveiled by the fog stalking its way over the ridge. It looked like the moon was moving, not the cloud. By degrees, the view opened. Ashley could see far enough to continue at a normal pace. She offered thanksgiving from her heart — Thank You Lord! — and hoped there wouldn't be any more murk.

Reaching the ridge, she saw the stars shining brightly. She could nearly imagine she was back in space. The path began to lead downhill, a bit. She wondered if it would take her back into the fog. Briefly, before leaving the ridge, she saw the dimly lit vaporous cloud to her right, hanging on the mountain, but to her left, along the path, it was perfectly clear. There wouldn't be any more visibility problems — she guessed, hoping she was right. The moonlight was almost bright enough that she could see to walk without the aid of the lantern.

Climbing through the fog had left her exhausted, but with the way clear, she began to feel new energy, and was moving along the path at a good speed until, rather unexpectedly, the lantern's light went out. Its somewhat bothersome hiss silenced, and the propane ran dry.

Ashley still had the flashlight and turned it on, looking for one of the propane cartridges. Instructions for changing the tiny cylinder were written on it.

After unscrewing and removing the old one, she securely tightened the new one in place, twisting it vigorously — she was eager to keep moving. When she went to light it, she saw the error of her way. The fine globe of the mantle had diminished and fallen mostly away into a fine white powder. She tried to light it anyway, but only a blue flame shot upwards, giving no significant lighting. She realized that she had read the instructions too quickly and cursed herself for having been so careful with the mantle before, but in the most crucial moment, when it counted the most, having been so careless. She sought for another, examining every pocket and every corner of the pack, but found nothing. She still had good starlight and a quarter moon. The flashlight would be bright enough for her to keep going.

An hour later, she came to a place where she couldn't distinguish the path from the ridge of deep black, jagged and porous lava. Jon's poor shoes — Ashley thought. They'll be sacrificed on this stuff.

Soon afterwards, the flashlight started to go dim. The richly black, nonreflective rock had so absorbed its light that it hadn't been very helpful, but now it was useless. With light from the moon, she managed to change the batteries. Once she had slipped in the new batteries she turned it back on, but it gave only a dim, useless, reddish glow — the batteries were old!

Ashley began to consider the possibilities of going ahead with the moonlight on the lava rock. It would be easy to trip, and the rock was sharp as a butcher's ax. Worse, she had no idea where the path was — it was black against black. Again, she was forced to move slowly and she started to feel cold, but not just cold; she felt frigid. A persistent breeze cooled her body even more. Since sweat soaked her clothing and jacket — she had been working hard — it was imperative for her to do something to combat hypothermia. She remembered the sleeping bag, but was concerned about lava. There wasn't any other choice, though.

If she slipped into the sleeping bag with her damp clothing, it would do little good. So she undressed, as fast as she could, being careful not to lose track of any of her belongings. Brrr! It was cold. Fortunately her damp skin dried rapidly, almost as fast as she undressed, in the dry mountain air. She shivered and took the chill as long as she could stand it, trying to dry out as much as she could. Her body dried, but not her hair. She didn't remove Jon's tennis shoes, or the rock would have sliced open her feet. She took the sleeping bag out of the pack, and shivering, she pulled it down over her. Stooping and unzipping it from the bottom up, she was able to cover herself and breathe too.

It wasn't too restful, standing, while holding a sleeping bag around your body, in the pitch black of night, and standing on lava rock, but she was feeling warmer, except, of course, for her feet, which were still covered with sweaty socks. She would just have to put up with it. It had taken a while, but her hair had dried, and she was able to warm herself inside the bag.

There was one other thing she would have to accept; at least until there was light, she wasn't making any progress towards James. What was she to do? Stand there the rest of the night? At this point, she didn't have any choice — the rock would cut through her sleeping bag. It wasn't fun, but she'd done worse things, and she would just have to accept the situation. She wondered why God had helped her with the fog, but left her stranded on the rock, and she hoped, and prayed, that she would reach James before the enemy did.

* * *

Quito, Ecuador

DAWN'S FIRST LIGHT started to appear to the east. Two Ecuadorian Air Force helicopters lifted off their pads at Quito's Mariscal Sucre Airport. Following the flight path a short distance, they started flying towards the sun's early light. The day was clearing, and having gained about 4000 feet, they had an open view of their destination — Mount Antisana.

Walker knew that another SAO would be coming to take charge, but he had decided to get the operation under way. It hadn't been easy to bite through the leather binding the witch had tied around the blasted guard. She had left him so well bound that the guard wouldn't have ever succeeded in freeing him. It had been rather humiliating. He had had two choices: to work on the guard's feet, or on his wrists, which had been disturbingly close to his large posterior and to the delicious smell of squashed pizza. The guard's feet had seemed like a better choice: Curse the boots — and the shoe leather too! Walker hadn't been endowed with jaw implants. The tech people hadn't ever thought of such a necessity.

It tasted terrible! — probably because of the black dye. His tongue was still dark. At least the strips hadn't been thick, but they had been wide, and it had taken him almost three hours to chew his way through the "delicious" leather — resting from time to time. His neck still hurt — because of the way he had had to hold it — and the jaw ache wouldn't go away. It made him wonder if he would have to go to an orthodontist. He had to support all of this, without considering the pain from the nasty blows the witch had given him.

There were several choice words he kept using to describe the hag who had been dressed in black with a dark gray, spotted, face. He comforted himself with the knowledge that the tech people would soon have the SPARQ's pictures ready. He wasn't sure how much it would help, but whoever *she* (and of that detail he was relatively certain, since he hadn't seen any boys shaped so exquisitely) had been, she knew how to fight — with implanted power. She also knew how to arm a PHENIX, and to arm it fast. Worst of all, she beat him. How humiliating! When they found her, he would personally inflict her! — he decided, making sure she lived long enough to suffer a dozen doses, or so.

His present mission was probably futile, but he hoped that by waking half of the Ecuadorian government and military, and getting Antisana sealed off, he might regain a trace of his pride. It hadn't been easy for him to get a couple of helicopters to look for a lost friend on Antisana. He would have had Quito sealed off too, but bucking bureaucracy and nationalism wasn't an easy assignment, especially at 4 AM. Besides, he didn't even really know who they were looking for. A shapely female was the only certain description he could give. He'd seen her eyes — they seemed blue — but under such circumstances it was hard to tell. She was fast. Alpha Force? — he asked himself. But that wouldn't help the police much: Look for a shapely, probably tall, perhaps blue-eyed, cat burglar. Or perhaps she was short, black-eyed, and dressed in black: for a funeral — *his*.

At one point he wondered if she could have been Ashley Brown — but isn't she dead? Could she have gone mad? Could she be suffering from amnesia? Her RSB was found in the Pacific — the serial number checked out. The RSB on Antisana is Smith's — that is an established fact. So why would Brown come all the way from the Pacific to pick a fight in Quito? Well, whoever she is, she's a witch! And she probably flew away on her broom. Maybe the SPARQ will show something, some clue — Walker hoped.

He also hoped it would absolve him of negligence. It was easy to see she had come into the office through the louvered windows, but the alarm hadn't triggered — he marked, and asked himself — or did she disarm it? If so, we will know who she was.

He wondered — Why didn't she just vaporize me? He couldn't answer the question, but decided — It won't be long and we will know. SPARQ pictures will come soon.

For right now he would dedicate his efforts — despite a headache, stiffneck, "lockjaw," and injured pride — to insuring proper troop deployment around Antisana, and in passing, he would check out the site where they had found the RSB. He asked himself — Does the RSB on Antisana have anything to do with the witch? But wasn't it Smith's?

* * *

"WELL," JON SAID, after a horrible sleep on the inclined car seat and waking to see daylight through the front window, "she wasn't back by midnight."

"I hope she's okay," Judy added.

About then they heard a roar from behind and Jon sat up and looked around, but it was passing overhead and he saw it sooner through the front window: a helicopter, and then another. "Wow!" Jon exclaimed. It was deafening.

"What's going on?" Judy asked as the flying machines finished their pass.

Then it fell — silence, like a storm had just moved through.

* * *

ASHLEY HAD GOTTEN her things together and dressed. As soon as there was enough light to distinguish the path, she had been on her way. It hadn't been far, and based on what Jon had found out, she had knocked on the door of the hut she imagined was Juan José's, but it wasn't. She had asked which *"casa"* and the older woman, with deeply furrowed dark skin, pointed back down the path.

It seemed that Juan José was her neighbor, so Ashley started back, about a hundred yards, where she was about to try again, when suddenly, from over the ridge, the roar of turbojets and blades bellowed. She had heard it coming a few seconds earlier, but had been concentrating on her objective and had ignored the warning. She looked towards the ridge. Two helicopters appeared, one after the other.

She told herself — Something isn't right. Why are military helicopters flying towards a small village? They were moving quickly. This must be the beginning of Nova Mundi's big operation — she decided — and the SAO is probably as angry as a stuck pig. She would have chuckled to herself, remembering how she had left him. However, it simply wasn't a good idea for her, a blond *gringa*, to be standing in open view in an Indian village, so she looked for cover. There was a fold in the mountain that formed, to some degree, a lean-to. It would do. Fully powered, she entered a *bio*, and slid under the overhang. She covered about forty-five feet in just over a second, and then pushed herself up into the roof of the opening — where she was well hidden.

What are they doing? — she asked herself. She guessed they would probably try to seal off the area around the mountain. It didn't take long for their thunder to pass over, and then silence returned to the village. She started down from her hiding place, knowing the next time her sound processors picked up the roar she would pay more attention. She ran back to the path, which widened into a narrow road that entered the village area, and moved, with increased urgency, towards the house.

"Ashley!" she heard from behind.

"James!" she answered as she turned.

He ran up to her. She stood, with her arms out to receive him. He came and wrapped his arms around her in a fraternal hug. "Where were you?" she asked.

"We went to the field early with Juan José, but when I heard the helicopters, I thought they might be looking for me."

"You're right! They're after you. They found the RSB. I was in their office last night. It's a major operation."

"But, didn't you turn yourself back in?"

"I tried, but failed. And now I don't want to."

"Really?"

"Of course, but it's a long story, and right now we need to get out of here."

James rushed to get his backpack and his belongings.

Chapter 6

Yes, Captain

BEAUTY IS one of the rare things that do not lead to doubt of God.

— Jean Anouilh

February 18 — That same day — Path to Talontag

WHEN JAMES came back out of Juan José's house, Ashley asked, "Where will we go?"

"We'll have to see. But now we have to get out of here."

"Too many people have seen us," Ashley added.

"How did you find me? The Whittens?"

"Yes, Captain," Ashley answered, feeling like James was in charge, and wanting him to know it. "They're waiting for us in Talontag," she informed.

"Do you think we should go back there?" he questioned.

Ashley understood. Their presence could endanger them. "It's your decision," she answered.

James considered for a split second. Ashley knew that this was his specialty — being right the first time when there wasn't time to be right. He would make the best decision possible. Then he said, "I don't know. It seems like the best thing would be to go somewhere else, but I feel like I need to see them again. That doesn't make any sense, but let's go back to Talontag."

"Okay, James," she answered, feeling confident of his decision, that it was the best one.

Then he spoke, as if giving an order. "Let's *bio* to Talontag."

"Yes, sir," she answered, ready to go.

Smith took the first step and they kicked into a *bio*. They would surely draw some attention from local eyes, but James figured that their mere presence had already drawn more attention than they needed, and the faster they left, the better. Since Nova Mundi's operation was just beginning, they might have time to beat it. However, a few more hours, and it would be too late.

In no time they were on the lava field and had to slow down. This was the worst kind of rugged terrain and it was like walking on razor blades. James had worn his general-issue Alpha Force shoes, but Ashley had Jon's shoes, which didn't have the materials and construction necessary for a *bio* on a lava field.

Ashley heard it first. "Captain, enemy at 7 o'clock."

James heard the roar too.

Ashley thought quickly and said, "I'll camouflage, sir. Get off the field!" she suggested, nearly giving an order. She yanked the black scarf and hair net out of her bag. James, seeing what she was trying to do, figured it would work, and knowing his blue jeans and light jacket could be seen forever (plus his golden hair and the scandalously bright backpack) he pushed the envelope and began running at maximum *bio*.

Ashley, having covered herself well, became a black dot on a black surface by folding herself together and looking downwards so that her white face wouldn't be visible. She crossed her arms and hands under her body while still squatting. She didn't want to touch the treacherous lava.

James ran — nearly at full speed; only the lava field slowed him.

Their sound processors gave them an edge, warning them ahead of time, but there was still reason to believe their effort could fail. Ashley's camouflage was a bit too shiny against the flat black rock, and though James's speed was great, he had a long way to go.

A helicopter appeared over the horizon. There was just one.

Ashley knew that James wouldn't be taking any time to look over his shoulder, but she caught a glimpse out of the corner of her eye, and said a prayer, "Lord, help us!"

WALKER LOOKED DOWN and saw the beautiful black lava flow. It made a striking contrast to the area around it, accentuated by the early-morning light. His vision enhancements were working perfectly, but he had already seen what he had gone looking for — the RSB site — and he didn't imagine that he needed to be looking for anything else and zoomed his enhancements back for normal vision.

He thought he saw something light, perhaps cream-colored, towards the edge of the flow, and he zoomed in. But it was gone.

ON THE GROUND, James just managed to reach the edge of the black field and dive into a muddy ditch — cold and wet — having thrown, as he plunged, his bright backpack under a bush that was a few feet away. He felt thoroughly humiliated, and chuckled to himself — *If I'd had this mud, I could've just stayed with Ashley.* It didn't take long before the helicopter was gone. James got out of the ditch, and tried to clean himself some, but it was useless.

Then Ashley came over the edge of the lava flow and saw him standing as he was trying to shake out his jacket. He looked up. As soon as she saw him, she began to laugh. He felt like a pig, and figured he must look like one. He had half a notion to grab her and throw her into the ditch, too. But they didn't have time, so the threat would have to do: "Ashley, quit! Or I'll throw you in!"

His words just made her giggle more.

"Stop, Ashley. We've got to get out of here!"

"Yes, sir!" she answered, as if she was at boot camp, and she raised her hand in an Alpha Force salute, which was close to a "Hail, Hitler." Then she drew her hand back to herself, and covered her mouth, continuing an obvious mocking laugh.

James looked at her. There were sunbeams streaming off her golden hair. He realized that he was seeing her better than he had allowed himself to see her before. She was beautiful. She came down to where he stood and looked into his eyes. Her eyes were blue and enticing. Her face came close to his and her golden hair glowed, in the backlight. Her mild cream features danced in the dark shadows cast by the radiant early morning sunlight that sparkled through her tousled, breeze-swept hair. She was engaging — flawless.

He didn't want to, but he had to say it, "We've got to … go … Ashley."

JUDY LOOKED out the back window of the Jeep as a helicopter landed about a thousand yards behind them. Something about it made her feel like it wasn't there to help them.

"What are they doing?" Jon asked.

"Beats me," she answered.

"Hope they aren't making some kind of checkpoint, or something. We'll have to go that way." Then he asked, "How long will we have to wait for them?"

"I'm hungry," Judy complained.

"There's stuff in back," Jon indicated.

"I want real food," she specified.

"There comes James and Ashley!" Jon exclaimed as he saw them appear over the top of the hill.

"They're both dressed in black?" she questioned.

"Look at them run. It's beautiful," Jon said.

"They're fast," Judy added, and about then they were beside the Jeep.

Judy opened the door and got out so they could get in, but James said, "We'd better not get inside. It looks like they're making a checkpoint. We'll meet you at the intersection, down by the highway."

Jon didn't have time to ask any questions. They took off again, descending towards the ravine.

"Well," he said, "I guess we'd better go."

Judy got back inside, and they both pulled on their seat belts.

"What was all that black stuff on him?" Jon asked.

"It looked like dried mud," Judy replied.

Jon started the motor and turned around. They moved slowly down the road that was full of mud and holes. Judy found herself nervously anticipating the possible checkpoint. She felt some relief when the helicopter lifted off and headed away, but she knew that there could still be trouble.

FOUR ECUADORIAN SOLDIERS in green uniforms — dressed for the march, with rifles slung on their shoulders and helmets in place — stood, two on each side of the dirt road.

Jon slowly pulled beside them as they signaled him to stop. He complied and rolled down his window to greet them. *"Buenos días* — Good day," he said, wondering if it really was.

One soldier looked carefully in the back of the Jeep, the other stood ready, like he was expecting something, as did the other one on Jon's side. The soldier who seemed to have the highest rank asked Jon, "What was your business in the area?"

Jon explained that they were missionaries and had been with some friends. Seeing it was late, they had spent the night. He prayed they wouldn't ask why he was driving without shoes.

Then the man pulled out a faxed picture. It was grainy, but Jon nearly fainted when he saw what must have been James's face. The soldier compared it to Jon. There wasn't any resemblance, so the troop signaled them to move on through.

Reaching the end of the dirt road, they were ready to start onto the pavement. James and Ashley popped out from behind a bush, running over to the vehicle. Judy let them inside. She moved with urgency and ignored the fact that she really didn't want that dirtbag of a man in her car. She remembered her living room and how James had been when they first met. She wished she could have sent him for a bath like she had on that occasion, but now that was impossible.

They exchanged few words. Judy knew they all felt the gravity of their situation.

James and Ashley arranged themselves, and got down out of view, but if there were any more checkpoints, there wasn't anywhere to hide in the Jeep.

"What now?" Jon asked.

Judy thought — Indeed, what now? I'd like a hot shower and a pleasant bed. And then she reprimanded herself, realizing that that was probably the wish any of them would have made.

Jon suddenly pulled over to the side of the highway and asked, "May I have my shoes?" as he turned to Ashley.

"Oh," she answered, "I'm sorry." And she started to untie them. In a moment, she gave them to Jon.

JON KNEW IT would happen. His shoes looked like they had been subjected to a consumer protection test. He opted, against all temptation to the contrary, not to say anything. It won't do any good — he told himself. She didn't have any choice but to use them. And a complaint won't fix them — he loathingly reminded himself. Besides, Judy will get mad if I say anything, so I'll just keep my mouth shut.

"They're going to be searching the mountain, and Quito," Ashley said, explaining to James what was going on, and what she had seen at the Nova Mundi office. When they had traveled about fifteen minutes, after discussing their situation, James asked, "We shouldn't go back to Quito, then?"

"No, I don't think so," Ashley answered.

"But James, don't you need to clean up? And the car — it's so dirty. Where will we go?" Judy asked.

Ashley offered, "To Manta?"

"To Manta!" Jon exclaimed. "That's a long way. Why Manta?" he asked. "Don't you just want to get away from here? Isn't that the object?" And he offered, "What about Colombia? It's close."

"No, Colombia wouldn't be good," James said. "Colombia is full of Nova Mundi; that's why they have so many problems. The whole drug cartel is Nova Mundi inspired. Drugs make a lot of money for them. There are SAOs all over that place."

"Manta's a long way," Jon said, trying again.

"But I've got friends in Manta," Ashley said.

"And it's a long way," James explained. "That makes it harder for them. It's also a small port, and maybe we can get a ride going somewhere on a ship."

"Okay," Jon answered, "but how are you going to get there?"

There was silence, until Judy looked at him. He knew that they were going to "volunteer." Besides, James and Ashley really didn't have any other option. Pubic transportation would give half of the country a chance to gawk at them, which was the last thing they needed in their situation. Besides, it made sense. Ashley had friends there, and they wouldn't have to get anyone else involved. Jack Kinderly had even been talking about bringing James to the States, so maybe that would be part of the plan. But it's massive — Jon considered. We're dealing with thugs who can search, and probably will search, the planet. They're after blood and they'll probably find it — *mine*. But I've come too far to stop. And he knew that despite his misgivings, he would help, and he continued, "Well, then, do we leave right now?"

"I'd really like to go to Quito, at least to get ready for the trip," Judy said, wishfully.

"We shouldn't go back, at least James and I," Ashley said. "If you want to go back, we can stay out here somewhere, between the mountain and Quito, maybe."

"It'll take us a little longer, but we can circle back around by Pifo. We have some great friends there. You can stay with them until we're ready for the trip," Jon offered.

* * *

Quito

"**Walker?**" López asked, identifying the man who was receiving his party.

"Yes, sir," he answered and started leading the SAOs — who were all dressed like they belonged in Quito, in dark suits for both male and female — away from the ramp.

"Good."

After they had taken a few steps down the tarmac, and having led Walker a few steps beyond the rest of the group who were still disembarking, López asked, "How are we doing?"

"I went ahead and began sealing off the Antisana area. I have a chopper waiting to take us there so you can see the crash site for yourself. Frankly, it seems that Smith must be dead. He couldn't have lived through it. The crash against the boulder would have been fatal. The vultures have surely cleaned his corpse. Perhaps there will be some bones. Maybe some implants. There's not much flesh for the birds up there, like the condor, so they probably started picking on him about as fast as he crawled out of the RSB. It looks like he tried to hide it, and cut a piece out of it, about the size of a blanket.

"However, I've speculated that he didn't do it at all. Perhaps a climber did it. Some chap on the mountain, you know, cut the piece and hid the rest for later. Or maybe a local looted the site."

By now, they were nearing a black limo.

"If you wish," Walker continued, offering again, "we can fly over there."

"What about Brown? Are you doing anything?"

"Yes, sir," Walker answered, embarrassed, and feeling some pain. The *techs* have been able to pick up the message she left on the phone. It was playing while we fought. Her bioidentification was also present on the demodulator record. Apparently she was going to turn herself back in and then changed her mind. Comparing the call from the airport with her actions, it would seem she must be suffering some kind of dementia — one moment trying to turn herself in, and the next, breaking into the office like a common burglar. Maybe she drowned and went into biosuspend, but by the time she got air, brain damage was setting in?"

"Do you think that's possible?" López questioned.

"Well, sir," Walker started, "I must say, I've thought about it quite a bit, and I can't imagine any reason for her behavior."

"What else? Have you done any follow-up around the airport and the office?"

"We have. She makes an easy target to track. Everyone from beggars to businessmen has seen her, and none can forget. It seems to be a memorable experience. We even have a description of a Jeep she rode away in at the airport, about three hours after she made the call to the office. It seems that she got in with a man and another woman and they turned towards the west, but after that, we run out of leads. We are still investigating, especially around the office. It seems one of the building's guards saw her leaving, but we know nothing else. She said she was 'lost,' " Walker pronounced bitterly.

"Have you checked with the local police about the vehicle? Did anyone get a license number?"

"Unfortunately, sir, no. Someone blasted their klaxon, loud and long, when the suspects stopped for Brown, but we haven't found anyone who saw the license. Everyone seems to think it started with the letter 'P.' "

"Does that help us?"

"Which, sir? The klaxon blast is typical fare in Quito. And most everyone's license starts with P; it stands for the name of the province. And Jeeps, like the one that was spotted, are abundant. I should say, we are quite lucky to know anything at all."

"How many Jeeps are there?"

"About six thousand."

"Six thousand! What is it? The most popular vehicle in Quito?"

"It seems quite so."

"So, what's your plan, Walker?"

"Two of the witnesses agree that the people who picked up Brown were foreigners, perhaps *gringos.* So that fact may limit the field."

"Do you have people working on it?"

"Yes, sir."

"Do you need more?"

"Not yet. When we get the printout of foreign owners of gray Jeeps, we can begin the footwork."

"And when will we have the printout?"

"That's difficult to say. The police computer is down."

"Down?"

"Yes, sir. It seems to spend much of its time that way. With power outages, communication shutdowns, sloppy programming, viruses, irresponsible operators, riots, changes in government, strikes, maybe even changes in the weather — perhaps it's part of being here: the altitude, you know. Everyone blames everything on the altitude. But they don't call it altitude; they say it's the *clima.*"

"Curse it! Walker, what are you saying? It sounds like a joke?"

"Indeed," Walker answered. Perhaps López had taken him too seriously because of his British accent. He resumed, "Most things are like that here, you know, sir. You are familiar with the region, sir? You know, '*mañana,*' and all. I assure you, I'm not joking."

López knew, and understood, the "region," as Walker called it, but that didn't make it any less frustrating. "Okay, Walker, do this: Pull some strings and find out why the computer is down. Maybe we can bring in someone. We could link the police data to Nova Mundi, or something."

"Yes, sir. Do we still want to tour the crash site?"

"Well, Walker, if you're right, a pile of dry bones will probably wait, but we'd better find Brown. She seems to be very much alive, and dangerous. She's got a PHENIX?"

"Yes, sir. She does, and must be considered dangerous, although I cannot think why she didn't vaporize me."

"Good question, Walker." The way López said it, Walker almost wondered if Nova Mundi might be considering finishing the job Brown had begun. Surely not — Walker told himself. He opened the limousine's large black door, which had been buffed to a polished glaze. López got in first.

Chapter 7

Pifo

O<small>NE MIGHT</small> well say that mankind is divisible into two great classes: hosts and guests.

— Sir Max Beerbohm

February 18 — That same day — Pifo, one hour outside of Quito

"H<small>ERE WE ARE</small>," Jon announced as he pointed to his right.

James looked up through the window. He and Ashley had been staying as low as possible. Perhaps he hadn't thought about what to expect, but his eyes saw numerous soaring objects, namely antenna towers.

"What is this place?" he asked, with a trace of unease, asking himself — Why all the towers?

"It's an antenna farm," Jon informed.

"HCJB, The Voice of the Andes," Judy added.

As they started to pull into an entrance Ashley saw the many towers. She asked, "What's that?"

"You don't know what HCJB is?" Jon questioned.

"No," Ashley answered.

"It's a Christian radio station and they transmit on many different frequencies to the whole world, in many languages," Jon explained.

Ashley asked, "Why do they need a radio station?"

"To tell people about Jesus," Judy answered.

Then Jon changed the subject and ordered, "Why don't you all sit up normally?"

"Why?" James asked.

"We're going to go past the guard house and we wouldn't want him to think we're trying to smuggle people inside their compound."

Jon wondered what the guard would think, seeing James black with mud and Ashley in black too. He told the guard they'd come as visitors and were friends of the Brooks. After a brief confirmation by telephone — the heavy iron gate started to roll back.

They drove on through, nearing the towers, which came in all sizes and shapes. Jon parked by a house.

"I don't know how I'm going to handle this, but maybe Judy and I will go first and introduce you and Ashley as best we can."

James wanted to tell Jon not to do it. We could just wait out in some field — he considered, but Ashley beat him to it. "We don't need to stay here. Why don't you just leave us out in a field?"

It made sense to Judy to leave them and she thought — We could just say hello and good-bye, a we-were-in-the-neighborhood-and-stopped-by, glad-the-family's-fine visit. Then the Brooks won't have to get mixed up in the whole mess.

Jon was also aware it would be easier, and they wouldn't have to be concerned with explanations, but then he would feel as if he had to get back to James and Ashley before they caught a cold, or something, out in a miserable field. Besides, it looked like it was going to rain. The alternative was to travel right away, as they were, but such a long trip!

Jon told himself — I'm tired. I barely slept last night, and my feet are cold. I deserve a shower and a good night's rest. He had one other motive, though he didn't admit it openly, or even to himself: He felt like he had caught the big one, and he had to tell someone. He wanted someone else to see his new toys, especially James, with his watch and his PLOT. It was the best science fiction since Jules Verne invented the genre, and he knew that Dan Brook would love to see his toys.

"No," Jon answered. "You don't need to stay out in some field. It'll be cold, and it could rain. Our friends will want you to visit them," he said, as Judy looked at him with anxious eyes.

"Let's go, Judy," Jon indicated.

Jon and Judy approached the door together.

STILL IN THE CAR with Ashley, James commented, "This is a big operation," and he admired the towers.

Ashley agreed, with a nod, and added, "We probably could have listened to them on Mars."

"Right. If they'd ever given us any free time, or let us listen to outers, but they would have inflicted us if we had tried."

"But would it have made any difference? We were convinced that we had all the answers. What could an outer have told us? We would've laughed at the fanatical Christian message," Ashley clarified.

James remembered the "absurd" tract about Jonah, and laughed to himself. She's right — he thought, and added — We would've called it a fish story, and called it an outer myth.

AFTER A KNOCK, Linda Brook came to the door and they exchanged greetings. The ladies hugged.

"Is Dan around?" Jon Whitten asked.

"He's over at the transmitter building."

"Oh," Jon said, with a now what accent.

"Why?" Linda asked with alarm in her normally pleasant voice. She made an inquisitive shift of her head, "I can call him."

"That's okay. No need to bother."

"Why don't you come in and visit. Maybe he'll be back soon."

"We have some new friends," Judy commented.

"Invite them in," Linda offered, and said, "You know us! You didn't even need to ask. Your friends are our friends." And she made a sweep of her hand, as if marking an open path, inviting all to enter.

But Jon knew that she didn't know what she was saying, in this case, and he explained, "They've been out in the mountains, and we've been over at Talontag. It's a really long story, but the guy fell into a ditch, and he's caked with mud. He's been staying with us the past couple of months. He made a decision for Christ in a meeting we had. His girlfriend met him by chance, just a few days ago, when we were visiting Santo Domingo, and she's with us too. She just made a decision yesterday, at our house. Excuse me for explaining like this, but they need a place to stay tonight, and we thought of you."

Judy spoke, refining Jon's explanation, and said, "If you would be able to have them tonight, that would really help us. We need to get ready for a trip, and I won't have much time to attend to them. Please forgive us, Linda, for asking. Maybe you're too busy?"

"Oh, no," Linda answered, having gotten a look at them, though from a distance. Jon could see that her curiosity was aroused. She invited, "We always love to have visitors."

Of course, entertaining guests was a mandatory part of a missionary's life, Jon knew, and felt himself a little crude for having taken advantage of Linda's hospitality, but he didn't have any other good choice.

After a few more brief exchanges, Jon went back to the Jeep to invite James and Ashley to come to the house so he could introduce them. James still looked as if he had been playing with the pigs! He looked like a walking clump of fertilized topsoil.

"I think I'd better change before going in," James offered, as they walked towards the house.   He had already noticed the look from the lady at the door when he got out of the Jeep. It was the same kind that

Judy Whitten had given him when he had first entered her living room after coming down the mountain.

Jon noticed it too. Linda's smile was a permanent feature – he couldn't remember when he had seen her without it, until now. The sight of James must be traumatic – Jon considered, and then chuckled to himself – Just wait until she smells him.

"Linda, meet James and Ashley," Jon introduced.

She was petite and attractive (though not a model for making mannequins), with neat light brunette hair (curled) that fell below her shoulders. Her good nature and good cheer won her many friends, but sometimes it opened the door to those who sought to take advantage of her.

Ashley and Linda embraced, but James felt ashamed, and nodded a weak greeting.

"Jon," Linda began, "there's a room around back. You can show James, if he would like to clean up, and change before he comes inside."

"Thank you," James answered with gratitude.

ASHLEY DWARFED LINDA, but Linda abounded in warmth, kindness, and confidence. It was one of those things that happened quickly, as though it had been foreordained. Ashley knew she wanted to be like Linda, and she felt like she had always known her.

James and Jon walked around, behind the house, where James would be able to clean up.

The ladies went into the house, which was pleasantly decorated with typical ornaments from Ecuador and the Andes. There was a thick rug made from alpaca wool hanging on the wall. It was white, with pleasant shades of brown, depicting an alpaca. Linda called her husband, Dan, telling him they had visitors. He returned right away, and with his approval, final arrangements for the stay of Smith and his "girlfriend" were made.

Ashley felt a little awkward being called, Smith's "girlfriend." The outers had stepped out to speak, but with her hearing enhancements, she was able to hear everything they said. It seemed that in the tone that Judy spoke, "girlfriend" wasn't a complement. She wasn't even sure what outers meant by the word, but it seemed like it shouldn't be anything offensive. Don't outers have boy and girl friends? — she asked herself.

Directly, the Whittens were on their way, returning to Quito. They were going to prepare for the big trip to Manta, and get some more things from James's apartment. Jon had also mentioned that he was going to contact Pastor Kinderly. Ashley wondered if it wouldn't be better to keep it quiet. Was it wise to tell so many? But James told her that the pastor was a good man, and that if Jon contacted him, it would be okay.

Ashley marveled at how everything in Linda's home seemed to run as if she had a degree in business administration, though she really was a nurse. Everyone in the family, one son and four daughters, had assigned duties — and it worked. It wasn't the impersonal world of TerraNova. The children had never experienced infliction, but they were obedient, from what Ashley could observe. She thought — This is the way it's supposed to be; this is a family!

Seeing the Brooks' home function in harmony made Ashley feel that her "parents" had deprived her, as if she had missed out on life. If only I'd have grown up in a family like this — she pined to herself.

JAMES, FOR HIS PART, had already been exposed to a wonderful family when he had stayed with the Williamses. But in Dan Brook, James found an example of a man who carried on missionary work at a level, and in a way, he hadn't previously considered. Brook was an electrical engineer who played a significant role in running the radio station. He was commanding, but gentle. James realized a person of Brook's talents could be living in higher material circumstances. It was apparent he had given up a lot to be in Ecuador.

That evening the Brooks gathered around the piano, and Linda masterfully played Rachmaninoff's "Prelude in C# minor." Ashley had commented, "Could I ever learn to play the piano so well?"

Linda had answered, "Sure you can!"

James stood close to Ashley and before the music finished he had taken her hand in his. She liked it, and she softly answered his touch with her own. James liked the family atmosphere, and he wanted Ashley to share it with him.

Later, when the children had gone their separate ways, destinations dependent on age — homework or bed, the Brooks finally had some time alone with James and Ashley. Sitting in the love seat, Dan and Linda radiated. They weren't as young as their behavior indicated. They carried their forty-plus, near fifty, years well. Dan still had all his blond hair, not one of which was gray, and Linda, if she dressed herself in jeans and a sweatshirt, might have been mistaken for one of her teenage daughters.

"So, James," Dan began, "what brings you our way?"

James knew that the tough questions were bound to come before the evening was over. He had been trying to figure out what he would say — and was disgusted, to some extent, that he had allowed himself to be trapped. We could have just sat out in a field somewhere and waited for the Whittens to come back — he told himself, but he knew that he really preferred being with the Brooks. He thought — I should just make up some story, something an outer would believe. I could say that I'm a pilot, or something. But he knew he couldn't lie. Jesus wouldn't do that. However, he felt he couldn't tell them the truth without endangering them also. I can't tell them the truth — he told himself. And then he thought — I've got to tell them the truth. However, the conversation was happening then and there, and he had to answer, "Well…" and he paused. It became suspenseful; everyone was waiting for him to speak. Ashley sat beside him on the couch, and he glanced to her, hoping she would somehow come to his rescue, but she was silent.

It took a moment for James to get going, but he decided that the truth was his best answer, and finished his sentence, "…that's a long story."

"We've got time," Linda invited.

James wished they didn't. "Well…," he began again, still stalling, but seeing no other option, he continued, "it's hard to explain. Do you remember that explosion out to the east of Antisana a couple of months ago?"

Ashley tugged James's sleeve, touching his elbow. He looked at her, and saw a change-the-subject look.

"My, yes," Dan answered. "How could we ever forget it? They said it was lightning. I really have trouble believing that. It was cloudy here, and rainy. We couldn't see anything, but the thunder, or whatever it was, was deafening. We even felt a wind, like some kind of atomic bomb. It lit up everything. It was better than daylight, if that's possible, and bluish in color. It was like lightning, or welding, but just so much brighter," and he paused for emphasis. "Some people who were outside said they couldn't see for a few seconds — it blinded them. They say it was about twenty miles from here, and really high up. Why do you ask?"

With reluctance James undertook an answer, "That was the explosion of our spaceship," James said, looking at Ashley, and then back at Dan, who, he could see, almost laughed.

James heard Ashley cackle, with a failed laugh, which lapsed into a curt giggle. He realized that she was trying to reinforce to Dan's disbelief by reaffirming unbelief.

Dan, however, asked, "Spaceship?"

James noted that Ashley looked concerned, but he couldn't think of a better way to deal with the situation, except directly. He answered, "Right, we were returning from Mars, and our reactor blew up. We had to abandon the ship. And it self-destructed when it came back to Earth. That was the explosion you heard."

"That's quite a story," Dan commented. "I'm sure you know it's hard to believe," and he chuckled.

"Yes, I know," James said. And, as if he knew he would need it, he had his watch ready, and pulled it out of the pocket of his blue jeans.

Dan and Linda seemed to become instant believers, at least sort of. James could tell that they were suspicious. His watch was believable, but it really didn't prove anything concerning the story of the exploding spaceship. Jumping from the watch to the explosion took some creative thinking.

But the 3-D projection made by the PLOT, showing both terrestrial and extraterrestrial destinations, was quite convincing, and left less work for the imagination, but James felt there was still a hint of doubt in his audience.

Dan was really up front, and after the demonstration, he said, "Well, if you do come from this secret world you've been talking about, you probably would have fancy electronic toys like this one you call a PLOT."

Dan's comment wasn't intended to draw any answer in return, and James didn't have anything to say, but he understood that the engineer was being as charitable as possible, trying to give him the benefit of the doubt, without saying something like, "Great technology, but it wouldn't fly that spaceship you're talking about."

They had a long evening together. By the time James told his story, and Ashley too, it was after 11:30 PM — late for the Brooks and the storytellers too, since they hadn't rested the night before. James didn't mention the search on the mountain. It was hard enough to convince his hosts that Ashley and he were from a hidden world, without complicating the subject and telling the Brooks that their guests were the objects of a massive manhunt.

* * *

Quito

THE AMATEUR RADIO phone patch was completed, thanks to Larry Williams and his ham radio station.

"Hello, Jack. How are you? Over." Jon asked.

"We're fine, and the church is great. Over." responded Jack. His voice sounded clear but slightly "twisted" — the pitch nearly normal, but lower. Larry didn't notice, but Jon did, since he knew Jack really well.

"Jack, I've got some interesting news. You remember our friend Jim? Over."

"Yes, Jon. What's going on? Over."

"Well, Jim found an old friend. She saw him in Santo Domingo. Seems they worked together. It's a long story; I'll have to write you more. Jim was her boss in his last job. But she decided to go back to her people, you know, the *others*. Over."

"You say she went back to the *others*? Over."

"Right, Jack. But then she decided she did the wrong thing and came back and accepted Jesus. Problem is, the others want to find her, and they're looking for Jim too. So we've decided to go on a trip. Over."

Jack paused, before answering. He couldn't say just anything over the phone patch. He had to choose his words. Besides, he was confused. It sounded like Jon was talking in circles. He answered, "Sounds like you need some help? Over."

"Affirmative, Jack. Over."

"Okay, Jon. It sounds like I need to call you. Over."

"I'll be waiting for your call — call me at home in a half-hour. Over and out."

"Okay. Got that. I'll be home in an hour. Over and out," Jack replied.

Jon thanked Larry and dismissed himself. It only took about five minutes to get home, so he had to wait a while for Jack to call, but the call finally came through.

"Hello."

"Jon?"

"Yes, Jack."

"What's this you're telling me?"

"James met his first officer when we were in Santo Domingo..." Jon went ahead, telling the whole story. Jack appreciated the concise version that Jon was giving him. They both knew how expensive long-distance time was for international calls. He began to get a clearer picture, and his desire to bring James to the States increased, as he began to feel certain that it was the Lord's will. With Jon's comment that "Ashley and James seem like a great pair and they seem to like each other (holding hands, etc.)", Jack suggested, "I think we need to get them out of Ecuador as soon as we can. Take them to Manta and help them arrange a trip to Mexico. Call me collect from Manta and I'll tell you what I've been able to work out in Mexico." Jack had already been thinking of ways to get James to the States. This would just move his plans ahead. And then he added, in jest, and full of sincerity too, "And maybe you can get them married so they won't be like hippies — just traveling together."

Jon laughed, "You want me to play matchmaker?"

"At least give it a try. It sounds like the match is made. Just instigate things, a bit. Maybe if you tell Judy, she would get a kick out of trying."

"But they aren't going to be able to have a legal marriage. They don't even have passports," Jon protested.

"Do the best you can," Jack encouraged. "And if anything comes of it, you can marry them before the Lord. This is an exceptional case, and the way James told us about his world, they really don't understand family and things. So don't push them. But if it looks like they're headed that way, help them along. You know, if someone hears about this, and thinks we're using church money for unmarried couples to travel together, they'll make a stink. It'll be hard enough to explain without making things worse than they are. It would have been easier with just James alone, but God knows, and He's sent us Ashley too. If they want to get married, it'll make it easier, but we've got to work with what God has given us."

When they finished making arrangements, Jack hung up and looked at his watch. They had talked thirty minutes. That'll be a hundred dollars — he figured — and the expenses are just beginning. Is it really worth it? Is this what God wants? Maybe it would be better to let Smith and his girlfriend go. Maybe we're getting mixed up in more than we can handle. Maybe I should call Jon back this minute, before this goes too far, or someone gets hurt, or something terrible happens, and tell him to backoff, and let Smith and his girlfriend do what they want.

However, Jack knew that he had a mandate. It's in my heart — he told himself. God wants me to bring them to the States. I've got to put my questions aside, and make it happen. But I really do need to know how the Lord wants us to do this. It could be dangerous. The others are looking for Ashley, and James too, so we've got to be careful.

* * *

Hotel Colon, Quito

LÓPEZ HAD HAD A LONG DAY. Walker took him out to the mountain and despite his initial distaste for the "chap," he felt like he could learn to like him. But now he was reporting to Novus Ordo.

"What do we have, López?" Weller asked.

"We're having trouble with the local police computers. Walker's people have done a good job, and they've gotten us a description of a vehicle and a couple, who apparently gave Brown a ride, near the airport, not long after her call to Nova Mundi, but the police computer is still down, sir."

"Still down! They've had all day. When are they going to get it running?"

"Good question, sir. We're trying to get them to accept our assistance. I'm sure they'll see it our way. We should have what we need by tomorrow."

"What about Smith. Any trace?"

"Not yet, sir. Walker has this idea that maybe some climber cut off the piece of RSB, and buried the rest for later use. He figures all that's left of Smith is bones. The vultures probably got the flesh. He says they're really hungry; not much to eat up on the mountain."

"Okay, López. Walker's probably right, but I want to know for sure. I want every blasted *outer* in that part of the world interviewed. I want them to see Smith's picture, understand."

"Yes, sir. We've begun. I'll let you know as soon as we get any answers. And sir, I think we are going to need more resources to go after Brown."

"You'll have everything you need, just give the word."

* * *

The next day — Pifo

DAN AND LINDA, not to mention the entire Brook family — especially one of the girls, Ann — had grown attached to Ashley. It was the worst part of missionary life. As soon as you made a new friend it seemed you were parting company. There was comfort in the thought that one day you would meet again in Heaven, but Ann and Ashley had truly become friends, even though they were together for only a short time — maybe an hour. Perhaps it was because Ashley shot hoops so well!

Dan had become a believer (mostly) in Smith's hidden Cosmokrators. His PLOT device was incredible, not to mention his watch. But maybe that's only advanced military stuff — Dan wondered. Then he questioned himself — Could it be *only* military? Maybe. Maybe not. The PLOT, and the watch are great toys, but a flying saucer would require far more advanced technology. The main thing that convinced Dan was that Smith sounded authentic. His words sounded like they came from a man who had walked on Mars. As much as Dan's intellect told him the whole story was preposterous, James sounded right. He also couldn't see any point for a person who, having access to such advanced technology, would find it necessary to exaggerate and to contrive a story. It simply didn't make any sense. And James wasn't going to get anything out of him. So it was with extreme reluctance that he let the Whittens take James and Ashley when they came early the next morning. He jokingly said, "I'll let them go, but only if they leave the watch."

James had even shared with him some of the prophetic implications that Pastor Jack had noted. And Dan had insisted they continue to correspond. James told him he would try. In parting, Dan gave James a postcard with a picture of Pifo's antenna farm. James, trying to give something in return, and to express his gratitude, let him have a patch that he cut from the piece of RSB material he was still carrying.

Ashley wanted to stay, and learn piano, how to cook, and other things that were fine arts in the Brook family, but she knew she couldn't.

With everyone refreshed and ready, their trip to the coast began. The travelers were careful not to tell the Brooks exactly where they were going. Not that they didn't ask, but James told them, "It would be better for you if we didn't say." Having been told a bit about the world that James came from, neither Dan nor Linda dared challenge his wisdom.

James finished with a joke, having found in Dan Brook a man of unsurpassed good humor, "If I ever get to Mars again, I'll see if we can pick up HCJB, and send you a listeners report."

Dan answered, "Just be sure it has an official postmark, and has stamped on the envelope: VIA DEEP MAIL."

On that note James and Ashley left with the Whittens, the Brooks waving as they departed.

Chapter 8

The Proposal

NONE OF US liveth to himself, and no man dieth to himself.

— Paul the Apostle

February 19 — That same day — The Road to Manta

JON WHITTEN was full of doubts and shaken from the checkpoint incident. He asked himself — Wouldn't it be safer just to turn them in to their people? But he figured not — The thugs would probably have me killed. I'm trapped. It'll be a long trip. And he knew, even if it would've been expedient to send the pair back to their TerraNova, he couldn't do it, and still live with himself. It had been nothing more than a passing thought, something he briefly considered — And it's rotten — he told himself.

During the first hour there was little conversation and they rolled along the highway, which was pitted and uneven, across valleys and over ridges. Deep blue sky with puffy white clouds contrasted with the powerful green slopes of the Andes that gracefully wore the stark shadows of the highlands. Furrowed plots covered the mountains, and made a towering checkerboard pattern. Occasionally there were ridges, and snowcapped mountains.

As to the highway itself, Jon always wondered how a middle lane would seem to appear — not that there really was one — and a truck or bus (or even whole lines of traffic) would come barreling at him with no apparent thought for life or limb — his or theirs.

It hadn't taken James and Ashley long to snuggle close together in the back area while lying on the floor, and staying out of view. The space wasn't long enough for them, and they were forced to cramp together. It was the better part of wisdom for them to hide themselves, as much as they could, especially as they drove back past the area where they had avoided the checkpoint the day before.

JON HAD TOLD JUDY about Jack's comments on matchmaking and Judy laughed heartily, but at this point, seeing James and Ashley acting as if they were closer than mere friends, but not quite newlyweds, she figured it wouldn't be a bad idea, and hoping to start a conversation, she asked, "Why haven't you two gotten married?"

In response to her question, Judy, with a woman's eye, caught James subtly shy away from Ashley. He's embarrassed — she chuckled to herself, and thought — Maybe there's hope!

Ashley answered, "There wasn't any marriage in Alpha Force."

"Did you used to feel like you wanted to get married?" Jon asked.

And Judy added quickly, "After all, they kept you boys and girls awfully close. If they didn't want you getting married, why would they do that? Wouldn't they want to have new '*Alphies*'? "

"Not really," James answered. "We were always busy. And they *inflicted* us if we even touched each other."

"*Inflicted?*" Jon asked.

"We have bioprocessor implants. Whenever we behaved in a way they didn't like, they would just press a button and make us feel like we were in the hell your Jesus taught about." And James explained further, "It makes you hurt and burn and ache all over, and inside too. It makes you feel like you're terrible and ashamed, all at the same time."

"Will they inflict you if they find you?" Judy asked.

"First thing," Ashley replied.

"So why are you touching each other right now? Aren't you afraid?" Jon asked.

Upon hearing Jon's question, Judy saw James flinch, though it was something she *felt* more than saw. Indeed, he probably hadn't moved at all. It was really her special way of seeing things — the things that other people usually didn't — and in this case, it meant that James must have felt some guilt, or shame, or whatever it was that an *"Alphie"* (as she had dubbed him in her mind) would feel if caught enjoying something he shouldn't. Since it was her thought, her own perception, she didn't have to account for it, but James did seem to have put a little more distance between himself and Ashley.

Ashley answered, "Maybe we always wanted to touch each other, but now we're free, and we can."

"That sounds like a good reason to me," Jon said approvingly. "But if they didn't allow marriage, where did they get…"

"Where did the babies come from?" Judy said, finishing his question.

"We were genetically engineered and *implanted,*" James answered.

"Implanted?" Judy asked.

"Into the womb of a surrogate mother," Ashley clarified.

"And did you know your mother?"

"Oh, no. We were taught that our mother was TerraNova. But now they've improved, and they don't need to use a woman's body; they have tanks."

"Tanks?"

"Yes, for the gestation of new personnel."

Judy was immediately repulsed by the idea, but it sounded like more sci-fi, and after DEEPs, and all the rest, it sounded reasonable.

Ashley continued, "They made us by *lots*. James and I are from a special lot that was genetically designed to be officers for Alpha Force."

"So they didn't need for you to reproduce. They did it for you?" Jon queried.

"We were too important to spend our time in that function," Ashley added.

"But why didn't they just make boys? It seems like they wouldn't need any girls in this Army you're talking about," Judy probed.

"Actually, they do use the girls for many things that boys don't do very well. There are missions where a man would be out of place. There are, you know, all kinds of covert activities, and boys can't do them all."

"But they could have made girl agents for those things, but left the army for the boys," Judy protested.

"I don't know," Ashley conceded. "I can't tell you why they do everything the way they do. Whatever you may think, the fact is they did, and do, include females in their army."

"Okay. I'm still curious," Jon began. "You say they didn't want you taking time for the 'function,' but excuse me if I'm getting too personal, or something, but didn't you want to do it — like getting married?"

Neither James nor Ashley answered. Judy began to feel awkward and embarrassed by her hubby's question, but she could tell that James was gazing into Ashley's eyes.

Then James answered, "I think we would've enjoyed marriage."

Judy thought — Yes! There's hope. She then said, "The others aren't here. You two can enjoy each other. If you want to talk about marriage, you have two experts here," she added with a wink that she made sure Jon caught by reaching over to tap his arm.

He smiled, and agreed, "Yeah, we're experts," and he winked back.

Everyone paused before continuing the conversation. Judy felt rewarded when James and Ashley snuggled a bit closer.

"When you were going to Mars, and all, what did you do when you wanted to be near each other, like now?" Judy asked.

James answered, "I think I've always wanted to be near Ashley — even when we were little — but they wouldn't allow it. As I said, they would inflict us. And it seemed like she really didn't want me—"

"What do you mean, James Smith," she interrupted, " 'it *seemed* like *I* didn't want you?' "

"Well, it did. You were always so serious, like you hated me."

"I just didn't want you to get inflicted anymore; that's all. I always wanted you to be close to me, but I was afraid for you. Then you became a commander, and acted so aloof. I couldn't even talk to you. When you wrote that book, they promoted you, and made you a captain, and then it was impossible to get near you."

Judy was losing hope. The pair had separated again, and weren't touching.

Then Ashley said, "I'm sorry you took it that way. I thought you knew why I acted like I did. I didn't have any choice."

"I know. I understood. But after they inflicted me I felt so ashamed, and you acted like I had a bad odor whenever I was around you. You were so invested, and I understood, but I wanted you to be like you were when we went to the closet together. I wanted to be close to you, but we couldn't. So I started acting like you. Besides, that was the only way to get ahead."

"So, you *do* love each other!" Judy affirmed.

"Love each other?" James asked.

"Don't you?" Judy questioned with a lighthearted giggle. She could see she was getting them to think. They looked at each other, penetratingly. Judy thought — They love each other. I knew it! Now we need to get them married.

JAMES HAD ALWAYS wondered what "love" really was. Was he in "love" with Ashley, as Judy said? Everything else diminished as he began to search for an answer to the question — the roar and the vibration from the road disappeared, as if he had fallen asleep. For an instant, there wasn't anything else, just Ashley. He was entranced, and watched as pulsating dashes of light, which shot through the eucalyptus trees they were passing, strobed across her clean features.

SHE WANTED HIM to enshroud her, to hold her — oh, so tight. Everything had changed. Her professional ambition dwindled into a fervent appetite for him. She wanted James and always had wanted him. Right then, she knew that she couldn't live without him.

Life in TerraNova's world was gone forever. She would never go back, and neither would he. She knew they couldn't. And, as a result, they had nothing left in the world but each other. She thought — Do outers call this love? Are we in love? We must be!

* * *

Hotel Colon, Quito — Novus Ordo

"WELL, LÓPEZ, what have you found?" Weller asked.

"Sir, there are about four hundred people who own the type of vehicle we're looking for, and are foreigners also — in this province — but if we take into account only the sections of town that are near the airport, we can lower that number to about eighty."

"Eighty!" Weller exclaimed, adding an oath. "How long will it take you to interview them?"

"With our present number of operatives, about a week."

"One cursed week!" Weller exclaimed, and then lifted his hand to his chin, thinking. After a pause, he spoke, "Okay, I'll mobilize some agents. We'll see if we can get things moving, and temporarily move all of our Spanish-speaking SAOs to Quito, but we can't do it for long. We need Colombian *powder* to boost our cash flow. To save time, we'll *deep* them in to a remote area. Have Walker arrange a place for delivery."

"Yes, sir. Sounds good, sir. That should speed things up."

"Fine, López. Anything else?"

"Not yet, sir. We have a vague report from a man who sells knives. He said he bought one from a *gringo* who looked like Smith, but he wasn't sure. He said that 'all *gringos* look the same.' " Obviously, his account is barely credible.

"We also have a report from a person in the Talontag area. She said that the morning Walker sealed off the Antisana area, a couple of *gringos* ran through the village, very quickly, but she couldn't identify them. They were dressed in black. It doesn't make sense that they would've been together — Smith and Brown — weeks after the crash, and still on Antisana?" he questioned. "Besides, Brown's RSB was found in the Pacific. Why would she go to Antisana? How would she know where to find him? Why would he still be on Antisana? And if he even survived the crash, he surely wouldn't be in any condition to be running."

"Imbecile, Brown was *in* the Quito office, of all places. She could have found out that we found Smith's RSB on that mountain and that we were going to search it. López, don't be so dense! Somehow, it seems like Smith and Brown are in this together. When Walker saw Brown in the office, she was dressed in black. Your lady said they were dressed in black. Open your eyes, López! Follow up on every lead!"

López thought — *He* said, "*my* lady." Huh! She's not my lady. He can have her if he wants! And then López answered, "Yes, sir. We will, but it seems the people in that area are reluctant to speak to strangers."

"Then make them talk! You know how to do that, López, don't you? Give them some serum. Do something! Do I have to send in a DEEP for something so simple? An abduction just to make some half-wit Indian woman talk! Surely you can handle that, López."

Weller's look filled him with fury, but he didn't let on, and kept his own expression calm as his boss continued, as if talking to himself.

"I'll see if we can get a better ionic scan for RSB material. Whoever cut that piece has it somewhere. We might be able to find it. I'll also ask about looking for the PHENIX. It could lead us to Brown."

"Yes, sir," López agreed, as he thought — Sure! No agent will want to trudge around in those mountains, going hut to hut, looking for something they'll never find. Besides, even if Smith and Brown were there, they were seen running away, so they're long gone. What's the point now? I'll just delay. Weller's just hot air. Maybe something will come of Brown and the Jeep incident. Then we won't waste our time chasing ghosts in the mountain fog.

"If Smith or Brown think they can get away from us, they've forgotten their inflictions all too easily," Weller finished, adamant in his tone, and again looked at López in a way that questioned, as if he was asking, "Would you like to try one too?"

* * *

Novus Ordo

"Jones," Weller began, "I've considered your request for a command position."

"Yes, sir," she answered while looking at him on the monitor in her quarters and standing at attention in uniform pajamas that were barely comfortable.

"Relax," Weller offered, and Nancy loosened her posture a bit. "As you know, thanks to your effort we've found Smith's RSB. However, a piece of it, about the size of a large blanket, has been cut off, and removed from the site. We may presume it's still in that general vicinity, but it could be anywhere. I'm willing to commit whatever resources are necessary to finding it, but I've been told, even with the improvement you made in our scanning capability, we can only detect a piece that's that small from the lower atmosphere."

"That's correct, sir."

He uttered an oath and then said, "Jones, I know! I'm not getting you out of bed to tell you things you already know. We did the low-altitude scan of Antisana, but there's no more RSB material in that area. So I want to make a deal. If you can improve the scan so that we can find the missing piece, you'll have your command."

"Yes, sir! I'll get on it."

"One more thing."

"Yes, sir."

"I know this will be hard, but can you come up with any way to find a PHENIX?"

"A PHENIX, sir?"

"Right. Brown took one from our office in Quito."

Nancy thought — Ashley, but why? She began to answer slowly, and without her accustomed confidence, "I'm sure, sir, you understand the technical problems related to your request. It's one matter to scan for a highly reflective material, and quite another to be looking for a well-insulated, and sealed, device — that's so small."

Weller responded, "Yes. I understand. But while you're working on all of this, if you have any ideas, it's really important."

"Yes. I see, sir."

Then the screen went blank.

EVEN THOUGH the conversation ended on a discouraging particular, Weller thought — There's something about talking to Nancy. All those blond Aryan gals in Alpha Force, but Nancy ... she's right. But if she comes up with the scan I'll have to give her a command. After a few months, I can have her retired — early. I'll unplug her processor and take her to an abandoned island.

Then he cursed to himself. He felt miserable. It couldn't happen. He was a Cosmokrator. Besides, he could have any "real" woman he wanted. Alpha gals with bioprocessors are freaks. They've been so *inflicted* they probably can't act human, even if they have to.

And he knew he couldn't do it either. He didn't have time to be human, and no one had ever taught him what acting human meant, anyway. Life under the sea hadn't ever been very human. Maybe that's why he felt attracted to her. She was as much a machine as he was.

ON THE OTHER END, when Weller closed the communication, Jones turned away from the screen, and allowed herself a chuckle, but only in her mind, lest the walls be watching. Her research had taken her much further into ionic scan technology than she had let anyone know. She hadn't even kept notes so *they* wouldn't know, but she had the key concept in her head. She had learned not to play her cards too quickly — to keep something back. An improved ionic scan was but a couple of weeks away, or maybe a month, she guessed, with a sly smile. We'll see. Maybe I can get something else from Weller. I'd give him the scan tomorrow, but it would be too soon. He might guess I've been holding back. He's playing with me — I'll play with him.

* * *

The Road to Manta, Ecuadorian coastal region

THIS IS ONE LONG TRIP! — Jon thought. Fatigue tightened every muscle in his body. Judy had driven a while, which helped, and he had rested several times, but they really needed to make it to Manta without any layover. Even at night the smoldering coastal heat (unlike the permanent "air-conditioning" of Quito) boiled around them. It was hard for him to hear everyone speak over the roar of the wind that was coming through the windows as they moved along at about fifty miles an hour. He estimated they had about two hours to go, and then they would pull into Manta — around 12:00 AM.

He had told James and Ashley that they could sit up just after sunset, a few hours ago; since they wouldn't be easily identified in the dark, and since the road had little traffic.

Jon listened with amazement as he heard James ask, "You think we should get married?"

Marriage had become the day's only subject. He was nearly tired of the whole thing, and it seemed like they had been over this point in multiple ways already.

This time Judy answered, and said, "Jon already told you. That's something you'll need to work out for yourself, between the two of you, but people who are in love and have known each other for as long as you two, usually do get married. Sometimes non-Christian people just live together, but we believe the Bible teaches that that's wrong."

"How do you get married?" Ashley asked.

"Well, outers have to do some legal things. Get tests. Do papers. Then, here in Ecuador, they go to a judge and he marries them, but Christians believe they must get married before God, and they go to a minister afterwards. There's usually a ceremony, and people come, and the bride dresses in white. There's a party and people have fun. But it isn't always the same. People do it differently," Jon explained.

ASHLEY WASN'T totally ignorant of the subject, and she knew that James also knew something about it. They had studied outers' behavior. But before, they had understood it as an ornithologist might understand the mating habits of hook-billed mergansers. But this was different, Ashley recognized — Things have changed. We aren't invested Alpha officers now. We're just outers. And the way things have gone, that's all we'll ever be.

Ashley remembered something about outers – The man is supposed to ask the girl to marry him. So she asked, "Is James supposed to ask me to marry him? Is that how it works?"

Hearing her words, Judy laughed and giggled. Ashley was beginning to feel annoyed, since Judy had been acting so ... so outer! Judy had been cackling at her questions all day long.

And Judy answered, "Why, girl, with a question like that, you just 'bout beat him to it. We're a little old-fashioned, and we think a man should ask the woman, but anymore a lot of people don't care who asks first."

NOW JAMES remembered his lessons on outers' customs almost as well as the ones on Mesopotamian art, but he had already seen that marriage would be good, and simply: It was normal for outers to pair up and live together. The Christian way was marriage, and the tradition was that the man should ask the woman. He wasn't totally sure if he considered himself a Christian, though since he had prayed the so-called sinner's prayer, according to what Jon said, he was a Christian — and he knew he had become an outer. There wasn't any way he could go back to TerraNova, and if he was going to spend the rest of his life as a fugitive, he wouldn't mind having a companion. He couldn't let Ashley beat him to it, and even if they were no longer Alpha Force he was the captain.

Based on his logic, he made the decision and immediately asked, "Ashley, will you marry me?" He spoke loud enough to be sure everyone heard.

It was pitch black. Haze covered the stars. There were a few distant lights. Black pavement absorbed the Jeep's lights. Some cabin light was available from the instrument panel, but it was nearly impossible to read expressions. James barely saw her surprise. She raised her brows, made a nervous turn of her head, and began to speak, and said, "Why?"

Then she paused, and James tensed.

After what could have been hours, at least in his mind, she continued, and asked emotionally, "Oh, James, ... does that mean you love me?"

He felt relieved and reached towards her. She received his hand in hers.

James answered her question, "Yes, it does. I guess ... if wanting to have you near me for the rest of my life is love, then I love you."

JUDY COULDN'T BELIEVE her ears. Her eyes had seen precious little. She momentarily wondered if they had made a mistake, and gotten James and Ashley together too quickly. Maybe our plan worked too well? — she asked herself. Shouldn't it have taken longer? But she wasn't about to let the moment escape, and announced, "After the man proposes and the woman accepts, he's supposed to kiss the bride to be." She could hear the glee in her own voice, and it made her even happier, to the point that she shed a tear.

JAMES WONDERED. It seemed repulsive. Kissing? That's outer! And then he confessed to himself — I'm outer! He rationalized — She probably doesn't have any germs I don't have already, so what will it hurt if we kiss? And he approached her. His lips touched hers, and they were soft. Time could have stopped. He didn't have any previous experience for comparison, except the closet, and they hadn't kissed. In the closet it had felt good to have her near, but this was better. Was it smoother than a DEEP? More revealing than a SPARQ? Devastating, like a PHENIX? Nothing seemed right, except her lips. Nothing else was left. He felt fully pleased ... and that was all.

DID ANYONE count the seconds? Judy tried, but in the dark it was hard to tell — Maybe it was a half-minute. She wasn't sure. No one said anything.

She didn't want to interrupt them, and she remembered a few moments of her own. Moments that could have gone on forever, and she leaned closer, and rested her head on Jon's shoulder. She felt him reach over and lightly touch her hand.

Warm, humid wind rushed through the cabin, buffeting and battering. The Jeep ground its way along, faithfully trudging over washboard-worn, pothole-riddled pavement. She was, as she imagined they all were, road weary and beaten, but somehow, it was wondrously passionate — and she loved it.

* * *

That same day — Worldwide

STONEFELL SEETHED as he thought over their situation. Being a Cosmokrator wasn't supposed to be so difficult, was it? Even his plush leather chair seemed to him to have hardened, as though it had fossilized. The seal fiasco really set us back — he considered. We're years behind schedule. It's almost as bad as the '42 disaster when we had to dump that slobbering demigod — Hitler. Who would've imagined the Soviet Union would fall apart so easily?

Stonefell gave Weller's holographic double only enough attention to know what was going on. The kid's report dragged on. Then Weller said, as he changed subjects, "We have recovered Captain Smith's RSB on the slopes of Mount Antisana in Ecuador. It's a snowcapped mountain, reaching about 5700 meters above sea level."

Stonefell thought — The kid got his wish. Now what?

Weller continued, "We haven't found a body, or any remains. There are a couple of possible sightings but the witnesses aren't sure. They seem to be dead ends. All of our experts agree that it would have been impossible for Smith to have lived through the crash, and had he lived, he certainly couldn't have walked off that mountain alive."

Stonefell questioned, "Okay, you found the RSB. Can we get on with more important things — like bringing Russia back into our sphere of influence?"

"Mr. Chairman," Weller answered with a smirk that Stonefell realized was a visible indicator of false respect. "There is one more detail. A piece of RSB, approximately three meters square, is missing. Smith's backpack is missing, along with other things — especially the PLOT."

"So, the captain did attempt to leave the crash site," Rennedy summarized.

"There are other theories," Weller explained, and went on to tell them the idea about the climbers. Stonefell wished he could move them away from the subject, but they were determined to continue. When they reached their conclusion that the search for the missing piece of RSB should continue, Stonefell wished he had more forcefully guided the Committee into a productive discussion, but once they had reached the consensus to continue the search, it would do little good for him to try to change their minds. At last, when it looked like they were ready, he asked, "Shall we move on?"

Weller spoke, "Please, Mr. Chairman, I have one more point."

Stonefell looked down in anguish, but tried not to let it show, as he asked, "What else? Weller?"

"A person identifying herself as First Officer Ashley Brown and quoting the correct Alpha Force serial number called our office in Quito on Sunday morning. That evening, a person, who was Officer Brown herself, broke into our office and took a PHENIX, after a fight with the local SAO."

This information provoked several shocked expressions.

"Wasn't she found dead?" Gernik asked, intensity in his voice.

"No, only her RSB was found. Circumstances indicated she couldn't have survived, but now we have evidence to the contrary," Weller answered.

"My, my," Rennedy pondered aloud, "and what? Have we captured her?"

"What the [explicatives deleted by editor] are we doing to find her?" Stonefell demanded, adding a few choice curses.

"Excuse me, Mr. Chairman, you asked?"

Stonefell immediately overheated. He could feel the heat on his face. He knew that Weller had heard him. It was just more of the kid's games, but now wasn't the time to humble him; that would come. Stonefell asked, "Okay, Weller. What are we doing, anything, to find her?"

"SAOs are being moved in from everywhere we can get them, and we have people walking the streets. We've gotten a list of suspects, people who may have picked her up in the vicinity of the airport. I doubt it'll be long until we know who they were."

"Then what, Weller?" Stonefell examined, "You said she has a PHENIX?"

Weller made a condescending snort as he answered, "Yes. But we'll find her! Dead or alive. A PHENIX won't save her."

Chapter 9

Flat Tire and Wedlock

THEREFORE SHALL a man leave his father and his mother, and shall cleave unto his wife: and they shall be one flesh.

— The Hebrew Bible

February 20 — The next day, about 1:30 AM — Near Manta

LIGHTS FROM MANTA started to appear in the distance. "We're almost there," Jon announced.

"Jack wants us to go to the States?" James asked after Jon told him about his conversation. Judy and Ashley both slept, and it had cooled down a bit, so they had rolled up the windows some. They didn't have to shout as loudly to talk.

"He thinks the Lord has a mission for you there, to help him start something to warn people about the others and their plan — how it compares with prophecy, and all."

James began to think — The outer God saved me. He answered my prayer, even when I was ready to turn my back on Him, and He saved Ashley too. The missionaries say I'm "saved," that when I prayed with them it made me a new person, and I am different — and I am really different. I don't like the same things I used to like. I don't talk the same. I don't act the same. I'm not really Captain Smith — not now. So maybe I should offer to help Jack. He's been good to me.

James, however, doubted that he could really do what Jack wanted, and asked, "But wouldn't that make me too visible? A target for TerraNova to see?"

"I'm sure Jack understands your situation. You'd have to be hidden from public view somehow. I know Jack will be concerned for your welfare. But if I were you, I'd be worried about all the computers, and Big Brother things in the States. Don't you think that would be a serious problem?"

James thought for a moment and answered, "Not really."

"Why?" Jon asked, wanting to understand.

"Well," James began, reasoning as he went, "it's a big country with a lot of people. There's still a lot of freedom there. You can hide, and you don't have to get yourself in the computers — if you're careful. Here, we can't hide. Everywhere we walk it's like we're carrying a big sign that says, 'I'm a foreigner. I don't belong here.' It's hard to hide in a country where you're taller than everyone else. In the States we would look normal."

"I don't know," Jon answered. "I think you two would look special no matter where you were."

James didn't quite understand the subtlety of the word "special" and the meaning Jon was giving it — a compliment. So he answered, "How will we hide, then, if we'll look 'special'?"

Jon was starting to become accustomed to James's lack of understanding when certain expressions were used and began to explain, "I mean that you're special — " But there was a small explosion and the Jeep suddenly swerved towards the center lane.

A car that refused to lower its high beams was speeding, and coming right at them. James watched as Jon released the accelerator, braked, and manhandled the steering wheel. Blaring at them, the horn of the other car made a Doppler shift as it sped past, barely swerving to get around them. Jon was too busy to answer. James was powerless to help, but he admired Jon. For an outer, he was doing a great job. He didn't even have nerve-pulse accelerators.

Judy woke up and, startled, asked, "What's happening?"

By then Jon was beginning to get the vehicle slowed down, and rolled to one side of the road.

Ashley had also awakened.

"Blowout!" Jon finally exclaimed. "I was thinkin' I should've gotten new tires before a trip like this," his voice was a little rattled.

"On a missionary's income?" Judy asked nervously and jokingly.

"Yeah," Jon answered.

From his voice, it was apparent to James that Jon was angry.

"Well," Jon began, with a greater degree of composure, and a hint of frustration, "we'd better change the tire. At least we're near town. A few more minutes, and we would've been there."

"May I help," James offered.

"Sure," Jon replied.

The men got out and James asked, as they began to get the tools together, "You said I'm 'special'."

"Oh." Jon laughed. "That just means you're a good guy."

It was a compliment. "Thank you," he answered.

Conversation continued as they changed the tire.

"So how did Jack think we should get to the States?" James asked.

"He mentioned something about going through Mexico, maybe by ship."

James, who didn't lack strength, was making a quick job of changing the flat.

"What are we planning, then?" James asked.

"I'm not too sure," Jon answered. "Jack told me to call him collect from Manta, and he would give us a plan."

" 'Collect?' " James asked.

"That means he'll pay for the call in the States."

"Oh, I see," James indicated. And he began to think. Perhaps it was the moment of silence, without the wind (although his sound processors had helped keep the roar out of his hearing) or perhaps it was the change in position, mixed with a bit of exercise, but for whatever reason, James saw a weak link in their chain of escape. Retreat is never easy. The military strategist in him told him as much. It's hard to watch your tail, and run at the same time. If the enemy has any intelligence that could lead them to the Whittens (a real possibility thanks to Ashley's phone call and her failed efforts at the Nova Mundi office), then Jon and Judy shouldn't know their next step — James decided. Indeed, they know too much as it is. I've got to break the chain — he concluded.

"Look, Jon," James began as he finished tightening a bolt, while Jon shone the flashlight, "I think we need to part company."

"What do you mean?" Jon asked.

"Well, I think it would be better for you, and us, if you don't know where we go from here."

Jon didn't take long to understand what James was trying to tell him, and he said to himself — I wish he'd been thinking like this before.

"But what are you going to do? Jack wants you to go to the States."

James thought and then spoke, "You said he wanted you to call him?"

"Right."

"Give me the phone number and maybe I'll call him sometime," James offered.

Jon understood. James and Ashley would have to go their own way. There wasn't any other choice. "What about you and Ashley? You proposed marriage to her. Will you go ahead?"

"We should," James answered. "I would like that. But how?"

"That's a long subject. In the beginning, boy and girl got together and lived the rest of their lives together. Now there are laws, and all. But you two couldn't ever get married by man's laws, since you don't

even have papers — and can't even get them. And you're on the run."
Jon wanted to soften the words "on the run," so he added "so to speak."

"Then what should we do?"

"Well," Jon said, trying to say the right thing. "If you two love each other, and you want to make a commitment to live together for the rest of your lives, and not go after anyone else or let anyone else come after you, then I figure we can work something out."

"What do you mean, 'go after?' " James asked.

He's not good at slang — Jon thought. "What I mean is you shouldn't try to love any other girl like you love Ashley, and she should do the same with you. The love you have for Ashley — that makes you want to hold her close, and makes her want for you to hold her close — that type of love is the one people get married for. Know what I mean?"

James thought for a moment and answered, "Yes."

"That's the type of love I'm talking about, James. You can only have it for Ashley, and no other woman, and she needs to have the same kind of love for you, and no other man. If you promise to love each other in that way, then you can enter into Christian marriage, which amounts to a promise, to God and to each other, to keep yourselves for one another and no one else. It means, if you have children, you'll care for them and teach them the things of God. It means you'll care for one another. The Bible says it's becoming one flesh. That means, in God's eyes you are like one person, not two. And you need to act together, and do things as if you're just one person." Jon paused, allowing him to think. And then he asked, "So, what about it? Do you still want to get married?"

"Yes," James simply and elegantly said as he lifted the spare onto the wheel.

"Well then, you should talk to Ashley about it, and see if she agrees. Maybe we can do some little ceremony, and you two can make your promises to God. Judy and I can be your witnesses. Most couples, when they get married, do a big thing and invite family and lots of friends, and that's nice, but you two have a different situation. If you were regular outers," Jon said (wondering to himself what a "regular outer" would say to his advice), "I'd insist you need to obey man's law and go to the judge. The Bible teaches us to obey the law, but it also teaches that God's law is higher, and if we have to disobey man's law to follow God's, then we just have to do it. You two can't follow man's law because you don't belong to any country. Ecuador wouldn't marry you without papers. And your country doesn't exist, as far as outers know, so you can't get any papers. If you want to do something, some little ceremony, just us, before you take off, I know God will be a witness, and that's all that really counts. Then, if someone asks if you're married, you can say, 'Yes.' "

James finished and the spare tire was secure. He stood up and looked Jon in his eyes that were barely illuminated by the distant city light. He said, "I'll ask Ashley."

* * *

Quito

WALKER WAS WORKING late again. Sleep wasn't a compatible choice, not now. They had knocked on forty doors, but at six addresses no one had answered. All the rest were ignorant of having ever seen anyone, in person, like the one pictured, although several made cracks about having seen her on the cover of a magazine. One asked, "Is she Miss Sweden?"

It made sense, though. Even if Brown is hiding with any of these people, and they are helping her, none of them would claim to recognize her — he thought. They'll all say, "I've never seen the lass." How disgusting! It will take forever to find out who the liars are. It will take work and resources. Imagine, PARASITES in so many homes, looking and listening for hints of Brown. Even then, we have no guarantee she has even been in any of them. The description of the Jeep could be wrong. The police computer could be wrong, and that's terribly likely, Walker reluctantly confessed, as he went on complaining to himself — a thousand things could go wrong and any one of them could slow us down for weeks, or months, or worse, forever. If we don't find her — they'll probably inflict me, and then send me to an office in Antarctica. I should have reached for my PHENIX quicker.

Tomorrow will be another day. There are still forty more doors, and then we will have to go back to check the ones who weren't home. Maybe we will get lucky and some fool will say, "Oh, that girl. Wasn't she sweet? We gave her a ride to…," and then we will know.

* * *

Near Manta

JAMES AND ASHLEY were in conference. Judy stepped out and walked around the Jeep. It was still warm, but cooler, almost comfortable, at 1:30 AM.

"This heat," she commented, standing near Jon, neither questioning, nor declaring.

He answered with a weak "Yeah." He was thinking. Judy knew it, and asked, "What are you thinking?"

"Oh…," he paused and looked towards the city, "James thinks we need to let them go."

"Why?" Judy asked.

"He thinks the *others* might come ask us about them, and he reasons it'll be better if we don't know where they are: for them, and us too."

"He's right, you know."

"Yeah…," he said, looking down. "I told him they should get married."

"How? You know they don't have any papers."

"Well, I told them it was important for them to get married before God. That in their case, that's all they could do."

Judy wanted to complain or protest, and say, "That's not right," but she couldn't think of why — it just didn't seem right. But letting the youngin's (as she thought of them, with her Southern drawl) run off like folks who are just livin' together wouldn't do. Having thought it through, she asked, "Are you going to marry them, then?"

"I guess, if they want me to do it. My, it's taking them a long time to decide."

"Long time? Hon, it's a lifetime decision. Maybe they have some questions. Should we ask them?"

"Not yet," Jon answered, not sure himself and wondering how he had managed to get into this mess. He was beginning to feel irritated, but was immediately distracted from overly pondering the degree of his vexation when Judy took his arm. He responded by pulling her closer.

It was too late for any traffic, and the road had been silent. Jon enjoyed his own bride for a moment, until he heard a rustle, and turned. James and Ashley approached.

"What did you all decide?" Jon asked directly.

"We wish to do it, like you said," James answered.

"Great," Jon replied. "Just a second, I'll get my Bible."

He wondered if he would even be able to read it in the dark. He hoped the batteries in his flashlight would work long enough to get him through the ceremony.

He soon returned to the place where they had gathered, with the Jeep between him and the road, and Judy stood at his side.

The four of them formed a small circle, so to speak, about five feet in diameter. James and Ashley had their arms hooked, and they were all dressed as they came — in jeans.

Jon began explaining Christian marriage to his audience, realizing that he had never performed a ceremony with so few present. He wanted to be sure they understood the meaning of what they were doing, and that they understood what it meant to make a promise to God, and to man. That, no matter what followed, they would be man and wife. It took him about twenty minutes. He had felt exhaustion when he began, but not now. It seemed like all were listening attentively, though the light from the flashlight was starting to redden, and it barely lit the Bible's pages anymore. For a moment Jon imagined they were the only people in the world. If any vehicles had passed, he hadn't noticed.

Jon instructed, "Let's bow our heads in prayer. Heavenly Father, we come before You in the name of Jesus. Perhaps someone will consider what we are going to do as irregular or irreverent, but we are certain that You are here, with us. We ask You, good Lord, to bless James and Ashley in the decision they have made."

Jon stood for an instant, contemplating his next words, and began, "We are gathered, the four of us, as witnesses to the union of two hearts in Christian marriage. The first couple married was Adam and Eve. God did the ceremony, so to speak, and made them one flesh. So we know only three people are necessary for this ceremony: You, Father, and the couple. Judy and I don't really have to be here, but we thank You for this chance to share with James and Ashley."

Having spoken about man and woman becoming one flesh in marriage, and about the bride of Christ, Jon said, "The vows you will make are holy. They aren't meant to be just fancy words. Even if others around you break their promises to one another, you must not. The security of your marriage isn't based on other people, or a church, but on the purpose of God's heart, His character, and your devotion to, and love for, Him."

Jon waited momentarily to allow his last words to penetrate. Then he asked, "James, will you take Ashley to be your wife? Will you love her, honor her, comfort her, and keep her — refusing any other woman, and keep yourself for her alone — as long as the two of you live?"

James answered, "I will."

Then Jon directed himself to Ashley and asked the same things.

"Yes," she replied.

"If you wish," Jon continued, "you may kneel together."

James started and Ashley quickly followed, with their bent knees in the sand. Jon placed his hands on their bowed heads and prayed, "Father, bless James and Ashley..."

When he finished praying, Jon paused and then said to James, "You may stand and kiss the bride."

Ashley and James stood. James put his powerful arm around her, drew her close, and kissed her gently on the lips. Jon was startled when Judy began to clap her hands. He looked her way. He saw tears in her eyes, and put his Bible under his arm, and joined her applause. He noticed that his own eyes moistened.

It was finally about 2:15 AM when James and Ashley gathered their things into his backpack. With hugs, the couples parted. The Smiths disappeared into the night. Jon offered them his flashlight, but James said, "It's close to town and there's some light. We can see for now."

Then Jon gave James an envelope and instructed, "Open this when you need extra money. Pastor Jack made a special deposit for your travel expenses. It should be enough to get you to your destination. His phone number is written on the envelope. You can call him collect, from most anywhere."

The Smiths walked off into the night. Jon had wanted to go into Manta, find a hotel, and get a good rest before turning around, but as things stood, he decided it would be better to turn around and start back. It would be a couple of hours on the road back before they would find a place for a layover, but at least, he remembered, there was a place that fixed tires a few miles back, and in Ecuador, with roads so bad, *vulcanizadores* were common. Usually the proprietor slept in a shack and worked all night — a fact that made Jon grateful.

Chapter 10

Preparation for the Voyage

WE ARE AS near to heaven by sea as by land.

— Sir Humphrey Gilbert

Febuary 20 — That same day — Near Manta

IN HER DREAM, María heard the children at play on the street. They were beating on her door, and she squirmed, trying to remain unconscious a while longer. She tossed. In her dream the naughty children didn't relent. However, they were no longer children; they had turned into chickens, pecking her about — or so it was for an instant. Then the sound got louder, until she realized it wasn't a silly dream — though she wasn't sure if her realization was anything more than a dream. Slowly, she connected to her consciousness. She realized someone, or something, was tapping on her window.

Having reached her present level of awareness, she turned quickly and looked at the window. A vague umbra filled its narrow view. Her heart raced. Then the rapping stopped and she heard, *"María, abre la puerta* – Open the door."

It barely registered, but the voice sounded familiar. María sat up and asked, *"Ashley?"*

"Sí, soy yo – Yes, it's me."

"Hija mía! – My child!" María exclaimed and pulled on her robe, turning on lights and moving towards the door as fast as she could, with a giant smile on her face. She opened it, and there stood Ashley with a big man, who looked to María like he could be Ashley's brother. She lost no time hugging Ashley, and then she reached to greet the man. He looked friendly, and she took his hand and felt its strength.

María immediately wanted to serve her guests, and was about to invite them to sit down and get them something for breakfast, when Ashley began introducing her husband…

"Mi esposo, James!" Ashley exclaimed, introducing him to María. This was Ashley's first opportunity to introduce him as her husband, and she felt proud, as if she had aced a DEEP navigational examination.

"Esposo?" María questioned with a big smile, and an expression that told Ashley she was surprised to hear the news, as if she was saying, "You didn't tell me."

"Sí," Ashley answered, and explained that they had just gotten married. However, she decided not to tell her about the early morning ceremony. It would be too hard to explain.

María's excitement was contagious and Ashley forgot how tired she was, and thought how good it would be to lie down on what had been her bed, back in María's guest room, but she knew they didn't have time, and she quickly advised María that they needed to speak to Pepe. Ashley never had found out where Pepe lived, but she knew it wasn't far. She hoped that María would take them there, and asked her if she would.

María consented and quickly dressed herself. They only had to walk about four or five blocks. Dawn's first light was starting to fill the east, but it was still dark. Some villagers were moving into the streets, going to markets and work. María warned Ashley that they might not reach Pepe before he put to sea, telling her, "*Siempre sale antes del sol* — He always leaves before sunrise."

Indeed, Pepe had left his home, so they rushed towards the docks. It was a long way. They barely made it, arriving almost exactly as Pepe was pushing off. They yelled as they approached, and Pepe waited for them. James and Ashley hugged María good-bye and got on the vessel.

Ashley could see that he was excited to see her, as well as the others who had participated in her rescue. When she introduced her husband, Pepe congratulated her and told her that God blessed her greatly.

For the Smiths, it had been a long day — sunrise to sunrise — and now they began another. So it was to be expected that — after a mid-morning talk with Pepe, as he worked, asking how much it would cost to make it worth his time to take them on a voyage of 1,500 miles, and if he would be interested in making the voyage (and he thought he could), that James and Ashley found a place to lie down on the deck. It was hard, and it was hot.

Ashley was glad that James still had sunscreen (Alpha Force standard issue) in his pack. She dreaded sunburn, and knew that it wasn't healthy. She still had some scars on her shoulders from before. The honeymooners applied it generously to one another and lay down beside each other, unable to endure any more time on their feet. Their hands touched. They hadn't thought of sleeping, but it couldn't have been any other way. Sleep would not wait for them. Ashley found it impossible to keep her eyes open another second.

HOURS PASSED. Pepe's men worked hard. They would've made Saint Peter proud, for they were superb, capable fishermen. But for the Smiths, a look at the catch would have to suffice, since they slept most of the day. Pepe had thought of waking them, and sending them below, so that they would each have a cot, but he decided to leave them alone, for waking them would have been like waking a baby, or babies, in this case.

He wondered if he should help them with his boat for the trip they were asking him about. It seemed like it could be a good way to earn some extra cash, but it would be a long trip. Later, he saw that the *gringa* was stirring, and he wondered why God had sent her into his life.

ASHLEY AWOKE. She felt a chill, and noticed the sun was flaring yellow and red on the horizon as it sank into the Pacific's blue. It took her a moment to remember where she was — on Pepe's boat. Her marriage, though not even twenty-four hours old, could've taken place a hundred years ago, or maybe it never happened at all. She knew it had, but in her memory, the night's ceremony seemed to be a dream that had faded with day's light. One look at her prince — his golden hair agitated by the breeze and firm accents in his muscular limbs — restored her presence of mind.

Seeing him lying on his side with an arm for a pillow, she knew that when he awoke, he would feel as if he had spent the day on a torture rack of medieval vintage, just as she did, even as her senses were returning to her. After a while she scooted beside James, and then slowly lifted his head into her lap.

JAMES ROUSED. As he felt Ashley's mild contact — softly holding his head and forming a cushion for him — he relaxed and didn't open his eyes as he savored her touch.

He felt it was growing cooler, and the sea breeze waxed stronger. By now, he had opened his eyes, only to find darkness. He sat up, and by now Ashley had found her way into his arms.

He almost hated to interrupt the beauty of the moment, but there were things that needed to be resolved, and he asked, "Ashley?"

SHE FELT as if she should answer, "Yes, sir," but she knew that she needed another response, an outer response. Alpha Force wasn't their life, not now. For better or for worse — like Jon had said — their lives were never to be the same again. Her tongue struggled to find an answer, one that would suit their context. She finally remembered a word she had heard Judy use, and responded, "Yes, honey."

MOMENTARILY, James paused, wondering what bees had to do with anything, until he remembered that outers talked in that particular fashion. He understood he was the "honey." And though he didn't know why, he felt as if he understood Ashley in a way he hadn't before. Taking the cue she was giving him, and realizing that she wasn't Officer Brown any longer, he remembered a word Dan had used when he spoke to Linda Brook. With it he began his answer, and said, "Sweetheart…" Saying the word caused him to linger, as though he was relishing the taste of a fine chocolate. When he had savored its taste, he finished, "We need to plan."

"You're the tactician. You have the best mind in Alpha Force."

James felt gratified. For the first time he could remember, she had given him a compliment. He reasoned aloud, "Well, the only thing we can do is put as much distance between ourselves and the focus of their search as we can. We have to break every connection they might follow. And we have to give them decoys to make them waste their time, but how? Pepe's boat isn't a DEEP."

James thought for a while, not saying anything aloud. Ashley breached the hush and said, distress in her voice, "We're traitors. We've become our own enemy." She continued intensely. "They taught us we would win and crush the Christians. Now we're Christians! They'll take us to the slaughter. One way or another, they'll get us. If not now, they'll get us when Operation Therion begins — and that shouldn't be long. They'll get us, James," she said with a trembling voice. "And if we go back, they'll trash us. No matter what, we're doomed."

Hearing Ashley's words made James realize that he would have to face up to his new faith, or reject it. He realized that Ashley didn't know he wasn't sure if he was a Christian yet, or that he hadn't yet really thought of himself as one. True, he had prayed the prayer, and the missionaries had told him he was now a Christian, but until this moment he really hadn't had to define himself. It had been easy to let others presume he was a Christian, if they so cared, but now, since Ashley had become one, and she was his wife, he reasoned — I might as well face up to my own Christianity. His thoughts continued — Some outers are

Christians because it's part of their society and their customs. They call themselves Christians, but they really don't care about Christ. Anyone can see it. They go to church, but they act like the outers who don't. They want people to think they're good, and they think that good people go to church, so they go to church. But it's different for the missionaries and Ashley. Their Christianity is … is what? – James asked himself. What is it? – he asked himself again, and continued to wonder. Is it "real"? Is that the word I'm looking for? And spontaneously he asked, after the long pause, "Ashley, is Jesus real to you?"

"Sure," she answered, but then she asked him with a frown, "Isn't He real to you?"

Her question made him feel ashamed of himself, but it was exactly the question he knew he needed to answer, for his own benefit, if not for hers. So he asked himself – Is He? Is He real to me? Should I tell her that I don't know? Would that offend her? They all think I'm a Christian. She even thinks I'm a Christian. Am I? I prayed that prayer. Right – he thought – I prayed that prayer. So I'll tell her that, for now. And he said, "I repeated the prayer."

"You mean like the one Jon helped me with?"

"I guess," James answered, and then questioned, "How was the prayer? How did it go?"

"I was so … so emotional, I guess … I don't know if I remember exactly, but I first told Jesus I'm a sinner. Then I asked the Lord for help. I said I believed that Jesus died for my sins on a cross and that He rose again. There was more, but I think those were the main things.

"You're right," James affirmed, and he thought – Yes, she's exactly right. "I prayed the same thing. I have to confess I've tried to forget, and to pretend that Jesus was just for outers. But it seems like ever since I prayed, my life's been different, like the missionary said it would be, so I guess I'm a Christian – an outer Christian at that! Imagine, a captain of Alpha Force turned into an inflicted outer Christian, and now I'm married and I suppose the next thing we'll be having babies, like outers."

At that, Ashley smiled. James saw her, and laughed. "You like the idea?" James questioned, taunting her with another chuckle.

Ashley giggled, and said, "Yeah. I do."

James paused, and laughed again, as he added, "I do too."

Only the palpitation of the boat, with the sea swishing against it, and the monotone sonority of the muffled diesel engine could be heard. Pepe's men had finished their jobs and were resting. Momentarily, when their giggles turned serious again, James began, "Sweetheart…" He spoke softly.

Ashley looked up to him from his arms; her expression was peaceful. James pulled her closer.

IT WAS GOOD. Ashley felt secure. Fear seemed so childish. When James said "sweetheart," it was enough. They were outers now, and James was talking about babies, and she liked it. It was absolutely contrary to everything she had ever been taught, but she liked it. She knew she did. It was all crazy, and she knew that TerraNova would get them; they had to! But it really didn't matter. She didn't know why it didn't matter, but it didn't.

James reasoned aloud and spoke, "We aren't what we used to be. Like you said, we can't go back. We've got to get through this as best we can. Both of us are living on borrowed time. Neither one of us would have made it to here if the outer God hadn't intervened. You know, we should both be dead. There's no way that either of us could have lived through the crashes and the storms. It was impossible. But here we are, together. The missionary said, what God puts together let no man try to take apart. He has put us together; so that's the way it is.

"Sweetheart," he said, and looked into her eyes, "they never let us have freedom, or love. Now, we have both. Jon said that sometimes the future looks dark, but the worst it can bring is brighter than the past that Jesus saved us from."

ASHLEY KNEW James was right, and she agreed with him, but she didn't know why. He didn't make much sense, but she felt satisfied, despite the fact that certain thoughts troubled her. Thoughts like: You can't beat Therion. Listen to reason. You're finished! Why run? Just give up. Call Nova Mundi and tell them to come and get you. Maybe they'll go easy on you. Maybe they won't inflict you. But another part of her, the part that didn't make sense, said — James is right. God will help you. Trust Him. Don't be afraid. God saved your life once. He can do it again. For now the latter voice prevailed. She felt peace.

Ashley, thinking of what they would do next, asked, "Who's this 'Jack' we're going to see?"

"He's the man who helped me pray," James answered.

"But you were here, in Ecuador?"

"He was visiting from the United States."

"Why does he want us to go there?"

"I think he wants us to help him tell people what Operation Therion is."

"But if we do that, TerraNova will find us for sure."

"I think he has some secret plan. He wouldn't want us to get hurt, and he knows about our problem. Besides, we're free now, and if we don't like what he says, we can go elsewhere."

"Is it a good idea to let Pepe take us?" Ashley asked with concern.

"I've tried to think through everything. We can't fly; they'll find us for sure. We can't drive; there are too many papers. If we go in buses we'll have the same problem, and leave a trail of witnesses as long as the continent. A small boat is ideal. I don't know how much it will cost, but I think Pastor Jack sent us enough money."

"I don't know," Ashley said.

"What don't you know?" James asked, wishing she had more confidence.

"I mean…," and she tried to figure what it was she meant. "I mean everything is so uncertain. We don't even know the prices, and outer things. If we had been SAOs, maybe we would know more; but frankly, I don't know anything about outers. SAOs can't fly DEEPs, but flyin' a DEEP didn't teach us much about the outer world."

"It won't be hard. We'll learn," James reassured.

"Yeah," she agreed, but she felt as if it was a complaint. It wasn't though, and she didn't want James to think she was whining, so she added, "The outer God must have some purpose for us, or we would have died when the DEEP exploded. He's brought us through so many things, and put us together. So we just need to trust Him." But even as she finished the phrase, she asked herself — Trust God? That's like a mist. I wished we had something more tangible, like a DEEP. She remembered the PHENIX she had from the SAO, but she knew it could only stun a few dozen times until it needed to be recharged and that it would only hold its charge for a few months. I'll just have to get used to things; after all, Jesus saved me when a DEEP couldn't or wouldn't, whatever the case may have been.

She began to wonder if she should tell James about the PHENIX, and decided that he needed to know, but now wasn't the time. It just didn't seem right to talk about it when they were talking about trusting God.

* * *

Quito — Novus Ordo

"López, what have you found?"

He hated to answer Weller's question. If only he had something to tell him, but he didn't, and there wasn't any way to avoid the issue. "Sir," he pronounced, in spite of himself, "we have nothing new to report."

"López! I should inflict you. What do you need? More people? This is already one of the largest manhunts we've ever had."

"I think, sir, at this point, time is the only thing I can ask for. We've knocked on all eighty doors; thirteen weren't at home, and the rest deny having seen Brown. Voice analysis indicates that they were telling the truth. So, if Brown is to be found, the clue we need might be in one of the empty houses."

"López. Send your people back out to the mountain area, and keep checking."

"Yes, sir," he said, as he thought — But the stupid natives are so backward! Most of them don't even speak Spanish. And it seems like they've made an agreement among themselves not to talk to *gringos*. "But sir, if I may?"

"What, López?"

Hearing Weller's sharp reply, López wondered why he had even bothered to say anything, but now he was committed and he would have to speak. "Sir, we really don't have any operatives who are fluent in the Indian language of that area, and who understand the culture there. Whenever we ask them anything, it seems like they're ignoring us."

After a few violently spoken words, Weller asked, "Can't we get someone to help? An interpreter?"

"Perhaps, sir. But I don't know if we can trust them."

"Why not?"

"The only people we know of, who have bothered to learn the Indian language, are missionaries, sir."

"I see," Weller answered.

For the first time since the conversation started, López felt like he had made some progress, and he took advantage, offering a suggestion. "Sir, I believe we have a better chance of success if we use our resources to search the houses where the occupants were missing. Perhaps we'll find something more conclusive."

"López," Weller said, "you have resources! Are you trying to avoid footwork?"

"No, sir. Not at all." As López answered, he felt demoralized.

"It shouldn't be so hard. You don't need very much language. Just make the ignorant Indians look at the picture. Do sign language or read lips, but if Smith or Brown was there: Find out! You hear me?"

López knew Weller was an intelligent man, and it seemed to him that even a grade schooler would've had better-reasoned instructions. Lip reading in Quechua? López nearly laughed. But Herr Weller was still the boss, and could press the inflict button. So he answered respectfully, "Yes, sir," wishing Weller would visit the village himself, and taste the mud, and feel the cold. Then he asked, "Should we also search the houses, sir?"

"Of course! … " Weller commanded, the glare in his eyes suiting the modifiers he added.

* * *

María's house, Manta

THAT EVENING Ashley and James talked at length with Pepe, while sitting around the small coffee table. María listened from the kitchen and would occasionally take a moment from her work of preparing a feast for her visitors to listen to the conversation while standing in the doorway.

At times Pepe figured it was easier to agree with whatever the *gringos* said than to be too concerned about understanding their rationale. He concluded that they must have good intentions. They looked like good people. Also, since he had saved the *gringa*, he felt a special attachment to her, and wanted to please her. Besides, they were Christians and he was certain they wouldn't ask him to do anything amiss, albeit certain details seemed strange. Why did they want to go in his small boat? There were big ships in the port, just a few miles away — cargo ships — but some of them carried passengers too. He knew they would be cheaper and better. Why did they choose his vessel? And having asked himself this question, he asked them, "Why don't you go in a merchant ship?" But they seemed to ignore him.

God had led him to the strange lady. Now she was asking a strange thing. It made sense. In Pepe's way of seeing things — strange ladies make strange requests. This became his justification. He told his crew, "It's for the *gringa rara*" — "Strange foreign lady." But he told his wife, Elena, it was for the *gringos raros* — strange foreigners. He convinced her to let him go by giving her three weeks of market money in advance. He rarely gave her more than a day at a time, but with the gringos' money, he could afford to pay in advance. And he gave her plenty — more than usual. It made him feel proud of himself, for there had been many days when he had only been able to give her a little money, or nothing but fish, and a family needed more than fish.

As to the legality of the trip — passport and visa requirements — Pepe was ignorant. Law wasn't a subject for a fisherman. He thought

— May the *doctores* (lawyers) know the law, and may the *pescador* (fisherman) know the sea. Besides, there wasn't an immigration office in Manta, so far as he knew — if he even knew what immigration might be — and Pepe hadn't ever seen a passport, let alone gotten a visa.

No one before the *gringos* had offered to pay him so well for his services. He would make more money in two weeks than in two months. Also, it sounded exciting, and Pepe was still young enough for an adventure to attract him. It was a chance to change his routine.

He was certain they could do it. Once, he had navigated all the way to Galapagos and back. Though that trip had been only a third of the one proposed by the *gringos*, it had been far enough for Pepe to have confidence in his seamanship, and the worthiness of his twenty-eight-foot vessel.

Pepe had one concern in particular. The *gringos* didn't want him telling people where they were going, and they didn't even tell him. They only gave him a distance. He was tempted to say, "Well, if you don't tell me, I won't take you." But he decided he didn't need to complain. If they didn't have charts, he wouldn't need to take them. He told them that they would have to bring the charts. They had told him not to worry, but he wondered where they would get them, since they were hard to get in his country.

* * *

The next day

PEPE BEGAN the morning with good intentions.

According to his calculations he needed eight barrels of diesel. James had given him the money and the *gringa* had told him to get it from several different providers, but it was too much effort — Pepe decided. Besides, it didn't matter, did it? What if people asked him a few questions? So what. No one would care.

He went to the first distributor and resolved — I'll just get the fuel.

No sooner had he ordered the diesel, and everyone became curious. They asked many questions. Why do you need so much? Where did you get the money? Where are you going? Pepe always answered with something about the *"gringa rara."* Someone asked if he was going to run some coke. "No!" he replied adamantly. "I'm a Christian. I don't do things like that. It's the *gringos.* They're going on a *luna de miel* (honeymoon)."

"Do they want to go to Galapagos?"

"I don't know," Pepe answered. "They haven't told me yet."

When he went to get food and supplies, people asked the same questions. Pepe gave them the same answers. He realized that he was being lazy, for Manta was big enough that he could have followed the *gringa's* instructions.

Chapter 11

Fumigation

THE PEST, in a sense, is a very superior being to us: he knows where to find us and how — usually in the bath … or asleep.

— Charles Bukowski

February 22 — That same day — Quito

JON WAS READY to collapse and he anticipated a good shower, the comfort of his own bed, and a rest. The trip to Manta and back had been barbaric. He told himself — I'll have to be careful about letting people rope me into things. I'm getting too old to drive day and night. He turned the last corner, and started rolling down the street where they lived. In an instant his house would come into view, but something was wrong with the picture. Parked on his street was a panel van. It looked *gringo.* It was white — *all white* — without any markings, except the fact that it was new. Indeed, it was too new, at least for his neighborhood, and it had a blue and gold diplomatic license plate. Being a capital city, Quito had a large diplomatic presence. So there really wasn't anything strange about a van with a diplomatic plate, except that there weren't any diplomats on Jon's street.

"Judy, look at that!" he exclaimed as they crept by. The van seemed wider than normal and the street was a little narrow, forcing him to drive with care.

But she had been asleep and didn't wake up until they had gone past. Jon got a good look at the occupant of the driver's seat — nothing out of the ordinary — just a typical chauffeur with a shirt and tie. However, Jon had a feeling. It was as if the driver had been expecting them.

They rolled on by and Jon parked in front of their house. "What do you suppose that van is doing around here?" he asked Judy.

"How would I know?" she questioned as she stretched herself.

"Strange, isn't it? Diplomatic people never visit our neighborhood."

JUDY CHANGED the subject, commenting on a warm cup of coffee she fancied. She didn't see any point in worrying about where the diplomats were parking.

Reaching their garage, Jon stepped out and opened the gates. He got back in the Jeep and pulled in the driveway. They unloaded, and went inside as quickly as they could, unpacking as little as possible. Jon made a dash for the shower. Judy made herself some coffee.

Perhaps they had been home twenty minutes when the doorbell rang. Judy answered. A man in a black business suit stood before her. She might not have thought anything out of the ordinary, but seeing the man — who seemed out of place — she remembered Jon's comment about the van and glanced down the street. It was still there.

The stranger said, *"Buenos días* — Good day."

Judy answered apprehensively, *"Buenos días."*

"We have a report of a missing person, and we have reason to believe the *señorita* may have been seen in this neighborhood. Could you please tell me; have you seen this young lady?" The dark man, with black hair that was slicked back, took a picture from his coat pocket and presented it, holding it where Judy could see.

Oh, Lord! — she exclaimed to herself. It's Ashley. She fought to keep any expression of alarm from reaching her face. It was her turn to answer and she reasoned — I can't tell him she's been here. *"No la conozco.* — I don't know her," she replied, and after a pause she added, *"Es muy guapa.* — She's very pretty."

The stranger told her to please call if she saw the *señorita.* He gave her a business card: *"Fundación Nova Mundi."* He said that it was possible that the *señorita* was suffering from amnesia and that she had been in an accident.

Judy couldn't take it much longer. She wanted to tell him to get lost, but that wouldn't help. After a few more repetitious instructions he excused himself. Judy closed the door politely, turned, and then raised her hand to her chest. She felt her heart thumping as if she was running a marathon.

She ran up the stairs and into the bathroom and announced with an imperative pitch, "Jon, they're here!"

"Who?" he yelled back through the rush of the shower, already concerned, noting her urgency.

"Nova Mundi!" she exclaimed.

THROUGH HER 3-D contact lens enhancements, the operator who was piloting the PARASITE saw an image of the female subject. She looked terrified. The operator maneuvered her bug to a better angle, from which she could see both of the Whittens.

The male subject pulled the shower curtain back enough to stick his head through. He asked loudly, "Say again?"

The operator switched the live feed onto the van's speaker for Walker to hear. He snapped to attention.

"I said Nova Mundi. They're here!"

JON HAD NEVER been one to spend much time watching movies; he was too busy. But he had seen his share. The idea of a panel van sitting out on his street, combined with Judy's announcement, immediately brought images to his mind of G-men sitting in dimly lit quarters while listening to an unsuspecting conversation.

Jon lifted his finger to his mouth and made a shush sign. He got near Judy, having wrapped a towel around himself, and spoke softly into her ear. He felt a bit proud of himself for being a good spy, and for realizing that they were probably being bugged, or something.

IN THE VAN, the operator hit a few buttons: SOUND PROCESSOR, ON; DIGITAL AMPLIFICATION, ON. But by that time, whatever the male subject had told the female was drowned out by the shower's roar.

Walker cursed. However, it wasn't likely they would have been able to hear much, for even with magical sound processors, it's hard to hear whispers under the cover of a shower's *white* noise. Walker watched the flat screen, which showed an unenhanced picture of the 3-D image the operator was seeing through her contact lenses. He watched as the female walked back to, and around, the bed from where she pulled back the curtain and looked out the window. It was obvious she was looking towards their van.

"They know," Walker spoke with the gravity due the reading of a death certificate.

He watched as the female stepped back from the window. She was visibly apprehensive, and she left the bedroom.

"Launch Unit 2," Walker ordered.

"Launched," came the terse reply of the second operator.

Operator 2 began to maneuver close to the house. He flew through the crack, between the door and the floor, and then up the steps, around the corner, and looked into the kitchen, where the female was now located. Perhaps he had entered a bit too fast?

JUDY LOOKED UP as the bug flew through the door and exclaimed, "Darn fly!" as she heard it buzz into the room. Her fine hearing noted that its pitch was different from a housefly's, though not by much. She stood, leaving her coffee again. She walked over by the closet and grabbed a fly swatter.

OPERATOR 2 was ready for some sport and would have loved to let her try to catch him, but it would be better to hide, so he circled around.

He and the other occupants of the van laughed when they heard her order, "Land, you darn fly!" As the operator laughed, he teetered, and the PARASITE flew as if it was a little drunk.

JUDY HAZILY NOTED she had never seen a fly, fly that way, and wondered — as it seemed to stagger in the air — Can flies get drunk? It must have gotten its fill at the neighbors, there's none of that stuff here — she declared to herself.

RECOVERING FROM his brief amusement, Operator 2 brought the PARASITE around and flew it out through the kitchen door into the hall. Finding a dark spot, he landed the bug. Its sticky feet held it upside down on the ceiling, where the operator was sure the female subject wouldn't pursue.

WITH THE FLY'S DISAPPEARANCE, Judy was frustrated in her attempt to cleanse the Earth of the filthy pest, so she went back to her coffee. She didn't want it to get any colder. She wondered what it could mean that the man came to their door with the picture of Ashley. She wondered if it meant that she and Jon were in as much trouble as James had told them could come to them if the Nova Mundi people came to visit.

PARASITE 1's IMAGE showed Jon dressing. As soon as he finished he headed down the stairs, wondering what he and Judy would do next. He was thinking he might need to take Judy and go somewhere else. But where? Surely they aren't as bad as James said they were. Maybe we can go out into the country, like James did. Or maybe they won't really bother us. We'll just tell them that James and Ashley were passing through, but they never told us anything.

OPERATOR 1 followed the male subject at a discreet distance. By now Operator 2 had walked his fly back into the kitchen, still on the ceiling, and upside down. The male subject entered. Operator 1's bug came flying in behind him.

"Oн! It's that darn fly again," announced the female subject with aversion in her voice.

Operator 1, not expecting to have drawn attention to the PARASITE so easily, momentarily released the pressure on her joystick. The PARASITE stopped and hovered in one spot, in midair. The male subject, alerted by the female's outcry, turned and looked right into the PARASITE's eyes.

When the operator saw the virtual image of the subjects, looking with set gazes, simultaneously and directly at her, she knew that her PARASITE needed to fly: For flies fly. It shouldn't have been seen hovering. It was clear that the subjects had noticed the PARASITE by the expressions on their faces.

Walker knew they had too, and was already formulating a reprimand for the bumbling operator, but he would save his words for now. Perhaps they would get by with only one mistake, and he didn't want the operator losing concentration at this critical moment.

THE HOVERING FLY — though by now it was moving around in a circle and soon passed back out of the kitchen — had, indeed, caught Jon's notice. If James hadn't told him about TerraNova's formidable flying robots, he might not have noticed, but the quick glimpse of its emerald-green eyes — a shade deeper and yet more fluorescent than what he remembered as being normal for a fly, combined with the sound of its buzz coming from one point — made an impact on him. Jon knew — It's not a fly at all!

When James first told him about the things — "PARASITEs," was that their name? — Jon had asked, "How can you stop them?"

James had told him, "Black ink works pretty well."

So — remembering James's words, and thinking it would be quite an accomplishment for an amateur spy — Jon decided to act. "Judy," he addressed, "let's go to the office."

She hesitated, so he ordered, "Come on," and took her by the hand.

SEEING THAT he had a chance to take charge, Walker commanded, "Operator 1, stand down. Your mistake may cost us dearly."

Operator 2 followed the subjects into the office and entered behind them, landing his PARASITE on the top edge of the door.

JUDY WASN'T sure what was happening, but she could tell that Jon wanted her to stand still after they entered his office. It was strange: He wasn't talking, and he didn't let her talk. He gave her a "hush" sign, and looked into her eyes. With all of this, Judy began to realize that Jon was acting this way because of the darn fly that had flown into the room after them. She realized that the ugly creature had been behaving in a strange way. About then she remembered James commenting on those PARASITE things. With this realization, her expression changed from seriously inquisitive to one of frightened understanding – her skin flushed.

JON HAD anticipated that the PARASITE would follow them to the office, and he watched for it. Sure enough, he saw it come to rest on the top of the door. He went over to the desk drawer, opened it, and artfully lifted a bottle of black ink into his pocket, while blocking himself from the robot's view, trying to keep Judy between him and the infernal contraption. Once he had the ink, he quickly stepped to the other side of the office and entered the closet. He grabbed a fumigator, and hoped that he would have time to carry out his plan before the thing flew to a position where it could see what he was doing. He ripped open the ink bottle's security seal, and poured its contents into the pump's reservoir. He pumped it a few times and a mist of ink puffed out. He loosened the nozzle to make the mix less misty and tried again. It looked as though it might work better than a squirt gun. This was going to be fun! – he smiled slyly to himself.

He stepped out of the closet while holding the fumigation pump behind him. He was ready to shoot, and stepped over to hold Judy close to him. He whispered, "It'll be okay." He could see that she was nervous.

He concentrated, and looked to see if the PARASITE was still on the door. It was. He could see its silhouetted form against the cream-colored wall.

He walked around Judy, trying not to stare at the thing, lest it fly away. He acted as though he was going back to his desk and said, "Judy, I'm going to get a phone number."

With his back to it, he moved as naturally as possible, keeping the pump out of the bug's view. When he reached a point that he felt confident that he was close enough, and having calculated in his mind exactly what he would do, he swung around, looked the bug straight in its radiant-emerald green eyes, and raised the fumigator.

OPERATOR 2 saw a black blob flying right at him. It covered his entire field of view. "What's he doing?!"

The operator watched in horror as blackness, thicker than night, fell suddenly, and blocked his view. "I can't see!" the operator exclaimed.

THE BUG SAT on the edge of the door, without moving, as the black ink soaked it. The force of the spray knocked it off the top edge, and it fell to the floor.

Seeing the show, Judy gasped in surprise, and exclaimed to herself — What a mess! The wall and the door were covered with ink, and the carpet too. That'll be hard to clean — she lamented to herself.

Jon picked the bug up from the floor. He tried to crush it in his fingers, but it was sharp and it cut him, drawing a drop of blood. "I'd better keep it inked," he said, as he opened the fumigator's reservoir and dropped it into the solution. "That hurt," he said. There was a dab of red blood that was set off against his blackened fingers.

He closed up the pump, and tightened it with an extra twist. He moved back around, and reaching Judy, showed her his finger, which he was squeezing.

"Don't you think we should get rid of the thing?" she asked with uncertainty.

Jon didn't answer her quickly.

OPERATOR 2 sent various commands; however, no matter what, he only saw black — deep virtual black — surrounding him. Then ugly snow from the dead transmission filled his entire field of view. When the screen went blank, Walker began blurting out a series of foul words. It was clear that the PARASITE was useless.

The operator ordered, "Visual off," and the virtual image of hypnotic snow he had been seeing through his contact enhancements disappeared. Now that he was able to see again, he hit rewind and carefully watched a slow-motion replay of the mission video on the cabin monitor. He saw a fumigator — and then a rich black liquid squirted straight out until it enveloped the screen.

"DID HE INK US?" Walker asked incredulously.

"It looks like it, sir."

"Why didn't you fly!" Walker demanded.

"Ah... I'm sorry sir. I wasn't expecting to be inked. Only our people know that kind of thing."

"Indeed," Walker answered, his inflection saying — Now you're getting the idea.

Walker then looked over at the other stall and ordered, "Operator 1, here's your chance. Ready a WASP." (Weaponized Arial Situation PARASITE.)

"Yes, sir," she answered excitedly.

Walker decided that the victims were familiar with PARASITEs, since the subjects knew how to ink them — probably, he guessed, because Brown had told them how to do it. Therefore, he decided that surveillance would be fruitless. He reasoned — For these subjects we need to do something else, like an abduction; but for now, a good dose of terror will teach the fools a lesson or two.

"Operator 1," he directed, hatred in his voice, "let them know we aren't happy."

OPERATOR 1 sent a programmed order to the WASP, which she had flown to a point where it hovered just outside of the office window. Upon receiving the order, the miniature robot began to gyrate in a small circular pattern. Its wings reached a speed that made a whine, like a dentist's high-speed drill. The maneuver was intended to terrorize. It also prepared the WASP for a "crashing" entrance, which was also meant to frighten the victims.

JON heard the intimidating sound coming through the window and looked out. However, he didn't have time to see anything. The window exploded and fine granular pieces of glass flew everywhere. He threw himself on top of Judy, pushing her down to the floor.

After the explosion, he looked up and saw the "insect," for lack of a better word, making an intense buzz as it hovered just a few feet above him. Momentarily, as his eyes focused, he realized that it looked like a wasp, a large one at that. It was making a sound that wasn't just a buzz. It was like a roar too, and it was bloodcurdling. This isn't a movie — Jon thought. It looks like something out of the book of Revelation!

Judy, her face white in fear, said, "It looks like it's demon possessed."

IN THE VAN they heard her, and laughed. Walker insulted, "Imbeciles. We shall teach you a lesson you'll never forget!" And he ordered, "Begin high-frequency broad-angle gyration."

Watching the screen with a view from another WASP that Operator 2 had deployed, Weller smiled, seeing the fear on the subjects' faces. Then he heard the male say, "Judy, don't be afraid. We've got Jesus!"

Upon hearing this one name, Walker exclaimed, "May he be eternally inflicted!" After a pause, he continued, "We won't play with them any longer. Let's finish what we have started." He looked at the operator, who answered him with an approving smile, and then he ordered, "Begin sting treatment — omega series."

An instant later, the WASP dove at the male subject as the operator controlled it with a joystick and multiple firing buttons.

THE ROBOT'S BUZZ, which sounded as like it was reverberating in a pit, reached a higher pitch. Jon tried to swat at it, but it was useless. It moved too quickly. Then it suddenly dove at him, and before he could react, it painfully stung him in his temple, bringing debilitating pain to him — first his head, then his whole body. Then the infernal insect dove at Judy so quickly that he couldn't have stopped it, even if he hadn't felt so terrible himself. His heart sank as he watched it sting her, also in the temple. He felt humiliated, being unable to protect her.

He already felt terrible, but the pain increased, and he also felt weakened and nauseated; then came delirium. It didn't take long. He began to feel that he was both burning and chilling, and began to twist in agony — powerless to do anything else. After several convulsions, he fell flat on his back and looked up through tear-filled eyes, to where the WASP hovered. It seemed to him that the ugly creature, with burning red eyes, was laughing at him and mocking him in his ruin. Then the device darted back outside through the broken window. A brief allusion came to his mind that this "insect" could be a prelude to the fifth trumpet of Revelation.

After several minutes, the initial intensity of the pain from the stings began to subside, and he started to feel a little better. However, the pain continued to burn. Jon, as he recovered, saw Judy crying, which just added to his woe.

He slowly recuperated his lucidity, and the gravity of what had happened began to weigh on him. *I couldn't do a thing to stop it! I've failed. I'm worthless. It's all my fault. I never should've brought that man Smith home with me. I shouldn't have let Kinderly overrule my common sense. Stupid me! Trying to play spy games. Driving that blond cat burglar around. Now look what I've done!*

JUDY SOBBED. She felt betrayed, and she asked herself — *Why did God let this happen? Is this what we get for helping people?*

And then she blurted out in her agony and humiliation, "You infuriated them! Didn't you? You should've left the darn bug alone! Why did you ink it? You should have known that you couldn't beat it. And what's the landlord going to say? Ink all over! Glass in everything. That big picture window will cost a lot."

Jon remained silent. She looked into his eyes. They were the eyes of a defeated man, and she began to ask, in silence — Where were You God? But she knew. He had been there from the beginning, which made her feel worse, as she wondered — How could He love me? I should trust Him more.

With that thought, and seeing her husband so defeated, Judy fell silent. She was bewildered. She felt betrayed and angry. The sting continued to torment her — it burned — and the headache continued, making any other she had ever felt seem trivial.

Jon's voice still seemed distant to her when he eventually said, "I'm sorry, honey. It's all my fault." She could hear the frustration in his every syllable.

"No, it's not," she answered weakly.

"Yes, it is!" he insisted.

"Oh!" she said, and paused, before sarcastically countering, "Let's argue about it.... Haven't we had enough?" Changing tone, she reconciled, "You did what you thought was right, Jon. Sometimes that's not easy. Sometimes it can cost, but your heart's right, dear. So don't condemn yourself."

"What about that darn bug thing?" Judy asked, looking over at the fumigator on the desk. "What will you do with it?"

"I don't know."

"Maybe you can just wash it down the drain, or something?" she suggested.

"James said they're expensive."

"Oh. So what are you going to do? Walk up to the van and give it back to make some point? " Judy asked with a caustic grin.

JON IMAGINED himself doing just that — trying to make a point — but he figured it probably wouldn't improve their situation. "I'll just take it out and dump it in the garden." And then he thought — Or should I preserve it in alcohol?

Chapter 12

Robbed

DEFEAT DOESN'T finish a man — quit does. A man is not finished when he's defeated. He's finished when he quits.

— Richard M. Nixon

February 22 — That same day — Manta

ASHLEY HAD TO say good-bye to María, again. It wasn't much easier than it had been the first time she left Manta — just days before. However, now that she was a Christian, she felt an even greater bond with the sweet Latin lady, whose full head of peppered hair added to her dignity, a dignity that Ashley hadn't thought she would find in the outer world and, indeed, she had never found in Alpha Force. Ashley judged that María's dignity was unique to her in that it demanded respect, but it didn't require a uniform. Not only that, but María had earned Ashley's respect by nursing her back to health when she could just as easily have been left for dead.

For now though, it was good-bye, and Ashley felt a tear on her cheek. She wished she could stay, and with James too. Life in Manta seemed like it would be right. But she knew they couldn't stay. They had to move on, and put as much distance between themselves and TerraNova as they could.

It briefly crossed her mind that it seemed more than just coincidental that it would be Pepe, the man who rescued her from death, who would carry her and James to safety. Although, she really wasn't sure they would ever find safety, since anywhere they ran, TerraNova was bound to follow. It was a sure thing — like sunrise and sunset. So, why try? She couldn't answer her own question, but they had to try. It was better than sitting around and waiting for the inflictors to come to get them.

PEPE CHOOSE his best shipmate to go along with him and gave the other a vacation. He had four small bunks below, so there would be one for everyone. Although he wondered, seeing his passengers so tall, if they would fit on the short cots. He had insisted on having the charts before leaving, but the *gringo*, James, had assured him that when the time came, he would be given them. Pepe didn't understand why, if the *gringo* had them, he didn't go ahead and give him the charts. He decided, though, that by using his own he could sail out of port and travel about a hundred fifty miles in any direction before he had to have better ones, so he said nothing else.

They hadn't sailed very far, though, when a port patrol, with Ecuadorian marines, started to approach. It was highly irregular. Why? — Pepe asked himself, but he felt like he needed to tell the *gringos*, who were still below arranging their belongings.

He ducked his head inside, and spoke out so they would hear him, saying, "*Viene la patrullera.* — The patrol is coming." He then stepped down into the chamber below.

Ashley, *la gringa,* asked him, *"¿Qué patrullera?* — What patrol?"

"Los marineros, guardianes de la puerta. — The marines, guardians of the port."

Then the man, James, spoke to the *gringa* forcefully, but Pepe didn't understand. Afterwards, the *gringo* told him, *"Si preguntan, no estamos aquí.* — If they ask, we aren't here." Then they moved topside, smoothly and gracefully, so quickly that Pepe could hardly believe his eyes. In an instant the couple had disappeared. He followed them topside as quickly as he could, but there wasn't any sign of them. The crew member pointed to the starboard side. Pepe looked, but didn't see anything. It seemed to him that if they had gone over the side, there should have been a splash, but he didn't hear anything.

He wondered, though, why they had told him to say they weren't there. Did the *gringos* think the marines would be looking for them? Why? Were they in trouble? The *gringa* had been strange from the moment he first found her, and now, the mystery deepened. However, at this juncture, he had little time to think any more, except to wonder why he had even bothered to tell them that the marines were coming.

The approaching cutter made a lot of noise. Pepe shut down his own motor when he was ordered to prepare to be boarded. Two Marines jumped over, into his boat. One of them had a mean-looking police dog on a leash that jumped across with him. They presented him with a document, which they said gave them permission to search his vessel, but Pepe didn't read quickly, especially the words of a lawyer, so he didn't bother to try.

Then the captain of the port also boarded his boat. He informed Pepe that they were going to search his boat for illegal substances, that he was suspect. The man stood erect with his arms crossed behind him, where he held his baton. His suit was immaculate white, and his presence intimidated Pepe.

"I have nothing illegal!" Pepe told him. Though his tone was exclamatory, his voice quivered.

The captain chuckled, *"Así dicen todos.* — That's what they all say."

JAMES COULDN'T IMAGINE why the port's authorities would be approaching Pepe's boat, unless they were looking for Ashley and him. Although, he guessed, there could be other reasons for the presence of the marines. Maybe Pepe hadn't paid some fee, or he was missing a paper. In the outer world there were many possibilities, all related to outer affairs. Even if they were checking Pepe for some reason unrelated to their presence, it wouldn't be good for the officials to see them, for certainly, TerraNova would eventually send SAOs asking for them and showing their pictures for people to identify.

Once he slipped over the side, with Ashley, he grabbed a piece of hose that was near, and with his enhancements aiding, he snapped it into two pieces — each about eighteen inches long.

He and Ashley would use the tubes for breathing, and hide under Pepe's craft. However, it proved to be quite difficult, even with bioenhancements, to keep themselves near the keel and to inconspicuously breathe through their hoses as they bobbed out of the water far enough to get their hoses to the surface and then bobbed back under. They would have released their breath under the water, which would have allowed them to wait longer between breaths, but they were afraid that the air bubbles would be too conspicuous.

THE MARINES searched every square inch. Their dog sniffed everything, but nothing excited him. At one point, one of the Marines looked over the side, as though he was trying to see beneath the boat. He wasn't concerned though, since he knew that the captain would order a dive later for him to search under the keel. For now, the captain ordered him, and the other marine, who had the dog, to search below.

Once below, in the cabin, a golden backpack caught his attention while the other guard moved further into the area where the cots were found. To the guard, the strange pack looked like something that could carry an illegal substance. It had a metallic sheen, and really appeared, to him, to be *"algo de otro mundo* — out of this world."

He began to feel around inside of the pack, and checking, he found an envelope with a telephone number on it. It seemed like it might have something green inside. He looked over his shoulder at his companion, to be sure he wasn't looking his way, and opened the envelope. It had money — lots of money. All in one-hundred-dollar bills, and he questioned himself if maybe there were ten bills? Maybe more? Could it be drug money? But the dog hasn't found any drugs. Well — he thought — Pepe's doing something, and wherever this money came from, it's probably illegal, so I'll just keep it for him. He took the envelope, and folded it into his own pocket.

He asked the other Marine if he had finished his search. He had. "Let's go," the thief said. "There's nothing here."

They climbed topside. It was a little difficult to get the big dog out of the cabin.

"*Está limpio.* – It's clear," the thief reported to the captain.

"*Entonces, vean la quilla.* – Then, check in the keel."

"*Sí, señor.* – Yes, sir."

"*Pues, ¿qué esperan?* – So, what are you waiting for?"

"*Sí, capitán.* – Yes, Captain."

PEPE TREMBLED inside as he watched the Marine step away, wondering what would happen if they found the *gringos* in the water.

The captain, observing, and pointing to the barrels of diesel, addressed Pepe and asked (their conversation in Spanish), "Where are you going with so much fuel?"

Pepe answered, "I bought it while the prices were low. I heard the government will soon raise the price." There was a hint of truth in what he said. The government was talking about raising the price. But Pepe knew that it really wasn't true.

Then the captain interrogated, "But you spent much money, and purchased supplies for a long voyage?"

"True," was all that Pepe answered.

"So, where are you going?" the officer pressed.

Pepe tried to think of something, and was unnerved as he glanced at the Marine who was stripping for the dive. He couldn't think of a good answer and said, "We are going to fish in deep water."

"You lie!" exclaimed the captain, his tone menacing. "Your boat isn't big enough for more than a day's catch."

The captain's cross-examination made Pepe shaky. "I'm sorry," he responded, for indeed, he was sorry. "You're right, Captain, but we are going fishing for sport. We will find a few barracuda."

The simple fisherman didn't have enough sophistication to make a believable lie, and the captain spoke forcefully, "Liar! Your boat isn't fast enough."

Pepe answered, "I'm sorry." Pepe continued, "My clients — newlywed *gringos* — have asked me to be silent. They are traveling to Galapagos and they have asked me to take them."

Pepe glanced, and saw that the Marines were ready, with scuba on their backs. They would dive any second.

"Where are your honeymooners?"

"They're in Guayaquil. They contracted me here, and then they traveled for supplies that we don't have here in Manta. I will pick them up there."

Now convinced he had heard the truth — it made sense — the captain told Pepe, who was well known to the whole community, "You are a poor liar!"

Pepe answered, "Yes, Captain. You're right."

And then, with a chuckle under his breath, having scolded him, the captain wished, "Good sailing," and an instant before the Marine would have entered the water, he ordered, "*¡Desembarque!* — Return to headquarters!"

After a short time the cutter pulled away. James and Ashley saw and felt it leave. They gave it time and distance. When they finally surfaced, they did so with caution. Once on board, they went below, where Pepe sat mournfully. James noticed it before Ashley. He walked over and sat on the edge of the bunk that was in front of Pepe.

"*¿Que pasa?* — What's going on?" James asked.

PEPE FELT as though he didn't wish to live. He didn't want to answer. He couldn't imagine what good it could do, except to inform that he was certain they should turn back. He finally said, "I regret — but we must turn back."

Ashley asked, "Why?"

Pepe answered in a voice that sounded piteous. "The bad marines have stolen my money. And it's all my fault. I didn't obey your orders. I bought all of the diesel at my supplier, and I bought all the provisions in one place."

James asked, stumbling with his Spanish, "So they were curious, wanting to know where you were going?"

"Yes," Pepe answered. "They thought I had drugs, probably because they saw me spending so much money. They searched. No drugs. But they found my money, and took it."

Ashley asked, "How much?"

Pepe told her, his voice sad, "Two hundred dollars."

"We'll help you," James offered.

James got up and walked over to see his pack — ready to solve Pepe's problem. He noticed it had been moved. He looked for the envelope, but it was gone. He started to feel sick. *Inflict* those rotten crooks — he thought. "They took our money too," James said, speaking heavily, and directing himself to Ashley.

Pepe understood some English and asked, "*¿Ustedes también?* – You too?"

Ashley quizzed, "All of it?"

"All of it," James replied, his tone dismal, matching the lighting and the mood.

Pepe, thinking to find an empathic audience, affirmed, "We have no money. They have robbed us. We must go back."

JAMES THOUGHT for a moment — Really, the money shouldn't be a concern. We have fuel and provisions. But Jack's phone number is gone. If we had his number, we could call and get more money. Although, during his brief time with outers, he had learned to appreciate the value of the green bills, and decided that even Jack might have trouble coming up with more. Starting to feel the gravity of their situation, and the injustice they had suffered, James exclaimed, "It's not right! We can't let them do this to us!"

Pepe didn't understand this time, and asked Ashley what James had said. She translated, and Pepe said, "We have no choice. The captain of the port is a powerful man. I fear him."

* * *

Quito, then Cyberspace

LÓPEZ COULDN'T BELIEVE IT. He asked, "Walker, how could your people ruin such a simple assignment?"

"Good question. I offer no answer," he answered, moving his head slowly from side to side. "My crew isn't experienced in fieldwork, and they do not use PARASITEs often. We have few assignments here."

López had watched the videos of the mission, and had especially taken note of the hesitation that had allowed the subjects to see the PARASITE. It was inexcusable. Then, the SAOs lack of response — just sitting there while the ink came! It couldn't be justified. The operator had accelerated nerve-pulse channeling and panoramic stereovision — he should've flown his fly and beaten the ink.

In a few minutes he would have to face Weller. So he went over all of the facts, thinking of the best way to break the news. After all, he was in charge, and his head would roll first. When he decided he had the right angle, he connected into Nova Mundi. Soon he was virtually present in Weller's office.

López began, as naturally as he could. He didn't want to stir the boss until he had had a chance to present his case. So he started politely, and said, "Good evening, sir —"

"Okay, López, let's have it," Weller snapped back. He was impatient and López couldn't imagine why, but his effort to get on the boss's good side had apparently failed, so he would just have to take responsibility for the mistake and figure out a way to fix it. With this in mind, he went right to the point and said, "It seems we've found the *gringos* who picked up Brown."

NORMALLY, such news would have been good, but Weller could tell that the SAO had something to say that he really didn't want to say. He could see it in his face and figured that there would also be bad news. He asked, "And? What else!"

"Well, sir," and he hesitated, "the operator handling one of the PARASITE units made a critical mission error, sir."

"Did he kill them before they talked?" Weller asked, imagining the worst, seeing López's expression and hearing his vacillation.

"No, sir. The subjects are alive and under surveillance. The problem, sir, is that the operator allowed the subjects to identify the PARASITE. He then lost the PARASITE to an inking. The subjects were aware of *anti*-PARASITE procedures. Because of this the SAO in charge at the scene, Walker, made the decision to *parasitically* intimidate the subjects and sent in a WASP."

"Sounds like they've been around Brown. How else would they have known about inking?"

"True, sir."

"These people are missionaries by profession?" Weller inquired, looking at the report on his desktop monitor.

"Yes, sir."

"What would Brown have been doing with missionaries?" Then Weller asked, "What kind are they?"

"Fanatics, sir. They're Christian, Evangelical, and their mission is 'Ecuador for Christ.' "

"Watch your tongue, López. That's an inflicted dirty word."

"Yes, sir." López answered.

"You're convinced the subjects picked up Brown?"

"Yes, sir. They seem to be the only candidates. Apparently the female subject had seen Brown previously. When asked to identify Brown, the subject showed signs of recognizing the picture. As soon as our agent finished speaking to her, she went to tell the male subject something about our agent's visit. Unfortunately, he was in the shower and we weren't able to hear what they said, but it was easy to see they were concerned. Considering their knowledge of PARASITEs and anti-PARASITE tactics, I believe we can conclude that they've been in contact with Brown."

"What do you recommend?"

"Sir," López said, his confidence showing that he had thought about it, "I recommend abduction. I think we need to treat these people as being hostile. Their present degree of knowledge warrants their elimination, but we can't sacrifice them until they give us the information we need to find Brown. Abduction would provide a high degree of intimidation, and with our advanced techniques they won't be able to resist our interrogation. They'll spill their guts and tell everything they know. We can then dispose of them — arrange an accident. You know, in Ecuador accidents happen all the time — especially traffic accidents."

"Sounds good, López. I'll get things moving for a DEEP to visit your subjects." Weller shuffled a few papers, looked over at his workstation's floating monitor, and then said, "We'll see if we can set it up for tomorrow night. Good afternoon, López."

"Good afternoon, sir," and López's virtual image disappeared, and the seat in front of Weller's desk was left empty, just as it had been all along.

* * *

Manta

THEY DISCUSSED the options for a long time. One, continue as is. Two, go back home. Three, recover what was theirs from the captain and his men. On the third option, Pepe repeatedly contradicted himself. With one breath it seemed like he was ready to march up to the captain and demand the money, but by the next breath he figured it would only get them into deeper problems. After all, it was cash, and the Captain had probably gotten his share.

James thought they could pull off the third option — recover their money. Indeed, he was certain they could do it. The problem was, he and Ashley hadn't seen the Marines, so they didn't know who they would be seeking. And risk would be involved. Chances were, James and Ashley wouldn't suffer, but could they do it without hurting anyone? In response to this event, Ashley told James about the PHENIX. They discussed using it, but stories of people being knocked out by a matchbox would leave clues for the SAOs.

Pepe had made it abundantly clear that he really wanted to turn back. He didn't want to sail without cash. James understood. But when Pepe confessed that he still had a hundred fifty dollars in his pocket that the thieves hadn't taken, and James realized that he still had over a hundred in his own pocket, the first option — to continue — started making sense.

It certainly wasn't advisable to travel with so little money, but they had everything they needed for the trip, and it was dangerous for them to stay in Manta. They needed to continue, full speed ahead. How would they persuade Pepe?

James took Ashley to one side and told her, "Convince him to go. If we turn back now, they will find us."

"But if we go back, just for a few days?"

"Why? We don't have Jack's number now, and I doubt that he has any more money. And we can't go back to Quito."

Ashley didn't like the idea too much, but she agreed — they had to keep moving — so she began, "Pepe?"

PEPE THOUGHT — The *gringa* is dumb. We can't travel without more money. But she is so pretty. God sent me to save her. She's like my own daughter. How can I tell her no? And it's my fault. If I'd listened to her, the captain wouldn't have bothered us. And so, against his better judgment, he was tempted to say yes to the trip, but he couldn't. *"Es muy peligroso.* – It's very dangerous," he answered, before she even asked.

James hung his head. Ashley, who had been squatting in front of Pepe, pleading her case, stood to her feet, turned her back, crossed her arms, and stepped away.

Pepe felt like a heel, but what could he do? It wasn't a good idea to travel without cash. What if there was an emergency? It was his boat, and that was the way it was going to be!

ASHLEY MOVED over to James, who was now stooped over, leaning against the cots on the other side. He looked so defeated. She had never seen him this way. It didn't seem like a good time to ask, but she went ahead, "What should we do?"

James raised his brow and looked into her eyes, and said, with resignation in his voice, "We don't have any choice. We'll go back."

Then Ashley thought — Shouldn't he give our money back? — and she asked James.

"He probably should," he answered. "But he's poor. And they've robbed him."

"Well. They've robbed us too!" Ashley said indignantly, and turned towards Pepe. She stepped his way and fell down on both knees before him again. She looked up into his face. His countenance was fallen; he looked so discouraged. She really hated to do it, but she had no other choice. She told him, "Okay, we'll go back. But you must return our money."

PEPE SQUIRMED. *Gringa!* — he thought. Why did God send you to me?

He didn't want to answer, and delayed.

The *gringa* insisted, "Well. What about it? If we go back, you have to give us our money."

"I'll take you to Guayaquil," Pepe offered.

Ashley looked around at James, and he responded, "But that doesn't help us."

"I can't sell the diesel here," he answered. "No one has money. In Guayaquil, I can sell it and give you back some of your money."

"Pepe," Ashley begged, "we can do it. You won't need money. We've got all we need. We'll give you another hundred dollars when we get to our destination."

Pepe figured — Another hundred? We shouldn't need to spend anything, like they say. With another hundred I'll have half of what the captain took. Pepe changed his expression, looked up, and said, "*Vamos.* – Let's go."

Chapter 13

Abduction

CURSE NOT the king, no not in thy thought; and curse not the rich in thy bed-chamber: for a bird of the air shall carry the voice, and that which hath wings shall tell the matter.

— King Solomon. The Hebrew Bible

February 22 — That same day — Whitten's home, Quito

JON AND JUDY hadn't been able to say much to one another. They felt defeated. All the words they could think of to encourage one another, words that would have been uplifting any other time, seemed hypocritical. Phrases like "Have faith," "Trust God," "The Lord will help us" seemed to have lost their meaning. They were flavorless.

Not that Jon or Judy felt less Christian or less saved, and they didn't love the Lord any less — it wasn't that. They trusted God as much as ever — maybe more. But the wasp's stings hadn't stopped stinging. They wondered how long the torment and the headaches would continue. Aspirin didn't seem to help at all.

Judy wanted to go home to Georgia. Get away. Hide. Do something! But what? They'd been over it together. Jon himself was ready for a break, and the pair was about ready to drive out to the airport, and take the next plane out. But they would think — All of our things? We can't give up so easily. It takes time to sell everything for good prices.

Several times they almost went to the Williamses' house, but the sight of Nova Mundi's van reminded them not to involve anyone else. They wanted to call, but figured everything they said, and even the numbers they dialed, were being recorded. Jon wanted to talk to Jack, but if he did, what would he say? And then Nova Mundi would know Jack's number.

Emotional overload was heavy. They had no good options, and there weren't any easy solutions. Worse, they were emotionally incapable of making the right decision, and Jon knew it.

He tried to busy himself by cleaning his office. He filled four sweeper bags with the fine powdered glass. He prayed it wouldn't rain until he could get a new window. At least their monthly support check would be deposited the day after tomorrow, and maybe he would have enough to replace the window.

He tried several stain removers on the ink, but decided he would end up having to paint, and maybe get a new carpet.

It had been a long day. Jon knew they needed to take some decisive action, like calling in the marines, he joked to himself, and wished that he could.

When Jon and Judy finally reached their bed, exhausted in every sense of the word, they neither conversed, for fear of bugs (a word that had taken on a new meaning for them), nor did they sleep, for fear of what could happen.

Perhaps they lay there an hour before Jon suggested, "Let's pray."

Judy thought — Good idea. Why didn't we do it a long time ago?

Jon began, "Heavenly Father, forgive us. We have been slow to speak to You. We have faced a power we didn't know existed. It has drained us and exhausted us. It has shaken us. Forgive us, Lord, for forgetting to call upon You. Mighty God, we ask You for strength. Precious Jesus, give us Your love …"

"…FOR STRENGTH. Precious Jesus, give us …" spoke the speaker in the Nova Mundi surveillance van, faithfully reproducing every word Jon and Judy pronounced.

It was on the word "Jesus" that the SAO ordered the operator, "Turn it down. We don't need to listen to that useless rot."

The operator responded quickly.

"Precious indeed," mocked the SAO.

Operator 1 snickered as she said, "We'll teach them a 'precious' thing or two."

"Indeed, we shall."

JON FINISHED his prayer. He felt better. He felt peace. He should have done it long before. He decided — I must remember to pray, even if they come back. Judy felt the same, and said, "That was good, Jon. Thanks for praying."

"Yeah," he sleepily said, "we have to pray if they come back." And he added, "There's just something about the name of Jesus. I felt so much peace after I said His name."

"I did too," Judy affirmed.

"Problem is, it's hard to remember to pray when you're being dive-bombed by a demonic *wasp*," Jon commented.

* * *

Quito

DEEP 43 was a small Unit, especially adapted to the mission now under way. Commander Roberts was practiced in urban DEEP exercises. He loved gliding over rooftops. He hadn't had many assignments in Quito. He enjoyed getting back. It was especially challenging, thanks to the mountains, and the way the city was laid out: in a long valley with an airport downtown, along with lots of low clouds, and fog to spice things up.

Based on experience, he programmed a course for Mount Pichincha. He would reenter using a low-speed stealth descent. Accordingly, he started the mission early. Power dives were great — especially when landing above water where a small error was inconsequential — but in the Andes it wasn't as easy. The high altitude and lower atmospheric pressure had to be taken into account. A power dive would probably have worked, but why take unnecessary risks?

It was two hours later when Commander Roberts brought his DEEP into a hover just a couple hundred feet above the eastern slopes of the mountain. Quito was lit up like a necklace around the lower edge of the mountain. It was a beautiful city. He notified the personnel on the lower deck, which looked like an operating room, to prepare.

He didn't have a first officer and didn't need one. The DEEP was all his. He enjoyed flying the compact Unit for that very reason. His DEEP was, to the former DEEP 1, what a subcompact is to a semi. DEEP 1 could have carried his whole Unit inside of its upper deck.

Roberts began a roller-coaster ride, so to speak, down the slopes of the mountain. No one felt the movement (a great way to avoid motion sickness) but it was fabulous to watch on the monitor. It was dark outside, but the picture that the commander had was computer enhanced, augmented by the amplification of the night-light, infarred, and radar, and ionic-meson scanning technology. With these views layered together, he saw them as one through his panoramic stereo visor. He couldn't have seen better, not even in daylight, and yet it retained a night flavor.

Swooping down over mountain cliffs, over tall grass and fields, then trees, until pulling up over city buildings and lights, Roberts approached the exact address indicated on his PLOT.

A couple, embracing on a dark corner a few blocks up the hill from the Whittens, felt a slight breeze. The teenager looked up, but there wasn't anything; it just seemed like there should've been. It looked like heat rippling past, over their heads, but the night was so cold. His girl-friend saw it too, but whatever it had been, neither bothered to ask, nor to concern themselves with it.

ROBERTS DEEPED at subsonic speed, ASCANS (Advanced Sound Cancellation Anti-Noise System) fully functional. The DEEP made no perceptible sound. Holographic Active Camouflage (HAC) had no trouble blending with the partly cloudy sky and occasional stars — better and faster than a chameleon. The Unit was nearly invisible.

Roberts pulled to a sudden stop over the Whittens' house, hovering there, inches above the rooftop. The Commander made a minor adjustment in the DEEP's placement to allow the crew to drop down onto the balcony.

"UNIT 43, you're on target," the SAO in the van communicated. His eyes were trained to know that the hovering "ripple" wasn't hot air coming from a chimney.

"Affirmative," Roberts answered.

"Situation quiet. Operation go. Subjects are in bedroom," the SAO informed. "We'll distract if there are any outers."

They had taken care of the neighborhood guard earlier — with an American candy bar — he would sleep until morning.

ROBERTS LOOKED out over the empty street below him, and saw the white van — there weren't any unwanted eyes. He ordered, "Begin capture."

A hatch opened and lowered. Momentarily the hatch area became visible as four "aliens" — or so they looked — with large gray heads and bulging eyes moved down the ramp and dropped onto the balcony. This part of the operation was difficult to totally camouflage, but the SAOs below were ready to distract anyone who came along.

The "aliens" knew exactly where to go to find the sleeping Whittens. Their PARASITEs had mapped the entire house. They moved into the bedroom. Jon started to wake. Perhaps he heard a sound when they came in the sliding doors? But he never achieved consciousness. Using needleless pneumatic syringes, the "aliens" drugged Jon and Judy while they still slept. Quickly, they carried their victims out to the balcony, and the DEEP crew hoisted their *packages* through the hatch — again their action was visible from the street below, but in the dark it would have been hard for an outer to figure out what was taking place.

"We have capture. *Packages* collected," spoke the Alpha Force officer who was in charge on the lower deck. An instant later he added, "Hatch is secure."

"Nova Mundi," Roberts spoke, "we have *packages*."

"Roger, DEEP 43. Proceed with operation."

"Thank you. Have a good evening," Roberts answered, and issued a voice command to initiate launch.

THE **SAO** in the van watched as the hatch closed and the "heat wave" disappeared. She stuck her head out of the van's window to see how well the Unit's ASCANS worked. She felt only a mild breeze that chilled her nose with a puff. She didn't hear a thing, even with her hearing enhancements. Pulling her head back into the van she told the PARASITE operator, who had been watching for traffic that might have entered the street, "They've got that DEEP well tuned. Not a sound." She leaned back in her reclining seat. "We might as well get a little shut-eye. They'll probably keep the *packages* most of the night."

ON BOARD THE UNIT, which now rested a hundred thousand miles above Earth, not quite halfway to the moon, the crew had strapped their *packages* to testing tables. A team worked on each subject. They each had a skull net, and sensors strapped to their extremities. Just millimeters above the net, around the back of their heads, slowly spinning plasma pulsated in color and intensity as it shifted ethereally in rainbows of pastel hues.

On large monitors, the mental images of the subjects were displayed.

Jon was dreaming about something that looked like a vast landscape. There was a tree trunk in the foreground with something like a city sitting on top of the plain made by the surface of the stump. In the distance was a red desert. It didn't make any sense and quickly disappeared into another scene that was just as senseless.

Such are dreams — thought the technician in charge.

Judy had more activity in her dream. Pulsating green eyes stared down at her. She saw herself running in the air. Looking at the images from her dream, the technician said, "She's ready."

The assistant agreed.

"Wake her," the technician ordered.

Another assistant entered a few commands on the control board.

JUDY FELT like she was waking from a nightmare, but no ... reality seemed worse. She was confused; and wondered — Am I conscious?

A movie began to play in her mind. Was it a dream? She couldn't tell. It seemed vivid. It was decidedly real, or was it? She gave up trying to decide.

She saw herself levitating out of her bed, inside a brilliant light. There were gray aliens watching. The thing, a shining light, levitated her. It moaned. Then she saw Jon, lying behind her, still in their bed. She tried to go back to him, but couldn't. She kicked, but couldn't resist the levitation, which moved her out of the bedroom. She screamed and cried. Tears welled up in her eyes, but she couldn't hear herself. The "beam" pulled her outside into the cold night air, and lifted her from the balcony, slowly, into the bottom center of a UFO. It was horrible. She fought, but to no avail, and watched herself as if it were through her own eyes, and yet from the eyes of an observer — all at the same time. Gray creatures laid her on a flat table, and automatically, straps pulled her down.

Then a robotic apparatus that looked like a drill started to lower slowly, directly over her mouth.

THE TECHNICIAN commented, "You'd think we could get a new video by now — something original. I think they've even had this at the movies."

"That's the point. All outers have seen this, so they believe it's a real alien abduction," the other technician commented.

JUDY SCREAMED with all that was within her, but there came forth no sound. Some clamps grabbed her mouth and opened it as the drill, or whatever it was, continued towards her. She was terrorized. She screamed again, but it was useless.

Then, in that moment of fright, she remembered she'd promised herself she would pray if anything happened, and began in her mind — Father, in Jesus' name, have mercy upon me…

"IT LOOKS like we have a problem," the technician reported.

"What's she doing?"

"She's blocking."

"How?"

"It's hard to say, but she's not concentrating on the illusion."

AS JUDY prayed she felt greater peace. The drill didn't even seem real. When it entered her mouth and passed between her teeth (which seemed to be held open while at the same time she felt certain her mouth was closed), a part of her didn't feel anything, but another part felt pain. She began to realize, though, that the harder she thought about Jesus, the less pain she felt. When the drill seemed to press against the roof of her mouth, the agony seemed unbearable, but she concentrated, in prayer, and the pain left her.

She discovered that the more, and the harder, she concentrated on the Lord, the less torture she suffered.

"I worship You, my loving Lord Jesus. Your name is above every name. I bow in Your glorious presence…" and she kept on, worshipping in her mind. She entered the throne room and sang, "Worthy is the Lamb who was slain to receive power and riches, wisdom and strength, honor and glory, and blessing." She cast her crown at the feet of the Lamb. She saw herself dressed in pure white linen, worshiping and adoring the King of kings, the Alpha and the Omega.

Her torture was distant. She didn't try to understand, for whenever she tried to reason, the torment seemed to increase, but as long as she kept her mind in heavenly places, her torment was nothing more than a vapor — an annoyance — a mosquito buzzing her ear.

"CURSE HER. She's blocking over 90%. I've never had such resistance."

"Well," said the chief technician, "I think this is an exercise in futility. Stop the video."

"Yes, sir."

He entered a command in the console, and the plasma donut around the female subject's head disappeared.

WHEN THE VIDEO STOPPED, abruptly, her awareness focused on the things around her and the torment ended. Her senses gave her immediate indications. She felt cold and wanted to shiver, but couldn't — unable to move at all. In her mind, she continued to praise and to worship, but unlike before, it made no difference in her perceptions. Distant mumbling voices sounded like they were on the other side of an empty room. It seemed as if they were speaking English.

She heard hollow footsteps, and then saw brilliant lights focused down on her. The shift in light hurt her eyes. Four people, two men and two women, came into her view. She could have mistaken them for twins of James and Ashley.

One of them began to speak. He addressed, "Ms. Whitten," with a quality of English that was distinctively American, the typical garden-variety, without even a good southern drawl. "You block us to your own detriment," said the distinguished-looking man with blond hair and blue eyes. He did look a lot like James, but he wasn't as tall or as "James," Judy summarized.

Now, let's get to the point. Do you know Ashley Brown?"

"No," Judy distressfully answered.

"You lie!" the blond man cowed.

The table started rotating her into an upright position and he slapped her with a backhand across her face. She reflexively twisted to avoid it, but couldn't, because of the straps. Her action left her neck muscles strained. She wanted to lift her hand and wipe away something. It felt like blood from the corner of her mouth, but it was hopeless, she couldn't move.

"I'm sorry!" Judy began. The technician thought — She's going to speak so easily? She continued, "Jesus, forgive me, ple…"

He slapped her again. I must have said the wrong thing — she thought. That's nasty! Surely I'm bleeding.

"I won't have it!" the tormentor spoke. "You are not to use the name of that dead man."

Judy was tempted to say, "He's not dead," but decided to save her reply until she better understood the situation.

"Now," he began, "we can make this simple, or we can take all night — as long as you wish. I already know you and your husband picked up Ashley Brown and transported her in your Trooper. Simply tell me where to find Brown and we can get this over with."

That's easy to answer — Judy thought, and said, "I don't know."

The technician looked over at someone, or something, outside of her view.

"You don't know," he affirmed, as if he had some way to tell if she had lied.

They must have me on a lie detector — she decided.

"Did you see Brown?"

"Yes," Judy answered.

"Did she teach you about PARASITEs?"

That's easy, James told us. She confidently answered, "No."

Again the man looked beyond her view. Again her word was confirmed.

"Could you then, please, tell me about your encounter with Ms. Brown?"

"She came to our house about a week ago, stayed a night, and left the next morning. We saw her walking that afternoon and invited her back. She stayed for a while and left."

Her interrogator received confirmation that she had told the truth and then continued, "You say she came to your house. How was that? She didn't just walk in?"

"You'll need to ask my husband. He brought her home."

"We will, you can be assured."

Judy felt terrible. I just betrayed Jon — she thought. One of the others spoke in a whisper to the interrogator.

"My answer caused you much distress," he said, and snickered.

Judy knew what was coming. They were going to threaten Jon. It probably would've come to this anyhow, but now she felt like it was her fault. Her nearly upright table rotated some and the lights came on in front of her, showing Jon, laid out.

"Let's show her how we can make him dance, shall we?"

Jon's body began to convulse. It was grotesque.

She felt terrible. She wanted to die.

After a few seconds, her table rotated back to the horizontal and the strong retainers that were holding her snapped loose. Suddenly, she too began to convulse. Pain ripped through her body; she had never known anything like it. She wanted to scream, but couldn't. She would have cried, but couldn't. Time was meaningless. If it was seconds, or if it was hours, she couldn't tell; it just seemed to keep going, without end. She tried to pray, but found it impossible to concentrate. She tried to say "Jesus," in her mind, and couldn't, though she knew that she wanted to say His name.

At last the infliction stopped. She was fatigued. Cold sweat had broken out all over her. The restraining straps snapped back around her. She was immobile. One pain, however, didn't stop. Her chest felt like it had been hammered.

"Do we need to show you more? Should we do something else to your husband? I'm sure we can think of something if you don't talk."

Judy wanted to scream, and tell them she'd say anything they wanted, but she was too weak. The interrogator's voice sounded distant, and then she faded out. Dismal blackness crushed in upon her.

"She's unable to answer," the technician reported. "There seems to have been a slight miscalculation on the infliction time. She'll need some rest before we can proceed."

"How long."

"Not too long. We'll give her a shot of epinephrine. She should be able to continue in a few minutes."

The interrogator didn't blame anyone. He knew how hard it was to get the mix of all the drugs and electrical manipulation exactly right. Sometimes they even lost the victim and had to send back a corpse.

She started to recover consciousness.

"Can you answer?"

"Yes," she said weakly.

"Are you ready? Will you tell us where you last saw Brown and everything you know about her."

Judy began, "Near Manta…"

A technician opened a direct link to Novus Ordo and piped Judy's words directly to Weller.

She labored to speak, and they gave her a little longer.

Weakly, she repeated, "We took her to Manta," and then began to fade.

The interrogator slapped her, trying to keep her conscious. She opened her eyes and he said, "You took her to Manta, then what?"

"She left us."

"Where did you leave her in Manta?"

Judy voiced her reply in feeble tone, "On the road … outside of town." Her chest felt so heavy.

"Who did you leave her with?"

"Uh…," she paused and then began to fade.

Again, the technician slapped her. She didn't respond.

Her eyelids snapped open and revealed a fixed, vacant stare.

"Flat line!" the technician shouted.

"She looked healthy," one said, as they rushed to help.

One dove for the defibrillator. The technician who had been interrogating grabbed the paddles. He held them while another smeared solution. One paddle went over the heart, the other, on her left side.

"Stand back," he yelled. "Three… Two… One… NOW!"

Electric current zapped through her, making her body convulse, but she lay there: dead.

"Again," screamed the man with the paddles.

The defibrillator whined. It charged in seconds.

Once more he placed the paddles on her lifeless body.

For a moment she thought she saw Jesus — in Heaven? Then, she knew she saw Him. It was Heaven! Jesus spoke, and said, "You have to go back, but only for a moment, My precious one."

Judy felt so good. She wanted to stay. She asked, like a child, "May I stay?"

Jesus said, "Not this time, daughter, but soon we will see each other, very soon."

"Three… Two… One… NOW!"

Her body jumped again. Every millisecond ticked slowly by, like the swinging pendulum of a grandfather clock making each second pass like a thousand.

Afterwards, the technician announced, "We have a harmonic rhythm."

"Curse her," Weller said. And asked, "Did she tell us anything else?"

The interrogator looked like he would enjoy a shower. He rejoined, "No, sir, but we still have her husband, and might be able to work on her some more later. She may come out of it ready to tell us everything."

"She said they took Brown to Manta?"

"Yes, sir."

"We'd better get our people down there."

It occurred to the technician that Brown's arrival in Manta would have been two or three days ago, and by now, she could be anywhere, but he decided that Herr Weller was smart enough to figure it out by himself; he didn't want to insult the boss.

He walked over to the other table and looked at the mind monitor. He asked, "What have we gotten?"

"Piles of useless imagery, as usual," answered the assistant. "But there was one dream, and its meaning would be anyone's guess, but he seemed to be by the ocean, at night. There was only one point of light. And there seemed to be three other people. One could have been his wife. The other may have been Brown, but we weren't able to identify the fourth. You know how mind images are."

"Yeah," he answered in a way that showed he was thinking — They're just about useless. They'll quicker lead us down the wrong path than the right one. Dreams are fickle. Never trust one.

"So what should we do? Run the video?" she asked.

Good question — the chief technician considered, and then answered, "No. He'll probably block. We'll just waste our time. He knows about us, probably better than the woman," he said, shrugging towards Judy, who had been stabilized. "He's the one who inked our PARASITE. Let's just get to the point. We all took off our gray suits; no need to put them back on."

"Shall I awaken him?" she inquired.

"Go ahead."

JON BEGAN to feel something hard. He thought — My, this bed's turned to stone. It's cold! He attempted to reach for a cover, but couldn't move. He opened his eyes. Figures of two men and two women, as if they were shadows, stood around him as he looked up into a bright light that hurt his eyes.

He felt himself being tilted into an erect position. The figures about him were dressed in the same scarlet and purple uniform James had. He didn't need anyone to tell him in whose company he found himself. His first thought was — I must pray. He remembered how prayer had comforted him earlier, and he closed his eyes and began aloud, "Heavenly Father," — he found himself pleased that he could speak, and not sure why he had spoken aloud — "in the precious name of Jesus..."

Crack. It sounded like a firecracker? My, that hurts — he thought, while moving his tongue around in his jaw, and twisting it to see if he still had one. It seemed to him that it was bleeding. Whatever had happened, it hurt. He was startled. He guessed that one of the uniformed people had given him a good backhand across his cheek.

"Shut up, Whitten. We don't need any of your religion! Now, pay attention."

Jon felt indignant. It didn't matter to him who the devils were, and he thought — I just took out a good life-insurance policy a few months ago. I'd probably do Judy more good dead than alive! He really didn't mean it that way, but he was angry. He knew his stubbornness was stupid — but he felt good about it (even if it probably would make them hurt him more), and in defiance, he said, "In the precious name of Jesus…"

Crack! Again it hit him across the same place — his cheek and his jaw. He had kept his eyes closed. He didn't want to look at their faces. He wasn't sure why he was subjecting himself to the punishment, except he kept remembering the Lord's teaching concerning the blessing that was to be given to those who suffered for His name's sake. And he thought — Maybe this is the first time I've ever really suffered for His name's sake. With this thought he prayed aloud one more time, "Wonderful Lord Jesus…"

Crack. That time it felt like it broke. He felt nauseated, but he began to work his jaw, hoping to enunciate his prayer again. He was exhausted. He could feel his glands squirting perspiration as if they were a fire hose. The cold dampness of the moisture on the skin of his armpits seemed to make the "faucets" open even more. It took a while for him to get himself together — he was feeling weak and woozy. They really don't like the name "Jesus" — he thought, wishing he could eat a candy bar.

THE INTERROGATOR felt that he would just as soon dump the subject out the hatch into the ice-cold darkness of space as to continue. He thought — It's obvious we won't get any cooperation from this fool. I'd better try a different approach. He began to speak politely, "Please, Mr. Whitten, let's make this easy. If you'll open your eyes for a moment, there's something you should see."

Well — Jon thought — the man's trying to be polite. Maybe I should do what he says. But holy wrath simmered in him. No! — he exclaimed to himself. They don't want to hear the name of Jesus. There's no communion between light and darkness. When they get what they want from me, they'll just murder me, so why play their game. And he began once more, yelling with all that was within him, "JESUS! – "

Something clutched him, as if strangling, and every fiber of his body tensed. His eyes popped open. He felt like they were bulging – like a goldfish's. Pain pulsated and riveted every nerve in his body, his skin crawled, and he couldn't think straight, let alone speak.

In it all, one image was burnt into his retinas. It was Judy's corpse, or so it looked. She's so pale – Jon thought, and the torture stopped. Her face was bloodied. His eyes remained fixed on her.

"Ah, Mr. Whitten. Now that we have your attention, perhaps we can talk in a more civilized fashion."

"Is she alive?" Jon asked.

"Oh!" The interrogator replied. "That depends on you? If we can talk, and you tell us what we need, I promise you, both of you will be returned to your comfortable home, right away."

"Where are we?"

"My, Mr. Whitten, you are one to ask questions, aren't you. But I'll ask the questions! Do you understand?"

Jon felt like saying the Name, but he paused for a moment.

"I'll take your silence to mean you are seeing things our way. Now, Whitten, I want you to tell me about Ashley Brown."

Jon reasoned – They want me to think that if I'm a good boy, and tell them what they want, they'll let me take Judy home, but I know how these things work. I've seen it in the movies. If I tell them what they want, they'll finish me just the same, and Judy too. If I don't tell them, they'll make me wish I was dead. If I tell them, I die fast. If I don't tell them, I die slowly. Only a miracle can save me. And if this is the cross I must be nailed to, so be it. I'll die with dignity – without denying His name. And Jon prayed silently – Jesus, help me to finish well. Give me the strength of character to die as You did. Lord, if they threaten Judy, if they do unspeakable things to her, Lord Jesus, give me character to endure, and give Judy peace to understand.

Facing the gravity of his situation, knowing they would likely use the one person he most loved to force him to comply with their wishes, he felt reduced to a heap of mud. In that moment, when Jon felt he couldn't be more useless, more worthless, and when he felt himself the most odious thing to have ever lived, peace came to his heart.

The interrogator was starting to get impatient with the *package,* and asked, "Will you speak, or do we need to do something else to convince you?"

Jon began, "I will speak— "

"Excellent!" his tormentor exclaimed and motioned for the assistant to open a channel to Weller. "Now, tell us everything you know about Ashley Brown."

Just as Weller came online, he heard Whitten say, "I will speak..."

Afterwards, the interrogator said, "Yes, Whitten, you said that. You've said it twice. Now, tell us what you know."

Before Jon spoke, a smile came to his face. He fixed his eyes toward the ceiling and he saw a brief vision: Jesus stood in glory. He was Almighty. He was clothed with a royal garment, and had a golden band across His chest. His hair was white, like wool. His eyes seemed to flame, like fire. He had a sharp two-edged sword and His expression was like the sun shining in its strength. He knew that it was John the Apostle's vision, but right now it was his.

His heart filled with confidence. He feared nothing they could do to his body, or Judy's, and he began, with a holy chuckle, and said, "I will speak," and he paused only an instant, and yelled like a kid, "JESUS!"

He would have done it again, but he saw Judy's body convulse.

"If you continue, Mr. Whitten, you will be responsible for your wife's death. Her heart already stopped once this evening, in our earlier session. Every time she convulses, she is weakened. Every time you say that stupid name, she will convulse."

Jon had already made the commitment. And he said, "I've said all I've got to say."

Violently, Judy churned again.

AN ASSISTANT tapped the interrogator on the shoulder, who turned to hear her whisper a message. The interrogator turned back and ordered, "Freeze Whitten."

The technician entered a command and Jon was frozen, motionless. He had a smile on his face (perhaps "smile" overstated his actual expression, but at least it wasn't horror, which would have been more pleasing to his tormentors) and his eyes were fixed towards Heaven (really, the ceiling).

JON COULDN'T move or hear. He only saw deep black, like night. But he could think and pray, praise, and declare the name of Jesus, and he saw things that eyes can't see. He saw seven lamps. He saw crowns of gold. He heard thundering and voices. And there was a sea of glass and a chant: "Holy, holy, holy is the Lord God Almighty!"

"YES, SIR," the chief interrogator answered, addressing himself to Herr Weller, who had called him to the monitor.

"You've got an idiot, a nutcase."

"It seems so, sir."

"Look at the mind monitor," Weller indicated.

The interrogator turned and saw an image that made his blood boil.

"The man sees that religious art so vividly. He doesn't even dream that well," Weller said with a face-the-facts look.

"Turn off the mind monitor. We don't need to see such trash!" the interrogator ordered, and the dynamic lifelike image of Jesus, with His hands extended and reaching out towards them, went black.

"The female has already provided a good lead. It will be useless to continue with this fanatic. We don't have to put up with his sordid ecclesiastical zeal."

"Yes, sir. Shall I terminate them?" the interrogator asked, hoping for an affirmative. It would make things simpler if they were able to dispose of the subjects in space. They wouldn't have to carry them back into the house.

"I don't think so," Weller said.

The interrogator looked disappointed.

Weller continued, "Until we find Brown, there's a possibility she might return to the subjects' house, since she's been there previously. Or, it's also possible they might do something that could lead us to her. We can't dispose of them just yet. Not until Brown is found. Drug them, *erase* them, and take them back."

"Yes, sir, but what about the lady? She may need more medical attention."

"Keep her alive. If Brown goes looking for her, we'll need her," Weller instructed. "Keep Whitten sedated until the doctors think the Mrs. is ready to go back, and then take them back together."

Chapter 14

Stopped Clocks

FOR TO ME to live is Christ, and to die is gain.

— Paul the Apostle

February 23 — That same day — Quito

HENRY LÓPEZ was having a good night's sleep, for a change. The hotel was plush, the bed was as comfortable as they come, but then his computer began to ring. Its warbling sound penetrated his dreams, and he jumped to open its panel and Herr Weller's face pixelated into view. He didn't relish the thought of visiting Weller's office in his pajamas, so he punched a key to cancel the virtual meeting mode. Weller could override, but he probably wouldn't, and would respect his request for privacy.

"López," Weller addressed forthrightly.

"Yes, sir."

"Those Whitten people are real religious fruitcakes."

"Missionaries. Yes, sir!" López affirmed, not entirely sure what Weller was headed for.

"Look, López. I think you're a good man, but your Quito job hasn't worked very well."

"True, sir. What do you suggest?" Henry asked, anticipating his own recall.

"I've been going over this whole thing. It seems like something out of a comedy. Why don't you just paint a big sign on the control van that says, "WE'RE YOUR FRIENDLY NEIGHBORHOOD SPIES.""

Henry began to feel anemic — weak. He could see this wasn't going to look good on his record and thought — It's Walker's fault. I trusted him too much.

"Imagine, a big white van with a stupid diplomatic license plate. Can't we do better than that? And PARASITE controllers who are as covert as fireworks on New Year's eve? Come on, López."

"Yes, sir."

"For now, stop the Antisana operation. Move everything to Manta. The Whittens confessed they took Brown there."

He finally sees the light — López considered, and asked, "Anything else, sir? Some other detail?"

"Thanks to your bungling, no. There's nothing else, yet. They'll be *erased* so they won't remember the abduction, and then returned to their house. We hope Brown will try to contact them. So I want discreet — do you understand, discreet — surveillance to continue. I want to know anything that could lead us to Brown. Anything at all. We have to let the subjects feel safe so they'll do something to show us where to find Brown. Do you understand?"

"Yes, sir."

"Good."

López asked, "Sir?"

"Yes."

"Manta is a small place. It would be easy to scare Brown away, or anyone who knows anything, if we go in like we did at Antisana."

"Or Quito," Weller added, to rub it in a bit.

"Or Quito, sir."

"Handle it, López. Just don't fail me."

"Yes, sir."

* * *

The next day — Quito

JON WHITTEN'S HEAD felt like his brain had been removed, compacted into a pea, and then converted into a microchip. That wasn't an adequate description, but he had no idea what would be better, and in his present state, he wasn't going to try to figure it out.

He found himself stumbling out of bed and making his way to take care of pressing personal needs. He detested taking medicine of any kind, but he found an aspirin in the medicine chest. They always kept bottled water in the bathroom, and Jon filled his cup, about halfway, and popped two of the white pills. He quickly gulped them down.

He went back to bed and, as he sat on the edge, and before lying back, he looked at his watch: 1:30 AM? There was bright sunlight outside. It was burning into the bedroom, even through the heavy curtains. The battery must be old — he decided, and began to lie down, his head throbbing.

Looking over, he saw Judy lying faceup. She never lies face up — he noted. Something about her caught his eye. She looked so pale. He reached over and touched her. She was cold. Ice cold. A corpse.

He shook her, and then held her. Tears started to fill his eyes. He prayed and screamed — cursing death. But she didn't move. She looked so natural, like she'd already been to the mortician — sleeping so calmly. "Why?" he shrieked. "Why? God! Why?" he yelled. But dead silence was his only answer.

He tried to remember, but it seemed like the harder he sought to remember, the more his memory distanced itself from him. Something happened last night! He knew it. But he had no idea what it was, except that Judy's death was the result. He cried. Jon cried until he had no more tears. And he asked, "Why? What happened?"

What now? He had to call someone. Do something. But he couldn't. He had long forgotten his own headache, for the pain that now filled him was far worse. He screamed again, raising his eyes to Heaven, "Why?" and cried some more with newly found tears, tears that wouldn't lack for many days.

Did it matter? Why didn't I die? He knew she was with Jesus. And it wouldn't be easy, but he would just have to wait his turn. However, the question didn't, and wouldn't, go away. "Why?" he cried.

It took some time, but he finally got the phone, and hit the memory button. One of the children answered and Jon tried to sound normal, but he couldn't. He heard the daughter say, "Daddy, I think Uncle Jon is on the phone."

"Jon. Where have you been, buddy?"

"Larry...," and he sniffled and cried, choking.

"What, Jon?"

And he started again, trying to force his mouth to say the words. His mind knew them, but he couldn't vocalize.

Larry finally decided he should offer to go over, "Do you want me to come?"

Even saying "yes" was difficult for Jon.

IT WASN'T SIMPLE for a missionary to die. Especially when the family wanted to move the body back to the States. It meant bureaucracy and lines, and that was the easy part. Fortunately there was a small life insurance policy that would cover most of the basic expenses, but it wouldn't be enough. Jon was grateful for all the support he received from many people. He couldn't have done it himself.

The police thoroughly examined the body for some sign of foul play, but the autopsy found its condition compatible with natural death — a heart attack. They said Judy had some undiagnosed problems, and it resulted in "sudden death syndrome."

Eventually, Jon quit asking why? Somehow, he knew. It had something to do with a trip to Manta, but even that had disappeared from his mind. It was hidden in an impenetrable fog — distant and warped, like a thick soup. And every time he tried to think about it, the memory receded even further, like brushing his balding head — with every stroke less hair was available.

The strangest thing was that all the clocks on the top floor of the house, except for one, in a distant back room, had stopped at the same time, 1:30 AM. Dan's watch had frozen, displaying the day and date — early Saturday morning. Later, when Larry took it to get the battery changed, since Jon didn't feel up to it, the jeweler measured the battery. It still had sufficient reserve. He put it back in and the watch ran like new. "Just needed to be reset," the jeweler said. "Maybe a gamma ray got it," he joked.

Somewhere along the way Jon realized he must have slept from Friday night until Sunday morning. He had no memory of waking, not once. Indeed, he felt like he had been somewhere else, but there wasn't any evidence to indicate he'd done anything other than sleep. The neighbors never saw him leave on Saturday, and the guard said no one had gone in or out.

Larry said he had called once on Saturday, but hung up after four rings, since it hadn't been anything important — figuring the Whittens had gone shopping.

It was hard to believe: Sleeping from Friday night until Sunday morning and not even remembering if he had been to the bathroom? But Jon hurt too deeply to pay much attention. If he had slept so long — he had no idea. But something, which he wasn't ever able to identify, made him feel that Judy's death, in some way, was his fault. At the same time, he felt a peace, a godly peace. Somehow he felt the Lord was proud to call him one of His own. He couldn't explain it, and didn't try. It didn't make any sense.

It seemed that with every passing hour Jon became less coherent. Even his short-term memory seemed to be affected. Larry found himself having to tell Jon every single thing — like a child.

The Brooks came to the memorial service, and they talked one-on-one with Jon, mentioning James and Ashley, that they had been in Pifo, but Jon couldn't remember. Trying to help him, they told him about how the two of them, Jon and Judy, had left James and Ashley, and then picked them up the next day. Linda said, "Judy was so sweet. So full of love." And she said many other kind things, until tears came to her eyes.

Jon gasped for air, but he didn't remember. And he wanted to remember Judy and everything about her. How she touched. How she walked — everything. But his mind was empty. He wanted to gaze on a memory of her lovely form, but it was gone — erased, and even the dust had been blown away; only a latent carbon print remained, dirty gray. Jon could feel the dampness of the Wite-Out brush, hovering above, with a drop of purging liquid ready to flow into the porous smudge of blotted memories.

Hearing Linda speak so wonderfully of Judy brought some distant comfort to him and he said, choking, "I... I... wish I could remember." And more tears came to his eyes. Dan Brook reached around him, and held him tight, closer than a brother, for a moment when words wouldn't do.

Dan was there, listening to the pathetic confession and thought — They've snuffed out his memory. It probably has something to do with Smith's Nova Mundi. Whatever, or whoever, it was, Dan hated it.

Indeed, there were suspicious details. The subject would become one of the most debated in the local missionary community. Who were the mysterious people who had been with the Whittens? Did Judy's death and Jon's loss of sanity have anything to do with their visitors — but why? How? Nothing was stolen. It didn't make sense.

Jack Kinderly, when he eventually had a better understanding of the whole picture, would counsel Larry and Dan Brook not to dwell on the subject — silence was probably the best policy. Having heard James's description of the hidden world, none of them could look on things in the same way they used to. Larry Williams and family would soon be due for an extended furlough, returning to the States for a longer visit than usual. A few weeks after Judy's death they would decide to travel. The Brooks, though having been involved, hadn't been as close, and were better able to continue in the field.

Jack went the extra mile and got things moving in the States to bring Judy's body home, and Jon too. It all happened so suddenly. "She looked so healthy when we were there," Mercy Kinderly mourned. It was sad, so sad.

After further police investigation, no criminal evidence against Jon could be found, or against anyone else, for that matter. Judy didn't look murdered. Besides, the coroner had a visit from a famous American forensic scientist who had been passing through. Since it was an American who had died, the coroner thought it appropriate, and asked the tall blond doctor to examine the body – just to be sure. Really, when the coroner reflected, it almost seemed as if the American had suggested it first. After the visit, he left a case of American candy bars – a goodwill gift. Officially – most officially – Judy Whitten died of a heart attack.

* * *

The next day — Quito

SURVEILLANCE AT THE WHITTEN's hadn't been conclusive, except for two things – Walker summarized – definitely there hadn't been any calls from Brown, and she had not returned.

They really *erased* Whitten – Walker considered, as he listened to the subject. He had the coherency of an advanced Alzheimer's case. Cases of overerasure, like Whitten's, could go away – Walker knew. Erasure didn't work the same in everyone. Most of the time, the technicians were able to do it correctly and eliminate only the memories of the abduction itself. But like trying to erase a point on a sheet of paper, sometimes, the eraser's head sticks and then, pressed harder, it wipes out other things, things that hadn't been targeted.

Erasure gave no long-term guarantees. Whitten's wits – Walker considered – could come back in a flash. But if the man's memory came back, it wouldn't matter. People will have him committed to an institution, and if he starts talking about alien abductions, and the Martians who murdered his wife, everyone will say, "Poor chap; he was an intelligent soul."

No reason for surveillance at the memorial service — Walker concluded. It'll just be religious nonsense. I get enough listening at his home. It makes me lose my concentration, and they've moved all of my people to Manta. How do they expect me to do it by myself? And the man is rarely home. They seem so friendly, inviting him *everywhere*. It is hard to keep up — he complained to himself.

* * *

Novus Ordo

"YOU MORONS!" Weller charged. "What in the Skotoi's universe do you think you're doing? An outer could have handled this better!"

None of DEEP 43's crew dared bat an eye. They stood at attention as Weller paced back and forth, spouting ill words with every other step.

"After she had the heart attack, you inflicted her some more! You knew we needed her alive. Then you started cleaning the man's mind like he would never need to remember his name again. Any more of this incompetence and I, personally, will inflict the responsible party until their heart stops. Then I'll revive the slob and erase until the only memory left is infliction!"

One of the assistants, who had been part of the botched interrogation, said to herself — Yeah, Weller. And if we would've treated her as gently as you're saying now, she wouldn't have said a cursed thing. You'd be threatening us for lack of decision and ineptitude, anyway. And if we had left that man with one memory too many, you'd have erased us. In this army, you're *inflicted* if you do and *inflicted* if you don't — she resigned.

Weller steamed back to his workstation with a few nervous twitches. Occasionally, perhaps every ten steps, he jerked his head with a left-handed, short-range recoil movement. By the time he sat down to talk to López, he was certain he would kill.

"Okay, López. What have you found?" he angrily demanded, addressing the virtual image that sat in front of his desk.

"I'm sorry to report, sir, but we have no concrete leads," he responded calmly, trying not to show that Weller was making him nervous.

Weller was ready to have López on a platter, but he decided to let the fuse on his anger-bomb stretch before detonation. After all, it would be more effective if he could actually find something that was wrong before he laid into the poor SAO. "How are you handling it?" Weller asked.

"Well, sir, we have every Latin SAO that we've been able to bring in, without shutting down the Colombian cartel, and we're doing footwork; we're going to all the places we can with Brown's picture."

"What do the people say? Anything?"

"Well, sir, some, especially the men, say, 'What a pretty *gringa.*' "

"Curse it, López, we need something concrete! How big is that town? It's just a village, isn't it?"

"Actually, sir, it is somewhat extended. There are about eighty thousand inhabitants, sir."

"That's a lot of people," Weller conceded, but still trying to find a point of detonation, he asked, "Do you have a plan?"

"We do, sir. We're checking all the points of embarkation first. We went to the captain of the port, but the only thing he mentioned was that a couple of honeymooners contracted a boat, but they were actually traveling from Guayaquil. Besides, we're looking for a lone woman."

"López! Curse it! You don't know that. You're presuming!" Weller lifted an infliction control and pointed it right at López's virtual image, which sat across from him, in front of his desk.

López tightened. Weller enjoyed seeing him fill with fear, and angrily exclaimed, "I'm ready to inflict someone! Don't you remember that other report from Antisana? What if Brown is traveling with Smith? Do something, López! Do it right now! I'd love to press this button," which he fingered — still pointing it at the virtual projection.

"Yes, sir! Please, sir," López implored. "But we *have* asked. We're showing Smith's picture too. The captain of the port couldn't identify the honeymooners, though. He never saw them."

Weller hated it, but it wouldn't do any good to inflict López. After an infliction the man would be useless, and there was precious little time to waste. Each day that Brown was able to remain on the outside increased her chances of escape. It would only force him to put someone else, who would only be half as informed, in charge of the search, so he concluded, giving a mandate, "Okay López. Keep up the pressure."

Weller lowered the control.

* * *

Novus Iridium

EVERY STEP I take is a monumental task, a masterwork — Janice thought. It has to be created, thought out, and schemed. It must have been like that when I learned to walk the first time, but I don't remember.

She vaguely recalled learning to ride a bicycle. Her entire body had trembled with the tension stretching through taut tendons and nerves to the cusp of each limb. However, her stress hadn't been because of the bicycle. Instead, the one who pushed her — Uncle Ralph — had induced it. He caused her to shy. And she cursed him once more — in his tomb. He had left her bitter. Thanks to him, she had never been innocent.

His abuse still held her, like the therapist who supported her. I'm harsh — she thought. The therapist hasn't touched me anywhere he shouldn't. Maybe it's because he's forcing me to endure so much pain, like Ralph — she pondered.

Not all men are "Ralphs" — she rhetorically advised herself. Sure they aren't — she told herself with the conviction of a cloudy day, a blinking yellow signal, or more aptly, a little girl in the body of a demolished woman.

They, whoever "they" were, had told her she was getting better and to be strong and courageous. But they wouldn't tell her where she was. And she hadn't seen the light of day in weeks. It could've been a hidden underground compartment of NHMI Siberia, except no one looked Russian or even spoke a word that sounded "vichy" or "somethingsky." There had been few opportunities to even hear someone speak. They looked and sounded like they had grown up listening to the Voice of America, "in special English," except for an occasional word that didn't make sense in the context they spoke.

One nurse she had heard, while pretending to sleep, had been talking about, *"deeping"* someone to the trauma unit. Janice asked one of her therapists what *"deeping"* was, and she answered, "Do you mean sleeping?"

Another day, a handsome blond gentleman in a scarlet and purple uniform stood outside of her door (again she was supposed to be asleep) and said, "He *overbioed*. Just needs a little rest."

She asked a nurse what *"overbioed"* was, and she questioned back, "Boiled?"

"No, *bioed!*" Janice insisted emphatically.

The nurse chuckled, and said, "You probably heard wrong."

It was useless to ask questions. Janice had a notion to do some *deeping* or get *bioed*, or better, *unbioed*. It was useless nonsense, which was also a good description of her self-esteem: worthless rubbish.

When she heard one comment about "a case of *extreme infliction* compounded by *erasure*," it struck her as funny. She thought — That sounds like me, and she would have laughed, but she didn't want the doctor to think she had been awake. It was all she could do to keep it to herself.

Chapter 15

Beachhead

AND WHAT'S ROMANCE? Usually, a nice little tale where you have everything As You Like It, where rain never wets your jacket and gnats never bite your nose and it's always daisy-time.

— D. H. Lawrence

February 26 — That same day — Twenty miles off the Mexican coast

PEPE'S BOAT had been small, but adequate. That didn't mean comfortable. And though it might have been called a honeymoon cruise, the Smiths had no such luck. It was too crowded. Ashley didn't have much problem with being the only girl since Alpha Force had been a unisex organization, although she was careful to use proper modesty among the outers. But there wasn't any need to pretend. Their trip had not, in any way, been for starry-eyed lovers.

The weather had been remarkably good, and hurricane season was still two months away. Considering the cramped quarters, and encouraged by the warm, dry nights, the Smiths had found themselves sleeping on deck much of the trip, except when they helped with the night watch. Then, they would rest below, away from the hot sun. At least they had been trained for, and were familiar with, life at sea.

"*Es mágico* — it's magic," Pepe said upon seeing the PLOT. He knew *gringos* had sophisticated things, but he hadn't ever heard of anything like the black slab. It even understood Spanish! The *gringo* gave it to him as a gift for his return trip, but made him promise never to show it to anyone, and as soon as he was back in the range covered by his own charts, to throw it into the sea along with everything else. He decided, after his mistake with the fuel, he would pay attention to orders.

JAMES ORIGINALLY planned on having Pepe take them as far northwest as possible, perhaps to Manzanillo, in Mexico, where he and Ashley had been on one of their more memorable field trips, visiting the beaches, and even spending a couple of nights in a gorgeous hotel. But with the theft of their money, James decided that getting out of Ecuador was essential, and that reaching Mexico, any part of it, would be sufficient. Originally, he had planned on a ten-day trip, one way, but four good days had gotten them close to southern Mexico, and with their cash shortage, Pepe would feel better turning back sooner than later. For the Smiths, and their own cash crunch, it all meant that they would have to cover a greater distance with less money.

James remembered another field trip — a DIDO (*Deep* In, *Deep* Out). They had gone to Paredon (located in Chiapas, south of Tonalá, in southern Mexico). It had had a beautiful beach, white sand and gentle Pacific waves — or so he remembered it. It was one of those places where they had been *deeped* in just before dawn, and they had left the group for the day. Then, that night, they were *deeped* out, an hour after sunset. It had been abandoned, and they had spent a pleasant day, but it had been twenty years ago. It's probably changed — James figured — but I hope it hasn't changed much.

This time wouldn't be a DIDO, but a SIWO (Swim In, Walk Out). The sun had gone down an hour before. Pepe kept complaining, *"No lo hagan* — Don't do it." James and Ashley nearly got mad at him. Pepe couldn't imagine that a twenty-mile swim at sea wasn't really extraordinary for the Smiths. Some Australian woman had swum over ninety miles, without implants, so Pepe need not have concerned himself about the Smiths. At least these waters weren't as shark infested as the Gulf of Mexico where the Ausi set her record.

Pepe repeatedly offered to move in closer to shore, but James explained to him, more than once, that he didn't want to draw attention to the two of them, and he didn't want Pepe's boat in Mexico's territorial waters. He and Ashley assured him, repeatedly, and emphatically, that they were going to be fine, and they really did know how to swim twenty miles at sea — no sweat.

James wished they had black wet suits for camouflage in the night, but as it was, black grease would have to do. They stripped down to the swim gear they had bought in Manta. Ashley wore a one-piece jet-black bathing suit, and James, a black Speedo-style brief — it had been all they had for sale. They put all their worldly possessions — clothing, shoes, New Testament — in layered black garbage bags; leaving behind James's backpack, Bible, and odds-and-ends. James made sure they had a bar of soap to be able to wash off the grease when they made shore. He wore his watch with its satellite-positioning module attached, something he would need without the aid of the PLOT.

Pepe kept warning about the sharks. Ashley couldn't tell him, but she had a secret weapon: her PHENIX. Though not as effective in water, it would knock one out at short range. She hoped she wouldn't need to fire, since it was likely the savage fish wouldn't be seen until after an attack. Chance favored them, and besides, they prayed and agreed together for a safe swim. Ashley remembered the two days she had spent in the Pacific, and though fried by the sun, neither shark nor jellyfish had gotten her. God had been with them, and both knew they should've died long ago — save His intervention.

Captain Smith decided the moment had arrived. Having tied and taped the bags shut, he secured a tether line to them.

It wasn't easy to persuade Pepe to leave them, and head back home. James instructed him, "If anyone asks where we went, tell them we left without mentioning our plans. If someone asks where you left us, say we wanted it to be a secret. But if you're threatened, tell them everything. It doesn't matter."

Ashley smiled and told Pepe, "Just say you dropped us in the sea." And then she gave him a brief embrace.

As she touched him, he thought – Dumb *gringa*, I'll have to fish you from the sea again. She's like a rebellious teenager – has a mind of her own. *Gringa! Gringa! Gringa!* – he exclaimed to himself, as if she should hear his thought. But he knew if she had, she would only have laughed at him; for she was young and carefree, innocent and beautiful – like a child. And he wished she wouldn't throw herself into the sea.

On the other hand, he had developed respect for James. The *gringo* will take care of her – he thought. Looking up profoundly into James's eyes, Pepe ordered, "*Cuídala* – Take care of her." Pepe knew the *gringo* would, but in some measure he felt better saying it, as if he'd done something for her – as if saving her life hadn't been enough.

James answered, "*Lo haré* – I'll do it."

But Pepe still felt sad, as if he was losing his only daughter.

A second later the *gringos* fell backwards into the sea.

A tear came to Pepe's eye, but he acted like he was brushing something from his face, lest his crewmate perceive him to be too sentimental and insufficiently *macho*.

The pair surfaced quickly and Pepe threw them the bundle. He watched as James tied the tether around his waist, and tried to arrange it so he wouldn't kick it. Then he yelled, "*Hasta luego* – See you later."

The *gringa* added, "*Gracias, Pepe!* – Thank you, Pepe!"

Pepe knew that these *gringos* were different. Of course all *gringos* are strange, he accepted, but these two were different — even from other *gringos*. It was hard to tell in the night, but it looked like they swam away, even with the bag in tow, faster than fine athletes.

He wondered why anyone would threaten him with violence. He also hated thinking he would have to throw the *plot* away once he got back to the waters covered by his charts. He would have loved to keep it, but he wouldn't fail the *gringa* this time.

He waited there an hour, hoping they would return, but finally decided he would start back.

* * *

Pacific Ocean, off the coast of Mexico

EVEN WITH enhancements it was an exhausting swim, especially since they had allowed themselves to get out of shape. James had the added burden of towing the bag. Ashley had to work more, too, since she couldn't swim efficiently while waiting for James. Adding the tension of watching for sharks in the darkness without visual enhancements — an impossible assignment — and ready to fire her PHENIX, the swim wore her down considerably.

When a jellyfish slid over the back of her leg, the excruciating sting shot through her enhanced nervous system, and was immediately processed as PAIN — burning and stinging — like multiple insect bites. It took her breath for a moment, but an infliction would have been far worse.

Fortunately, they had no schedule. Theirs was a simple assignment: Reach shore, if possible, unseen. James had memorized the coordinates, and with the satellite system he was able to track their progress. The navigation aid also helped them avoid getting turned around in the dark. However, there were several soft glows coming from different points on the coast. About twelve more miles, James estimated. He prayed silently as he swam, asking for the Lord's protection and guidance.

It was a very long swim, two hours. Many things could have gone wrong, but they didn't. A jellyfish sting was a small price to pay, considering. So it was, when they finally made their way onto the deserted beach, falling flat on their backs on the white sand that lazily scintillated in the moonlight, they rolled beside each other, exhausted. The sky looked alive, like a vast organism, its stars gleaming and twinking. The moon was over three quarters full — just a bit out of round. You could've seen its face — looking down with personality — if you thought about it.

They looked into each other's eyes, and James said, "Let's thank the Lord."

And they did, rolling closer, holding hands, and leaning against one another. White sand stuck to the black grease and water, caking itself to their bodies.

James whispered, "Heavenly Father, thank You for keeping us from harm and bringing us here. Thank You."

James looked at Ashley, her eyes still closed. She's beautiful — he thought.

AN INSTANT LATER she opened her eyes and the image of his powerful features, glazed by moonlight and black grease, made him look sculptured — in glowing Renaissance bronze.

His lips couldn't resist hers, and they touched. He tenderly held her.

Time was locked out of their embrace, or perhaps it enjoyed watching? It didn't dare interrupt. They were the only two people in the world and all the stars of heaven were witnesses. Could it have been Paradise? Romanesque light bathed them with just the right touch, as if the Creator had adjusted the dimmer's dial Himself. Faint waves with churning edges, foaming and bubbling, marked their season — as though it would never end.

But it did.

"WE'D BETTER get cleaned and dressed," James said, as if he regretted having a mouth.

They had managed to cover themselves with white sand, a good disguise, that blended perfectly, and served them well for the satisfying season they had just shared on the lucent beach.

Standing, they began walking, hand-in-hand. James dragged the bag behind them, over the sand. If he had navigated correctly, they wouldn't be far from a stream of fresh water — perhaps a hundred yards. To approach it, James had to lift their bag to keep it from being ripped open on the rocks, which seemed to be growing out of the sand. A few more paces, and the rocks dominated the terrain. They worked their way up the stream, following it inland, and found a shallow place where they could wash and prepare themselves for the next phase.

It was 1:00 AM by the time they had bathed and dressed themselves. By then, they felt ready to be seen by outers.

"Okay," James began, "do you like Jean for a name?"

Ashley answered, as if she had no other choice, "Yeah. It'll do. And you can be Roger."

"I'm Roger. Then we're Mr. and Mrs. Roger Baker. I think that's how outers say it."

"I wish we could be Mr. and Mrs. James Smith. I like that more."

They had found a "couch" in a large rock. It was a bit hard, but they found comfort in each other's embrace. The stream made a low, cheerful sound, as if it were telling jokes and laughing, at the same time.

"If someone asks, we're on our honeymoon. That's what outers say, isn't it?"

"Right, James."

"I'm not James," James said, with mild reproof.

"Right, Roger." And then Ashley laughed, "Get it?" and she looked at James, though it was difficult to see much in the dim light. She nearly wished she had her light amplifiers, but then decided not; it was much more fun this way — in the moonlight.

James repeated, "Right, Roger." He paused and said, "Roger..." and then laughed too. A moment later he questioned, "Maybe I should think of another name?"

"Oh, Roger. I'm just now starting to get used to Roger. Right?" and she giggled.

"We're visiting Tonalá, and we walked down to the beach, but when we realized it was getting late, it was too dark to walk back."

"Roger, you sound so outer. It's marvelous," Ashley continued with the fun. They felt total freedom to be themselves. The night slipped away quickly. Ashley leaned on James's strong chest.

It must have been 4:00 AM before they slept.

* * *

MORNING CAME too suddenly to be comfortable. The heat reached uneasy figures before the sun had risen fully.

"We'd better start," James instructed.

Ashley found the small mirror and brush she had packed, and tried to arrange her hair. James did the same.

They started walking back to the beach, over the rocks. It was still abandoned, but there was a small fishing skiff about a halfmile out. James and Ashley headed west, along the beach, back to the point where they hoped to find — as shown on the PLOT and as James's memory served him — a small road that would be just a little bigger than a path.

It would be a long walk, and they decided to *bio*. They found the path, and continued north, moving along at a good speed. Thick vegetation, so very green, surrounded them on both sides of the narrow "road." Occasionally there were brilliant flowers, blue, red, and yellow. At times there were swarms of butterflies, as bright in color as the flowers. They would have made it to Tonalá, fifteen miles, in just over an hour, but they couldn't keep it up too long because the path widened, and they started finding more and more outers. There were a few jeeps, and lots of people — *mestizos* — all moving along the road. It was a long, slow walk; the hardest part being, they knew they could do it more quickly, but they'd have to have patience — a morning's worth.

Tonalá was little more than a village. It wasn't lunchtime, only 11:00 AM, but the Smiths, alias Bakers, were famished. James knew he could eat a cow, something he became convinced of as soon as he saw a vendor in the small plaza preparing tortillas with strips of barbecued beef. He had a few fresh ones ready.

There was a problem, though. James's smallest bill was a twenty. The man with the tortillas didn't want to give him any change — maybe because he didn't have that much since he just started work. So they decided to look for a place to get pesos. There was a small hotel, with a restaurant, which made the exchange.

Once the two famished travelers, who surprisingly didn't look horribly out of place because of all the tourism, had finished eating, they sat down on a park bench to decide on a strategy.

"We could try to call Jack," Ashley suggested.

"But the thieves took his phone number."

"There must be some kind of information service. The telephone company can get us the number."

"You're probably right," James agreed.

They asked the man who had sold them the tortillas and guacamole where they could find the phone company. As was everything in Tonalá, it was just around the corner.

TELEMEX was written on the sign. The lady wanted ten dollars just for the information call. James hated to use the money, but she did get him a number in Orlando, Florida, for a Jack Kinderly.

When James asked to call collect, the little chubby lady, with a dirty white dress, pulled too tightly around her — as if to be a body girdle — informed him that they didn't accept collect calls.

Then Ashley, trying to help solve the problem, asked how much it would cost. It was six dollars for the first minute and one and a quarter for every minute thereafter.

"We'll have to keep it short," James said.

Ashley agreed.

They told the lady, who seemed to take it as part of a normal day's work, to go ahead and place the call. She asked them for a twenty-dollar deposit. James forked it over.

When the call went through, a voice answered, "Thank you for calling the Kinderlys. We are out or unable to take your call at this time ..."

"It's an answering machine," James said, defeat in his tone.

But Ashley took it much more seriously. "An answering machine!" she exclaimed with no small note of wrath in her voice. And she repeated, "An answering machine!"

"The tape said, 'Please leave your name and phone number after the tone and we will return your call.' " A couple of seconds later it BEEPED.

"This is James Smith," he began, having nearly used his alias, but Jack wouldn't have known who he was. "I'm in, ..., I'm in," and he thought better of saying. Surely they don't have his phone tapped – James wondered – but I'd better not take a chance. With this in mind, he said, "We're traveling ..."

"James, is that you, my friend?" Jack Kinderly greeted him with a rich and friendly voice. Jack had heard the call just before leaving, and ran back to pick it up. He had been quite occupied with the Whitten situation.

"Jack! Yeah. It's me. We're traveling."

Ashley nearly jumped up and down with excitement.

"Jim, I'm glad you called. I've been anxious for you to call."

"Well, I can't talk long."

"What's happening?"

"They robbed us when we left, and so I don't have much money."

"Where are you?"

James knew he would have to say, and went ahead, "Mexico, in Chiapas."

"You've come a long way." And Jack thought aloud, "But you've got a long way to go," and lingered before saying, "Jim, do you have something to write with?"

"No, but we'll try to get something." James signaled Ashley. She quickly asked the lady at the desk, who, finally, slowly set aside her knitting, crept to open her desk drawer, and leisurely elevated the items, giving them to Ashley as if they were held by an invisible ooze. Her motivation level left one with the idea that maybe she shared her meals with a tapeworm, or some assortment of parasites — not the mechanical variety — perhaps a small zoo of the creatures?

Ashley rushed the pencil and paper to James, who had hung up already.

"What happened?" Ashley asked with surprise.

"Jack realized that he didn't have a phone number he needed. He said we should move on up the coast with the money we've still got, to Acapulco. He thought it will be easier to help us there. He said to call when we get there and he'll have the information ready."

"So we're going to Acapulco?"

"Well, that's what he said," James confirmed.

"That sounds like a honeymoon!" Ashley said.

They passed by the desk, and the lady didn't have any trouble billing them. Could it have been that her lack of motivation in loaning the pencil and paper was really a reflection of the fact that she had lost many of the yellow sticks?

Sixteen dollars! — what a bill! It was more than James cared to count. She gave him his change in pesos.

Chapter 16

Acapulco

A FISH is caught by its own mouth.

— Ecuadorian proverb

February 28 — The next day — Acapulco

IT HAD BEEN a long six weeks, although, at times, it seemed to move right along. Some girls, some drinks (plenty of drinks), some coke, a puff of Acapulco gold — expensive. And the girls — he liked them young and clean, which was more expensive. The old hags, like Norma — he thought with a laugh — are cheap enough, but they probably have more viruses than even I could program.

However, things had changed. He had no idea how it had come about, and the bankers wouldn't return his calls. Indeed, it seemed that so far as the Swiss bank was concerned, Atler Redclift never existed. His code was invalid, or so he was told, and there wasn't any record that he had ever made a deposit, or had a code. He assured himself that it would certainly show up in an audit and any day he would have his money. It was his money! VICE (Virtual Internet superComputer Emulation) had earned it for him. They had no right! If they took his money so easily, he would spend the rest of his life denouncing the Swiss banking industry. But who would believe him? And in publicly denouncing them, he would likely have to explain himself to those who were either looking for him (Doug's people) or would come looking for him (the IRS). All things considered, it wasn't a good idea for it to be known that he was a millionaire, or once was, as the case may have been.

Due to the impossibility of accessing his Swiss account, he had been living on his credit cards, but he had managed to fill his meager credit lines rapidly — in just twenty-four hours. His cards had been issued to Atler Redclift, the "nerd," the one who had worked in a "past" life at the Jet Propulsion Laboratory. Yes, he had had a respectable credit line, but before he left it had been mostly filled — since he was planning to pay from his Swiss account. He had carried the thousand in cash, but at this juncture, he had nearly run out. It was proving impossible to get to his Swiss money, and his credit line was overextended.

He really hadn't put a lot of thought into what would happen when the cards' issuers decided that his accounts weren't worth further extension. He wasn't even sure when it would happen, since he was already over the limit, but it didn't take long for him to find out. His answer came when he was asked to approach the desk. The lady was very polite. She asked, "Do you have another credit card, *Señor* Redclift?"

"Why? What's wrong with that one?" he questioned indignantly. Of course he knew what was wrong, but he wasn't about to stand there and say, "Oh, I'm sorry. They're right. I don't have a penny to my name." It would be too embarrassing.

"It seems you need to speak with the issuers," she answered coolly.

Atler knew he had probably reached his credit limit. At over five hundred dollars a day, he probably should consider himself fortunate it had lasted as long as it had. After all, his credit card issuers didn't know about his Swiss accounts.

"Can I call them?"

"Collect?" inquired the petite Latin with medium-length black hair, blond streaks, and soft brown eyes and features — especially her nose — that hinted a mixed heritage of Spanish and Mayan. Not bad — Atler thought.

"Yes," he said, and read her the number from the back of the card.

"A collect call from Albert Wilson Redclift; will you accept the charges?"

The card's agent accepted.

"Yes," began Atler, pleading his case, "I'm traveling in Mexico and it seems you've stopped approving charges?"

The man took a minute and confirmed, "That's true."

"Is there anything we can do to change this situation?" Atler asked.

"Paying off your balance will restore your creditline," came a chilly reply.

"Could you extend my creditline?" Atler hopefully asked.

"I can take your application right here on the phone, and we'll send you the result in the mail."

"But I need something now," Atler pleaded.

"Mr. Redclift, I'm sorry, but with your history, and two late payments, I can't help you. You'll have to wait for the decision on your application." The agent already knew Redclift would be denied, and sent a letter demanding immediate payment of the entire balance of the account.

Atler knew it too, but not in so many words. He could see it was useless. He looked through his other cards and didn't see any that would do him any good. He could almost read the words "LIMIT OVEREXTENDED!" written across the top of each. None of them really had those words written on them, but he knew, as soon as they were swiped, the reply from the processing center would be definitive. He felt defeated, and was beginning to realize that he had a mess — a serious mess. He gave the phone back to the *señorita* and said, "I need to make another phone call."

"Collect?"

"No. I'll pay," Atler replied.

"I'm sorry, *señor*. Any money you pay will be applied to your hotel account. Once your balance is clear, the hotel will continue providing new service."

"Then...," and he didn't know what to say, until bossing, "just give me the key to my room."

"*Señor*, it is the hotel's tradition, and our right, to keep your luggage until your bill is paid. And you must pay your account before we can provide further service."

"That's not right!" Atler began, just a little hot — his tone — but it was hot, even with air-conditioning and it would be hotter on the street.

The *señorita* signaled for the guard, who soon appeared, standing behind, and beside of, *Señor* Redclift.

"*Señor* Redclift, please leave our premises until you are ready to make full payment," she said, looking him flatly in the eyes. She seemed to be such a sweet little thing, but she must have really been a fire-breathing dragon. He saw no choice but to leave.

Atler felt the guard's hand on his elbow, and turned to see that the thug's other hand was on his gun. Obviously, it wouldn't do for him to make a scene. So he turned, in obedience to the guard's leading, and walked across the lobby, out the door, and onto the hot pavement, into the suffocating air and the burning midday sun, but he didn't need to begin perspiring — his nerves already had him drenched.

It struck him that he had lived through the wreck, and escaped to Mexico without a sign of nerves, but now, facing that *señorita*, and the agent on the phone, with the guard behind him, he had turned into a worthless bundle of short-circuited synapses. He wished he was back at his workstation, and he wished he'd never met Doug Burnside, for whom he had only contemptible thoughts. It wasn't hard for Atler to imagine Doug dressed in red with a pointed tail, pointed ears, and a pitchfork in hand, flames leaping about as he wickedly and mockingly laughed back at Atler.

At least I have a few hundred dollars cash — he remembered. I need a drink — he decided, but it wouldn't be at the hotel's bar — and where then? Instead of wasting his time in Acapulco, he should have gone to Geneva — though he doubted that it would have changed anything. They would still say he didn't have any money, and now, he really didn't have any money, and he was stuck. How could it have happened? He even had the original deposit certification — back home, for all the good it would do him here.

Atler walked past a young man on the corner who wanted to talk to him. It was something religious. Atler told him, "I'm too busy." The young man, who was also a tourist like Atler, gave him a small folded paper, written in English, and told him, "If you will read this, it will change your life. It will give you the answer you need. God loves you."

Atler stuffed it in his shirt pocket and marched on.

He told himself — I've got to get some money. I wonder if Norma would loan me any? But I shouldn't call her — her telephone could be bugged. Doug's people could trace my call. However, his need for cash changed his perspective, and he figured — No, I'm being paranoid. It's been six weeks. Doug's forgotten me by now.

Atler had trouble finding his way to the local office of TELEMEX. His search was complicated by language difficulties. He hadn't tried to learn any Spanish, since everyone at the hotel understood him, but here, in this pit — with dirty floors and whitewashed walls that looked like they needed paint (for they were smeared with black streaks from hands and bodies that had waited in endless lines) — he realized that a few phrases of the local language would serve him well. His frustration mounted with every second he lingered in the queue, and the phrases he began wishing he knew would have been those of a vulgar classification.

When he reached the window, he found himself unable to communicate. They told him to wait. Someone who could speak English would take his call, after lunch, or so he guessed.

He had found a space along the wall where he could lean, and he stood with his arms crossed. He felt himself out of place, and realized that he looked like a tourist — dressed in his shorts with a bright Bermuda shirt. The Mexicans, he noted, wore, for the most part, jeans and short-sleeve shirts. He felt the paper in his shirt pocket, against his chest, the one that the guy had given him back on the street. He pulled it out, and having absolutely nothing else to do, he started to read it.

He had heard the words before: Believe on the Lord Jesus Christ. Jesus saves! etc., etc., etc. Imagine, me, a religious freak! He wadded up the tract and crushed it, dropping it on the floor behind him. I don't need any Jesus. I need cash!

About then, he looked up and a couple walked in. They were tall, not a little, but really tall, and really blond — dressed in jeans. She had a simple white short-sleeve shirt blouse, and he wore a cream shirt with thin maroon stripes, running parallel, up and down. Atler debated if he should hide. It could have been Doug, and she looked like Doug, too. Mr. and Mrs. Doug — Atler thought, with a nervous snicker. Doug wasn't a funny subject. They seemed like they were getting their bearings, trying to figure out what to do. The tall guy carried a bundle that looked like a black garbage bag.

They seemed to know Spanish, since they read the signs, and fell into line. Maybe they're speaking English? — Atler questioned himself. But he couldn't tell for sure. He tried to move closer — within earshot. They were saying something about how uncomfortable the bus had been, and that it had been a long trip — a whole day — and sleeping on the boat had been easier than on the bus.

Atler decided to introduce himself — something that was out of character for him (a recluse and a non-people-person) — for they might be able to translate, and then he could get his call through. "Hello, I'm Atler Redclift," he said, and extended his hand towards Ashley.

"We're the...," and she hesitated, and then said, "Bakers. We just got married, and I must remember my new last name," a note of apology in her voice.

Atler, as usual, didn't care anything about them. If they were just married, or just sleeping together, it didn't make a bit of difference to him. "Mrs. Baker…," he began, "could you, or Mr. Baker," he said, glancing up at James, and seeing that indeed the man was everything Doug had been, and more. Frankly, Atler never liked looking upwards into someone eyes, although he had done it most of his life. Even Norma, when she put on high heels, was an inch taller than he was.

The woman seemed like she would be easier to approach, but since they were together, he would have to treat them as a unit, so he finished his sentence, "…please help me with a call? I need someone to translate for the operator."

"Sure," the man said in a voice that while in Atler's hearing had some of Doug's inflections, it was decidedly different. Friendly? Yes. This guy sounded friendly. Atler thought – I need a friend. The man's one word sounded so amiable and Atler looked up, despite himself.

Mr. Baker continued, "We'll be glad to help, if we can."

Atler thought – I wish they could help me. I wish someone could really help.

The line had shortened; it moved quickly. Arriving at the window, Mr. Baker helped him place a collect call to Norma. Atler began to step away, and Mr. Baker placed his own. Atler could have sworn that he heard the man say "Smith," not "Baker," but that wasn't any of his business.

They were allowed to move into the waiting area where there were about fifty chairs. The Bakers found two chairs together, not far from where Atler sat. The tall man sat the bundle down on the floor in front of him, where they all sat in silence. Atler was too busy thinking about his own problems to be talking.

A child, perhaps five years old, jumped out of his mother's arms, probably no longer able to hold still, not even another moment, and without looking, ran, tripping and falling over the Bakers' bag. Atler noticed a watch, and a few other odds and ends, and something that looked like it could be a uniform, bright purple, that came out of the top of the bag. Atler normally wouldn't have been concerned about helping, but the watch looked curious, and he jumped to pick it up.

Atler was quick of sight, being used to digesting entire screens full of complex information, and he saw the mysterious letters on the watch, "UDTC," and on the back plate he noted the words "Nova Mundi," which were engraved with a symbol that looked like the same one found on the dollar bill.

The big guy's hand was out, ready to recover the watch, in a flash. It startled Atler, who wondered how a person could move so quickly. He handed the watch back, and in doing so, the realization came to him that his "friends" were Nova Mundi people, like Doug, and he felt a sudden wave of nausea. He wondered — They're on a honeymoon in Acapulco? But if they're Nova Mundi, why are they calling from TELEMEX? Are they here looking for me?

Just then the loudspeaker called, "*Señor* Redclift," and told him which cabin to go to for his call. He didn't understand, but Ashley translated. He thought — Well if they're after me, why don't they just grab me? Why are they helping me? And he got up to take his call. He walked over to the cabin, pulled the door closed, and heard the operator. She repeated the number, but he didn't understand, so he said, "I speak English."

She answered with a heavy accent, and repeated the number, in English. He confirmed it, and the ringing tone came back. He heard Norma's voice, and said, "Norma…" But the operator blocked him. He heard her ask, "Collect call from Albert Redclift; will you accept the charges?"

Her accent is so bad — Atler thought — will Norma even understand her?

"No, tell him to pay!" she said.

Atler could hear the wrath in her voice, even through the distant connection. By the way she said no, Atler figured she had understood his name. Rejection's all I need — he lamented.

"*Señor* Redclift, will you pay for the call?" the operator asked.

Considering everything, and the fact that Nova Mundi people were sitting outside, he decided that it wasn't a good time to talk to her. He concluded — if she didn't want to take my call, she wouldn't loan me a dime. So he told the operator, "No, I'll cancel."

* * *

Pasadena, California

"REDCLIFT CALLED!" the operator in the Nova Mundi van yelled. They were parked less than a hundred yards from the Redclift home.

"Where did he call from?"

"Acapulco, Mexico."

"Do you have a local trace?"

"No need; the call's coming from the main trunk. Apparently he's at the phone company."

The SAO placed a call on his cellular, and from the other end came a response, "Yes."

"Redclift is in Acapulco, at the phone company's office, right now!"

The answer came, "Okay, call our people in Acapulco."

The operator in the van dialed the Acapulco office, which was a small operation, even smaller than Quito. At least it was a weekday and during regular office hours, someone would be there.

STERLING, who had just taken the call from the agents in charge of surveillance at Redclift's, called Doug Burnside into his office, and ordered him, "Get down there to Acapulco, now! Don't let that lowlife, Redclift, escape again. We can't have a time bomb like him running around! If he finds the right jerk of a journalist, they'll publish his story everywhere. Then we'll have to explain things away. It'll be easier if we eliminate him. And it's hard to tell what evidence he's got. He might have something in a safety deposit box, so don't finish him until he talks! It looks like cutting his funds and closing his Swiss bank account did the trick. We've forced his hand. It shouldn't be long until we have him."

"Yes, sir," answered Burnside, who handed Sterling a paper, and explained, "Redclift is using his credit cards."

"But he was over the limit?"

"It seems that he was able to get a few charges through before they put a clamp on his account."

"Well, this confirms that he's in Acapulco. We'll nail him."

* * *

Acapulco

ATLER WALKED OUT of the phone company as fast as his toothpick legs could carry him. He wished he had Doug's legs, even if he hated the thug. He didn't want to be around Mr. and Mrs. Doug any longer, even if they weren't looking for him. He knew he had to do something! But what?

Call the press. That was the only thing he could think of — Tell someone my story. Then, if they kill me, everyone will believe me — but I'll be dead! So what, if people believe! Anyway, I don't have a thing to prove my case. I don't have any evidence. They gave me all that money, and even opened the Swiss account for me. But it's gone. The bank doesn't have any record that I ever had a penny. Surely that points a finger? Yeah — he told himself — right at me. It proves nothing. And I'm still broke.

In his mind he had gone over everything many times. Tell them about the Viper — he would think. There must have been something that made it go off the road? They could find the evidence if they look, but Doug's probably cleaned it up — he answered himself. Try as he might, there was nothing, no way to prove his case. What little proof he had, the program code for VICE itself, with dates and notes from his conversations with Doug, were all back in the hotel, with his luggage, and ultimately it was his word against Doug's. Given the choice, who would people believe? Doug, no doubt! Atler knew. He had never found himself very high on the believability scale. People didn't trust him. Nobody would pay any attention to him; they never had.

Just call the press, anyhow — he told himself. They'll want to hear your story. Then you can find proof later. And Atler answered himself — Sure. They'll rush right out to hear the story of a missing scientist who claims to have programmed a virus that will make the coming

Internet that most people don't even know about yet into the world's largest and fastest supercomputer. He laughed to himself, and added his own sad commentary – I don't even believe it. If I didn't know better, I'd say it was impossible. And if someone did pay attention, Doug's people would have a dozen experts denying my story, and saying that it's nothing more than a hacker's fantasy.

He urgently walked the hot streets – nearly running into several people. He saw what looked like a cheaper place to stay, and went in to ask, but they still wanted eighty dollars a night! And there wasn't any air-conditioning, just ceiling fans. Worse, they barely spoke English.

He figured – I don't have anything to lose. I might as well try another fancy hotel and another credit card. Maybe the charge will slip through unnoticed like it did the last time. Down here, not all of the merchants have instant credit verification modems. I'll just find a hotel. Someone will take me.

* * *

It hadn't been long since Redclift left, moving past as though something had bitten him, without even waving bye or nodding – not that Ashley had expected him to – but he started acting strange after the incident with their bag. Concerning herself with the enigma, she asked James, "You think he recognized the watch?"

"Hard to say," he answered. "But he didn't look like anyone who would know anything about Nova Mundi."

"He acted so strange after he saw it."

About that time they heard a voice over the loudspeaker, "Mr. James Smith, *acérquese a la cabina ocho* – come to cabin eight."

Ashley thought – So much for our alias.

They moved into the cabin; there was room for both of them. James took the handset and the operator began to establish the connection.

Soon James was talking with Jack, and they went on for about ten minutes. This time James had something to write with. Jack told them to go to a missionary's house, there in town. He gave James the phone number, and the address. Jack had arranged to make a deposit for the

Smiths through the missionary's account. He asked James to please try to avoid thieves, because it was hard to come up with more money. James apologized for what had happened, explaining it in as few words as he could. Ashley reminded him to tell Jack about their new names. When they left the booth, they started to walk towards the exit. About then, a tall blond man, who was dressed in a dark suit, came into the office, as though he owned it.

Ashley held James, pulling him back, and said in a low voice, "That's Tim Parker." She knew him from an assignment. "He's a SAO."

The agent moved towards the line. They were behind him. James saw they could make the door, but what if there were *others* outside? He remembered a WC to their right, and pulled Ashley through the door into the men's room — not that he even bothered to notice if it were men's or women's. There was a gentleman standing at a urinal, who didn't even look around; he was occupied. They moved with stealth to the end of the room, where there was a window. James opened it, forcing its latch, and looked out. It was an empty alley. A small group of men at the far end were talking. However, at this point, it wouldn't matter much — as long as they weren't SAOs.

James lifted himself up and through. Ashley was only a split second behind. The man in the room never noticed.

They moved smoothly, and wouldn't have been seen, except for a small accident. When Ashley passed their bag through the window to James, it ripped open, and her mirror fell out. It crashed, resounding notoriously in the alley, and broke into more pieces than anyone would bother to count.

In testimony to their speed, James and Ashley were planted firmly on the ground by the time the men turned around and looked their way. Fortunately, at least for the moment, it didn't look as though they had just escaped from the phone company.

From the expressions, Ashley wondered what the men might be thinking, but she really didn't care, so long as she and James were gone before a SAO asked if they had seen any strangers. They moved, walking normally, towards them.

Coming to the street, now on the other side of the block from the phone company, the Smiths tried to eye around the corner inconspicuously. Their way seemed clear. There was a taxi stand just fifty feet away. Approaching, they got into one, and James gave the driver the address that Jack had given them. Pulling out, the driver started to turn back towards the phone office. James spoke quickly, and asked him to go around the other direction.

They didn't say much, for fear the driver might understand English. Ashley wondered, as she knew James did also — Why had Parker shown up at the phone company? Did it have anything to do with the incident with the Redclift man? Did it have anything to do with their presence? Had they been found so quickly?

JAMES DECIDED it could've been entirely coincidental. The telephone company is a public place, and Parker may have had some business there. He could have been checking up on most anything. James knew it would only play to the enemy's favor if they became paranoid. But he remembered the look on Parker's face. He had entered the office like he was after something, or someone, and he expected to find them.

For now, they seemed to have missed whatever it was. They would soon get their money and be on the move. Forget any honeymoon in Acapulco!

Arriving, James paid the fare, and the taxi drove away. They approached the house and rang the bell. A few moments later, a big dog bellowed out.

"What a dog!" James exclaimed, admiring the animal.

"He's beautiful."

It was a purebred German shepherd that looked like he wanted them for lunch and he looked like he had enhancements himself. The animal was powerful. His bark had the report of a small explosive — even the windows rattled, and seemed to shake the ground. He was so perfect. Was Rin-tin-tin as impeccable? Its golden hair crowned, and wove into his glossy black coat. It looked like, if they tried to enter, the beast would rip their limbs asunder with his powerful jaws, and a set of teeth that could have filled a dinosaur's mouth. James, even with bio-electromechanics for defense, knew he would think twice before provoking the elegant canine.

A voice answered over the communicator, "Hello."

James suddenly thought — Which of their names would Jack have given the missionary? Reasoning, he decided to try their old name, since the arrangements had been made before he last talked to Jack. James replied through the communicator, "Hello, we're the Smiths."

"Excuse me," the voice shouted back. It was impossible to hear over the sound of the shepherd's fierce bark, booming without any respect for the conversation.

James answered again, trying to make himself heard.

No answer came.

He wondered if they had been rejected so quickly, until a tall man with light brown hair — that receded slightly from his pleasant long face, and whose facial folds indicated he knew how to smile, and loved to laugh — came to the door. Wire-rim glasses covered his sparkling hazel-green eyes.

He calmed the shepherd, "Quiet! Puppy. Quiet! Be a good boy, Schubert."

Panting, slobbering big drops, Schubert looked like he was smiling. James wondered if the carnivore was smiling because he anticipated some good white flesh. It turned out that Schubert was a happy dog, and made quick friends — not even half the monster that he had imagined.

ASHLEY NOTICED the late-model four-wheel-drive Suburban in the driveway, dark blue. It looked like some of the ones they had *deeped* into Colombia for the cartel. Soon they were in the house, and Jerry introduced his lovely wife, Debby. Her face was full and oval, and her wavy dark brown hair was cut just above her shoulders. Her features were soft. They sat together on the couch. They make a beautiful couple — Ashley thought. Sitting with James in the love seat, in response to the Kirtlands' invitation, she wondered if perhaps they knew that their visitors were still on their honeymoon.

It didn't take long for the Kirtlands' four active children — ages ten, eight, seven, and one (girl, boy, boy, and girl) — to introduce themselves, or to be introduced.

JAMES WASN'T sure how to advance the conversation, without seeming rude, but he needed to find a way. The phone company incident was still fresh in his memory. After all the pleasantries were accomplished, he began to speak in a voice that he knew had an edge. He said, "I'm sorry, but we really need to keep moving."

"Please don't go so soon," Debby answered. "You're welcome to stay for dinner."

"Thank you so much, but we need to get back on the road," Ashley replied.

"Well, then, I suppose you've come for this." And having spoken, Jerry lifted a white envelope from his shirt pocket and handed it to James. "This is what Jack Kinderly talked to me about."

James nodded his head in recognition and said, "Thank you for helping us."

"No trouble," Jerry said. "I owe Jack more than I could ever pay, so a little favor — a small transfer of funds for travelers in need — is no problem at all." Then he offered, "Can I take you to the station to catch a bus?"

James declined, having decided that if there was something to the phone company incident, it wouldn't be long until a SAO found the taxi driver, and if that was the case, it might not be long until Agent Parker found his way to the Kirtlands' home. It would be better for them, and us, if we leave soon — he told himself. So he answered, "No. Thank you for the offer, but we can take a bus."

"You don't need to. I'll be glad to take you," he offered once more.

"Thanks, but we can take a bus."

JERRY STARTED to insist, but Debby felt that he should respect their wishes — they had their reasons. She touched his arm. He looked into her eyes, and she knew he got the message. "Then … if you must leave … let's pray before you go." When they were ready, he led, "...Father, we declare that every unseen power of evil that could keep the Smiths from reaching their destination be bound in the name of Jesus — that they have traveling mercy, and that the eyes of harm be blinded, in the name of Jesus."

IN THAT MOMENT, when Jerry prayed for the eyes of harm to be blinded, an image came to James and Ashley, each in their own way, of the blind Skotoi. They both hoped that, indeed, darkness would be unable to see them during the remainder of their trip.

When Jerry finished, James said, "Thanks for the prayer."

The Kirtlands told them how to get to the bus stop, and the Smiths left.

Chapter 17

REJECT

To be shelterless and alone in the open country, hearing the wind moan and watching for day through the whole long weary night; to listen to the falling rain, and crouch for warmth beneath the lee of some old barn or rick, or in the hollow of a tree; are dismal things — but not so dismal as the wandering up and down where shelter is, and beds and sleepers are by thousands; a house-less rejected creature.

— Charles Dickens

February 28 — That same day — Novus Ordo and New York

It shivered, and then the holographic image froze — Stonefell's replica couldn't quite keep up. After its hesitation, it jumped forward as Novus Ordo's quantum computer labored to correct the momentary overload on its resources.

Weller, seeing that such glitches were becoming more frequent, thought — We need more processing power. It seems like there's never enough. Will we ever have enough to run a whole fleet of DEEPs and keep everything else running, while presenting Therion too? He knew they would, but it wasn't coming together as quickly as any of them wished, and that was precisely the reason for the high-level meeting he was having with Stonefell.

"Okay," Weller answered, accepting Stonefell's position. "I understand your concern. We are going through a critical time. We've lost the USSR. Our computers have to be upgraded to a new generation, and that's expensive. We have to stock Novus Iridium with millions of improved cashless point-of-sale systems to prepare for Therion's next window. We need the cash flow, and we can't afford to let the Colombian cartel fall apart. And there's the Middle East and OPEC! Africa's a never-ending problem — and Asia too! It's a big world. I appreciate what you're saying, but you know that finding Smith and Brown is a priority too."

"Hans," Stonefell spoke in a patriarchal vein, which got under the boy's skin, "I understand. You see it's important to find Smith and Brown. You want to send a message to the rest of Alpha Force: that they won't find life outside of the New Order. That's understandable. But right now, as you can see, we have to concentrate our resources on much greater projects. If we let Smith and Brown play house for a while, it won't hurt us if, indeed, they're together as you theorize. They'll make some mistake, and then we'll get them. Time is on our side. They can't hide forever, and when we have our new equipment, we'll bring the whole world on line. It was your idea, Hans. You should be proud of it. Only a genius like you could have come up with such a masterful plot: letting people buy computers as easily as groceries. We could've kept the technology hidden, but this way we don't even have to pay for it. Now they're all linking together through the new Internet. We'll have access to every home, every business, big and small, and be able to combine the world's processing power for our own ends. We can rob a few... 'cycles,' that's what you call it?" Stonefell asked, and Weller nodded. "You know, I'm not up on all of that cyber stuff. But like you explained, we'll be able to get all the computers in the world to work for us. Hans, you're the man who had the original idea. Dietrich would be proud of you. Imagine, linking all the world's computers together, and people won't even know their puny home machines are really part of a supercomputer that's working for us."

Indeed, that's one thing Hans did know. His dad would've been proud of him. And as much as he hated to confess it, Stonefell was right. He knew he should give up on the Smith-Brown search and stop squandering resources. Besides, they were AWOL and they knew it. They'd never have a happy moment, waiting their inevitable capture, infliction, and death. In a sense it was better. Let them live their hell, waiting to be found — what a life.

But I can't give up, not yet — he told himself. "Fine, Irving," Weller answered. (Being called by his first name bothered Stonefell about as much as it bothered Weller.) "I understand what you're telling me, but it seems like we're getting close to them. We're fairly certain they hired a fishing boat in Manta. When the owner gets back, we'll check him out. That shouldn't take many resources — maybe a whore. We should be able to keep the search up without making a big commitment. We've finished in Quito, for now. There were only dead ends. The only real leads we had have been *erased* and killed. I think, if we keep the search for Smith and Brown within our regular budget for daily SAO operations, we'll be fine."

Stonefell could tell that Hans was asking permission without asking. He would have loved to have heard Hans say, *"Please,* may we continue playing the game. We're having fun. We get to do abductions and use our toys." But Stonefell knew the word "please" wasn't in the brat's vocabulary. I'll just have to pretend I heard it — he told himself, and said, "Okay, Hans. Let's not argue over this point any longer. You *may* continue the search if it's within your regular budget. Unless you find a smoking PHENIX, or something really concrete, let's avoid mass SAO movements, especially out of Colombia. Your last operation cost us over a hundred million dollars. I know — that's not much. But it all adds up. Agreed?"

Hans wanted more, but he knew it wasn't time. His Internet was the greatest technological innovation in history. With it, the New Order would have all the processing power it needed and a universal presence throughout the world. Coupled with improvements in computers, Therion would be able to do anything. It was a simple idea. Therion wanted everyone to speak the same language, and Weller knew that one day they would. But the world's computers already spoke the same language — zeros and ones. In the right hands, that meant power! Therion would be content. While all the world's computers just sit most of the time, running, and waiting for people to do something, we can put them to work, and no one will have any idea that their computer has been working for us. They'll be ours — Weller proudly pondered.

"Okay," Weller answered, "I'll accept. I've already sent the SAOs back to Colombia. I'll keep the search within our regular budget, until I find a 'smoking PHENIX' as you say."

"Good choice, Hans," Stonefell said as he thought — He's really a good boy.

* * *

Acapulco

"**PARKER**," Burnside greeted as he got off one of the Nova Mundi Foundation's private jets.

"Burnside," he answered, "good to have you here."

"What have we got?"

"Redclift will be easy to pick up. He's had problems with his account at the hotel and they've rejected his credit card. The fool is leaving a trail of unending charge rejections at other hotels. All his credit cards are maxed out."

"Yes, it was a good idea to have his funds eliminated. We should have done it sooner, but closing someone's Swiss bank account isn't easy — even for us. Without his Swiss money, he's in bad shape," Doug noted, knowing that Atler's financial condition was one of the reasons they had chosen him in the beginning, since he would likely have done anything for some money.

"We've tapped into all the computers for his different credit cards and we're ready. We could've had him earlier, but I was alone. Now, with you and the reinforcements, we can grab him. Should we terminate him at the earliest convenience?"

"No," Doug answered. "I wish we could, but we have to be sure he hasn't left any time bombs — documents in safety deposit boxes and such. But I doubt it. He's so stupid."

"You know him?" Parker asked.

"I managed him at JPL."

Parker almost said, "Oh! The one who got away. He was yours?" But he figured his comment wouldn't flatter the senior agent.

Seeing the look on Doug's face, Burnside said, "I know. The story's gotten around. I let him walk, but this time he'll pay."

"Yes, sir," Parker answered.

* * *

ATLER HAD FOUND a restaurant with a bar. He would have to use some cash. He was "famished" after walking so much. A few drinks would fix things. And they did (or so he felt). They worked quickly on his empty stomach.

He had been rejected at three hotels, after being kicked out of the first one that morning. He was beginning to feel like there was a big stamp written in red ink across his forehead which said — in capital letters — "REJECT."

Atler didn't want to give up his lifestyle. He liked it. A little crack, some Acapulco gold, but not too much; after all, he wasn't a dopehead. He liked girls, now and then, too. Everything in moderation — he laughed. But he wanted his air-conditioning, and his hot bath too. Curse Doug! Atler wished he had his Viper and told himself — I've got a right to comfortable living. I'm a Ph.D., a computer scientist.

There was one more really good hotel in town, and Atler wasn't *really* drunk, yet, so he decided to try one more time to beat the rejecters. He had to take a taxi; it was too far to walk. It was a beautiful place; had everything — beach and pool — it was fine. He walked up to the main desk, like he owned the hotel.

The *señorita* took the first card and slid it through the verification slot.

Maybe it's like pinball: Shoot and then see what happens — takes a while. Thirty seconds? And BUZZ! The big difference was that with a pinball machine, at least you could shake it, and maybe coax the steely into a slot, but that was in the old days. Now they're computerized, like the credit verification system. Once the ball's rolling, you can't do a thing, just wait.

It didn't take long: BUZZ! REJECT! The rejecters were winning. Score: 5 to Atler's 0.

The *señorita* said, "Sorry, *Señor* Redclift, but you need to resolve your problem with the issuer. Do you have another card?"

Atler hadn't tried more than one card at the other places. This place was his last hope. He gave her another, certain that the rejection buzzer would sound. But what the heck!

* * *

PARKER WATCHED as the data flowed in. "He's at the Reina del Mar!"

"Let's go!" Burnside ordered the driver of Nova Mundi's black limo, which had been driven down from Mexico City earlier in the day. It had some special equipment (like a high-speed satellite link to Novus Ordo's quantum computer). "Look," he said, directing himself to Parker, "can you get Redclift's credit approved? That way, the next time he tries to charge, he'll be able to stay, and we won't have to play cat and mouse. We'll be able to get him at our leisure."

"Good idea," Parker answered. "I'm on it."

Nova Mundi's quantum computer meddled, in one way or another, with most of the world's information flow. Soon, Parker had all of Atler's credit lines kicked up an extra five thousand dollars.

* * *

IT WAS TAKING longer than usual. Was the ball getting a few favorable bounces? — Atler wondered. Two minutes had gone by, and the verification system still hadn't spit back a rejection. Why's it taking so long? — he wondered. Three minutes? (He hadn't timed it.) Maybe it's the alcohol? But it sure seems to be taking a long time.

Then the *señorita* stepped over to a supervisor. It seemed like she must have asked, "Isn't it taking too long?"

The supervisor walked over to look at the verification device. Written on its small window was the word, *"PROCESANDO."* She picked up a handset and dialed a number. Atler knew she was asking for a supervisor at the card company. About the time the hotel supervisor got through to the other one, the verification modem wrote, *"APROBADO* – APPROVED."

The supervisor spoke to the credit people. They told her, "Sorry it took so long for approval. Mr. Redclift had reached his credit limit, but his line was just increased by five thousand." The hotel supervisor walked over to personally give Mr. Redclift the good news.

"Señor Redclift, the credit card company just increased your line by five thousand dollars. Congratulations. Do you have any luggage?" she asked.

"No," Atler said, barely able to keep the excitement out of his voice. Thinking – I beat the rejecters! I won! He was drunk enough to ignore his suspicions. He thought – an increase of five thousand? Wow! Something's really wrong with their computer. Maybe I could get a new job there. I was thinking of just getting one charge through. I didn't imagine any increase in my limit.

He was shown to his room. He flipped on the TV. This is a great place – Atler thought. This is better than where I was. I can go back over there and fix my bill, and get my stuff. I'll do it tomorrow. On the screen, direct from the satellite, smut appeared. His eyes fixed, and he thought – Girls will like it here. I'm not a reject anymore.

His good fortune seemed too good to be true. He knew it was. But for now, ignoring that fact was easier than trying to figure it out.

* * *

"Redclift's charge was approved at the *Reina del Mar*," Parker confirmed.

"We have plenty of time, now," Doug summarized and added, "He knows me. I think he must have overheard me phoning in his extermination report. That's why he ran. So we need to send in someone to find out if he's got anything hidden away, that we need to know about."

"Does he like boys or girls?" Parker asked.

"Girls," Doug confirmed, and ordered, "find out who we have. See if there are any SAOs in Mexico City we can get down here. One who will light his fire."

"Yeah," replied Parker, "one to light his fire, and burn him down."

"Send the jet. I want her here. ASAP," Doug commanded.

* * *

Road to Mexico City

ANOTHER LONG BUS RIDE! But James had decided to break it up into shorter trips. Their immediate destination was Mexico City. There he would change bus companies, and anything else he could, to make their trail harder to follow. They needed to think of different aliases for every change, so their tactic would be more effective. The problem was that they always asked for identification. So far, the Smiths had been able to bluff their way through. "We were robbed," they'd say, which wasn't a lie. And in a bus station they could get by with such an excuse, since few ticket agents really cared to see passports or identification cards.

But James was already thinking about the border. There, things wouldn't be as simple. He didn't have any reference points from which to develop a strategy. He'd never had to cross a border the old-fashioned way. DEEPs didn't have border problems. James figured — We'll have to cross that bridge when we get there. (And, if his memory of geography served him correctly, they would, indeed, cross a bridge.)

It had been a long day. Sleep was the one thing the Smiths really needed. However, the seats were inordinately cramped (for their measure).

Seeing the garbage bags had more miles than their combined layered skins had been able to tolerate — and after the phone company incident — James bought a couple of travel bags. Their few possessions fit well, with some space left over. James also bought Ashley another mirror, which he used too.

When circumstances permitted, they took turns reading the New Testament. Together they discovered the truth of the Word. Obviously, this wasn't like any other book they had ever read. It certainly wasn't the Secret Doctrine. But for now, partially because of their honeymoon status, and partially because there wasn't any other way for them to fit in the small space they were allotted, they slept tangled together

* * *

The next day — Acapulco

NICE BED — Atler complimented, waking fresh. He'd slept like a baby. Permanent vacation. What a life! And I beat the rejecters! — he chuckled aloud — though still wondering how. One thing was to get one charge passed, but it was quite another to have your credit line raised five big ones. He couldn't think of any good explanations and asked himself — It certainly couldn't have anything to do with Doug's people, could it? Maybe I should move on? Go somewhere else?

But he would face his problem later. For now, he realized that he was actually hungry. Breakfast sounds good. Shall I call for room service? No, I think I'll get out and look around some. Then I'll get my "luggage" — he told himself, pronouncing the single word "luggage" aloud while mocking the accent of the *señorita*. She'll be surprised to see me. Probably thinks I'll never be back. I should take her a flower. Maybe she'd like to try a bed at the competition's place with a former client who's not a reject. "Buzzzzzzzzzz!" he verbalized. Maybe a rose or two for the *"señorita,"* which he also pronounced aloud. His *gringo's* accent so ruined the word that it could have sounded, to the Spanish ear, like he'd said, *"sin yodita,"* which really means, "without iodine." Yes, for the *"sin no dita,* a hundred-dollar bill," he said to the mirror — brutalizing the Spanish even further.

* * *

SAO MIRIAM SAVEDA nearly rolled on the floor. She hadn't had this good of a laugh in a long time. The first thing that came over the Redclift bug was the single word "luggage," but pronounced in a way that said: The man's a nutcase. Then, "Buzzzzzzzzzz!" as if to confirm her diagnosis.

"He's pretending he's a bee?" Parker asked with a chuckle.

A moment later Redclift said, *"Sin yodita."* It took the agents a while to figure it out. Parker got it first: "He's trying to say *señorita.*"

"GOOD," DOUG SAID, "we've got just exactly that." And he looked at the very *señorita* Miriam. She was just the one for the job. Even Doug, who considered himself too disciplined for such indulgence, had trouble taking his eyes away from her — hemline about as high above her knees as the neckline of her black body-hugging satin dress was low — and all her other lines! Let me count them — he chuckled to himself — especially the ones best drawn with a French curve. She's perfect — he admired. And not just the lines — but every item: seductive long black teased hair, green eyes and tantalizing smooth face, polished green toenails, five feet eight inches (a bit short for a SAO, but you need 'em in all flavors and sizes), a little tall for Atler. She's a perfectly designed machine (implants included).

But Doug knew that this particular machine could take a man, rip open his heart and make him reveal his deepest secret, and then tread the poor devil to a pulp. The fool would enjoy every moment of it, and even go back asking for more, if given the chance. However, Miriam's fame was to devour her prey the first time. Rarely did they get a second chance, and never a third.

A physicist and a SAO, Doug couldn't, and wouldn't, indulge himself in Miriam's curves, but Atler would. That was the important thing. She's too good for that slob — Doug thought — he'll probably faint.

WHEN, the loudspeaker repeated, *"Sin no dita,"* Miriam couldn't take it! She convulsed in mocking laugher. She already hated the jerk. Nothing new: That's the only kind they gave her — jerks. Perhaps it made the job easier. It didn't hurt to hate the victim. She thought — *Sin no dita,* yeah, buddy. That's you when I'm finished: without a thing. I'll have it all.

Chapter 18

Border Crossing

"Do not let your left hand know what your right hand is doing."

— Jesus Christ

Two days later — Reynosa, Mexico

Five buses and five aliases later, and it felt like that many days had past, but it had only been two. The Smiths arrived with the sunrise. "Reynosa, here we are," Ashley announced.

Why James had chosen this point for crossing — not even he knew for sure. It wasn't too far from Matamoros, and if nothing else, he thought — We can jump in the Gulf and swim a hundred miles, or so, north to Corpus Christi. (He was at least half serious, though not much more.)

During one of the bus rides, James had gotten into an interesting discussion with another passenger on the subject of illegal border crossings. It was all hypothetical, since the honeymooners (alias Michaels for that particular ride) were true *gringos*, as the Mexican called them, and he, the Mexican, was above illegal crossings — having all of his documents is order.

In the discussion, they dealt with specific options: falsification of papers, tunnels, and swimming, getting a "ride," even walking across. The gentleman mentioned that the United States was a nation quick to grant asylum to refugees who were being persecuted for their religious beliefs.

James figured — Now that we're Christians, we fall into that category. We'd be terminated if we returned to our own "nation." However, he knew that simply walking up, and asking for asylum, might get them to the other side, but it would also get Nova Mundi's attention.

James had no idea what they should do, but they'd reached their last stop. Fresh morning air, desert dry and desert warm, met them. It was most refreshing after being locked in the bus atmosphere that had gone flat hours ago. They began to walk, arm-in-arm, aimlessly — sort of. Really, James did have an objective: to learn as much about the place as possible. He contemplated the need to find somewhere to stay for a night, or two.

"Isn't that *hermanos*?" Ashley asked, distantly hearing hands clapping, and a song of praise in the distance.

James heard it too. They began to follow the sound, and after a few blocks, they stood at the entrance to a church. From the music, and from the joy on the faces, they knew they'd found *hermanos*.

Being a border town, it wasn't unusual to see, or even have, *gringos* in church. James and Ashley weren't your typical *gringos,* though. He was a little too tall and handsome, and she was the same. So, when they entered the concrete structure, painted white, there wasn't any shortage of eyes watching them. There were perhaps three hundred people in their Sunday best. In that respect (lack of Sunday best) the Smiths were a bit out of place, but they (the Smiths) didn't notice. Those who eyed them weren't looking at their clothing. Such a nice *gringo* couple — thought one of the older *hermanas*. They look like newlyweds.

With all their traveling, the Smiths had forgotten it was Sunday morning.

The service didn't seem long (they had missed part of it). When it was over, a man, whose appearance showed he had a few years to his credit, with well-kept white hair — a good bit of it on his face, making a well-trimmed thick beard — approached them. He wasn't short — six feet and inches. He was clearly a *gringo*, wearing a spotless white shirt, and dark pants. The gent walked up and presented himself without ado, "Earl Killian's the name. You folks?"

He caught James off guard, without time to think through their list of aliases. Besides, there was something about being in church — where they had just been worshiping God — that made all of the fear and every thought of the evil that pursued them disappear. Added to those elements, Earl's confidence, conveyed by his few words, made it impossible for James to answer with anything besides the truth, "James. I'm James, and this is my wife Ashley."

"Newlyweds! Don't tell me otherwise. I can spot 'em a mile away," Earl declared with a big smile that even his beard couldn't hide.

James and Ashley smiled, almost bashfully. Earl knew he'd pegged them right. He was an excellent judge of character, he would tell you himself. He could see it in a person's face. And, yes, he had a habit of being right.

"And to what do we owe this fine honor?" he asked.

"Oh," Ashley offered, "we're just passing through."

"My," Earl began, drawing out the word with admiration. "Isn't she sweet," he said, giving James a slap on the shoulder, "Boy, you've got yourself a real prize. You better take care of her! Hear me?" Earl asked, "Ya all a-comin' or a-goin'?"

"Guess we're coming."

"Back home?" Earl questioned.

James had to think a moment. Home? "We really don't have one, yet," he answered.

"I mean the States."

"Oh! Right. The States," James agreed, shaking his head back and forth with negative inclination.

Earl took it to mean that James was a bit mixed up. The boy's been traveling, probably wore out — he told himself.

"Where's home a goin' a be?" Earl asked.

"Florida," James answered.

"You have an offer there?" Earl asked.

"We do," James affirmed, thinking of Pastor Jack's invitation.

"So, what are you fine folks doin' now? Plannin' on crossin' back over?"

"That's where we're headed," James answered.

"How'd you get here? Walk across?"

"ACTUALLY, WE SWAM," James said, glancing at Ashley with a "Laugh, honey" look, which she did — a giggle. Seeing Ashley giggle, Earl fell in love with her and, as if he had room on his face for a bigger smile, he managed to join Ashley.

"Well, would you like to come back across with me?" he offered generously.

James hesitated as he thought — Without papers? We can't do it so directly, can we?

He almost said no, but Earl saw he was uncertain and said, "Lovely lady, tell that man of yours to get movin'. I want to have you with me for Sunday dinner."

Ashley looked up at James, smiling, though she wasn't sure it was something to smile about, but she didn't want to change Earl's opinion of them, or his offer, if it was what they needed.

Seeing that it could look suspicious, not to take the man's offer, James answered, "Sounds great. We'd love to join you, Earl."

Earl led them to his long white Suburban, parked around the corner from the church.

James thought — Well, if they want papers, we'll just have to go back and try another way. It didn't occur to him they could take them prisoners for attempting an illegal entry.

Earl began to tell them about himself. It was very entertaining. The man had been around, and done many things. It turned out he liked building churches for people, and the church they had attended was one of several he had help make. He visited it often, since he lived in Brownsville (across the border from Reynosa).

It took only a few minutes, and they pulled through the Mexican immigration, right across the bridge. They approached United States Immigration. There were a dozen stalls — not too much traffic — and the cars were moving right through.

Earl knew all the guards since he crossed frequently. "We'll take Jake's stall," Earl indicated; it was number seven.

"Hello, Earl," greeted the tall, fiftyish, sandy-haired, hazel-eyed agent.

"Jake, my friend. Lot's of work?"

"Just the usual. Things are moving along. And where are you folks coming from today?"

"Church. Sunday you know," Earl answered.

"Do you have anything to declare — food, seeds, alcohol?"

"Nothing at all, just, Jesus is Lord!" Earl said with a smile.

"Everyone's a United States citizen?" Jake asked.

"Why, certainly," Earl confirmed.

Jake smiled. "Your friends?"

"Ashley and James," Earl answered.

"WHAT STATE?" Jake asked.

"Florida," Earl replied, Jake thinking — I wish he'd let them speak for themselves. Oh, well. Earl's a good man.

"Mr. and Mrs.?" Jake asked.

"Smith," James offered.

"Do you have anything to declare, Mr. and Mrs. Smith?"

"No."

"Have you been on a farm or ranch?"

"No."

"Are you bringing any alcoholic beverages, seeds, fruits, alcohol?"

Jake always thought that that question was an insult, but they had to ask. Earl had told Jake, "Do you think a man that can only declare Jesus would touch that slop?" so many times that Jake had it memorized. And Earl had it memorized too. Jake would answer, "I'm sorry, but I've got to ask the question; it's part of the job. Are you bringing any alcoholic beverages?" And then Earl would answer, "No, sir," to be courteous.

James answered, "No."

"Welcome home," offered Jake, dressed impeccably in his blue uniform, and signaled with his hand for them to pass on..

THEY ROLLED out onto the Texas highway.

"He didn't ask for our passports?" James asked.

"Yeah," Earl said, "they only ask suspicious people. You two look and sound as American as apple pie. Made in the USA." He pronounced each letter in USA with unmistakable pride.

Earl took them to a steak house. It was "mighty good food," as Earl said.

Then he took them home, for a spell. Beautiful home. He told them about the different churches he had helped build in the Philippines, Guyana, Bolivia, and Mexico. The Smiths didn't ask many questions, for fear he might start asking them things they would have trouble answering, so they just let him talk. Something he said made James think Earl had made some money from oil. Earl got choked up when he told them about his wife, who had passed on to be with the Lord the year before. He still missed her. He knew she was fine, "up there a praaaaaisin'," but things weren't so easy without her.

It started getting late. James and Ashley had managed to say little. When Earl talked, he took his time. No hurry. He could take a minute a word, James guessed, but he didn't sound slow. At least it made it easy for them to keep quiet.

"Maybe Ashley and I need to get back on the road," James said.

"You don't need to leave so soon! You just got here. Why don't you spend the night? I have a spiffy guest room. I insist. Ashley, you tell that man of yours to stay. It's too late. You won't get far, anyway."

James knew he was worn out. He couldn't remember the last really good night's sleep he'd had. He knew Ashley felt the same. And he figured — Nova Mundi can't trace us that quickly.

"Well, Earl," James began, "I guess we can't refuse your offer," he answered with a smile.

It was a pleasant time. Yes, pleasant. And the guest room! Earl hadn't lied. It looked like a honeymoon suite. He had a pool too, but the Smiths were too tired to be finding ways to use more energy, and Earl could tell. They needed to rest. After a light snack, some odds and ends, Earl sent them off to bed.

Chapter 19

Loser of the Month

ALL TH' WORLD loves a good loser.

— Kin Hubbard

March 3 — That same day — Acapulco

"HERE, TAKE THE SLOB," Miriam ordered with disgust as she walked away. Her smooth hip and body motions magnetized Atler's eyes. He stared after her in disbelief.

Doug grabbed Atler's arm, "Let's get this over with," he exacted, jerking Atler out of the bed, and commanding him to dress — something Atler could barely do. Anxiety severely set itself upon him. This was worse than losing the Viper — and to happen now! — he thought — just when I was ready to marry Lady Luck herself. This is the pits! He knew he would've cried if they'd given him time.

The limousine was around in front of the hotel, and they marched him out. Miriam led the way, and the SAOs, escorting Atler, followed, like ducklings after their mother.

Inside the limo Doug commented, "Good job, Miriam."

"Redclift? That [expletive deleted]. He was too easy," she derided, as she looked into her prey's eyes with revulsion. Atler couldn't believe it! It was worse than any heartbreaker tragedy.

The limo started moving, and Doug began to inform Miriam, "Your next assignment..."

Atler reflected, thinking back over the events of the evening. He couldn't believe it! Only ten minutes ago he and Miriam had been planning marriage. She was the greatest thing that had ever happened to him. She was sweet and soft, loving and kind, warm and tender. I must be having a nightmare — he told himself. I'll wake up soon. Why, the things, the favors she did for me. I love her! I've told her everything; every secret I've got — Atler reflected. I even told her that Nova Mundi is after me, and I'm here in Acapulco, hiding. She listened, and made me feel like a man. She gave me self-confidence, and told me that I should go to the press and tell them my story. She said she believed in me, and the press would too. Then she asked me, "Do you have any proof?"

I told her the truth. "Not really," I said. "Just my notes and the virus program."

She asked, "But honey, Atler," and rolled her eyes with enticing charm, fluttering her eyelids, stroking my body. Oh! It was good, and she asked, "Didn't you keep some kind of proof? You know, hide something in a safety deposit box, or something, anything? Anything at all?"

I told her, "No."

"But, dear," and she caressed me some more, "nothing at all? Don't you have *something* to prove it was those Nova Mundi beasts?"

"No, nothing at all," I answered.

And she repeated, "Nothing at all," with such regard.

She looked at me with her bewitching green eyes. I was hypnotized. I still see her eyes. And I told her, "No, sweet thing. Nothing at all."

Then she pushed me away, jumped out of bed, laughed, and asked — with her back to me — *"Sin no dita?"*

"What language's that?" I asked her.

She pulled on her dress. I've never seen a woman who could dress herself so fast! And she said to the walls, "Come get the fool."

About then, Atler came out of his instant replay of the night's events. He saw Doug pass a picture to Miriam. It caught his eye. It showed a beautiful blond, and he recognized her.

Doug was explaining, directing himself to Miriam, "Your assignment is to proceed to Manta, Ecuador. The jet is waiting for you at the airport. They've given your new assignment an alpha priority. Ashley Brown, Alpha Force, is the subject. She's AWOL. They believe she was last seen in Manta. They want her alive. They need to find out what she's been doing, you know, the standard."

"Why are they calling me? It sounds like a job with a lot of footwork."

"I guess they think it requires your talents," he said, taking a fair look at her curves.

By now they were driving out of town through an abandoned area, headed for the airport. The limo came to a stop.

"Parker, is your PHENIX ready?"

"Sure, boss; you want the honor?"

Doug answered, "Yes. I'll take him. I started this. I better finish it."

Parker handed him a little black box. Something about the situation told Atler that whatever the PHENIX thing did, it wasn't good.

"What's a PHENIX?" Atler yelled, as Doug pushed him out the door of the limo, and kicked him about twelve feet. What Doug had begun in California, he would finish in Acapulco.

That hurt! He looked and saw Doug aiming the box at him — like a sci-fi movie. "Wait!" Atler yelled, "I've seen ..."

"Wait," — Doug mocked to himself, and silently pronounced — Yeah, jerk! He pressed the button and a concentrated blast of energy hit the loser. But hearing, "I've seen...," Doug released the button and the burn was cut short. Doug wondered what he'd seen, and walked over. He touched Atler's carotids. There was a pulse. Doug slapped him and shook him. "Wake up, you slob."

Atler's eyes came open in the dark of night. "What did you see?"

"The ... the…," he faded.

Doug slapped him again, "What?" he yelled at Atler.

"Uh," Atler weakly answered.

"We'll let you live if you tell us," Miriam said as she crouched beside him and softly stroked his cheek. But she knew he was living on borrowed time, though. The internal molecular disruption he'd suffered from the short blast would bring certain death, probably within minutes, if not seconds. At least he didn't know that fact, and maybe she could get him to talk.

Alter gulped for air.

She loosened his collar.

"Tell us, Atler," she invited seductively.

His eyes began to close.

"Atler!" Miriam shouted, slapping him gently, and then a bit harder. She yelled at him several times.

His eyes opened an instant more. "Atler, tell us," she pleaded, and touched her cheek to his, whispering in his ear, "tell us, honey."

"Uh ... ," he said as he faded.

Miriam shook him, "Come on, Atler!"

"She …," he slurred in a whisper, and then his diaphragm collapsed. The death rattle sounded like it could have been heard a mile away. Miriam tossed him down and stood with disgust.

The dead man's eyelids opened, and he stared towards the heaven he had rejected.

Doug stood, and then turned away. He walked back about three paces. Miriam moved too. He pulled out the PHENIX, aimed, and fired. A momentary flash, like a camera taking a picture, and the corpse disappeared — consumed by fire so intense that even the fire itself was burnt away. It was the kind of thing that had a real permanency about it. Nothing was left. Not even for the insurance people.

DOUG, PARKER, AND MIRIAM got back in the limousine with the sobriety of having attended a funeral. This wouldn't have been the case. Elimination of a worm like Atler was a good deed for humanity in general — so they considered — and though his passing wasn't worthy of celebration (he was such a disgusting vermin), he certainly wasn't worth the present solemnity. Indeed, the mood had nothing to do with the person of the deceased, but everything to with his last words.

None of them wanted to talk first. Doug, as the boss, at this point, knew he should say something, so he asked, "Did he say anything?"

Parker was ready and flipped on the recording, "I've seen ...," and there was a sound like a welding torch. It only lasted an instant.

"Who's he talking about?" Doug asked.

"Or what?" Parker noted.

"Or was he just trying to save his skin?" Miriam asked. "He was a nut case. He mourned his Viper as if it had been his only friend — "

"It was his *only* friend," Doug interjected.

Miriam continued, "And then he got on this thing of being a reject. But the way he said it; he was really into it. And he told me how they finally approved his credit card, after he'd been kicked out of the other hotel. He said he beat the rejecters at their game."

"That wasn't his luck. We did it for him," Parker mocked.

"He felt like he could beat us?" Doug asked.

"Yeah," Miriam confirmed. "He felt like one lucky stud. He said, 'Miriam, you're living proof that I'm the luckiest man alive,'" she quoted, ridiculing his every word, rolling her eyes as if she were quoting the *Journal of Losers*, the "Loser of the Month" column.

"Well, the world's a better place without him, so we don't need to worry about this anymore. The reject was just trying to save his life," Doug summarized.

Chapter 20

Haven Quest

In skating over thin ice our safety is in our speed.

— Ralph Waldo Emerson

March 4 — The next day — Brownsville, Texas

Earl nearly cried. Actually he did. When he got back in the Suburban, and drove off, leaving the bus station's parking lot, and them stopping a couple of blocks away. He let his tears stream, for a minute or two. I'd just as well drive 'em to Florida — he figured. I'm so lonely. Oh, my. Life is lonely without Linda. I've got nothing to do. It wouldn't be hard. They listened to me. Gave me someone to talk to. They probably could use some extra money, too. Newlyweds always need extra money.

Back in the lobby of the small bus station, Ashley said, "He was so kind."

"A kind man," James agreed, as they found a seat. "Okay, who are we now?" he asked in a low voice, near her ear.

"This is hard. Changing names all the time is work!" she exclaimed, keeping her voice low.

"Well? How about 'S'?" he submitted. "Just call me Sam. And, I'll call you..."

"Sandy," Ashley offered.

"Okay, Sandy. Now what's our last name?"

"Brown is common," Ashley offered.

"That's your name." But James knew it would do. "Very good. Sam and Sandy Brown. We must get to know them," James guided.

"They're returning to Florida," Ashley indicated.

"Orlando," James confirmed.

James stood to walk over to the ticket counter, and just about then, Earl came through the station door. His gait was a bit faster than usual. He called, "James!"

Forget the aliases — James decided. But he couldn't be mad at Earl. He had been so kind. He hadn't wanted to let them leave, and told them just to have the rest of their honeymoon right there at his house, which was an attractive offer.

The Smiths had thanked him, but they told him they really did need to move on to Florida. They had insisted, and he finally brought them to the bus station. But leaving him had been like getting away from Pepe. The main difference being, they could swim away from Pepe, but it didn't look like Earl was going to let them go so easily.

"Earl," James greeted, as he approached. "Everything okay?"

"Everything's fine, son. I just got to figurin'. But let's go over to the Mrs., so she can hear too."

There was something about this whole thing that made James nervous. He liked Earl, and the kind old man had helped them so much. Actually he had been like an angel sent from God, but now, James wasn't sure.

"James and Ashley," he began like he just had an idea for a new invention, "I was thinking, and I don't have much to do, I would love to give ya all a ride to Orlando! I'll pay the whole trip!"

"Uh…" James began, "uh…" he stuttered. "That's so kind of you, Earl, but we wouldn't want you to put yourself out. It's a long trip."

"No trouble. I enjoy travelin'. And you know the roads are so good here in the US of A, not like other countries I've been to." Earl put his characteristic emphasis on each letter of the abbreviation, as if it were the official name of the country.

"But Earl, don't you think it'll be a long trip back?" James tried to get him to give up.

"Ah! Not for me. Highways are fun. Ya all know, I've been drivin' since 1938! And I'm better now than ever."

"Earl, you're a fine man…" James began. Earl lowered his head, like he was feeling a bit ashamed.

"What's wrong, Earl?" Ashley asked, already feeling sorry.

"Oh. I know. I'm a fine man."

"But Earl? Why? What's wrong?" James asked.

"Well, you're goin' a tell me that I'm a fine man, and all, and then you're goin' a tell me that you best go in the bus."

James was flabbergasted. "Okay, let me talk to Ashley a minute."

"Okay," Earl answered, with a pinch of hope.

James turned, his back to Earl, putting his arm around Ashley, and stepping away a few feet. "What do we do?"

"I don't know, honey."

"If we go with him, we'll be leaving a big link for TerraNova to follow, right to our door."

"Yeah. And spending all that time with him, we'll have to tell him who we are; you know how it was with the Brooks."

"So, what do we do?" James asked again.

They both felt it at about the same time. Earl, from behind, put his hands on their shoulders. They turned as he said, "I'm sorry." He smiled, but it looked like he might be forcing it some. "You two are right. I'm just an old geezer tryin' to play a kid's game. Look. Let's just pray, and I'll leave ya all. Maybe you can write me, ya know. Maybe I can come visit sometime. Okay?"

James felt sorry for Earl. He sensed his loneliness. With a trace of remorse, James agreed, "Good idea. Let's pray. Go ahead, Earl."

It was a simple prayer and it didn't take long. When Earl finished, James knew he had made a mistake — not accepting his offer.

After a hearty, "Amen," Earl paused and said, "Well, folks, I better be lettin' you get your tickets."

"You mean we need tickets for your Suburban?" James asked with a smile.

"Changed your mind?" Earl asked, surprised.

"I believe so, Earl. I believe so," James affirmed.

* * *

Brownsville

EARL TOLD THEM about one exploit after another. They didn't need to worry much about saying anything. He did all the "talkin'." They doubled back so that Earl could leave word with the housekeeper, and pack a few things. Then he started to say something about, "I'll be takin' the Sm..."

James touched his arm, and said, "Excuse me, Earl, but we need to talk some, please."

"Go ahead, son."

"It's private," James said, trying to be polite, but speaking firmly.

"Okay," and Earl thought an instant, "let's go to my office." He led them around through the short hall.

"Earl," James interjected, knowing that if he didn't, he might never be able to tell the man, much less, get started on the trip. "I've got to tell you some things, and I need you to listen, because it could make you change your mind about helping us."

"I doubt that, but go ahead, son."

"Things in this world aren't what people think they are," James began.

Earl interrupted, "Amen. Ya ain't tellin' me nothin' new. I knew that."

"Ashley and I aren't what we appear. We aren't United States citizens."

"You mean you lied?" Earl asked, concerned.

"I don't remember. It seems like you did it for us," James said.

Earl laughed a spell.

"Well, you aren't Mexicans, so who are ya, where ya from?"

"Okay, Earl. Try to hold your questions for a few minutes, and I'll try to explain, but believe me, by the time it's done, you'll probably think it sounds like a lie."

Earl thought — I'm ready for a good story.

"Ashley and I are from Novus Ordo. It's a city underneath the sea, in the rock of the ocean floor, in the area known as the Bermuda Triangle…"

An hour later, James finished, "…Well, Earl, that's our story, and that's how we got here."

James paused for a moment.

"Finished?" Earl asked.

"I have," James answered.

"Mighty good story. Bet you could sell it. Okay, so lets get goin'. Oh! That's why you called me in here. We need to think up some alibis to tell the housekeeper, to throw off the TerraNova, or Nova Mundi people — whatever they are — if they come around."

"Right," James said, and then he thought for a moment, and asked, "You believe us?"

"Why wouldn't I, son. I can spot a liar a mile away," Earl spoke with a voice that sounded like he actually could see liars — as if they turned purple, or grew longer noses.

"Don't you want any proof?"

"Well, son, I don't reckon ya all got any, from what ya said. Besides, when we get to Orlando, and meet that Jack fellow, I'm sure he'll have something to say about all of this."

"But Earl, I do have some proof. Well, its not much. But everyone thinks it's proof."

"You mean that watch and the gadgets in your story? Naw. That won't prove anything by me. That tech-NO-logical stuff," and he pronounced it with lots of emphasis on the NO, implying that he probably didn't think it so "logical." "Why, that tech-NO-logical stuff," he repeated, "I don't know anything about it. Comb-P-U-ters, and all, just 'blow my mind,' like the kids say." He emphasized the "P" and the "U," pronouncing them separately. "Naw," he continued, "I believe you, son. You don't need to prove anything by me, but I would like to hear more. We'll have lots of time; drivin' back East on I-10. I'm sure those people in Florida are gettin' anxious to see ya all. Do you think you want to call this… Pastor? Jack, was that his name?"

"Right, Jack. Maybe when we're on the road, from a pay telephone, or something, but it would be better not to let his phone be traced to yours."

"Oh," Earl said, thoughtfully. "Well, we better get on the road."

They moved out of the office; the housekeeper was in the kitchen. Earl gave her some instructions, and finished, "Now, Juana, I want you to pay attention. Our guests, if anyone comes askin', and I don't care if he's the Pres-SI-dent of these here United States of America, don't tell 'em that you've seen 'em. Understand?" She shook her head reverentially.

"Remember, you've never seen 'em. And if anyone wants to know where I've gone, tell 'em he said somethin' about San Fran-SIS-co. Any questions?"

Juana understood perfectly.

By the time they had been on the road for an hour, Earl was still talking about some incident with police who wanted a payoff when he built a church in Bow-LIVE-e-i-a (as he said, pronouncing the letters e-i-a.)

Earl stopped speaking for a while. James and Ashley were tight together. Sunset, behind them, was a pleasing red, and before them, the long open road pushed into the veil of night.

"It's a lookin' like we need to be a findin' a place to stop — haven for the night." Earl said.

"Sound's like a good idea, Earl," Ashley confirmed, while wondering — Will our *haven quest* save us from Nova Mundi? They're probably closer than we think.

Chapter 21

Orlando

March 4 — That same day — Novus Ordo

WELLER'S SECRETARY had pulled in all of the border Immigration and Naturalization Service fax numbers from the database, and methodically her computer dialed each office along the Mexico-USA border. It was automatic and foolproof. The computer would keep trying until the fax went through.

Three pictures each — a full frontal, a close-up, and a sideview — of James Smith and Ashley Brown started appearing in INS offices from the Gulf of Mexico to the Pacific Ocean. Weller had ordered her to notify immigration authorities in the Americas just in case their AWOL Alpha troops were attempting a border crossing. Arbitrarily, the secretary started with the West coast and began to work eastward. It would take all night. As far as the offices along the border were concerned, the missing-person alert (high priority) came from Immigration and Naturalization in Washington, DC. As far as the INS in Washington knew, the faxes were being sent from their own office. That they came from under the Atlantic and not from Washington was of little consequence.

"Suspected terrorists" were two of the words written on the pictures' caption. Also written were the words "MAY BE CONSIDERED ARMED AND DANGEROUS."

* * *

Two days later — Orlando, Florida

JAMES ESTIMATED that they had traveled nearly a thousand miles. He guessed they could have made the trip in two days, but Earl had broken it into three. James got the idea that Earl wasn't in a hurry — that he was enjoying the trip. More than once James found himself puzzling over Earl and his motives. He had paid every single bill for the "fine sleepin' establishments" and for the restaurants, and everything else — including flowers for Ashley, which she had endeavored to keep fresh, much to James's lack of understanding. Why? They were already cut and destined to ruin.

Approaching Orlando, Earl asked, "Hadn't ya better be a callin' that Pastor Jack fellow?"

James agreed, and Earl pulled into a gasoline station to fill up while James went to a pay phone and called.

Jack was expecting the call. James had phoned the night after they started on the road from Texas. At times, Earl's ways annoyed James, but he still liked him. Earl always had something to say, and then some, about most everything. He would leave a healthy tip for waitresses, cashiers, and cleaning personnel, and would leave the money inside of a Gospel tract. His abundance of energy was extraordinary for an outer, and for a man of his age. James wondered if he ever breathed, he talked so much — without stopping. Earl, in James's estimation, was an outer religious fanatic, but he still found the elder gentleman to be knowledgeable and entertaining, even interesting, to listen to.

James was beginning to understand Earl's ways of expressing his feelings. For instance, to Earl, computers stunk. He said, "Them com-P-U-ters are destined to the promotion of world evil" and pronounced the "P" and the "U" distinctly, right in the middle of the word.

There were times when James almost told him to be quiet. Earl talked about the Bible hour after hour, and it was interesting, but some silence would have provided a pleasant change. Earl said he liked to talk about the Bible, "from Genesis to Revelation, and back again." He said that you could find Jesus on every page. It was mostly in respect for Ashley that James didn't tell Earl to change subjects, or to be silent. Ashley seemed to like what Earl had to say, and would ask him questions that James wouldn't have thought were relevant, but Earl always had an answer, and despite James's inclination to dismiss whatever he said, James always found himself listening carefully. The net effect was that he began to understand some things about Christianity that he had, until that moment, presumed didn't make any sense and weren't supposed to. Earl had made a convincing case that the crucifixion of Jesus wasn't fictitious, but rather a historical event, and that the resurrection was an absolute fact.

In particular, one of Earl's explanations stood out to James. John in his Gospel noted that the burial cloth had been folded up. If grave robbers had stolen Jesus' body, they wouldn't have bothered to fold up the burial cloth. Earl had a great deal more to say, and was capable of defending his religion. He repeatedly reminded them that Christianity was a matter of "heart belief." Hearing all of this made James wonder if he really had believed, as the missionaries said, or if his continuing skepticism indicated that he didn't have the "heart belief" that Earl talked about. He found himself wanting to believe, as Ashley seemingly did.

James also noted that Earl didn't seem to care that he and Ashley came from TerraNova. To the other outers, as soon as something from his former life came to light, there had been no other topic of conversation — TerraNova became the sole theme. But Earl was different. He didn't talk about it at all.

After James finished speaking with Jack, and had the instructions for reaching his place, they proceeded. His instructions were easily followed into his suburban neighborhood where houses were separated by large lawns and swimming pools and "little green fields with personality" (as Earl called them). Identifying the correct house, they pulled into Jack's long driveway.

Jack and Mercy met them at the door.

"My, James, look at you!" Jack welcomed. "Introduce me to your girlfriend!"

"Ashley, this is Jack and Mercy," James answered obediently.

"Girlfriend?" Earl asked, "Ain't she your wife, son?"

James answered resolutely, "She is my wife. Doesn't that mean she's my girlfriend too?"

Everyone laughed. James realized that he hadn't understood that outers make a distinction between "wife" and "girlfriend."

Mercy greeted Ashley, and the ladies hugged.

"When did you get married? Before you left Ecuador?" Jack asked.

"About two weeks ago, near Manta. Jon married us," James answered.

James noticed that Jack's expression grew solemn, but he wasn't sure why. "Jack," James said, motioning towards Earl, "meet Earl Killian. He brought us from Texas."

"Well, Earl, thanks for taking such good care of James and Ashley," Jack said.

"Why, pastor, seein' such a lovely couple, I just had to do my part to help 'em," Earl said, with a big smile.

"Care to join us, Earl? I think Mercy has lunch ready for everyone," Jack offered, and Mercy showed her approval with a big smile.

"Why, certainly. I'd be honored," Earl answered.

Not long after their initial exchanges about the trip and the weather, and having settled into couches in the living room, Jack asked, "Jim, you said Jon married you?"

"Of course. Why?" James asked, seeing heaviness come to Jack's expression again. "What's wrong?"

"Apparently, not long after they took you to Manta, on the following Monday morning, Jon woke to find Judy, dead, beside him, in bed."

James felt shocked. A moment of silence followed. "What did she die of?" James asked.

"Well, the coroner there, in Quito, said it was just a heart attack. They said the same thing here — sudden death syndrome."

"But she looked so healthy?" James said.

"She did," Jack agreed.

"There's something else," Jack added. "Every day since Judy's passing Jon has been getting progressively worse. At first, it seemed like he was taking her death hard, and he would get over it, but then, he started to act as if he had some mental illness. Now, it's gotten worse and reached the point that he only lies in bed, staring. He's in a coma."

"Coma?" James asked with disbelief.

"The doctors don't understand. They can't find any reason for it."

"Was there anything else?" James asked.

Before Jack had time to answer, Mercy called them to dinner. Although, at this point, James wasn't so sure he wanted to eat.

Jack paused the conversation long enough to bless the food, and added a note of prayer for Jon.

Ashley asked, "Was there anything else about the death?"

"Did anyone report anything strange?" James asked, probing.

"Like clocks a stoppin', " Earl added.

ALL EYES TURNED to Earl, who was innocently lifting a bite of steak to his mouth. Noticing that he had gotten everyone's attention, and not having sought it, he asked, "Well?" looking at the others with an expression that said, "Let's have it."

Mercy asked, "How did you know?"

And there was silence. Earl realized that he had inadvertently hit the nail on the head. "I didn't, Ma'am. I just said it to be a sayin'. I was thinkin' about them Naughty Moon-DIE-ers and their DEEP things. They always say that clocks stop around U-foes. And figurin' how those good missionaries knew our friends here," he said, while giving James and Ashley an admiring glance, "it just seemed to me that clocks could be stoppin'."

Jack began, "True, Earl. Jon said he'd been asleep since that Friday. All the clocks, and even a neighbor's, stopped at 1:30 Saturday morning. The jeweler didn't even have to change the battery in Jon's watch, though. Jon had gotten a new battery just a few weeks before, so the jeweler checked it. It was okay, so he slipped the same battery back into the watch and it started again. So does that mean a DEEP stopped the clocks?" Jack finished, and looked to James for an answer.

But Ashley answered, "DEEPs only stop electronic clocks and watches, but common watches, even ones with regular dials, are battery powered."

HEARING ASHLEY, James's thoughts returned to the conversation and he added, "A DEEP can stop anything that uses an electronic oscillator."

"What does that mean, son?" Earl asked. "You mean the DEEP things don't stop time?"

"Oh, no," Ashley explained, "their field can stop the crystal in a watch. That means it stops vibrating until it's reset, but they don't actually stop time." James caught her smirk. He knew it was in response to outer ignorance, and he knew that she had realized it wasn't appropriate, for she immediately changed to a solemn expression.

But Earl caught it, and said, "Ashley, Ashley. I'm just a country boy. Them DEEPs are really *deep*, no pun intended."

James began to explain, "Oscillatory cessation is a rare effect, but a DEEP can dampen the ether sufficiently to cause it."

"What language is that?" Earl interrupted.

"Sorry, Earl," James replied, and began again, "What I mean is that stopping a clock isn't something that happens frequently. It only happens if a DEEP's captain forgets to turn on field isolation. Generally, it should be on all the time, but a DEEP can achieve greater acceleration when it's off. Without it, a DEEP will stop electronic clocks, and some other things, if they're within range."

"What other things?" Jack asked.

"Well, a computer. Some control systems. Most anything that uses an oscillator, especially a crystal."

"A radio station?" Jack asked.

"Well, yeah, it could shut down a radio station, until they flipped the transmitter switch off and on. It could also stop a cellular phone call."

"Disrupt communication?" Jack asked.

"It could," James confirmed. "But that would be a gross mistake. If it's a clandestine operation, like abduction, you don't want people to know about it. You only stop the clocks when you want someone to know — or be afraid."

Ashley agreed, "If they wanted to intimidate and get information, then they'd stop the clocks to let people know that 'aliens' had visited."

"True," James answered. "But if they killed Judy…"

On that word, Mercy gasped for air. James stopped.

"I'm sorry," she said, "go ahead."

"No," James said, "I'm sorry. Forgive me."

"Please, go ahead, we've got to talk about it," Mercy encouraged. She then said, "Maybe we can move to the living room? It looks like everyone's eaten all they're going to. The subject doesn't lend itself to increased appetite or improved digestion."

After they moved, James said, "If they killed Judy, they wouldn't have wanted to stop the clocks. That would be hard to explain, and they wouldn't want to leave any evidence."

"But James, you know that mind monitors and mind intimidation, and everything they use when they do an interrogation can, in some cases, kill the subject," Ashley clarified.

"So, the *deepers* went to in-TERROR-gate the sweet lady and killed her by AX-so-dent?" Earl asked.

"Yes. I would guess so," James said, and continued, "and it's likely, too, since Jon's now in a coma. They probably tried to *erase* him, and someone was careless, and let it go too far."

"Will he die," Mercy asked.

"It's hard to say," Ashley said, solemnly. The two were sitting beside each other, with arms comforting one another. "He could remain in a coma for hours, days, or years, and then die, or snap out of it, but still be a mental vegetable, or he might even remember everything that happened, and be normal again."

"Which, I'm quite sure, would have the psycho people sayin', 'Poor man, tut, tut, tut. He was so fine. But now he's a talkin' about U-foes and green men. We'll just have to keep him locked up,' " Earl assessed.

"Gray men," Ashley said.

"Gray men?" Earl questioned, and then agreed, "Oh. Gray men. Yeah. They aren't green anymore. Aliens are gray now days."

"Is it certain that the Nova Mundi people did this to the Whittens?" Jack asked.

"I don't know," James said. "A lot of things don't make sense. Why did they abduct him? An abduction is a major step."

"So, you think this could have happened to Judy, naturally, as they've said, and it's just a coincidence that Jon's gone crazy," Jack said, with sarcastic intonation, and starting to show anger in his voice. Mercy, who was on the couch beside him, touched him gently. "Okay, I'll calm down," he said. He paused and twisted his neck to relieve tension, and continued, "And then the clocks stopped too, and all of this, just after they took you to Manta?"

"I guess not," James resigned, as if beaten, and feeling as if he was being blamed.

Earl questioned, "If them thugs went after the Whittens, and it's a lookin' that a way, what was it that gave them poor folk away? From what I hear, you two weren't there anymore. How did they know you had been there? And if they knew you had been there, why haven't they come here?"

IN ANSWER to Earl's question, a blaring horn when off in Ashley's mind. "It's my fault," Ashley began, speaking in a low voice. Her head sank shamefully into her hands; Mercy turned to comfort her. James rose and went to sit beside her, so that every seat on the couch was occupied, with husbands on the ends and ladies in the middle. "When Jon and Larry brought us up from Santo Domingo, they tried to get me to accept Jesus, but I just wouldn't. The next morning I left Jon and Judy's. I was going to turn myself in to Nova Mundi. I saw a plane land, so I walked to the airport and called Nova Mundi. An answering machine answered. Then I walked around the airport, and everyone saw me. When I realized it was Sunday, and that was the reason why Nova Mundi hadn't come to get me, I was mad, and started walking, without knowing where I was going. Since Jon and Judy lived near there, they saw me on their way home from church. They stopped to get me. And some … some, *person*," she said with a demeaning shrug, "started blowing a horn at Jon. It was just one continuous blast. There were people everywhere. They all saw me get into the Jeep. Nova Mundi could have traced it back to the Whittens. I thought about it at the time, but I was planning on going back to TerraNova, and if I did, the Whittens would have been eliminated anyway, so I didn't care."

Ashley stopped. There was silence for a time, until she began again. "After that," she added, as her voice started to choke, "the Whittens took me home and helped me pray to receive Jesus." Then she began to cry, outright. She thought of her conversion. She began to doubt. How could God have allowed Judy to be killed? How could God have allowed Jon, who had been so kind to her, to be *erased*. The price the innocent missionaries had paid was so great. They hadn't done anything wrong. Their only crime had been in knowing her. And now she asked herself if this would be the fate of all the outers who had known her, and her own fate as well. Wasn't God supposed to be greater than everyone and everything?

REALIZING THAT Judy's death was really murder and that Jon's sickness wasn't an accident, made Jack want to explode in anger. He controlled himself, but boiled on the inside. He knew that it couldn't have been any other way, though. They had done the right thing, and they weren't the first people to have been killed because they had done the right thing, but that realization didn't change his feeling of hurt and anger.

"I'm sorry," Ashley said, slowly and deeply.

"It's a terrible thing," Earl said. "A terrible thing to feel guilty for something like someone gettin' hurt. Ashley," he addressed, "you shouldn't feel guilty. God knows things better than we do. Judy's in Heaven."

"And I … I sent her there," Ashley sobbed.

"Don't say that," James ordered. "It's not your fault. I sent you to their home, knowing that you might go back to Nova Mundi. I should've known better. I knew how you had been conditioned, and how hard it would be for you to break away from Alpha Force. It was my fault for leaving you alone. I should've stayed with you."

"Oh, James," Ashley said, between gasps, "but if you would have been there, I might have killed you, just to be able to escape."

"Or I'd have killed you?"

"No, you wouldn't. I could tell that you were too outer. And I would have felt like I was doing the right thing by killing you. I almost killed Jon. He even told me to go ahead and do it. And then he prayed, and left it all up to God."

"It not your fault, Ashley," Jack spoke reassuringly. "And James, I believe God sent you to us, and you have a mission. It's not your fault. If anyone's at fault, I am. I should've told the Whittens to leave Ecuador once we realized that they might be in danger—."

My! That's shrill! — Mercy thought.

Earl whistled, as if he was out in a field, with two fingers for best effect. He had everyone's attention. "Okay, children" (for even Jack and Mercy were young enough to be his children), "it sounds to me like we're goin' a have a fight to see whose fault this cotton-pickin' mess is. Well, from what I'd a gather, it's all God's fault! Why, God could have stopped it! With His little pinkie He could have poked that evil DEEP right out of the sky. Flicked it like a fly." And Earl went through the motion, "flickin' " with arm stretched out, about waist high, making a show of how easy it would have been for God, and then flicking it with his little finger — dancing around after it, like it was a gnat. "So, just blame God, cause that's where we're a goin' a end up about an hour from now, after we've all blamed ourselves. So let's do it now, children. Everyone shake a fist! Look to Heaven, and say, 'God, it's your fault!' " Earl waited. Everyone's head was inclined.

"Well, how 'bout it? No one's a goin' accuse God?" Earl looked them all in the eyes, only to see tears.

"Okay, folks," Earl resumed, "it's a sad thing, all this that's a happened to those mighty fine Whitten people. But ya all know, blamin' ourselves, and each other, ain't a goin' a fix a single thing. From where I'm a standin', we've got a divinely a-POINT-ted mission, and I don't think any of us knows exactly what it is, yet, but we here people, in this room, we're goin' a be principals.

"And it ain't no game. Might cost our lives. It's cost some already. That Judy must have been a fine girl, but she weren't the first martyr, and I'll a promise ya all, she ain't goin' a be the last one."

On that note Earl paused, took a breath, and continued.

"So, folks, if you ain't ready to follow her to Glory, you better be a findin' someplace to hide your head in the sand. Won't do ya no good, though. Them TerraNova devils will git ya, anyhow. They'll just chop your head off, and leave it buried there, in the sand, and the rest of ya will make a fair feedin' for the vultures."

THIS GUY really has a way of saying things — Jack thought. But as crude as he is, it's the truth. We've engaged the enemy, and the enemy isn't going to offer a truce. And, as Earl said, the only one to be blamed for our predicament is God! Are we going to resist Him? Of course not! So we're in this thing to the glorious end. If that means seeing Jesus sooner than we planned, so be it.

"I think Earl has made his point," Jack began. "The Bible says our enemy isn't flesh and blood. But we all know that someday we might have to give our lives for our faith, especially James and Ashley, who received Jesus knowing full well that if their previous employers ever found them, they would be terminated. Jon and Judy also knew. They went to the mission field ready to give their lives to save the heathen. So let's face our situation, as Earl has exhorted.

"I think we should take a moment to repent of our shortsightedness. God has a great plan for us. I believe we all feel it. And then, we'll ask Him for supernatural strength and wisdom for our next step."

Earl inclined his head, and everyone followed. Jack began, praying, "Father in Heaven, I ask Your forgiveness. I've been so shortsighted. Sitting here, blaming others, and myself, when You, mighty God, have a great plan. I've been so quick to judge and to blame. Forgive me, Lord. Help us now. We pray that You will show us our next step. What do You want us to do? If You have a cup of martyrdom for us to drink, as Judy, Your servant did, then give us strength to do it for Your glory, that You would not be shamed by our deaths. And if it is within Your design, for us yet to live in peace, give us wisdom and strength, from above, for Your purpose.

"And Father, if it be within Your sovereign purpose, restore Jon. We ask that You would touch him and heal him. Thank You, in Jesus' sweet name."

There seemed to be more tears than tissues. The box that Mercy always kept in the living room (since, as pastors, they were accustomed to occasional tearful meetings) had been emptied. Mercy rushed to bring another box.

After noses were blown, and reddened eyes dried, smiles started coming back to faces.

JAMES COMMENTED, "I think it will be easy to know how successful Nova Mundi has been in tracing us from Ecuador. If they know we're here, or if they've suspected the Kinderlys at all, this place is bugged

— and they'll probably come through the door anytime. If they haven't gotten us by now, it's because they have no idea we're here. If they had been listening, they would have been here. They wouldn't wait to listen to all of this we've been talking about."

"That makes sense, son," Earl said. "But with that Whitten incident, I think we need to be takin' extra precautions. Ya all should decide on new names, and a new look."

"We've already given them new names," Jack said. "Like Revelation," he added in jest. "We rented the apartment in their new names, Steven and Sarah Jones."

"That's Ashley's new name?" James asked with a note of protest.

"And about half, of a half, of the other half, of the folk in these here United States of America. But don't you think them thugs should have traced us here through the Whittens' friends?" Earl asked, looking directly at Ashley, as if he knew she had the answer.

Ashley answered, "Probably not, unless they knew people would be talking about James and me. If they have to listen to something religious, they try, but only if they have to. They dislike everything that's religious. If they have some overriding reason, they'll listen. But they can't stand to listen to prayer or any talk about the Lord. They'll turn it off."

"Is that *anything* religious, or just Christian things?" Earl asked.

"They hate everything that's religious, unless it's New Age, or Hindu. They like some mystery religions too. If it's Islamic, it doesn't bother them too much, just a little, because they talk about the God of Abraham, but when it's Christian, especially fundamental, or Jewish, they turn it off. Listening to Judeo-Christian religious talk can make them feel physically sick, especially if they hear Jesus, Jehovah, or any invocation of deity. They can swear up a storm, but they never use the name of Jesus. In fact, if they're listening to nonreligious people, and they start swearing with Jesus' name, they might even switch them off for a while, until they get on with what they're saying. Before I got saved, that's the way I was. That's one of the reasons it was so hard for me to get saved. It was hard, just to get to the point I could hear the name of Jesus without shutting it out. I think the only reason I started paying attention was because, when I was at sea, and I knew I was going to die, and there was no other way out, I said, 'If there's a God, save me.' And He did, so it was hard for me to deny Him, even though I hadn't really used His name. I reached a point when I knew in my mind that I had to accept Him, but my conditioning kept me from it. When Jon and Judy risked their lives to help me, and they told the devils to leave me, in the name of Jesus, then things started to change."

"Your testimony is interesting," Jack said, directing himself to Ashley. "Do they teach you any reasons why you should hate Christians?"

"We were taught that Asmina, that's what we called Yahweh, is our enemy and that He has kept Therion from his 'glorious reign,' " Ashley noted with sarcasm. "There were 'incidents' they talked about. The one was the incident of Shinar…"

"Right," Jack interrupted. "I remember. James wrote me about all of that. So, it's really a spiritual matter, isn't it?" Jack asked. "I mean, their not wanting to hear Christian talk doesn't make human sense, does it?"

"Right," James noted. "It really doesn't make sense. When I received Christ, my whole outlook changed. I stopped hating Christians."

"Well, children, it sounds to me like we best be a prayin', since them thugs don't like to hear it," Earl said with a smile.

"Yes," Jack agreed. "It sounds like they're so full of demons they can't stand to hear a prayer."

"Oh, they'll listen if they think it'll do them any good, but unless they've got a good reason, they won't bother," James clarified.

"Anytime you're going to talk about something serious, that you don't want them to listen to, it won't hurt if you pray first," Ashley advised. "I remember one job we had, and the subject started praying, I ordered it shut off, right then."

James nodded his head, agreeing with Ashley.

"What's our next step, then?" James asked, deciding that they probably shouldn't stay at Jack's too long.

"Pray!" Earl said, which they did, Earl leading, and asking for guidance.

After prayer, Jack offered, "We have an apartment ready for you, as I said. It's a good distance from here. If Earl wants to stay the night, with you, and you all wish to have him, there's a guest room too. We have a meeting tonight with a member of our church who helped to pay for the expenses of your trip," Jack said, directing himself to James and Ashley. "So if you all want to go on to your apartment and get ready for this evening, I'll give you a little map I made."

* * *

Brownsville

"MACHINE NEEDS CLEANING," the technician informed.

Jake looked at the overworked beast. It had seen plenty of abuse. A fax machine in the INS office didn't have as high a status as an illegal immigrant. The technician had been called to clean and repair the hopeless contraption two weeks ago. He said, "I've been so busy. I'll need to take it back to the shop. I'll leave you another machine while I fix it."

Jake saw a fax coming through, just as the technician stepped out to get the replacement machine. Even from the other side of the room he could tell that it was little more than a black smear. Whatever Washington had sent, it wouldn't be legible. As he approached, to rip it off, he could tell it was a high-priority missing-person bulletin, but it looked like ink blotches that a shrink would use. Momentarily, he looked for recognizable trace, but it was useless. If he didn't already know the format for such documents, he wouldn't have even known what he was seeing. He laughed to himself — How do they expect us to find these people if they can't keep the fax machines clean? Any more budget cuts, and we might as well open the border and tell 'em to come on in — the water's fine.

Maybe it would be a good idea to call Washington and tell them to send the fax again — Jake considered. Novus Ordo would have gladly obliged him. But Jake didn't see the point in wasting the taxpayers money (even if Nova Mundi didn't have any trouble squandering it).

The chances of these people coming by right in Brownsville, along a thousand-mile border, and coming through his stall, and him recognizing them from a fax, and remembering it too, weren't good. Besides, he couldn't remember when he'd found anyone that way. And the board was already covered with such faxes, several deep.

Jake took one last look at the black splotch, and forthrightly wadded the inkblot, tossing it into file thirteen. About then, the technician came back through the door with another fax machine under his arm. Jake turned around to walk back to his stall.

At Novus Ordo, the fax reception confirmation tone came back from Brownsville and the computer, which had sent the fax, moved to the next number. The fact that it had printed out as nothing more than an inkblot wasn't one of the errors it checked. So far as Novus Ordo was concerned, Brownsville had the fax. (And indeed Brownsville had it, at the bottom of the wastepaper basket.)

The technician tried the new machine. It worked beautifully. Jake went to work, never to see the pictures of James Smith and Ashley Brown.

Chapter 22

The Meeting

NASA WILL EMBARGO the release of all imaging, and no live television will be provided. Selected prints of interesting features will be released within a week or two of acquisition. Further data will be released in several increments within about six months of acquisition. All transmissions from any of the outside Shuttle cameras will be electronically scrambled.

> — Excerpts from the new NASA policy for releasing pictures, implemented after the September 1991 live Shuttle transmission that showed what many considered to be UFO activity.

"EVIDENTLY, the Shuttle's cameras, on the night of September 15, 1991, showed what might be an active Star Wars weapons system. From the ballistics, we have concluded that possibly hyperdimensional technology is being employed. The video shows objects zooming into space at hundreds of thousands of miles an hour — accelerating in seconds. While we are unable to conclude with certainty that the origin of these devices is American, the video seems to provide plausible evidence of what is probably the most secret military program on Earth. It seems likely that it is also proof of a struggle inside NASA's bureaucracy.

The question must be asked, 'Who allowed it to be viewed on live worldwide television and why?' Could it be that the Americans are trying to scare us? While we concede that Star Wars technology is indeed very advanced, we are not convinced that they can do what this video possibly exhibits. Has the video been doctored to fool us into believing that the Americans are so progressed? Or must we look for another explanation. As disturbing as our analysis may prove, we are certain that the video clearly shows some type of UFO activity and does not show a urine dump or conform to any of the other 'explanations' being offered by NASA."

— Anonymous KGB military analyst

March 7 — That same day — Orlando, Florida

"Jack, you're so great!" Ashley complimented, wishing he were there to hear.

"The apartment is beautiful," James added, with admiration in his voice as he gazed at the living room's twelve-foot ceiling, plush carpet, and French doors that led out to a small, well-manicured garden.

"My, Jack's a treatin' ya all mighty fine," Earl complimented.

Earl found the guest room, and said, "Bein' we all's a goin' out on the town, I think I'll catch a wink, or two. This bed is a lookin' like it wants someone to keep it company."

It didn't take the Smiths long to see things the way Earl had — their bed, king sized — looked too inviting to avoid (even if it had more space than they needed). Kicking their shoes off, they found immediate comfort in the horizontal. They weren't sleepy, so conversation began.

"People have been so good to us," Ashley remarked.

"They sure have." James paused, and looked into her eyes, continuing, "I love you, Ashley."

"James," she said remorsefully. I'm not going to be able to call you that anymore." Then she declared, "Steven Jones!"

"Yes, my lovely Sarah Jones," James said, trying her new name, but it just didn't have the same flavor as Ashley. Not that there was anything wrong with Sarah, it was a good name, but Ashley had always been Ashley, and that wasn't going to change easily.

James pulled her close to himself, and cupped her cheeks, so mild in his hands, and his lips touched hers.

"He makes a better husband than a captain," she whispered to herself, eyes closing, his tender strength holding her close.

* * *

Six o'clock came and Jack, with Mercy, both dressed for the evening and right on time, as promised, pulled up to the apartment. The three were ready, and they all got into the Kinderlys red Pontiac.

"You look much better," Mercy observed.

"We had a great rest. The apartment is so beautiful. Thank you!" Ashley said wholeheartedly.

James joined Ashley, and added warm thanks of his own.

"Pastor Kinderly," Earl addressed, "ya all's a treatin' my children mighty fine. I thank ya."

Jack began, "We'll be having dinner with Robert and Jennifer Towley. Robert knows a lot. I've told him about you, James. He was responsible for much of your support while you were in Ecuador, and he's anxious to meet you."

James, somewhere in the back of his mind, remembered hearing about a Robert Towley, but he couldn't quite place it. It was when Jack said, "He worked with NASA," that James remembered, and asked, "You said he worked for NASA?"

"He was a Shuttle astronaut and became NASA's director, until President Bush asked him to step down. The press said there was 'no apparent reason.' He was the one who brought NASA back after the Challenger disaster."

"When did he resign?"

"When was it, Mercy?" Jack asked.

"Just a few months ago," she replied.

"You say his name is Robert Towley?" James questioned.

"Yes … Why? Do you know something?"

"Perhaps. Let's say that I may have heard his name."

"Well, that wouldn't be hard. Robert is well known."

"I hope them thugs aren't a watchin' him," Earl noted. "After what Ja—," he stopped after the syllable, and restarted, "After what Steven, my son, told me about how them thugs hate NASA."

Ashley looked alarmed, "Do you think they're watching him?" she asked, looking at James.

"I don't know? Something came across my desk about monitoring NASA frequencies before Ether Craft operations. It said there was a group of belligerents who permitted the worldwide transmission of a training exercise that showed a DEEP speeding into space. Towley was named as being responsible, and we were told to jam NASA channels until the problem was eliminated."

There was a hush in the car.

"Should we change plans?" Jack asked, directing himself to no one in particular, and before anyone had a chance to respond, he made an unexpected left turn.

"Where are you going, honey?" Mercy asked, with inquisitive voice.

"I'm not sure, but we should do something. If Robert is being watched, they might see James and Ashley."

"I guess they could be watching him, but now he's resigned, you said?" James asked.

"He resigned, that's true," Jack answered.

"So, there probably isn't much chance they're following him," James reasoned. "They have too many things to do without watching former bureaucrats."

Jack could have felt insulted, hearing his friend described as a bureaucrat.

"What can we do?" Mercy asked.

"We'll change plans?" Jack half affirmed, and half questioned.

"Maybe you can leave us somewhere else?" Ashley indicated.

"That's what I was thinking. I'll drop you all, and Mercy, by another restaurant."

"Then what?" Mercy examined, as if to say, "Why me?"

"If the 'thugs,' as Earl calls them, are following the Towleys, it will be better if I'm alone when I meet them."

"Then what?" Mercy asked, once more, hesitantly lifting her long auburn hair back over her shoulder, to one side.

"I'll pick up Robert and Jennifer and drive around some. If we're followed, I'll take them home. If I'm not with you by 8:00 PM, I'll call a friend from a pay phone and tell him to pick you up."

"But we shouldn't go back to the apartment," Ashley cautioned.

"Then what?" Jack asked.

"He can come in my Suburban. I'll leave the keys with you, Jack, and we can mosey back to Texas."

"Then, this is the plan. I'll drop you at the restaurant and see how things are with the Towleys. If it goes well, we'll be back. Otherwise, I'll send someone after you in Earl's car."

"I'd really like to stay. We just got here," Ashley uttered.

James heard the sincerity in her voice, and he wished the same. He didn't want to travel anymore. Not at this time.

Ashley added, "Being with you, Earl, is enjoyable. You've treated us well. And the Kinderlys too, have been so kind, and given us a beautiful apartment. I'd hate to leave."

Hearing Ashley, James remembered the four confining walls where he had spent much of his former life. He remembered Novus Ordo, Mars Base Aquarrian and DEEP units. They had all been the same – prisons.

"If we have to go back to Texas, I'll treat you well, my daughter. Couldn't let them thugs touch ya," Earl emphasized. "I think Pastor ought to pray, so we won't have to travel tonight. I certainly enjoy havin' my children with me, but I feel God wants you here with the pastor for a spell."

Momentarily, Jack found the restaurant he was looking for, and pulled into its parking lot. He then prayed briefly, but forcefully. He asked for victory over every power of evil that might try to harm them or keep them from their meeting that evening.

Earl, James, Ashley, and Mercy stepped out, and entered the restaurant. Jack pulled away to go on to meet the Kinderlys.

It was only about five minutes to the other restaurant. When Jack entered the dimly lit establishment, Robert saw him first and solicited, "Jack, where's your group?"

"Our man knows about your difficulties with NASA and he thought you might be under surveillance, so I decided to come alone."

The conservative gray suit he wore accented Robert's green eyes. Hearing Jack's words, he looked distressed. Jennifer, his wife, with Barbie doll features, from her pouring golden hair to her lush black heels, through soft blue eyes, saw her husband react, and asked, in a somber tone, "Honey? —"

Jack realized that she may not have known, and that Robert hadn't told her.

Robert swallowed, "It's all right, sweetheart," and paused, gathered himself, and resumed, "What are we going to do?"

"I left them elsewhere. I figure we can walk out, get in my car, and drive around. If someone is following, we'll see them. If that happens, I'll bring you back and you can go home. Otherwise we'll go ahead and have dinner at the other place."

"Sounds like you should have been a spy, Jack."

"Yeah. Sure," he answered with a nervous chuckle. "Okay, we'll walk out and get in my car, as if we had planned it that way."

Robert left a healthy tip on the still clean table and followed Jack. They wound their way to the door.

Pulling out of the parking lot, they watched closely. There was nothing to be seen, even if they'd known what they were actually looking for.

"Back when I first resigned, they followed me everywhere," Robert confessed.

"You didn't tell me," Jennifer complained distressfully.

"I didn't want to alarm you," Robert said, looking into her eyes. "They didn't do it for long, but since then, I've spotted them once, about a month ago."

"So they were following you?" Jack asked incredulously, as if a malefactor had just walked into an otherwise pleasant dream.

"Yeah … but it only confirmed my suspicions. I always thought they were with National Security until you told me that we have friends from the red planet. I knew that something was going on; I've seen it when I've been in space. I was convinced it was our own government, with hidden money, but your explanation, with the New Order, sounds much more convincing."

"I don't like the sound of this," Jennifer commented, her voice trembling. "It sounds like you're in danger."

"Sorry, honey. I didn't want you to be burdened, but now you know. I really don't think I'm in any danger. They removed me. That's what they wanted. If I'd stayed on, perhaps they would have been looking for ways to get rid of me. But now, I'm a nobody."

Having driven for ten minutes, Jack figured, "It looks like everything is clear. I've given them plenty of chances to show themselves." Jack had made several maneuvers that he hoped would have flushed out anyone trying to follow them.

"From what you told me, they think our friends are dead, so they wouldn't be looking for them."

"True, but there's been another incident. You know the Whittens?" Jack asked.

"The missionaries," Jennifer noted.

"Did you know that Judy died and her husband has gone into a coma after going crazy?"

"No. My, that's terrible. Why? Does it have something to do with us?" Jack asked.

"It seems it might have something to do with the New Order people looking for our people, so we need to be extra careful," Jack affirmed.

"They're powerful people with powerful interests," Robert added.

"You mean they may have killed Judy Whitten?" Jennifer asked. Her voice again trembled.

"It's possible." Jack really wanted to say, "They did," but he knew that it would be a little harsh for Jennifer, and maybe for Robert too.

"Well, it won't hurt to be cautious," Robert added.

"Right," Jack confirmed, "we've got to be cautious." And then thinking of some of his own pastoral teaching, he added, "But we can't let the enemy make us walk in fear."

THAT'S EASY for him to say — Jennifer thought. Just sweep it away with a teaching! We're talking about people dying and going crazy, and they're after my husband, and we aren't supposed to be walking in fear? But Jennifer knew, in her heart, Jack was right. It just wasn't an easy thing to do: be intrepid and face the facts at the same time.

At last they pulled into the other restaurant's parking lot, and soon the anxiously awaited meeting began. Robert Towley compared notes with the former Captain James H. Smith, with close observers Jack, Earl, and Sarah. (James and Ashley were introduced with their new names.)

They chose a darkened corner of the restaurant, in a position from which they could see anyone who might be trying to listen. Having exchanged greetings and other formalities, Jack asked Steven to start telling his story.

Jack knew that Steven had something that would speak more than words, and instructed, "Show him the watch."

Seeing it, Towley exclaimed, in a whisper, "Amazing!"

"You haven't even seen how it works," Jack responded.

"I don't have to. Just to touch it is to have a shroud pulled away."

Robert held it like a fine jewel, adjusting the angle of his head to see it better with his bifocals. He could tell that the plastic band wasn't plastic, and the back of the case that looked golden metallic, wasn't made of any metal he had seen. The tiny markings on the back plate came into his view as he turned the face around slowly. There it was: the unfinished Great Pyramid and the All-Seeing Eye, and then the incredible marking — 10000M, no less.

"Are you kidding; surely this watch can't take that kind of pressure?" he questioned.

"I assure you, Mr. Towley, it can, and more," Steven confirmed.

He looked Steven in the eyes. "Just call me Robert." Towley said.

Jennifer knew the man she had married was resolute and intuitive, a leader. His gray hair mixed into auburn. His features were friendly, but decisive, pleasantly balanced in his oval face. She loved him, and she could see that Steven respected him.

Steven went on to demonstrate. Robert exclaimed, "This is unbelievable!" He tried not to make a show.

Jennifer nudged him. Don't tell everyone in the restaurant! – she told him with a silent stare. And asked, deliberating to herself – What has Robert gotten himself into now? Maybe he's looking for thrills, since he can't ride into space anymore, piggybacking a burning bomb. God have mercy!

The elder gentleman said, "Why, it's better than a com-P-U-ter!"

Who's he? – Jennifer asked herself. Although she had been introduced, and it seemed like his name was Earl Killing or something, she couldn't see any barn doors in the well-lit restaurant with contemporary decor. The man seemed too country for the décor.

"You could tell the world a lot," Robert mused, looking artfully at Steven.

"That's the whole problem," Steven answered. "But most people wouldn't believe it, even if we told them, but we would get Nova Mundi's attention. They would hear, and find us."

"And them thugs won't be a figurin' how to give ya a happy birthday," observed the country gentleman.

While they talked about the Nova Mundi "thugs," Jennifer started a side conversation with Mercy in which she learned more about the Whittens, and she allowed her own fears to be fed, wishing all the time that Robert would just walk away from the whole conversation, but knowing that, being the man he was, he wouldn't. He was good at causes, especially the All-American kind. She knew he had to do it, and she would stand with him, and pray for him too, but she wished he would find a cause that wasn't so dangerous. A cause that didn't have thugs, and didn't chase you, and wasn't ready to exterminate you at its convenience.

Church was supposed to be a place of refuge, a place where you acquired strength for life. It wasn't supposed to be a place where the pastor introduced you to strange people whose problems threatened your existence. But Jennifer knew she really loved Pastor Jack and Mercy. She knew they were right. And she knew, as much as she hated it, she would support Robert, and he would do the right thing.

As much as she wanted to tune out, and let the men talk, she couldn't, and found herself listening to Steven when he said to her husband, "NASA is a problem for TerraNova. It's too open, and sometimes it gets an honest man, like you, Robert. When that happens, it jeopardizes their secrets."

"You mean, like the incident of the live pictures from the Shuttle?" Robert inquired.

"Exactly. You showed the whole world something that isn't supposed to exist."

"I suspected as much, but I never imagined that it was at the level you're saying. I thought that it had to do with Star Wars and the SDI projects. I thought they were using covert funds to make unimagined weapons, and that the video of the projectiles, UFOs, or whatever they were, had been made by secret government projects."

Robert continued, "For years I've heard of close encounters, UFOs, and such, from reliable sources, other astronauts for instance. Then we'd explain it away. I don't know how many times we've used 'urine dump' as an explanation for things that don't have reasonable explanations. If there had been a dump, then maybe that would suffice as the explanation. Problem was, there hadn't been any dump at all, of urine or anything else. But we didn't want to let the public know. It could've caused a panic, we reasoned. However, it reached a point, with so many things going on, that I decided we should show something to see if the government would take responsibility."

"Uncle Sam fess up? Don't you count on it. It's hard to get ol' Sam a talkin'. Tryin' to explain things, he might trip over his own coat tails," Earl observed.

There were a few chuckles. Jennifer even began to think she might learn to like the country gentleman.

"Robert, you need to know," Steven began earnestly, "Nova Mundi was responsible for the Challenger incident…"

Jennifer gasped, interrupting Steven. "But why?" she implored.

She saw that Steven's mood changed, and his exuberance was staid. He answered, "They wanted to slow down the space program. NASA was getting too much time in orbit, and starting to send people into space over whom TerraNova had no control."

"Like a school teacher?" Earl asked.

"Right," James answered.

With this revelation, Robert protested, "But, wasn't it because of cold O-rings?"

"Do you think that TerraNova would have just popped up on worldwide television in a flying saucer and blasted Challenger out of the sky? Not that they couldn't have done it that way."

"Of course not," Robert said.

"So TerraNova wanted to slow down NASA?"

"Right," Steven answered.

"Then Pre-SI-dent Reagan appointed you to put Humpty Dumpty back together again," Earl remarked, looking into Jack's eyes.

And Steven added, "You gave Nova Mundi a hard time, and that's why the president asked you to resign."

"You mean President Bush works with them?" Jack asked.

"No," Steven began, wanting to be careful to choose his words well, "Some presidents have had better relationships with TerraNova than others, but they all have served them, unwittingly, one way, or another."

"What did you mean that I gave them a hard time?" Robert asked.

"They figured it would have taken three or four times longer for NASA to get back into space, if they ever did," Sarah revealed.

"What does that do to their plan?"

"That, and everything else that's happened, delays it," Steven said. "Things have really changed. The Soviet Union shouldn't have fallen, but in the same month that our DEEP exploded, Gorbachev lost power. The Committee didn't like Yeltsin, so things aren't working the way they planned. And I don't understand how, but it seems it had something to do with the explosion of our DEEP. They should've picked up Sarah in the Pacific, but they didn't. So whatever was wrong with our Unit, it must have caused them to ground their other Ether Craft, and TerraNova lost control of the Soviet Union. Now, please don't think that Gorbachev served them knowingly. They are manipulators. Some people are easier to manipulate than others. Sometimes it has nothing to do with who's the easiest, or even with who's the president. Sometimes it's simply because TerraNova has things and people in place, and if a new leader suddenly takes over, and they haven't had time, or ways to influence the new one, their cause can be delayed."

"What do they do? Change plans when things go wrong?" Robert questioned.

"They do, and they have, many times. They teach that adaptability is an important part of their philosophy. They say it's like evolution. We must adapt."

"We're different. We Christians have a plan than never changes," Earl observed.

"They have a goal," Sarah qualified.

Robert looked at her for further explanation.

"They have a goal that stays the same even if the Plan adapts. They want to rule the world, and eliminate any person who keeps back the 'harmony of universal consciousness,' as they call it. They think they're going to carry mankind to the next level of evolution."

"Which is?"

"To become gods, without any need for bodies. But for that to happen, they say that Therion must reign for a thousand years and purify mankind, returning it to Aryan purity."

Jennifer listened in disbelief. Why Aryan? That was Hitler's fixation.

"Excuse me," Robert began with a telltale mock, shown by a facial movement, and he finished his question, "why Aryan?"

"Aryan is the purest form of the human species," James answered with matter-of-fact note.

Robert's consternation was apparent when he asked, "But why Aryan? Why don't they think that Asian or black, or whatever, is better? Why have they chosen blond, white-skinned, pale faces, like you two — no offense intended — why?"

"I don't know, I guess," Steven admitted with a hint of disgust. "That's the way we were trained in the Secret Doctrine."

"It's like your saying what Christians say," Robert surmised. "Christians say they believe because the Bible tells them so — so they believe. You're saying that the TerraNova people believe because the Secret Doctrine tells them so."

"I suppose you're right, to a certain extent. But it seems like it's more than that. It seems like the Skotoi blind them, in some way. Now that I'm away from them, living as an outer, I really can't make much sense of it myself. But you've got to admit, however hard it may be for people to believe something that is so absurd, Hitler found millions who would cheer his plans."

"Now, son," Earl began. "I'd say that tryin' to figure out them devils, and why they chose Aryan as better, would be like tryin' to figure out the devil himself. I'd say the devil likes strife, and likes havin' people tearin' at each other's throats. Maybe they like racism. Maybe that helps them keep everyone at war."

"I think you've got something there, Earl" Steven answered. "There wouldn't have been half the wars there have been if it weren't for Therion. I think it's a fact that over half the wars in history can be attributed to him. The Secret Doctrine teaches that a violent and sudden death releases a burst of what it calls 'consciousness energy.' The Cosmokrator believe they can control and channel this energy, and that it illuminates them. But an ordinary death won't provide this release. It must be violent and quick, and the deaths must be massive in number."

"Steven, wouldn't you say, then, that they're behind most forms of mass murder, like war and abortion, and any kind of human sacrifice?" Jack asked.

"Yes," he answered simply, lowering his head momentarily, but then raising it and gazing around to look at everyone. He then added, "Therion is a blood-thirsty god. He requires a constant expenditure of 'consciousness' to maintain his own."

"And don't these Cosmokrators, as you call them, see that one day Therion will demand their consciousness, too?" Jack asked.

"You know," Sarah offered, "I think they've already given their wills over to Therion, and his Skotoi, so I guess it really doesn't matter to them."

Jack began to summarize, "It looks like racism is a way of keeping human sacrifice alive by war and strife, and that the purpose of the sacrifice is for Therion to be 'illuminated.' Their Secret Doctrine says that Therion will make everyone Aryans, and that's why they bred you two as Aryans?"

"Right, Jack."

"Does this all go back to Hitler?"

"Oh, no. It goes back, long before, to Babel."

"But then, why didn't we see this Aryan tendency before Hitler. I don't remember anyone before Hitler who had this fixation. If the Cosmokrats have been trying to do this since Babel, why didn't we see it before the Nazis?"

"The Secret Doctrine teaches that the Atlantean supermen were Aryans. This goes back to the beginning. TerraNova has always had this doctrine. It's not new. Everyone who has ever been part of TerraNova has known this. However, Hitler felt that he could use this to his advantage to justify the extermination of the Jews. Hitler had gotten ahead of himself. He was certain of victory, and that Therion would possess him and rule through him. He knew Therion as the Superman. He was thoroughly convinced that he would live one thousand years, reigning as the Superman.

"His predecessors had never been as near to success as he was. None of the Skotoi's previous attempts had come as close to success as Hitler's. And he was certain that he would be victorious, and so he began to act as if he was initiating the new millennium.

"The Secret Doctrine mandates the eventual elimination of all those who worship Asmina. By extolling the virtues of the Aryan superman, Hitler was able to motivate the destruction of the Jews, the chosen people of Asmina. Therion cannot achieve maximum power until all of those who truly believe in Asmina are terminated. The Doctrine teaches that the belief of only one individual is enough to power Asmina. Therion will not have achieved victory until the very last believer in Asmina has been removed from the face of the Earth."

"Really?" Jack asked with incredulous voice. "You're saying that if Hitler had been victorious, he would not have left anyone alive who believed in Asmina, who is the One we call Yahweh. That means that they would have eventually exterminated all of the Christians too?"

"Without a doubt," Steven confirmed. "That's what they taught us."

"Well!" Robert exclaimed. "And they call their failures 'incidents.' Do they keep a record of these incidents?"

"They do."

"How many incidents have they had?"

"Probably over two hundred, wouldn't you say, Ashley?"

"That sounds right," she confirmed.

"So," Robert began, "if we guess that Babel was about five thousand years ago, there've been about two hundred of these incidents since then; that makes one about every twenty-five years, on the average."

"That's probably right," James affirmed.

"That means that these Cosmokrats, or whatever you call them, have been working on this Therion's project tirelessly, incident after incident, and they just keep trying. Don't you think they would get tired and give up?"

"I suppose that by the time they are ready to give up, they've spent most of their lives working on the project, and they don't have anything else left to do. It's up to the next generation to try," Jack conjectured.

"That's true," James confirmed, "but there's another reason. The Skotoi, Therion's group, always provide well for those who obey their purpose. Now, I don't see it that way, but when I was with them, I was convinced that their purpose would ultimately triumph."

"So," Robert spoke, obviously thinking aloud, "These powerful people are really weak. And they have to change their plans all the time, because things go wrong. And you think that the fall of the Soviet Union indicates that their plan has changed again?"

"Right," Steven affirmed.

Having heard Steve mention Asmina, Jack asked, "You had told me that the One we call Yahweh is who they call Asmina. What is Asmina? Where does the name come from?"

Steve replied, "Asmina is Sanskrit and means 'I am not.' I guess, now I'm a Christian, and I believe that Yahweh is God. From what you told me back in Ecuador, I should call Him 'Asmi — I AM.' "

Earl jumped in and declared, "Yes! He is the I AM! Or simply call him God, like all us regular folk."

"Now, Robert, remember what we were looking at, concerning Therion and Revelation," Jack reminded. "Therion must succeed — eventually. The only reason he hasn't, is because it isn't God's time yet. When the time's right, Therion will get his chance, but he won't reign for a thousand years, just seven."

"How will we know when Therion tries again?" Jack asked.

"Since we aren't on the inside, it's hard to say," Steven answered. "I wish I could be more specific."

Sarah added, "But we can be sure he won't give up. He's been working on it for thousands of years. He has better technology, and more people and resources than ever before."

"If I may, please, folks, but it's a lookin' to me that we're missing the point," Earl began. "Ya all are tryin' to figure out when the devil will be a comin'. But God's plan never changes. And we know, seein' the signs of the times, that this Therion beast is a goin' a come, when God says so, and it's not a lookin' to be so long away. Now, gentlemen," and Earl looked at Jack and Robert, "if I may say so, I'm convinced that God has put us together for these last days. This meetin', tonight, isn't no accident.

"At this table, I see a man that has influence in government, and another that is known by much of the Body of Christ. Why, I'd even heard of Jack Kinderly back in Texas. Felt like I knew ya, Jack. I'm just a humble servant. I've built a few churches. I'm not important like you two fine gentlemen. But God's given me a gift. I know that a powerful, big church, like yours, Jack..."

"Excuse me, Earl, but I must protest. It's not my church; it's the church of our Lord Jesus Christ," Jack clarified.

"Excuse me. I mean, a powerful big church, like the one you pastor, Jack, can do a lot, and you don't have many financial concerns, but I feel like God's put me here with you two fine men 'cause I've got a gift of givin'. I can't compete with the likes of them TerraNova thugs, with all their banks, and all, but I ain't done too poorly. Havin' a little land in the right spot in Texas has allowed me to do some givin', and I thank the good Lord. Now, I don't like to talk about my money. And I don't like others a talkin', but I think God's put the three of us together for a reason, like I said."

There was a moment's silence, while Jack and Robert thought over the import of what Earl was "sayin'."

"What do you propose, Earl?" Jack asked.

"I believe this Therion is like you've said. He's Antichrist. Personally, I'm a lookin' to be gone from this here Earth about the time that devil shows his face, but the more I read my Bible, the more convinced I am that before the Lord takes us all home we'll have seen that devil, and he'll have killed some of us, like our fine departed sister, Judy. If that's the case, and I think it is, since that's what Paul says in his second letter to the Thessalonian folk. Excuse me, but I happen to know it from memory, King Jimmy's version if ya all don't mind..." And Earl was going to tell them, even if they did mind, but no one did. "Let no man deceive you by any means: for that day shall not come, except there come a falling away first, and that man of sin be revealed, the son of perdition." Earl didn't have the inflection of a Shakespearean actor, but he almost allowed himself to sound educated. "It seems to me that Paul was tellin' us that we'd see the beast, even if we get raptured soon after. I sure hope it won't be long till Jesus takes us to Heaven, but we might see that devil first.

"Now, the good Lord has sent us this fine couple, and they're a tellin' us how Therion is a tryin' to take over. It seems to me, even a person who's a mite slow to catch on, like me, will see that God's tryin' to get us to do somethin', like tellin' people 'bout Therion and his *deepers*. We need to expose the devil for who he really is.

"Now, we can't just run around yellin' 'the devil's comin' — "

Jack and Robert laughed. Jennifer thought — Earl's a blast!

"But we best figure out some way to tell people, clandestine, ya know. So, Pastor, I propose that we begin a ministry, this very night, whose purpose it is to let people know what we know.

"I've got the gift of givin'. If we're needin' any, I'll put my checkbook where my mouth is."

"Well, Earl. It seems you've put some thought into all of this, and I have too. That's why I wanted the Joneses to come to the States, so we could tell people, and give them living proof. God has spoken to my heart the same things you've mentioned. I've shared them with Robert, and we've already thought of a name for this ministry, not too original, but it's simple, and it worked for the early Church, so it'll work for us: Fish.

"We are, then, the founding members," Jack said with the authority of a senior pastor, "and this is our first meeting. Like it was for our forefathers in the faith who met secretly in catacombs, the full impact of what we decide tonight may become history.

"How many souls will be saved from Therion because we warned them, or how many lives will be delivered from persecution, because of what we decide tonight, only the Lord can know, but I think we all agree that God hasn't sent the Joneses for us to ignore them. We're called to find ways to let the Body of Christ know about Therion, and his Skotoi. This will require boldness. It will require dedication and sacrifice — perhaps to the point of death. But if we're ready to accept this challenge, then every talent, and every asset we possess, we must be ready to commit. We need to be visionary. It's going to take a plan — not Therion's, but God's." And then Jack looked Robert straight in the eyes, and said, "It's going to take an administrator."

"It sounds like a good job for an old bureaucrat, like me," Robert offered.

"My, after what you did with NASA, this shouldn't be too hard," Jack agreed.

"It'll be harder, and it's bigger. Excuse me, Jack, for differin' with ya. But savin' NASA was a piece of cake compared to this job: tellin' Christians about somethin' they don't want to hear. But I agree," and Earl addressed, looking at him directly, "Jack, if there's a person on this here Earth that's shown themselves able for such a task, it's you. But let me warn you proper, NASA swims easier than a *fish*. The problem with Christians is that they're all so feisty, and they all think they know 'er all, and they're the best. Everyone knew NASA was messed up, and needed help. But when you go to start Fish, people will be tellin' ya, 'Why ya tryin' to fix something if it ain't broke?'"

"Well, Earl, I can't say that your comment is very encouraging," Jack said. "But I suppose it's better to say it now, than to be finding it out the hard way a year from now. I think we should pray."

Jennifer thought — Had we better! And Jack began to pray.

WITH THIS MEETING, FISH hatched. It was little more than an idea. It would need a head to plan with, a tail to propel it, and fins to guide it, but its body, Christ had given.

The waiter returned. Jennifer said, "Should we allow the young man to take our orders?"

* * *

The next day — Orlando, Florida

TEN **AM,** and hot, it was great Florida weather.

A horn sounded a couple of brief, well-tuned blasts, and Sarah looked out the apartment window to see, and called Steven, "She's here!"

Outside of their air-conditioned comfort, about 60 feet away, on the street — which was generous with floral embellishment, both around their apartment and on neighboring properties — sat a pink Mercedes coupe, which had hurriedly parked a second before, and from the driver's door, a redhead emerged. Sarah gazed at her a moment longer. *She looks like she owns everything Jack said, and more. Maybe she'll give me her look. I wonder what Steven would think of that* — Sarah pondered, with a smirk.

"Is it her?" he asked, entering the living room and catching an eye-full through the picture window. Sarah saw his eyes lock on the approaching form.

"Must be," Sarah remarked, feeling a trace of jealousy. But it didn't last long, since he then contemplated her with his tender gaze.

They went to the door to greet their visitor. Earl had left to have his Suburban's oil changed, and to take care of a few chores.

SHORTLY, STEVEN AND SARAH were speeding off to the appointment that Jack had arranged. Chelsa, their host, told them how she had been delivered from drugs, alcohol, and, as she put it, "the grueling competition of life in the fast lane." She had come to know Jesus at Jack's church, and had attended for two years.

It wasn't far, and soon they were in a large mall. A fluorescent sign — burning brilliant red and purple, catching eyes as quickly as the owner — announced, "Chelsa's." It was one of the most successful, upscale hair salons in the state.

When she entered, it was easy to tell that she was in charge. She knew how things were supposed to be, and she let everyone else know. But she had a tender place in her heart for the Lord and His people. As soon as Pastor Kinderly had asked, she took charge of helping the Joneses.

He had said, "I'll give them your address."

She had replied, "No, don't bother. I'll pick them up."

Chelsa wanted to serve, and this was her chance. She would give her guests the best, and she had the best to give.

Pastor Jack had told her, "The Joneses need a new start and a new look."

Seeing, for the first time, the prime material, Chelsa asked herself, "How can I do this? Anything I do will ruin them."

Arriving at the salon, Chelsa decided she dared not make a suggestion about a new hair color, or anything else. I'd better let them choose — she told herself. Then they won't be able to blame me when they see the change. They aren't going to like themselves.

After thinking about it a moment longer, she decided to be sure and asked, "Sarah, Steven, do you really want an alteration?" Chelsa even thought of making them sign a release form, absolving her from all responsibility. They had what everyone else was trying to get — beauty. Any other look, for them, would be a step down.

SARAH PERUSED the book of hair color swatches. Seeing the choices, which weren't lacking, she began to understand Chelsa's concern. Steven and I probably won't be happy with anything, and she thinks we might blame her, so Sarah said, "We have to do it, so don't worry; we'll take whatever we get."

Sarah reluctantly chose a color two shades darker than her own. Briefly she had contemplated Chelsa's red, but decided the last thing she needed was to draw more attention to herself. But she joked, just to see what Steven would say, "I think I like Chelsa's hair," trying to sound serious.

He answered, "I wish you didn't have to change at all, but wouldn't red draw too much attention?"

Sarah laughed, and Steven did too, but she noticed that he seemed to fade into his thoughts.

SARAH'S LAUGH, and Chelsa's, seemed distant, even if he had also chuckled. A memory flashed into Seven's mind, and he saw Sarah standing, with her hair shining, while she laughed, mocking him, back on the lava field. He was covered with mud and felt like a Beta, or even less. But she was beautiful! And her laugh? He saw himself laughing with her. I love her taunt — he told himself. Then, in his reminiscence, the scene changed, and the stage, including time itself, was at Sarah's orders. They were 14 years old, that day back in '76. He could feel her taunt driving him to chase her and pull her down with him on the soft tundra, to the chagrin of Master Teacher. Then, in his daydream, the tundra ripened into a field of hay, as golden as her hair, where they rolled and played. She ripened into the woman he loved. In his mind, one picture remained: Sunbeams streamed from her golden hair. He wished the scene had been recorded on a laser disk, but the memory was so vivid it would never leave his mind.

In that moment he realized that even though her appearance would change that day, her unblemished essence wouldn't. She would be Ashley — Sarah — always. What he held precious wasn't her hair, or her eyes, but that chiding, taunting little girl — the enticing, captivating woman — his bride.

The ladies finished laughing, and Chelsa asked Steven what color he would choose. Towards the end of the catalogue, there was a shade of purple. He pointed to it, and in response, they all laughed together. Then Sarah told him to get serious. He had a notion not to, but there wasn't any choice. It was time to take the medicine. So he handed the samples to Sarah, and told her to choose for him.

She protested, "Do I have to?"

To which Steven didn't reply, but she knew she did. She chose a shade a bit darker than the one she had chosen for herself: light golden brown.

WHEN THEY LEFT Chelsa's, their dazzling blonde brilliance was gone. At least fewer eyes followed them, which had been their purpose.

Chelsa had given Sarah a pair of clear-lens glasses from her fashion eyewear department. The dark blue frames complemented her new look. Later that day an optometrist fitted Steven with contact lenses. His light blue eyes became gentle brown. Having worn vision enhancement devices most of his life, he had no trouble adapting to the lenses, but what a letdown! The contacts had no telescopic vision, much less any light amplification.

When the former Smiths returned to 321 Floral Lane, a neighbor could have mistaken them for a different couple, not the one that had left that morning.

Chapter 23

The *"Man"*

WHO WILL pity a charmer that is bitten with a serpent?

– Apocrypha, Ecclesiasticus

March 8 — That same day — Manta, Ecuador

IT HAD BEEN a sultry day with a dark sky, but as sunset approached, a few rays escaped from under the cloud cover and painted the sky above the vast Pacific a subtle shade of orange.

A week had gone by since Pepe had returned to Manta. The very day after coming back from *"el viaje* – the trip," as he called it, a stranger, but not a *gringo*, came by and asked him about a picture. He knew it was the *gringa*, but it really didn't look like her, at least not the way he remembered her. The *gringa* in the picture looked joyless and miserable, but the *gringa* he had known was pleasing and refreshing. They really weren't the same person.

He had put a lot of thought into what the *gringos* told him about people who might come looking for them, and he had told his crew, "Let's stay out of trouble. If anyone comes looking for the *gringos*, we haven't seen them."

It had been in that spirit that Pepe told the *Señor*, "I haven't seen her." It really didn't occur to him that his answer was less than truthful. He didn't even think to justify himself, not even in his own mind, since it was evident that the stranger who had confronted him, with dark glasses and a black mustache, his black hair swept back and laid down with grooming solution and a mild trace of expensive lotion lingering, wasn't looking for the *gringa* for good, or moral reasons.

In Pepe's simple shrewdness, this "*man*" — a crook (pronounced MAH-nah) who flashed his golden watch — not merely yellow in color, but made of the authentic metal, his rings the same — wasn't to be trusted. The *man* had accepted Pepe's denial of having seen the missing woman in the picture, and left.

That was a week ago, to be sure, but Pepe hadn't forgotten. However, now a woman stood on the pier, a woman, whose striking figure could simmer any man's blood. As Pepe passed her way she moved seductively. Pepe hoped she had nothing to say to him, but why else did she stand on his pier? He looked at her and prayed, "*Señor, ayú-dame* — Lord, help me, for her very manner of dressing shouted "Take me. I'm yours." She was wearing a body hugging skirt, with a wide black band pulled tight over her hips and falling in a "V" shape that showed flesh nearly to the vertex of the sparkling belt (lined with tiny diamonds). She had pleasantly teased black hair, falling wildly over her shapely shoulders, shamelessly revealing flawless skin. There she stood, as tall as Pepe, an obstacle that commanded him to pass no farther.

As she leaned, sensually, on the rail, she looked into his eyes and spoke, "Pepe."

Upon hearing her speak his name a cold chill swept over him. Her dark green emerald eyes and her long nose spoke of nobility — features never seen by a common fisherman's eyes. Even her manicured toenails, painted the color of her eyes, told Pepe that he was in trouble. There wasn't any way around her, he had to stop, or go through her. Being a gentleman, he stopped, which wasn't extraordinary — a jerk would have done the same.

Hesitatingly, he answered her inquiry, "*Sí.*" It seemed to him, though, that even in limiting his response to just one syllable, he was speaking more than he should. It seemed to him that he could almost taste blood in his mouth, blood coming from the wound that her "hook" had made. And like a hooked fish the mere opening of his mouth betrayed him to the angler.

MIRIAM SAVEDA heard the filthy, stained, smelly fisherman respond with a monosyllable, and she knew that he was already under her spell.

This should be easy, she thought. I'll talk about the sunset, and try to get a conversation going. "*Que belleza...* — How beautiful...," she said as she pointed to the horizon.

He turned his head and looked. Seeing how easy he responded to her, she concluded that it would only take a minute. I won't even need to get in bed with this greasy muck. They didn't need to send me for this one. They could have used a local girl for him.

PEPE WONDERED WHY the strange woman spoke to him so informally. She even called him by his first name. As a pang of indignation rose in him he thought, "What right did she have?" He answered her rudely, "*¿Qué busca?* — What are you looking for?"

He immediately felt guilty, but he didn't want to let her know, so he kept his expression staid. It was obvious to him that something strange was happening. Why would such a beautiful woman be found on his lonely peer? One who knew his name, and had nothing better to do than talk about the sunset.

MIRIAM WAS SURPRISED. He's so direct! His voice sounds like an executive working on a tight schedule. He's just a miserable fisherman? How come he's acting so elite? Then she noted that he hesitated. I'll press my advantage – she decided – and reached slowly to take his wrist. She did it desirously; she was acting, but it always worked. In this case she loathed the very idea of touching the pestilent fishmonger.

She began to think that he might have been handsome in another life. He was almost tall, for a Latino. His eyes weren't so dark, and his features were decisive. He was pleasantly muscular, and his build was well-proportioned. If a good bath could remove the stench, he might not be so bad, but he would still be a simpleton.

Why were they wasting her talents on such trash? At least, she knew, this wouldn't last long.

PEPE WAS PERCEPTIVE. He knew that her touch was false. He was also keenly aware of his wife whom he loved and his children who worshiped him, and he was determined that he would not fail them. But… oh, her skin was so smooth. He nearly prayed, "Let her touch me no more," but not quite; her gentle contact felt too good to pray it away. Momentarily he forgot what prayer was, and he felt like a hypocrite. It was shockingly sudden, but for that moment he would have gladly given everything he owned just to have her. It would have been so easy to take her hand, then her shoulder…

But she's not real. She can't be! This is just some trick, and the devil is tempting me. He had to shake himself. The incident made him want to curse something, or someone. He had a notion to call her a slut. He knew she was there for something – for a price. Her every movement and her every expression told him as much, and it took every ounce of will he could muster, while fighting lust and a rush of hormones, to call out, as if he were speaking aloud, "*¡Jesús, ayúdame!* – Jesus, help me!"

Pepe jerked his arm away from her touch. With this, the woman's sultry, seductive look, turned momentarily harsh. However, it was only like a bit of dust that had gotten into her nose, and she sniffed it away.

SAVEDA THOUGHT – I won't let this crud go so easily. Why is he doing this? Men don't act this way around me.

She decided to try again. She reached back, and softly took his arm. She put her other hand to his shoulder, and facing him, and with all her charm said, "Please wait. I need to ask you a question."

PEPE HAD ALREADY OVERCOME temptation once, and now he was faced once again with its alluring pull. It was so beautiful. Shouldn't he have gotten a prize for resisting the first time? Shouldn't God have rewarded him? Why was he facing her again? As he looked into the woman's face, she drew close enough for him to feel her breath, and a fierce desire began to waken within him. Oh! How he wanted to cave-in to temptation, but he remembered the scripture promising that God wouldn't let him be tempted beyond his ability to resist, and he took strength, telling her resolutely, "*Tengo que ir* — I must go," and he began to move away from her.

MIRIAM COULDN'T FAIL. She wouldn't fail. She never failed! This oily man, so foul with perspiration, would not do this to her! She stepped back from him and said, "*Lo siento* — I'm sorry," in a such a genuine tone that it would have torn the hardest heart. She went on, talking fast and sweet, and pulled out a picture, "Do you know this woman? She's missing and her family wants to find her."

PEPE HAD ALREADY seen the picture. He already knew his answer. The devilish seductress wouldn't have her way with him, and now he knew that it had been as he suspected — this woman was no more than an enticing version of the "*man*" who paid him a visit the week before.

"*No la he visto* — I haven't seen her," Pepe answered, and sought to walk past her, quite nervously, still feeling the allure of her fleshly appeal, but he resolved that he would resist.

"*Mientas* — You're lying," she answered. He heard her mocking charm.

He didn't like being accused of lying. Actually, he was lying, but at this moment, saying he hadn't seen the "gringa" didn't seem like a lie. However, if someone from the church asked, or a local official, he would have answered truthfully. Somehow it seemed to him that in his current context, speaking to this strange, devilish woman, telling her a falsehood didn't cause him any remorse, nor did it make him feel any guilt. It even seemed like the right thing to do.

MIRIAM PERSISTED, SENSING she had him on the line, and that he was only struggling in vain, tugging as she reeled. He was fighting her and losing. His fluttering, unsettled speech told her so. She wouldn't let him go, and she stepped in front of him to block his exit. She pressed right against him. She knew of no man who could resist her treatment, not when flesh met such attractive flesh.

NO! GOD. PLEASE NO! – Pepe prayed silently. He pushed to slip around her, but she seemed uncommonly strong for a woman. Feeling her against him, he did want her to touch him. After all, no one was watching. He paused a moment, long enough to feel a caress. It had been a long time since he had felt a touch from his wife that excited him as much. Elena will never know. If this seductress wants me, what can I possibly do? After all, if it's not God's will He could stop her.

There was a distant voice, or maybe it was just a remembrance, or a thought, but for an instant he heard, or maybe he saw, his bride Elena, before him in her wedding gown, still a virgin, beckoning him towards her. But it was so distant that he was able to ignore it.

MIRIAM TOLD HERSELF – I've got him. She looked into his deep brown eyes, and put a cute smile on her lips. She giggled, and thought – He's a man, like all the rest. She almost forgot that he was such a pathetic slime. She was drawing hard on her line, reeling in her fish. Resistance was diminishing. She pressed in to him just a little tighter, and could tell that she was getting the response she was expecting. He's mine – she told herself, and invited, "Shall we go somewhere where we can talk?"

OH, GOD! Pepe cried, part of him enjoying every instant, the other, hating himself. Pepe lifted his eyes and lightly gasped for air, trying to hide his tension. Hearing her invitation, he could imagine how Adam must have felt at the tree. But Adam didn't have Jesus. I'm not going to let the serpent win! He lowered his eyes, and looked into hers. He hoped he would see the devil himself, but her eyes were lovely, a glimpse he would never forget.

THIS WAS IT! She had fully enticed him. She asked, seeing him delay in answering, "Shall we?" and caressed him again. All the tension in the line was gone. Any second she would be able to pull her catch ashore. It didn't look like she would even need to take him back to the hotel. In a few moments she would ask him about Officer Brown, and he would tell all, and she would be finished.

PEPE had allowed this incident to go too far and he sensed that this was his last chance. If he didn't break now, she would have him in the frying pan. He could already feel the heat, and see the flame. The form of her body fueled his passion, and the flame in her eyes ignited his lust. This was his last chance. He had to break this very instant, or he would be *pescado*.

Suddenly, he took hold of a strength that he found not within himself, and said, "NO!" to her question, as he jerked away. He tried to think only of Jesus. He focused himself on His blood-stained Savior, and he walked resolutely away, with long strides, though he could still see seductive green eyes in his mind as they still tried to seduce him and make him turn back, but he didn't, and wouldn't, return. He looked beyond, to the cross.

SAVEDA STARED odiously after him. He'll turn around — she told herself. Yet she could see that his stride only became more resolute with every step, and soon he was gone. She almost decided to chase after him. She would insist that he tell her about Brown. She questioned herself with disgust — What makes him think he's so good? I know he wanted me. Why did he run? Curse him! Why did he reject me?

* * *

Lópᴇᴢ ᴊᴜᴍᴘᴇᴅ back into his rented white Honda Accord which, as far as cars went, was nearly too ostentatious for Manta. He snickered under his breath. "I never fail," he could hear Miriam saying. She's going to be hot — he thought, still amused at the fire he saw in her eyes as she glared after her escaping prey.

Crossing the hundred yards, or so, of sandy beach that separated her from the car, Saveda arrived, and opened the passenger door. She slid into the front seat with the defeated attitude of a smitten boxer ready to demand a rematch.

López waited for her to say something so he could scoff.

Sᴀᴠᴇᴅᴀ ᴋɴᴇᴡ he was waiting for her to speak. She knew that he would deride her. So she sat in silence until she decided to attack, and blurted out, "You bungling idiot!"

"Me?" he asked incredulously.

"Yes, you!" she accused.

Hᴇ ᴡᴀꜱ ꜱᴜᴘᴘᴏꜱᴇᴅ to ask, "And what did I do?" But he saw through her diversion, and simply shook his head, engaged first gear, revved the engine, and popped the clutch, with squealing tires on the old worn pavement that had been scuffed from black to gray by the weather.

After initially feeling anger, he began to feel amused, thinking about how the assignment had gone. Saveda had failed. She could no longer boast a perfect record. He could use this to get favors from her. He liked her favors. She had best keep him happy, or he would let everyone know that she had failed. But she was too hot right now. It wasn't a good time for him to gloat. So he kept quiet.

Sᴀᴠᴇᴅᴀ ᴄᴏᴜʟᴅ ꜱᴇᴇ that trying to manipulate a fellow SAO by using her female rage would give her about as much success as she'd had with

Pepe, so she changed her manner, and demanded with sedate expression, "I want you to find everything that can be found about that slime. I want to know how he was toilet trained, and if he likes his yucca fried, or boiled. I want to know which hand he uses to hold a fish's head when he slits it open. No detail is too small. He will not mock me!" She said resolutely, pronouncing every single syllable in every word. "I will have him," and she paused. Then she affirmed, "He knows. He's seen Brown. I can tell. He's going to tell all! I'll have him."

LÓPEZ REALLY WANTED to say something like — He got to you, didn't he? — but it would only cheapen his victory. It was interesting that her failure was somehow his victory. Wasn't he on her team? But at this point he didn't want to get too philosophical, and he answered professionally, "Why don't we tell Herr Weller to go ahead and order abduction? Let the pros interrogate the fisherman? There's no need to waste time on the likes of him."

"What? Interrogate him like they did the missionaries?" Miriam questioned, her expression asking, "Are you crazy?" in a way that only a beautiful woman can, for in the eyes of another, it would have been trite, but in hers, there was an atmosphere — a storm with a haunting personality. López hated her for it as much as he loved to see her in turbulence.

After she paused, she added, "Besides, I have a better record than your 'pros,' and I haven't lost, yet. This was just the first round, and I won, on technical points. I had him! He just walked out of the ring, but he wants me. I'll get the information. If you turn him over to the 'pros,' " she said, ridiculing, "they'll *erase* him and we'll never find out anything."

López knew she was right.

* * *

March 14 — Six days later — Novus Ordo

"BY MULTIPLEXING SCANS, we can increase our resolution two hundred percent," Jones explained. "It has to do with the inverse square law; we just need to make it work for us, and not against us."

Weller didn't care for her explanation, he wanted two things: the missing piece of RSB, and her, but he would've settled for her.

Considering that he could have a *geneda* (a genetically engineered woman), exactly to his specification, adult and programmed, he was wasting his fantasies on Jones. Considering that with her bioprocessor and her infliction record, he would have just about as much fun with her as he would in solitary confinement. Such, though, is the nature of fantasy – it's not meant to come true – for if it did, it would be little more than stark reality. Could it be that for that same reason he didn't order a *geneda*? All the other Cosmokrators had several, each. They said that *genedas* made nearly perfect companions. Maybe they were right, though Weller's fantasy Jones was better for him, for indeed, she was perfect.

"When will you be ready with the multiplexer?" Weller asked, with satisfaction in his timbre and tenor.

"It's ready," Jones answered bluntly.

"You're marvelous," he sincerely complemented.

"Thank you, Herr Weller," and immediately, without hesitation, she asked, "Need I remind the Cosmokrator of the promised promotion?"

This wasn't part of his fantasy's script. Weller nearly hit the switch to terminate the transmission. Now he would have to deal with the real Jones. "Right," he answered, coughing. "I'll put it before the Committee. Perhaps there will be an opening in a few years."

"Need I remind the Cosmokrator that a new DEEP, to replace Unit 1, will soon leave dry dock?"

Weller, for a dime, would have hit the inflict button, and then Jones would learn her lesson, and cringe in pain, but it would also impair her future cooperation, and her genius was more than a little valuable. Even the threat of infliction had to be avoided in her case. Perhaps also, it was her spirit, her drive to advance, that made the fantasy Jones and the real Jones one person?

"Keen observation, Jones. I'll mention your petition to the Committee."

Later, Weller noted the situation in Manta. It was taxing many resources. The Committee depended on the Colombian cartel, and white powder was a significant ingredient in the fuel mixture that powered TerraNova's hungry bank accounts. With so many Colombian SAOs in Manta, Weller considered, *our ability to keep snow (coke) falling in the North will diminish. Is this inflicted search for Brown so important? Stonefell's probably right. We're devoting too many resources. Sometime Brown, and Smith, if he's still around, will make a mistake, and show their ugly heads; then we'll get them.*

Weller went online and rung up López on the computer. He answered, waking, "Yes, sir," obviously trying to get the sleep out of his voice.

"I've got your report here."

"Yes, sir."

"I think you've made the right choice. Saveda will get the information from the fisherman. She's never failed us; we'll just have to give her a little more time."

"Yes, sir," López said.

"López," Weller said, as he paused to rethink what he was going to say next.

"Yes, sir."

"I'm ordering all of our people back to Colombia. Everyone, except you and Saveda, and one other SAO, of your choice, should return to their habitual stations."

"Yes, sir. Anything else, sir?"

"That's all for now."

"Sir?"

"Yes," Weller answered.

"I'm sure you realize, sir, this could extend the time we need here."

"I do, López. I do. Chief Jones has improved the ionic scan. Perhaps, if we find the missing piece of RSB, it will show the way to Smith."

* * *

Two days later — Manta, Ecuador

SAVEDA STUDIED everything they had on Pepe. He was a López too. There really wasn't much. It was all that the team had put together before they left. He was a simple man, too simple to be causing so much trouble, but she began to see that it was that very simplicity that made the greasy fisherman so hard to catch. The worst thing was that he was religious. A simple, religious man of profound conviction, she had been taught, was a SAO's worst nightmare.

They had studied about two classes of religious people: hypocrites and true believers. The former were the easiest of all: like Atler. A true believer, on the other hand, couldn't be defeated by a frontal attack. That's why she had failed.

The manual stated, "When dealing with a true believer, especially a Christian in which moral priorities are well-established, the SAO should examine the subject's record for signs of propensity to perversion, especially sex and money. If, however, such propensities are absent, then the agent should consider other sources for the information sought. The time and energies required for success when dealing with true believers can surpass derived benefits.

"If it is imperative that the subject be broken, then covert action is preferred, not overt. Open interrogation will likely fail. The SAO may become a member of the subject's sect, gaining the subject's confidence. Once the SAO achieves trust, it is likely that the subject will yield information without seduction or threat. Often, the subject will provide the information gratuitously.

"It should be noted, however, that this type of mission can require commitments of months, and in some cases, years. It is likely that the SAO will suffer some degree of indoctrination by the religion, and it is recommended that agents who have been so contaminated be restored through a process of decontamination."

Miriam could see why she had failed. The fisherman, a deacon of his church, never missed a meeting. He even gave up work, and took a loss, to go to church, so he wouldn't be bought. And she could see that he wasn't going to be trapped in a bed — she had tried that, and had failed. Catching him was the ultimate assignment. *If I get him, I'll be the best.* And she scoffed at the idea that some mere religion might contaminate her, telling herself, "They won't need to decontaminate me. I'll see Pepe, on a platter."

López didn't like the idea. He said, "I'd better tell Herr Weller." But Miriam wanted it her way, and she would do López a favor, or two, whatever, but she was obsessed with the challenge. *No slime of a Christian, as nauseating as a rotten fish, would beat her. I'll have Pepe López and SAO López, too, and anyone else who gets in my way. Even Herr Weller himself, but I'll take Pepe López and flush him down the sewer.*

Her mind was set.

She began studying the "religion." How it worked. It was ridiculously simple. *Just believe on Jesus?* She hated it, but she could say it, "I believe." And she would say it, if by doing so she could fry her catch.

When she finished all of her homework, her mission — her very personal mission, and now her vendetta — began.

The fishmonger often preached at the religion's street meeting. Miriam determined that she would be there.

* * *

Manta

"BELIEVE ON THE LORD JESUS and you will be saved," Pepe's words blasted out of the speaker. It was a simple and direct way to begin a message. He wasn't really a preacher, he knew. He didn't pretend to be one. But he was a lay worker in the church and he loved to participate in the regular Sunday afternoon meeting. He loved to win souls.

He looked up, and in the back of the crowd, he saw a face, as if it were the devil herself. What a way to start a message! His throat tightened and his concentration wavered.

"Let's pray," Pepe said, more for his benefit than anyone else's — and he prayed.

ELENA, PEPE'S WIFE, felt that she had never heard him pray so powerfully. She could tell Pepe was fighting something. Petite, mestizo, black hair, dark brown eyes, she was ordinary. Dressed modestly, with her hemline below her knees, but she had *"una belleza sencilla"* (a simple beauty) that her simple husband always admired, even when she herself didn't believe his flattery. She was the mother of his three children and she knew he loved her — he always made her feel proud.

MIRIAM SAVEDA LISTENED. She had taken a lesson in modesty and her hemline, too, was below her knees — like a fine Christian girl. All she needed was a Bible in her arms, but that would come later. She had to get "saved" first, and the pestilent fish man needed to do the "saving." Then he would be her "spiritual father." Not a bad idea, she laughed to herself. He was nearly old enough, and she had never had "a father, natural or spiritual," she told herself, scathingly.

She stood there and watched. Modestly. Discreetly. She listened well, for she wouldn't miss her cue.

PEPE tried not to look her way. Her emerald eyes stood out in the crowd of black and brown irises, their luster keyed by the low afternoon sun. She looked so "Christian," with a lovely olive green dress, its neckline well closed. She looked fresh, but he knew she was a *man* — the same serpent that coiled herself around him on the pier.

He didn't attempt to understand, or figure her out, for now, he had to preach the Gospel, but he did it with decisive authority: Not trying to impress her, but trying to keep himself from her coils. By concentrating on his message he could ignore her snaking squeeze that encircled him, even from a distance.

MIRIAM HAD TO FIGHT to keep her attention focused on the words of the simple fisherman. His style had questionable eloquence — it even tugged at her heart. But she fought to pay attention — not because he was boring, quite the contrary — rather, she had to hear without listening. She couldn't miss her "cue" (the call to accept Christ), but she didn't dare allow herself to be convinced.

A strange thought crossed her mind, "What would it be like to really give my heart to this Jesus?" An illusion! Analogous to wondering, "What would it be like to find a man who really liked me and wasn't after my body?" Or, "What would it be like to have a real father and a real family?" Truth, as per Pepe's message, once filtered through Miriam's perception, was but a dream, a fantasy — violet razzleberry ice cream served in a fluorescent green cup, while sitting at a pink table with a stunning rainbow umbrella covering, surrounded by maroon vapor. Absurd! It couldn't be so easy. It just couldn't be! Believe in a mere dead man? NO!

The cue came, and in obedience to the call she walked forward, through the crowd, and stood there, first one, before Pepe, humbly, with religious contrition, waiting to pray — For all the infernal good it will do — she thought.

ELENA LOOKED ON and thought — How *guapa* — beautiful. Such a well-groomed *niña*, so shapely. She had no idea that this was the *"man"* whom Pepe had told her about.

Several others came forward, but the *niña* had everyone's eyes. Elena felt proud that her husband could preach the Gospel so well, and that even fine people, like the *niña*, would receive the message. She had to be a very special person. The *niña's* dress must have cost more than Pepe gave her for the market, even in a year. Her shoes were finer than anything Elena had ever seen, even when they had gone to the big cities. A person of such obvious status had accepted Christ at her husband's meeting. She felt proud.

It was also apparent to Elena that because of the *niña*, more people had passed forward than usual. She had observed that when someone who stood out in a crowd came forward, it was easier for others to do the same.

PEPE TRIED NOT to look at anything, or anyone, else. He tried to keep his eyes closed in prayer, but still, the emerald eyes, beautiful green, penetrated the veil beyond his eyelids where he could not escape their stare.

He wondered — What is this *man*, this degenerate temptress, doing? Mocking God?

He had to fight bitterness, if for no other reason, for the benefit of the others who had come forward. Perhaps, some of them had even been inspired to come forward, following the example of the *man* who passed so willingly. Elena had shared with him her observation, and he could tell that she was right. The *man* was adding to the number of decisions just because of her presence at the platform.

And, could it be, that even this serpent, this *man*, could know Jesus? Had He not died for her, also? Wasn't this the promise of the Gospel?

Pepe invited the group of eight to pray aloud with him.

"Señor Jesús... — Lord Jesus...," Miriam distinctly repeated each word, her eyes closed. She knew that the fishmonger could hear her, but now she had to keep her eyes closed. Before the prayer, she had noticed that López purposefully avoided looking her way. She had asked herself — Am I not modest enough for him now?

She had done her homework, and she repeated the prayer like any good parrot, adding a tear or two, and choking some. Her act would go a long way towards making the fisherman believe she'd gotten religion. But it wasn't as easy as she had thought it would be. She could have laughed, mocking. Or, she could have laughed at her wretched self. She shed tears because of the stupidity of it all. Or, her tears were shed in shame. It was a hard role, but the foolish task would soon end. So she let her tears come — Hollywood ready.

It was a strange thing. She almost felt different as she prayed, "Lord, forgive me... Make me a new person..."

It seemed that she only needed to *want* to feel different, and she would. If she really wanted it, she could have it — a new life and all the other fables that Pepe's religion promised. It was hers for the asking. It was an illusion, of course — she told herself. It couldn't be real. It's like hypnotism, perhaps. I'm strong. I'll resist.

WHEN PEPE made an end of praying he opened his eyes and the *man*, with glistening tear-streaked paths on her mild feminine accents, lifted her hand to wipe them away. Her hand moved smoothly. She looked innocent, virgin and vulnerable. Pepe wanted to think she looked Christian, and at the same time, he wished the slimy reptile would show herself as the *man* she really was.

Then he had a crisis of conscience — Maybe the poor *niña* really did receive Jesus? She had prayed the prayer, and sounded earnest, and even shed a few tears. Now she's saved — a new creature in Christ. She's changed. There won't be any problem now. She won't be after me.

Moments later, he saw that Elena had come up beside the *niña* to counsel her. He watched as his wife embraced the new convert, and he saw the smile on the well-dressed lady's lips.

Pepe wondered — Does she smile because of Jesus? If he hadn't met her at the pier, he would have said, "Yes." He realized that his eyes were clouded by the prejudice that came from their first encounter. He decided — I must give her a chance. He wondered what she would say to Elena.

* * *

Over the Pacific and in Novus Ordo

"YES!" Jones exclaimed resolutely. She felt like she deserved it. Even with the improved ionic scan, it had taken three months to find. But there she saw RSB material on the projected holographic display. It was pinpointed four hundred miles off the Ecuadorian coast under a mile of water on the Cocos Ridge.

"Computer," she ordered, "*com* Novus Ordo, priority alpha, Cosmokrator Weller."

An instant later his image was before her. "I have a positive location from the ionic scan. We have found RSB material."

"Where?" Weller asked excitedly.

Jones gave him the information.

"Sunset is only ninety minutes. With your permission, Herr Weller, I will dive at nightfall."

"Permission granted. But what is it doing out there?"

"It would seem to require a reworking of theories on the possible whereabouts of Captain Smith," Jones advised.

"It sure would," Weller agreed. "I'll be waiting for your confirmation on retrieval. We'll need to have it examined."

Chapter 24

At the Pier

THE PURPOSE of polite behavior is never virtuous. Deceit, surrender, and concealment: these are not virtues. The goal of the mannerly is comfort, per se.

— June Jordan

March 27 — The next day — Manta

EVEN WITH the air conditioning, in Manta's finest hotel, which wasn't too bad, she boiled. How frustrating! — Saveda considered. I can't touch him. That woman of his won't let me near. She's always around.

It used to be, she couldn't have even thought the words — That woman of his... — without inserting at least some foul language. Being around the *hermanos* had forced her to clean up her tongue. It hadn't been easy, and now, it seemed easier not to use such vernacular.

Her effort, her very personal effort, was growing more frustrating all the time. The worst thing was: Elena had already told her everything. She knew that Pepe had taken Smith and Brown to Mexico. She knew they had swum ashore in the dark of night and that they were masquerading as "husband and wife," pretending to be Christians; at least that was the way she saw it. She figured — They couldn't really have gotten married. Alpha Force troops weren't capable of such.

That was one reason she had always enjoyed being a SAO. With all the hype about how exalted members of Alpha Force were, it looked like a prison to her. Life, confined to a DEEP, wouldn't be life at all.

She was free, or so she told herself. But "free," in her case, was merely a mordant description of refined servility. For instance, she knew she wasn't free to become a real Christian. And the game she was playing, if someone found out, would surely bring infliction, for she had completed her mission: Pepe's wife had told her everything she needed to know, and more. But she hadn't told López or Weller, because she wanted things her way.

I want Pepe — she told herself — and I'll have Pepe. He wasn't a stinking fishmonger in her eyes, not now. He had become the symbol of everything her world wasn't. He was nearly a god to her. Unless she could have him, and make him "fall" (as those of the religion said), she would never be content with herself again. If she didn't succeed, life as she knew it would end — at least in her notion of what it was all about. Failure meant that he, and his God, would win, and she would be a loser. She couldn't allow that to happen.

In her fantasies she could feel his sweaty, slimy body against hers, crushing her tenderly in his arms. Her fantasy had to become reality. Then, once she'd had him, she would trash him, cutting him open and tearing his guts out — like a fish. She would be sure that all the *hermanos* knew. Elena, if possible, would find them in bed together — that was Miriam's plan. He'll *fall* — she told herself.

For now, I'm the only one who knows Smith and Brown are alive. It's my little secret. When "my man" has been shamed and smeared in slime, then I'll tell.

Her vendetta had to be settled.

There had been other work, though. Favors for the cartel, seducing a minister of government in Chile, it was work, and it had to be done.

Finding Brown became a low priority. As a result, Herr Weller had her flown in and out of Manta's dinky airport as needed, but he kept sending her back. Finding Brown, though not a top priority, was important to him.

She told the brothers that she was an investigator whose work was to find missing people and that there were a few cases in the Manta area. She promised, "Whenever I'm in town, I'll be at church with my hermanos." She even testified before the whole congregation how Jesus saved her — gave her a new life and changed her heart — "Thanks to my beloved spiritual father, Pepe," she said with charming gesture.

Her act was good. At times she began to believe her own rhetoric, especially while speaking to groups, but once she got back to the hotel, maybe about the time López would come after her for a report, and a favor, usually in that order, but not always, she would slip out of her Christian hallucination and become SAO Saveda — Pepe's *man*. Thanks to Elena, she had even found out that that was the way he thought of her — a *man*.

It really left her wondering if she would get him or not. He had even told his wife about their encounter on the pier. Any other man she had ever touched would have paid with hard currency to keep his woman from knowing, except that obnoxious Atler, whose elimination had been "a good work," she said to herself acidly, phrasing her thought religiously.

The more she knew Pepe, the deeper she wanted him: in her arms. She had to ruin him. At least, it seemed, he had been shamed to the point that he hadn't told his wife about her caresses, or if he had, Elena hadn't said so.

Sleep that night had been a dream (in that it never happened). One more day and they would fly her to an assignment in Venezuela. Something with an oil company's big shot. But Pepe was getting to her, and she knew the whole affair was diminishing her effectiveness, and causing her to make mistakes. She had almost refused to take liquor from a target who offered it to her. She had nearly said, "Christians don't drink." That would have been a mistake!

It must have been 1:00 AM, and still she lay face up, with legs crossed, when there came a pounding at her door.

"*¿Quien es?*" she asked, as she got up.

"López."

Miriam knew his voice but looked through the peephole just the same, in case he was with someone, which was doubtful. Having confirmed that he was alone she opened the door.

He passed through as she stood behind. Once inside, he began to speak, only to hesitate at the sight of her scantily dressed body as she flipped on a dim light. He had seen her many times, with even less, but it always had the same effect. Thoughts on any other subject became impossible for him.

Miriam realized that men looked at her that way all the time, goggle-eyed. Sometimes she got it while fully dressed, even while dressed like a "nun" (that's how she thought of the way she went to church). Even a few of the "good" Christian men did it. She figured Pepe would too, but he simply refused to look at her. If she could get him to look, even for a moment, she was certain he would fall.

López finally collected his thoughts and began to speak. Professionally he intoned, "Herr Weller wants you to press this case. They've found the missing piece of Smith's RSB in the Pacific."

"They have?" Miriam asked, sounding surprised. She couldn't let López know she had been holding back, and that she knew Pepe had been instructed by the "*gringos*" (as Elena called them, probably because Pepe had also) to throw their things overboard.

"Yes, and there's evidence that Brown was with him."

"Then the story about the fisherman taking newlyweds on a cruise fits," she concluded, making it sound like she had just experienced a new perspective in thought. Continuing, she added, "I'll have him soon." And she looked up at López's eyes in confident assurance.

"It'll have to be tomorrow," he replied.

"Why?" she asked, innocently.

"Herr Weller will order an abduction if you fail. He's only giving you one more day."

"He can't!"

"You want to stop him?"

Miriam bit her lower lip. "They'll just *erase* him," she finally spoke.

"That's their problem," the SAO answered, and then chuckled, "and his."

Indeed, it was out of her hands. They had already given her more time than usual. In light of the RSB discovery, she probably should consider herself fortunate that they were even giving her a last chance. "Okay," she pronounced, abdicating, but with a trick, or two, in mind.

Tomorrow would be Saturday. Pepe would be back early. They were supposed to have a prayer meeting at María's home, a sweet old lady. Miriam actually liked María. She had learned that Pepe had brought the *gringa* to her. There was a longing in Miriam's heart, whenever she was around María, to let her be the mother she never had, and it seemed that María would have enjoyed filling that role.

María always makes me feel so loved, not like a slut — Saveda thought.

About then Miriam felt López, pulling her towards him. She exclaimed, "Not now!" and wiggled away. Then seeing his eyes, knowing she still needed a good working relationship with the brute, she added, "Listen. I'm sorry, but I've got to prepare myself for tomorrow."

López almost said something sarcastic, like, "How? You look ready to me," but he didn't. She had been good to him and it wouldn't do to ruin their "working" relationship. It would be unlikely that he would ever be paired with anyone like her again.

They dismissed. He pecked her on the cheek in obedience to the custom, and left.

Miriam turned out the dim lamp and lay down once more. Sleep was at least twice the dream it had been. She thought and schemed. It would be tomorrow (really, today), or never.

* * *

The next day — Manta

BY MORNING she might have slept some, but even in her dreams, she was awake. She spent the better part of the morning trying to work through the whole thing. Trying to make a plan — something the whole night had failed to give her. Abduction was useless; they wouldn't find anything. Pepe would resist. She knew her Pepe. And, she told herself, I already found what they want. And I've got to keep them from abducting him; they might find out that I've been holding back.

Why do I have to fight this thing? If I tell Weller that I had Pepe, and he told me everything, the boss will never know the difference and I'll still be Queen of the SAOs. But she was a driven woman. After all, a third-rate human muck, a Christian at that, couldn't be allowed to mock her.

Before sunset, she had her plan. She was on the lone pier, once again, and had taken care to let the crew leave first, without seeing her. This time she didn't dress like a whore, and she didn't dress like a saint, rather, in shorts (cut just above the knees) and a white blouse, tied at her waist, with only a pinch of flesh bare. She looked like one of the girls, maybe even a little modest — depending on your way of seeing things.

WHEN PEPE started walking down the pier, he saw her, right off. His heart jumped and he felt a knot in his throat. His hands turned sweaty. Why does she do this to me? — he questioned himself. He nearly walked back to the boat, like he had forgotten something, but that wouldn't do any good. What if she follows me?

He kept his pace, but he knew he shouldn't be rude. Elena and María like her. He would probably get a lecture if Miriam reported that he had treated her crassly.

She leaned on the same post, but her posture wasn't a chosen pose, like before. She looked like the neighbor's *niña*, her eyes looking out to sea, off the pier's side. A breeze passed through her hair, and a few black strands went across her face. She lifted a hand in smooth fashion and pulled her hair back, turning to face Pepe, and said, with a smile, as Christian as they came, "*¿Que tal?* — How are you?"

"*Bien* — Fine," Pepe answered with a dry throat, trying to think of what to say, or better, how not to say.

"Are you going to the prayer meeting?" she asked, knowing that that was the Christian thing to do.

"Yes, with Elena," Pepe said, hoping that by invoking his wife's name it would bring some mantle of protection. Too bad she wasn't there! He looked into Miriam's eyes again. No one else was near — just the two of them, and it would seem strange if he didn't. She looked good. The smile on her face said so much. She really did look like a changed woman, but why had she come to the pier?

As if to answer his question, "I was near here, trying to track down a lead on one of the missing people, and I looked at the time, and knew you'd be coming. So I thought I'd stop by and let you know that I'll be leaving." She waited. She had to get him talking.

"You won't be back?" he asked, trying not to seem content, as they stood about three or four feet apart.

"No. I've finished here. Thanks to Elena. She helped me a lot. You two have been like the mother and father I never had." Pepe already knew she was an orphan, and that immediately touched him.

"I'm glad we've been a blessing to you," he answered, the lump in his throat growing bigger.

"You're my spiritual father, and I just wanted you to know how much I love you."

She stepped closer, but in a nonthreatening way. She kissed him gently on the cheek, and stepped back. "Wherever I go, I'll try to find *hermanos.*"

Miriam really seemed like a daughter. Her large emerald eyes were juvenile in the receding evening glow. She made him feel like a proud father.

"Well, I'd better go," she said.

"Will you be at the meeting?" Pepe asked.

SHE HEARD IT in his voice — I've gotten a hook in him. "Yeah. I'll be there. Can't miss my last meeting. María is so sweet," she said with a broad smile. "And I have to say good-bye to Elena."

"Good," Pepe replied.

She had clasped her hands in front of her, and stood coyly. She's become a sweet girl, Pepe thought — worthy to be a daughter.

In silent motion, Pepe gave her a perfectly respectable kiss of dismissal, in line with custom, and they walked side by side for a short distance to the end of the pier.

Miriam said, "I'll see you soon."

"Okay," Pepe replied, and waved as she stepped away, to go towards her car.

She waved back, looked away, and Pepe stood watching her as she turned and began to walk away.

I've finally got his eyes! — she thought. She knew that timing was everything — an instant too soon, or too late, and the whole scene would evaporate. She wished she could see out of the back of her head. Two steps, three. Is he still looking?

PEPE WATCHED her with pride. She was his true spiritual daughter, and she would go places. She was an important person. Maybe she would tell others about Christ, people in high places. He watched her, five steps, maybe a few more, and turned to finish his walk home, about a kilometer.

MIRIAM FELT like his eyes were beginning to leave her. Of course it was a guess, but it had to be right. She turned, sure to be wearing that charming Christian smile. Yes! — she exclaimed to herself. His eyes were just turning. He had been watching her the whole time.

"Pepe," she called after him, and he looked back.

Seeing her smile, he couldn't help but smile himself.

Miriam saw his smile. It's good — she told herself.

"*Sí,*" he answered, without any nervous flutter.

It's working! She could see it, and thought — Now, don't blow it. Think Christian. Don't come on to him too strongly. Be polite. "Would you like a ride?" she asked, trying to sound like the *niña* she had become in his eyes.

"Oh…, don't worry. I'll walk. I'm close," he answered.

Play hard to get! — she emphatically reminded herself. "Okay, but if you want, I can drop you by. And later, I can pick you and Elena up to go to María's." She made sure she invoked the name of Elena.

"**Well, okay,**" Pepe said. Hearing the name of Elena. By now he knew that she didn't have any bad intentions.

She smiled. Pepe saw it as a fruit of the Spirit. Not long ago, he would have been tempted to think that her smile was the fruit of a spirit, but not the Holy Spirit. Now, she was his daughter.

Pepe stepped after her, as she beckoned with a gentle motion. Together, they walked towards the nearly abandoned access road. The municipality had expected expansion, but it hadn't happened as fast as they had planned. The sun was nearly on the horizon and, in a moment more it would sink into the ocean, one more time.

The sky turned brilliant. It was romantic, Miriam thought — just right.

They talked about the prayer meeting. Miriam spoke kindly of María. Indeed, María was like everyone's mother, even those that had a mother already. Every time she spoke of her orphaned condition, she could feel Pepe getting closer to her, and could almost feel him wanting to put his arm around her shoulders and tell her that she was his daughter. A lot can be said in a hundred yards, especially when the steps aren't very big. Sand slows some, also. The breeze was refreshing, and just before they reached the bank of the rise, and the path to the road, in the lowest part, well hidden from view, in what was already an abandoned area, Miriam said, with a tear that squirted out on cue, turning to Pepe, "I'll miss you and Elena so much. I've never had people treat me so well. I never knew my parents…" A few more tears fell, timed flawlessly, the perfect time and place to stop, which she did.

PEPE LOOKED at her. It was terrible to see his daughter cry. His heart was ripped from his chest. He reached, both arms, and pulled her close to himself, and held her. "Don't cry, my tiny one," he said.

MIRIAM WANTED to tell herself something sarcastic. She wanted to say, silently, "Yeah, fool! I won't cry after I've had you. If it takes tears to lay you out, I'll cry my miserable head away." She really wanted to gloat in her victory. The finish line was close. She was going to have him, curse the prayer meeting, and Elena too.

But Miriam couldn't! She had trapped herself, and stumbled into her own pit. Her tears became real. No more were they choreographed. She couldn't stop. And she cried. Pepe held her tighter.

"Jesus loves you, child," he said, soothing.

He's the only man who's ever held me without lust — she would have said, in thought, but couldn't, for she couldn't think clearly — but she knew it.

"Miriam…" he began.

That one word penetrated. It tore and gave life at the same time. It was spiritual. No, not that she felt her name deserved reverence, but the voice that spoke. Not really Pepe's at all — and the first time he had ever called her by name — she wasn't a *man* anymore. No one, man or woman, had ever spoken to her with such love — love like what Christians talk about, not the bed kind.

"Let Jesus be your daddy and your mommy. The Bible says He takes care of orphans. Let Him comfort you."

She felt his arms release her a bit. A breeze made her tear-soaked face feel fresh. He then let her go gently.

Miriam came back to her senses. She still felt like she could do it. Probably, at this point, even get him to the hotel or in his own bed while Elena was at the meeting. Just a thing of timing, and Elena would come back and find them, like she had planned in the beginning. With the right moves, the right words — play shy — let him make the advances. She knew he would be hers. He would "fall." She had him hooked. The fisherman was *"pescado,"* hers for the taking.

But her agenda didn't seem so important. His God had won, at least this time around, and the boss probably wasn't going to give her another chance. At this point, it would be like taking her own father, the father she never had, to bed. She couldn't do it, at least not then. Maybe, once she got away, she would change her mind, but she could still feel his paternal arms embracing her. She had allowed her act to be too good, and had trapped herself.

Miriam gained control of herself, and Pepe started leading her up the path. The sun had set, amber twilight still glowed.

They got in the car, and Miriam let him off, a block from his house (so she wouldn't have to turn into the dead-end). She promised she would pick them up, Pepe and Elena, but she knew she wouldn't. She couldn't stand any more Christian love.

Maybe the Christians did get Brown and Smith, too. If I get any closer, they'll have me, really have me — she figured. A prayer meeting with María would finish me. I'd be a Christian, and have to run, like the "Smiths," she told herself with sarcastic intonation on "Smiths." It was still hard to believe they got married. It sounds like a fairy tale — she snickered, as she pulled back into the hotel's parking lot.

Why? — she kept asking herself, time after time.

A SHOWER really didn't make her feel any better. López came. He wanted more than information, but he wouldn't get it.

"Did you crack him?" he asked.

"Don't I always?" she answered, wishing she could stir some seductive charm, or at least give a sensation of proud superiority, but instead, her words sounded like, "I wash clothes."

"What did he say?" the SAO asked, excitement in his voice, as he reached into his shirt pocket for a CARD (Continuous Audio Recording Device). It looked like a credit card, which in fact it was, from one of the major issuers, but it was distinguished by a few hidden enhancements, and would record about thirty hours of digital sound.

"He took them to Costa Rica…" she lied, and since that was part of her profession, she did it well. She gave López a story — a real story, but not *the* story.

Why? — she kept asking herself. I lost? The Christians won? Maybe not. But Pepe gave me something I've never had — a father and a family.

"They jumped overboard and swam in, about twenty miles. Or so he guesses, since they never came back."

"Does he know anything about Nova Mundi?"

"No, he's just an ignorant fishmonger," she replied, saying it like a curse, and feeling his arms, fatherly arms, around her, embracing her without lust "in the holy fear of the Living God" — she knew the jargon. Maybe I'll need decontamination? — she asked herself. I should give myself a few days to shake this religious stuff. If I need a vacation, they'll probably tell me before I tell them.

BUT THEY never said a thing. Miriam successfully distanced herself from her brief flirtation with Christ and His Church, though she never did totally forget Pepe's fatherly embrace.

Rahab would have been proud. Miriam and she had at least two things in common. One, their profession, and two, they had both lied to save God's people. Rahab, however, was in heaven. Miriam was likely destined for the flame, but she knew the talk, and if she wanted, she could walk the walk.

Aside from any speculation concerning her eternal destiny, Miriam helped insure that the Smiths (for she didn't yet know they were now the Joneses), of whom she was terribly jealous (for reasons that weren't even clear to her) would live a long and prosperous life, as long as they didn't get in trouble with the law, or buy anything on credit — at least until Therion came. Then nobody would be able to hide.

THE JONESES little imagined to whom they were indebted for their serene life in the land of freedom. Of course, to God, they knew that; but that

His instrument for providing their season of peace was a woman of ill repute — they would never have guessed.

So Steven and Sarah found their new life most satisfying. They sometimes wondered why Nova Mundi never caught up to them. Sometimes they even discussed contingency plans, and they wondered if they shouldn't move away secretly, going to some remote town and starting over — where no one knew them, or anything about them. It really seemed like they should, but the Lord gave them peace where they were — they had found their haven, their rest.

However, they both knew that the season of normalcy wouldn't last forever. If nothing else, Therion, the beast, would eventually come, and then no one would be safe, much less former Alpha Force troops.

In the meantime they decided it was best to Fish (as Earl said, knowing that the word "fish," now had, for them, a greater meaning). They would wait until God showed them to do otherwise. But they both knew their tranquillity would come to an end. They had only to read the newspaper to know that the New Order hadn't given up its relentless quest for domination. Therion would have his hour, and clearly, another volume of their life's story was still before them, yet to be lived.

The epic continues:

Before the Apocalypse

Book Three

For Such a Time

Information about publication dates and more may be found at:

www.beforetheapocalypse.com

About the Author

Kepler Nigh served for 23 years as a missionary in Ecuador, where he lived with his wife Blanca and their three children. His travels have taken him throughout Latin America, including extensive visits in the Amazon region and in the Andes, where he often lived with the resident people. He is the author of *Manual de estudios proféticos*, which was published in both Spanish and Portuguese by Editorial Vida (Life Publishers) and has returned to print under the McDougal & Associates label. In it Daniel and Revelation are studied extensively, and the volume was used in his classes at Quito Bible Institute and at Cristo al Mundo (Christ to the World), coming from the fruit of over 15 years of investigation.

After returning to the USA, Kepler served for a time as editor, typesetter and equipment manager for McDougal Publishing of Hagerstown, Maryland, then taught classes in Information Technology at Hagerstown Business College (now known as Kaplan University), served as an adjunct instructor at Blue Ridge Community and Technical College and, later, managed all IT and computer networking for Cedar Ridge Ministries in that same region. He and Blanca have now moved to Martinsburg, West Virginia, where he again is dedicating his time to writing and otherwise serving the Kingdom's requirements.

www.ingramcontent.com/pod-product-compliance
Lightning Source LLC
Chambersburg PA
CBHW030244030726
47493CB00023B/583